The Millionaire

A Maureen Gould Legal Thriller

Keenan Powell

Three Hooligans Press

To She, and He, Who Persist

Newsletter Sign-up

Sign up: Home - Keenan Powell (keenanpowellauthor.com)

Praise for Implied Consent

Powell has written a book that dares to be legal thriller, family drama, and polemic. Remarkably, she succeeds at all three. – Booklife Reviews, Editor's Pick

Keenan Powell has penned her most memorable heroine to date. Powerful and authentic. *Implied Consent* is a must read! — Bruce Robert Coffin, award-winning author of the Detective Byron Mysteries

Sharp-witted, big-hearted and authentic, *Implied Consent* is a knock-out of a novel from a writer who knows both the letter of the law and the messiness of real life. Treat yourself - you won't regret it. — Catriona McPherson multi-award-winning author of *In Place of Fear*

Contents

Prologue		1
1.	Chapter 1	5
2.	Chapter 2	13
3.	Chapter 3	19
4.	Chapter 4	29
5.	Chapter 5	35
6.	Chapter 6	47
7.	Chapter 7	57
8.	Chapter 8	67
9.	Chapter 9	73
10.	Chapter 10	85
11.	Chapter 11	91
12.	Chapter 12	101
13.	Chapter 13	111
14.	Chapter 14	121
15.	Chapter 15	131
16.	Chapter 16	137
17.	Chapter 17	139
18.	Chapter 18	147
19.	Chapter 19	157
20.	Chapter 20	167

21. Chapter 21   173

22. Chapter 22   179

23. Chapter 23   183

24. Chapter 24   195

25. Chapter 25   203

26. Chapter 26   207

27. Chapter 27   217

28. Chapter 28   221

29. Chapter 29   231

30. Chapter 30   235

31. Chapter 31   241

32. Chapter 32   243

33. Chapter 33   249

34. Chapter 34   257

35. Chapter 35   259

36. Chapter 36   261

37. Chapter 37   265

Hope You Enjoyed The Millionaire!   269

Author's Note   271

About the Author   273

Acknowledgements   274

Also By   275

Sneak Preview: The Pied Piper   276

Maureen

THE SECOND HAND CRAWLED across the wall clock, then everything happened at once.

A door concealed in the courtroom's wood paneling swung open. A security officer pushed my client in on a wheelchair. As he was rolled in from the dark hallway, Tony blinked rapidly under the bright overhead lights. Handcuffs that secured him to the frame dangled from his bony wrists as he leaned forward to knuckle hornrims back up his nose. When he searched for me, he whipped his head around as if to shift his bangs out of his eyes, but his hair had been shorn. It was barely long enough now to cover the scar from the jailhouse beating.

I gave Tony a nod, then touched Granny O'Shaughnessy's string of pearls at my throat, my good luck talisman. "You're as smart as any of them," she used to say, "and smarter than most."

The guard locked the chair wheels, unlocked Tony's cuffs, and helped him to stand. Tony braced his hands against the counsel table as he shuffled into position before his chair. The guard stashed the wheelchair in a closet hidden in the paneling, then struck a stance a few feet away, easily within reaching distance, as if Tony, in his present condition, was any kind of threat.

I held the chair steady as Tony lowered himself and noticed the scar beneath his eye looked inflamed. When he reached for water, he miscalculated the distance, upsetting the half-filled glass. I caught it just in time and offered it to him. He grasped it with both hands and took a sip. The liquid rippled in his trembling grasp. He carefully set the glass down.

I squeezed his hand. "Breathe. You'll pass out if you don't."

In the next few minutes, the world would shift on its axis for all those involved in the case. Tony would spend his life in prison or go free. The victim's widow, who had sobbed through most of the trial, would see justice done – as she believed it to be – or feel twice cheated, first by the murder, then again by the system. The assistant district attorney's win/loss record tilted in the balance.

An old glory hound once told me that if you want to own the wins, you got to own the losses too. It's the difference between being attached to the outcome and doing the next right thing, he said. I wasn't so Zen – I wanted to win this case – badly. Not just for me, but because I was certain my client was innocent. If I lost, he would most likely die in prison sooner, rather than later.

The clerk strode in. "All rise!"

When I reached out to help Tony to stand, he waved me off. "I can do this myself."

We stood in sync, like well-rehearsed ballerinas rising for the grand finale. I shifted my weight closer in case I needed to catch him. Another door opened and Judge Han flowed onto the bench. She spun her chair into position and gazed into its depths for a long moment before she gathered her robes to sit. Once settled, she scanned the room, her face a mask of dread, only pausing for a slight moment when she made eye contact with me. "Madam Clerk, I understand the jury delivered a verdict."

"It has, Your Honor."

"Then please bring the jurors in."

As the jury filed in, the air behind me, filled with the anxiety of the onlookers, was so dense it pressed against my back. Behind the prosecutor, a paralegal comforted the widow now scraping at her reddened eyes with a tissue. Beside the widow stood her adolescent son and daughter.

Behind me was my husband, Jake, and my daughter, Quinn. They had a vested interest in the outcome. This was my first murder trial and, as befell lawyer's families, it had been the hub of our lives for months. To be more accurate, it had been the hub of my life. If I was physically present in the condo, I was mentally living in the case. I wouldn't hear Jake or Quinn talking to me. I had forgotten my night to cook or bring home take-out. I had fallen asleep on the couch still wearing my suit, my laptop charge dribbling away, surrounded by files. At one point, Jake thought it was funny to leave me messages written on stickies, stating things like "brush your teeth."

My most enthusiastic cheerleader, paralegal, and office mom, Yolanda Martinez, was in the first pew as well. The only person missing was my investigator, Eli Conroy. He should have been here. He had been with me when this case first started.

"You may be seated," the judge said. I held Tony's chair still as he lowered himself, then I glanced at the assistant district attorney. Before the trial started, she had gotten a court order that there should be no "indicia of disability displayed" to the jury lest its verdict was swayed by sympathy. Ergo, Tony was brought into court by wheelchair out of the jury's view and the wheelchair was then hidden. I was admonished not to be over solicitous. There was an entire hearing about whether Tony should remain seated when the judge and jury entered and exited, thus hiding his frailty, during which I argued the jury may dislike him if he was seen to disrespect the court. It was then agreed that he could stand and sit again but only if unassisted while the jury was in the room.

With my look, I dared opposing counsel to object to my holding his chair. She gave me a slow blink instead, then faced the judge. The verdict was in. Nothing I could do would sway them now. She knew it.

Now settled, the jurors stole looks at the widow, who now sobbed uncontrollably as she grasped at the hands of her frightened children for support.

"Madam Foreperson," the judge said. "Please pass the verdict to Madam Clerk."

The clerk walked across the room, took a document from the foreperson, then carried it to the bench. The judge read the verdict silently.

"Very well," she said. "Mr. Paredes, please stand."

Chapter One

Maureen

Four months earlier

I pulled up in front of my former home in Pacific Heights, a Classical Revival mansion, complete with rounded portico and columns, and now the Elizabeth O'Shaughnessy Foundation for Abused Women and Children, just before seven a.m. When I was little, I thought it looked like the White House, and I pretended John and Jacqueline Kennedy were my parents. I mentioned my fantasy to my father one day, as we walked from his Jaguar up to the house, to which he replied, "So, I'm not good enough for you?"

I never mentioned it again.

As I cruised for parking, the top was down on my new yellow BMW M-5, a gift from my husband Jake, which I'd named "Sunny II" in honor of my first sports car. The crisp, moist San Francisco air filled me with joy for just being alive. A loving husband, a brilliant daughter, and a successful career – I had a lot to be grateful for. Thoughts of my father's disappointment evaporated.

My daughter, Quinn, was in the passenger seat. We had tied scarves around our messy red curls, a la Grace Kelly, to keep the wind from whipping our hair around. As I turned the corner, I spotted activity in the park across the street, where a stage was set up with a tent, a stage, and large speakers. Men busied themselves assembling booths and running cables across the grass.

Large trucks lined the street. I couldn't find a spot and ended up double parking in front of the mansion's brand-new gate. There had been a hedge there before, but it burned when Sunny was firebombed. The sidewalk was badly damaged too, so I'd had it removed and replaced when we built the gate and pathway to the front door.

"What's going on?" I wondered aloud.

Quinn pulled off her scarf and ruffled her hair. "That's the Rick Stevens rally. We got a flyer about it a few days ago."

"Who's Rick Stevens?"

"Some guy. Owns a car dealership. He's running for the state senate against the incumbent, Foster Heiki. All the moms say they can't wait to meet him. They say he's 'really cute'."

"What do you say?"

"I say he's all fluff. Nothing but a collection of populist soundbites. No substance." She took in my expression. "But cute enough if you like that sort of thing. Heiki seems much more capable. He has two master's degrees, one in public management and the other in business, but he's kind of a dweeb. It's like pitting a movie star against a book worm."

"I didn't know you were political."

Quinn was my biological daughter, but she had been adopted because I was fourteen years old when she was born. Only recently she had re-established contact with me. I was thrilled, a dream I had not dared to dream come true, and Jake and I moved her into our condo shortly after she arrived. In some ways, it was like we were never parted. We had many of the same preferences, like watching old British crime dramas and peppering our french fries. But in other ways, she was a stranger to me.

"My parents – I mean the people who raised me – believed politics was important. They had me stuffing envelopes when I was still in a highchair. It was a big deal when I got my own staple gun so I could build signs."

I caught myself holding my breath, so I rummaged around in the console for lip gloss, hopefully to distract her from my anxiety.

Her adopted parents, good, kind, loving people, were educators. The mother had died when Quinn was in high school. The father when she was in college. That was when Quinn started looking for me.

I was dropping her off at the mansion because she volunteered for childcare while the mothers assisted by the O'Shaughnessy Foundation took classes to improve their employability. In the fall, she would start law school. She would be a lawyer someday, just like me. We were still getting to know each other but, with her interest in law, I was pleased that we had more in common than messy red hair.

A car behind me beeped its horn. I motioned for it to go around me. When I opened the tube of lip gloss from the console, I found that it had melted. Warm coral goo clung to my fingers.

"We're holding up traffic," the ever-considerate Quinn said. She gave me a kiss on the cheek. "Have a great day, Mom." The gratuitous "mom" was added because she had mentioned her adopted parents. Sometimes I felt they had been her real parents and I had just been a host. I reminded myself that she looked like me. She was my height and had my hair. But the next thought that always sped in after this reminder was that she had her father's gray eyes. I needed a new affirmation, something that removed her father's existence from my thought pattern.

If only I could.

With that, Quinn climbed out of the sports car and grabbed the grimy backpack that was in the passenger seat well. When she lifted it, the sound of fabric tearing was followed by pens clattering to the floor. She gathered them quickly and stuffed them into a pocket on the bag, the zipper of which had fallen off.

"You need a new backpack," I said.

"I'll just run down to the thrift shop. No problem."

"No," I said. "Let me buy a new one for you. A gift for starting law school. You need something sturdy to protect a laptop."

She scowled. She didn't like buying new things when the earth's resources were already strained.

"It would make me happy." Was I guilt-tripping my daughter? I'd ponder that later.

"Alright. But no leather. And it needs to be made from recycled materials."

That's my girl, saving the planet.

"You got it."

"Love you." She waived as she turned to punch in the security code on the gate post I had programmed, her birthday, and the automatic gate swung open.

The car behind me beeped a second time. I motioned again. I wasn't leaving this spot until I knew she was safe inside. I found tissue in the console and wiped my hands while Quinn loped up the path.

A flash of red caught my eye. It was a parrot sitting in the monkey puzzle tree in the mansion's front garden. My father hated that tree. But my mother refused to cut it down – it had been planted by Elizabeth O'Shaughnessy herself. Such was the force of my grandmother's personality, that even long after she was dead, no one dared to change anything she had loved.

Except me.

I had sold her treasured Diego Rivera painting to finance the O'Shaughnessy Foundation. She would have approved.

My cell phone chirped. I pressed a button on my steering wheel and answered. It was my paralegal, Yolanda Martinez.

"Tony Paredes called."

Tony had been a client of mine a few years prior. I hadn't heard from him in months.

"It's seven in the morning. Why are you answering the office phone?"

"I came in early to catch up on filing."

Sometimes eliciting information from Yolanda felt like cross-examining a hostile witness. The problem was mine. I had asked her a specific question and she had answered precisely.

Yet, I persisted. "So why is Tony Paredes calling the office this early?"

Quinn dragged the heavy mansion door open.

Yolanda's voice was obscured by the car horn behind me.

"What was that? I couldn't hear you."

"He's been arrested," Yolanda yelled.

Tony was given to emotional outbursts, but I couldn't imagine him committing a crime.

"Tony? Our Tony Paredes? What for?"

"Murder."

Quinn turned to wave at me. I waved back.

I couldn't have heard that right. "Wait, what did you say?"

"They say he murdered Oscar Wenderholm," she yelled even louder. "That's all I know."

Oscar Wenderholm was a high school chess coach who had sexually abused Tony repeatedly and left him the emotional wreck that he was. The authorities never prosecuted. By the time the crime was reported, they said the evidence was lost and memories had faded. So, Tony filed suit and I agreed to represent him. The jury awarded him millions of dollars. But a juror had researched the case online during deliberations and had shown inadmissible evidence to the other jurors, which tainted the verdict. The defense attorneys found out and had the verdict set aside.

Afterwards, Wenderholm went on with his life, while Tony continued to struggle daily with functioning in a world which he believed was rigged against him. But murder? And why, after all this time? It didn't make sense.

The car behind me lay on its horn, a long loud blast. The mansion door was closed. Quinn had gone inside.

I pushed the stick shift into first gear and popped the clutch. My tires squealed as I pulled out into the street.

▼

WHILE I WAITED FOR Tony in the jail visiting room, I searched through my phone for news about the arrest. The story was everywhere, complete with a perp walk video, Tony being escorted from his apartment building to a waiting police car. The crawl along the bottom of the screen said, "Anthony Paredes arrested for murder of abuser." So much for trial by jury.

When Tony entered, he whipped his surfer boy bangs away from his face as he surveyed the surroundings before he sat down. The door behind him banged shut. He flinched. Through the glass pane, I saw the guard smirk. A key ring jangled when it turned in the lock. The guard jerked on the door to make sure it was secure before he sauntered down the hall.

Tony looked at me, his mouth open, but no words came out. With the yellow light and the orange jumper, he looked anemic. Through his hornrims, I could see his eyes were red from crying.

"What happened?" I asked.

"I don't know. It was like five o'clock in the morning when the cops came. I had just gotten to sleep. I work nights now. There was all this banging at the door. When I opened it, they pushed me to the ground and handcuffed me. They said I had murdered Oscar. I told them it must be some kind of mistake."

I held up my hand. "Okay, first things. No more talking to anyone about anything unless your attorney is with you. Got that?"

"Okay, fine. That's all I said anyway, promise. I don't see how that can hurt me."

"Not a word, Tony. I'm warning you."

He made a twisty gesture at his lips, then asked, "So, like, what happens next?"

"You're entitled to a public defender if you can't afford to hire counsel."

"I don't want a public defender. Everyone I talked to in here said their PD sold them down the river, not to get one."

"Stop talking to the other prisoners. They count. You never know who's going to rat you out."

"I didn't lie to them."

"The fact that you talked to them at all gives them a chance to say you said something incriminating – even if you didn't. See what I mean?"

"Whatever. I don't want a public defender. You know me. You know Oscar. You know the case."

"Tony, I have never defended a murder case, or any kind of criminal case for that matter, not even a traffic ticket. I was a prosecutor, not defense counsel. The public defender's office does nothing but. And they are very good at what they do."

"What's the big deal? You just have to do the opposite thing, right? And you know what the prosecutors will do, all their dirty little tricks."

I would prefer to think prosecutors didn't use dirty little tricks, but the truth was, there were some who do.

"Maureen, I didn't do it. You have to help me. I wouldn't even know how to kill someone – how stupid is that? I can't spend the rest of my life in prison for something I didn't do. That stuff you see on TV doesn't even come close. These guys are really scary, some of them are just like crazy animals. And the guards! I heard they look the other way when someone they don't like is going to get hurt. You know what they call me? The Millionaire. They know about the case, and they think I got all that money. You know me, Maureen. It was never about the money. I just wanted to get the truth out. Now these inmates are circling me like wolves. I need you to get me out of here. Please, I'm begging you."

"I'll step in long enough to apply for bail. After that, we'll need to talk again."

Tony grabbed my hand. "Thank you. Thank you so much. I knew you'd help me. You're my angel."

A mechanical voice came over a loudspeaker. "No contact."

I pointed at the fish-eye camera in the ceiling.

Tony let go of my hand. "Can they hear us?"

I wasn't so sure. "They're not supposed to eavesdrop, but its best if you don't say anything."

"No problem."

"Have you talked to Isaac since you were arrested?"

Isaac was Tony's roommate and best friend. They had known each other since the Lafayette Academy, where Tony was abused by Wenderholm. Isaac didn't testify at the civil trial. He said dredging up those awful memories was emotionally hard on Tony. Isaac believed it was better to look forward, not behind, and forget about what had happened. Besides, he said he didn't see anything, so he had nothing to contribute.

"I talked to Isaac for a few minutes on the phone," Tony said.

"No more phone calls. Or if you do, don't talk about the case. The jail records those. Understand? No talking about the case to anyone, anytime. I'll call him myself as soon as I get back to the office."

Chapter Two

Rick

RICK STEVENS SUNK INTO an oversized leather armchair as he swirled a tumbler of vodka tonic. He'd selected the furniture and décor for his home office, all midcentury modern. Clean lines. Neutral colors This was his space. Appollonia, his wife, had decorated the rest of the house in some old French style with a lot of gold, silk, and crystal chandeliers.

But this room, his room, was clean lines. Over the drinks cabinet was an enlarged studio photograph of his long-dead mother holding one year-old Rick. Rick was just a kid at the time, he didn't know any better, but even then, she looked sick.

Umberto Salazar, Rick's campaign manager, hiked a hip up on Rick's desk, and pointed a remote at the wall-mounted television. The black screen flared to life in a blaze of color, then resolved into a video of Rick's primary night party.

A handsome young reporter stood beside Rick in a two-shot. The kid was a little shorter than Rick, but he had an athletic body and the chiseled features that would turn him into a network star one day. He held the microphone loosely, exuding the kind of self-confidence that some people were born with.

"I'm standing next to Rick Stevens, the upset winner of today's senate primary. Mr. Stevens, what do you owe your success to?"

The kid flicked the microphone towards Rick's face. At the time, Rick thought the gesture was suggestive. Watching it now, he was pleased with how quickly he aimed his sincere look directly into the camera. No one would have detected the innuendo. "Clearly, the voters are tired of politics as usual. No more behind-the-doors deals. No more kowtowing. The people of San Francisco want a fresh voice in Sacramento, and they see that I am that person."

The boy reporter tilted the microphone to himself. "The pundits predicted that your primary opponent stood a better chance of defeating the incumbent, Senator Foster

Heiki. Yet, the party turned out for you. Why do you think the voters would risk sending you to the November election?"

Umberto stabbed the air with the remote. The video froze. "There! Did you see that?"

The image was blurred.

"See what?" Rick asked. He hadn't been watching. He'd been wondering where he would have been if his parents had lived. Would they be sitting right here next to him, faces beaming with pride as they watched their boy accept the nomination?

Umberto thumbed the device. The video spun in reverse at high speed. Images raced across the scene. Rick looking sincerely into the camera. The boy reporter pointing the microphone at Rick. A long shot of the crepe-paper decorated ballroom filled with half-delirious supporters.

The real-life Rick needed more booze. The drink in his hand was low. He leaned across the armrest to reach the decanter that Umberto had set almost out of his reach. He poured two fingers into the glass.

"Pay attention," Umberto said.

"I'm all yours." Rick took another sip and pushed deeply into the chair, the leather squeaking expensively under his butt. *This was the life*. Fame, fortune. Good booze. People sucking up to you. And he wanted more of it. Lots, lots more.

The video began again. Boy reporter. Question. Microphone thrust. Rick's sincere face. Answer. Next question. Rick brushing his bangs out of his eyes.

Umberto lunged at the screen, pointing with the remote. "There!"

"What?"

"See how you push your hair back? You're hiding your face. Rick, your face is a gold mine. You have movie star good looks. Blonde, blue eyes, square jaw. The slow, easy smile with glistening straight white teeth. Women love you. Gay men love you even more. Straight men want to be you. We don't want that million-dollar face covered, ever. Every photograph, including paparazzi shots, needs to show" — here he jabbed twice at the television screen with the remote for emphasis – "That. Face. Foster Heiki can't compete against you."

Foster Heiki might have been the senator for San Francisco, but Rick had never heard of him before because Rick didn't care about politics. From what he understood, Heiki was an overeducated pencil pusher. No personality. Not unattractive but nothing going for him. Where Rick had a thick blonde mane, Heiki had brown hair, buzz cut to hide the fact that he was balding. Where Rick had dimples, Heiki had chipmunk cheeks darkened by a perpetual five o'clock shadow. Rick was the blue-eyed boy. Heiki looked like an evil IRS auditor.

Rick knew he was handsome, and people reacted to his good looks. Still, it tickled him that Umberto, no slouch himself, made such a big deal out of it. Umberto was almost six feet, not quite as tall as Rick. Lean. Black suit. Black hair. His thick black curly eyelashes framed puppy brown eyes and made him look feminine. He looked like a hip undertaker. He carried himself like a dancer.

That's what Rick wanted in a campaign manager. Someone who could appeal to anyone, mostly rich old white guys even as Umberto played the Spanish charmer with their wives with a suddenly adopted accent, and who had his fingers on the voters' pulse, white and Hispanic. He'd come very highly recommended. Combining his Spanish heritage with that of Rick's wife, there was a whole group of voters Rick could pull in that Heiki could not. Without Umberto and Appollonia, Rick was just another ambitious white guy.

Okay, a movie star handsome ambitious white guy. When he was approached to run for office, politics had never occurred to him. But, why not, he thought. He was successful, hardworking, likeable. It was his likeability that made him a great salesman. He could sell anything from busted-up old beaters to shiny new luxury sedans. Selling himself? No worries.

He'd made millions. The problem was, and he was the first to admit it, he didn't have a head for business. For some reasons he never understood, the more he made, the more he owed. When he won the election, he could sell the dealership and get out from under the debt. Start new. Good things come to those in office. Look at all those saps who get elected when they're dead broke and die rich. That could be him, too.

"So, what do you advise, compadre?" Rick asked.

Umberto winced. He didn't like Rick's Spanish. Rick didn't know why. He was trying to bridge the gap, show that he cared to go that extra step. But Umberto had told him to never speak Spanish in public, claiming Rick's accent was embarrassing.

Umberto said, "You're booked into a salon tomorrow."

"You're cutting my hair?"

"This isn't a barber shop. We're styling it. We'll keep the thickness. But we'll trim it enough that it doesn't fall in your eyes, so you won't need to brush it away."

People loved to run their fingers through his hair. The last time, a fist closed, then slowly pulled his head back. Rick had playfully resisted, but for only a moment.

He felt a wriggling in his pants and adjusted his legs to camouflage the movement.

"Settle down, Romeo." It was Appollonia talking. She had entered the room without Rick noticing, even though he had made sure to close the solid wood double doors when he and Umberto had returned from the rally. It was a wonder she could walk on the thick carpet in those spikey high heels without turning an ankle, much less without making a sound. Rick couldn't.

Without standing, he took her hand and pressed his lips to it. "My love."

She snorted and pulled away. Her own glass, a champagne flute, was full. As she moved across the room, her hips swayed more than when she was sober. If not for Rick, then for Umberto? Did it matter? She was entitled to her own diversions too.

She draped herself across a couch, then motioned to the television screen, now frozen on a close-up of Rick, an earnest frown ever so slightly creasing his brow. "What's this?"

"Umberto thinks I should get my hair styled."

She cocked her head as she studied the image. "He's right. Expose those blue eyes. They are what made me fall in love with you. They are," – she searched for the word – "electrifying."

So, it wasn't the promise of a lavish lifestyle north of the border? This time it was Rick who snorted.

Umberto interrupted, "I'm lining up an interview, the loving couple, Mr. and Mrs. Stevens, in their dream home. Just a typical American man and wife. So, no more driving the Bentley."

Rick slammed his tumbler onto the end table. "What!" He loved that car. He loved the looks it got when he pulled into valet parking, how the drivers trembled when he handed them the keys. He loved how, as he entered the hotel after handing off the car, women who'd seen his entrance, would turn themselves ever so slightly, presenting their breasts to him with wet smiles on their faces. He swore their perfume was stronger, heated by a sudden surge in their hormones. He loved how, after he politely smiled back, he could feel their eyes on him as he walked into the building. "Then what the hell am I supposed to drive? Foster Heiki's car?"

"He drives an electric mid-size," Umberto said. "You are going to drive one of those American cross-over things, like everyone has now."

"A mommy mobile."

"That's right."

That could work for him. Rick liked mommies. There was that one –.

Umberto frowned as he scanned his cell phone. "I need to speak to the next California senator in private, Mrs. Stevens, if you please."

"Sounds mysterious." Appollonia teased as she coyly crossed her legs.

Umberto opened the door and stuck his head out into the hallway. "Javier, would you open a bottle of champagne for Mrs. Stevens?"

A skinny, young Mexican man appeared. "Yes, sir. Mrs. Stevens?"

Appollonia upended the champagne flute over her open mouth. Umberto extended a hand to her, helping her to her feet. She sashayed into the hallway, purring to the boy who was waiting for her. "Thank you, Javier."

Appollonia liked the good life too.

After she had left the room, Umberto closed the doors.

"Bad news?" Rick asked.

"Remember Oscar Wenderholm?"

Rick had hoped to never hear that name again. He scanned the room as if to search his memory. When he caught his reflection in the sliding glass door behind his desk, he saw fear. Umberto met his eyes in the reflection. Rick looked away.

"You know who I'm talking about. Your friend. The one who called here looking for a favor."

"Oh, yeah, him. Now I remember. You said you handled it. So, what's the problem?"

"He's been murdered. It's all over the news."

Chapter Three

Maureen

MY OFFICE CONDO IS in a historic Jackson Square building, two flights up from the street. I bought it with what was left of my Granny O'Shaughnessy inheritance, just after I left the DA's office. I filled it with big heavy furniture, wooden desks, cabinets, bookcases, leather chairs and couches. Being young, and a female, I felt like I had to compensate to match client's expectations of what a lawyer should look like. Even though television courtroom dramas are veering away from the old white guy stereotype, most people expect to see Perry Mason when they walk in the door. So, I wanted my office to convey tradition and history.

When I returned from seeing Tony in jail, Yolanda was already at her desk. She was wearing the fringed black and white checked tweed suit she wore when we had first met at a legal clinic. Her purse would be stashed in the bottom drawer of her desk.

"I need an entry of appearance for Tony's case," I said. An entry of appearance is the formal document that an attorney signs and files with the court informing everyone concerned that she represents a party.

"You're taking the case." Yolanda's tone was efficient. And cold.

"Is that coffee I smell?" I asked brightly.

She gave me a hang-dog look. Clearly, she wasn't interested in small talk. But until I had coffee, I wasn't ready for big talk. I was exhausted and dehydrated from visiting Tony, not just the emotional drain, but also the long shuffle into the depths of the institution and back out again, during which time it was best to have an empty bladder.

I wandered into the kitchenette, and before I filled the biggest mug I could find, I piled a small plate with brightly colored sugar cookies that Yolanda had been bringing in lately, and then carried the lot to my corner office.

By the time I'd settled into my chair, put away my briefcase, took a bite out of a cookie, and drank half my coffee, she was standing in front of me holding a single page. She ceremoniously slid it across the desk for my signature.

I signed and offered it back to her with a smile. "Thank you."

"Since when do we take murder cases?" She perched on the edge of one of the visitor chairs without accepting the document. I laid it down on the desk between us.

She said, "When I signed on, it was because you said you wanted to help victims find justice. We were fighting the good fight. Making things right. And now you're defending a murder case? Who's the victim here? It's not Tony. It's Oscar Wenderholm. And his wife and children."

"Tony's innocent. I'm certain of it. He doesn't have it inside of him to kill someone."

"Then let the public defenders handle it. Why does it have to be us?"

How could I explain it to Yolanda? When Tony's civil jury verdict was vacated, he was worse off than if we hadn't filed suit. He told his story. He had been vindicated, but only for a little while. To him, it had to feel like he didn't matter. So, I hadn't made things right for him. My mission was a failure, and I felt an unsettling sense of incompletion. Now he was in real trouble. I had the skills he needed to see him through this case.

"Look, I told Tony I'd handle the bail issue, just for the time being. Then we'll reevaluate, see if the Public Defender's Office can do a better job."

"You never leave anything half-done."

Yolanda might be my office mom, but this was my practice. "Yolanda, you know how important you are to me. And I would hope to have your complete support with any case I accept."

She recoiled as if she'd been slapped. This was the first time I had felt the need to establish a boundary. Without a word, she picked up the document and walked out of the room.

When I called the DA's office to see if they would agree to bail, I was put through to Vivian Thandi, a senior prosecutor who I had known when I worked there. We had both started at the same time in the misdemeanor unit, then she went off to homicide when I went to sexual assault.

Vivian was African, originally from Britain, but she had moved to the States with her family as a teenager. Tall, lean, and graceful, she was elegant in a way that made me feel awkward and clumsy. Her perfectly formed head was shaved and made her look regal. She spoke with carefully chosen words and said as little as possible. In court, she was deadly. She spoke with such authority that the juries naturally fell into line. When we were both prosecutors, I was grateful that I would never be on the opposite side of a case with her. And now I was.

"Maureen," she drawled. "How good it is to hear from you. To what do I owe the pleasure?"

"Anthony Paredes."

I could hear her tapping her keyboard. "Ah, yes, murdered his abuser."

"Accused of."

"You received quite a nice jury award for him a while back."

"The verdict was substantial," I said. "But the judgment was set aside, and the case dismissed. He doesn't have any money."

"How can I be of help to you?" Vivian asked.

"I'm calling to see if you'll agree to bail."

"Hmm. You're representing him? I thought you'd gone into personal injury when you left the office." Personal injury was DA code for greedy ambulance-chasers.

More tapping on her keyboard.

"I represent abuse victims," I said. "As I did when I worked for the state. But this isn't about me. Tony has no priors. He's a lifelong resident of San Francisco. He's not going anywhere. He has no means at any rate, he's living hand to mouth."

"We have a very strong case, Maureen. I don't know if the DA would agree to house arrest."

"What case? All I know is the man is dead."

"The victim was shot in the driveway of his home as he disembarked from his vehicle at approximately 1: 30 a.m. The murder weapon was found in the trunk of your client's car."

"Witnesses?"

"His victim's wife found his body. She had taken sleeping medication and didn't hear the shot."

That would be no eyewitnesses, then. "How was time of death established?" I asked.

"Preliminary report from the medical examiner. Also, it was the victim's habit of returning home from work at approximately that time."

It wouldn't take a lot of knowledge to kill a man with a gun, it's literally just point and shoot. "I assume you tested my client's hands and clothes for powder."

More tapping.

"His hands were clean. But that doesn't mean anything, he could have worn gloves."

"Did you recover gloves?"

"No, but we recovered a hooded sweatshirt that your client admitted belongs to him. The gun was wrapped in it. Significant evidence of gunpowder was detected."

"Transference." It was a knee-jerk rebuttal. The real problem was the gun was found in Tony's car. It may have been planted. Or Tony was lying.

"Ah, but we have a witness."

I suddenly felt cold.

"I thought you said –"

"Not to the shooting, but to the argument the afternoon before the murder. Your client showed up – just a minute, here it is – at Mr. Wenderholm's residence, just as the victim was leaving for work. It appears Mr. Paredes had been watching him and knew his routine. Your client was angry and irrational. He stood behind the victim's vehicle, blocking the driveway and yelled for some period of time, preventing the victim from leaving the premises. When the man's wife emerged from the house and informed your client that she had called the police, he threatened to kill Mr. Wenderholm, then climbed into his car, which was parked in front of the house, and drove away. The wife identified Mr. Paredes from a photo line-up. She said she was positive it was him, having attended the civil trial."

"Did the house have surveillance video?"

"There is a device. My investigators are looking into whether it recorded anything useful."

"I trust you'll send me a copy of what you find."

"In due course."

"Have you tracked the gun?"

"We tried," Vivian said, then let out a huff. "It's a ghost gun. Untraceable. Regardless, Maureen, we have fairly strong evidence. The DA takes a dim view of releasing an accused under these circumstances. Sorry I couldn't be more help."

A judge might grant bail anyway. There would be no harm in trying. "You can do me one favor. No more perp walks for the television reporters. My client is entitled to a fair trial and that means an unbiased jury. You know as well as I do, showing him cuffed and escorted makes him look guilty to anyone who watches television."

"Sorry about that, Maureen. I will have a word. But to be honest, I'm not sure this is the right case for your first murder defense. Losing couldn't be good publicity for a new practice. Are you sure you want to get involved?"

I wasn't. I had only promised to cover bail while an experienced criminal defense attorney could be found. I was terrified that if I took the case and made a mistake, Tony would be unjustly convicted. But the longer Vivian talked about the evidence, the more intrigued I became. If the DA's case was that good, why did she need to work so hard to convince me?

"See you in court, Viv."

QUINN MADE DINNER THAT night, which is to say, she picked up Chinese food. We gathered around the dinner table in the great room of my loft, now our loft, in the neighborhood known as South Park, a former industrial area just south of the Bay Bridge. My open-concept, urban chic condo was in a converted warehouse, all concrete floors, granite counters, and overhead pipes that I'm not sure did anything except collect dust. I loved it.

Jake, my tall, dark handsome husband, brought three bottles of Tsingtaobeer from the kitchen while Quinn bustled around, setting the table with chunky stoneware she and I had picked up at a fair earlier that summer. Before she came to live with us, he and I would have eaten out of the cartons. But with my daughter in the house, we tried to act a little more civilized. We were a family now, not just a pair of exhausted trial lawyers.

Germaine Greer, the Siamese cat Jake had given me, complained in the kitchen that her dinner was late. The cat barely tolerated me, loved Jake, and adored Quinn. I heard the grinding of the can opener and Quinn murmuring.

Jake handed me an opened bottle. "Did you see the mail, Red?" When we were first married, he started calling me "Red" in a Jimmy Cagney voice, a term of endearment between a gangster and his gun moll. We thought it was cute, especially since we were both lawyers.

I'd noticed a stack of mail on a sideboard in the front hall, next to the vintage Bakelite phone my mother had given me as a housewarming gift, a not too subtle reminder to call more often. "Is there something important?"

"Nothing that won't wait until after dinner."

Quinn came out of the kitchen with three lager glasses. She took the bottle out of my hand, expertly poured the beer, then handed it to me. "Saw you talking to someone on the phone this morning before you peeled out from the mansion. Is everything okay?"

"Peeled out?" It was so long ago, I'd forgotten.

"Laid rubber? Is that what they say on the West Coast?"

My dramatic gesture had been childish. I'd wanted to irritate the driver behind me, who had every right to honk his horn. I was double-parked and blocking the road. He couldn't get around me without driving blindly into oncoming traffic. Besides, by driving fast, I was only going to get to the next stop light quicker.

"I got a call that an old client of mine is in jail."

"Which old client?" Jake asked.

I'd just opened my practice a few years ago and had taken a handful of cases. Jake knew all their names.

"Tony Paredes."

"What did he do to get arrested?" Jake asked.

"He's *accused* of murdering Oscar Wenderholm." I emphasized "accused" to remind Jake of the presumption of innocence.

"No way," Jake said.

Quinn finished delivering the food and sat down. "Who is Tony Paredes and Oscar whathisname?"

"Wenderholm," Jake offered.

I explained while I piled rice on my plate. "In high school, Tony Paredes was a student at Lafayette Academy. His chess coach, Oscar Wenderholm, abused him multiple times. When Wenderholm was caught, the school let him go with a letter recommendation and kicked Tony out. We sued Oscar and the school."

"Which you won spectacularly," Jake said.

"If you won the trial, why would your client kill the guy now?" Quinn asked.

"That is a very good question, Counselor," I said. "You're thinking like a lawyer."

Jake gave me a look from beneath a lowered brow. Quinn was thinking like a defense lawyer, tearing a case apart. Jake, the former cop and now prosecutor, does the opposite. He builds cases to put away bad guys.

I responded. "He said he didn't do it and I believe him. He never lied to me before."

"Right," Jake said. He knew that virtually one hundred percent of defendants claimed they didn't do it when they're first arrested. He also knew that most of them eventually confessed. "So why is he calling you?"

"He wants me to take his case."

At this Jake's chin jutted in my direction – in silent disapproval.

"Why shouldn't she?" Quinn asked.

Jake put two eggrolls on his plate then passed the carton to Quinn. "If we have enough evidence to charge him, he probably did it. Any assistant public defender can get him a good deal."

When Jake used "we," he meant the DA's office. He wasn't just the loving spouse giving me his unvarnished opinion of my cases, which, earlier in our marriage, had been a source of misunderstanding, arguments, and almost a divorce. But now he was slipping into the role of my opponent.

I didn't like it.

And I don't back down from a fight.

"You know as well as I do between four and six percent of people incarcerated in the United States are innocent. There are exonerations on the news all the time, even years after the convictions. Not only that, but people are also sometimes acquitted."

He didn't back down either. "Less than one percent are acquitted. That doesn't mean they didn't do it. That means the prosecutors didn't prove it to the jury's satisfaction. But, assuming for the purpose of argument, that all those acquittals were innocent, that leaves in the neighborhood of ninety-five per cent that were justly convicted. What makes you think Tony is in that rare five percent who should walk away Scot free?"

"Assuming for the purpose of argument" was a legal brief term meaning even if the facts were as argued by the other guy, the other guy was wrong.

Fight on.

"I talked to Vivian Thandi. There are holes in her case. She knows it, I can hear it in her voice."

"Oh, geez, Maureen. Are you sure you want to go up against her?"

Not Red anymore. Maureen.

Quinn passed the eggrolls to me. "Why is she so bad?"

"She scares the shit out of everyone in the office," Jake answered, "even the detectives,"

"But not you, right, Jake?" Quinn adored him. Tall, dark, square of jaw and broad of shoulder, he held a bit of Prince Charming alure for her. He was intellectual and compassionate, but someone who would bravely challenge a dragon with nothing more than a sword and his trusty steed.

"I wouldn't want to go up against Thandi, let me say that much. Did I ever tell you about the time she made a rookie cry when she was prepping him for court?"

"At least twenty times." I'd heard the story from another assistant DA who had been in the room, so I knew it wasn't exaggerated.

"Okay, she's scary," Quinn said. "But why, that's what I want to know."

"She's that intense," Jake said. "And determined. And she doesn't like to lose."

"No one does," I said.

"Yeah, but her win-loss score is sacred to her. Every time she comes back from a verdict, she goes straight into the supervisor's office and the first words out of her mouth is her score. Last I heard she was 72-1."

I knew all this. Vivian Thandi was famous throughout the office.

"What happened in the case she lost?" Quinn asked.

I knew the answer to this too, but Jake was on a roll, so I let him answer. "The defendant committed suicide while the jury was deliberating."

"Technically not a loss," I said. "Really a mistrial."

"Technically. But she likes to mention it so everyone will remember, or ask if they don't know, why she lost that one trial. It makes her sound even more intimidating. If she tries a case, it's because she honestly believes she's going to win it. Otherwise, she'll offer you a deal."

"Sounds like a bunch of mind games to me," Quinn said as she reached for soy sauce.

Jake picked up his chopsticks and started in on his chow mein.

"Mom?" Quinn asked. "How come you aren't eating?"

That honeymoon high was gone. It felt like Jake and I were back where we had been during Tony's civil case, when his criticism chipped away at my self-confidence. I understood now it wasn't the case that drove us apart, it was how I reacted to what he said. His statements inflamed a pain I'd kept secret from him and instead of being honest, I retaliated in defense. I wasn't going to do that again.

Before I agreed to taking Tony's criminal case beyond a bail motion, I had wanted Jake's support. The new less reactive me decided to ignore his self-righteous prosecutorial pronouncements and reframe his comments as loving concern.

"I get what you're saying, babe," I said. "And I appreciate your advice. But someone will be at his side. I know the players and the facts. So that person should be me. Hey, Quinn, do you think you can make some time before fall semester starts to help me organize the case?"

"For real? A murder case?"

"All hands on deck."

Jake half stood out of his chair, grabbed my hand, and pulled me up to a kiss.

"I knew you were going to say that, Red. Quinn, that's the thing about your mother. Tell her she can't do something and she'll attack it like a bulldog."

"Oh, gross, you guys. Get a room," Quinn said, smiling.

After dinner, Jake and Quinn settled in front of the television. He had recorded a San Francisco Giant's game to watch with her. Sports bored me, but I treasured each moment when we built our little family shared history.

I picked up the mail on my way to the couch and thumbed through it. Bills, ads, and one letter in a thin envelope addressed in my father's handwriting. The return address was California State Institute Snowden. That's where Frank had been incarcerated following his conviction for money laundering. The District Attorney didn't get him on child abuse – it didn't have enough evidence.

By the time he was charged, everyone in the District Attorney's office knew that I had an adult daughter and they appeared to have done the math, but I wasn't asked to testify. Nor did I volunteer. I didn't want Quinn to be famous for being the result of an incestuous rape. I hadn't told her who her father was then and still hadn't. She only knew that it was a trusted family member. I suppose she could figure it out for herself. Even so, that's something that should be discussed and not left to conjecture. When I was ready.

I tore the envelope in two and took it to the recycle bin in the kitchen. Jake watched me and said nothing. Quinn didn't notice, absorbed in cheering along with the television crowd. When I returned to the couch, he wrapped a big warm arm around me and pulled me close. I wiped my eyes with the palm of my hand and snuggled into him.

The scars on my arm itched. I tried to ignore them, focusing instead on the steady thump of Jake's heart beating in his chest, the smell of soap he'd used when he took his after-work shower, and the rustling of his chest hair beneath my cheek, but the burning intensified. The pain was nearly as searing as when I'd first got them.

I drifted to sleep wondering how people could be so cruel.

Chapter Four

Maureen

AT THE BAIL HEARING, Judge Cranston, an older white male who looked as if he was fighting sleep after a big lunch, gave Vivian and me exactly one minute each to state our positions. Vivian, poised in a tailored black suit, was sitting at her table with a young male attorney. Her paralegal sat in the front row behind her. Tony, dressed in an orange jumpsuit, had been brought in chained to several other defendants, and was waiting in the jury box.

Behind us, the courtroom was packed with attorneys, clients, and loved ones waiting for their turn on the docket.

Vivian Thandi asked for no bail. She argued Tony had been charged with murder, a witness had heard him threaten Wenderholm's life, and the murder weapon was found in Tony's car with his powder-stained hoody.

I touched the O'Shaughnessy pearls at my throat for luck and stood up. "Your Honor, we request house arrest. Anthony Paredes has no criminal history. He is unlikely to flee the jurisdiction as he was born and raised in San Francisco. Gun ownership is untraceable because it was a ghost gun. The powder stains on the sweatshirt could have easily been caused by transference when the gun was placed into Tony's trunk, the lock on which is broken so anyone could have planted the gun easily." I couldn't have gotten the bit about Tony's broken trunk lock into evidence unless Tony testified, and I had no intention of putting him on the stand.

Judge Cranston understood my evidentiary problem. "Ms. Thandi, does the State agree that the vehicle lock was broken?" he asked.

Vivian stooped to whisper to the policeman sitting behind her, then returned to her table. "We agree, Your Honor."

It was too good to be true. Sometimes the judge will nudge the other attorney into concessions, knowing that ultimately, he can ignore the evidence when making his decision. Manipulating the attorneys in this manner cuts down on fighting and moves cases along more quickly. With a packed courtroom, his primary goal was efficiency.

It turned out the Wenderholm home surveillance camera had not recorded because it was only there for looks. It wasn't connected to any recording devices or applications, so the proof of whether Tony visited the premises. made threats, or committed murder, hinged on the testimony of the victim's wife.

Vivian called the widow to testify. Brita Wenderholm was a stout woman with graying blonde hair and a fleshy face. She wore a navy-blue shirtwaist, the belt of which looked uncomfortably tight. As she crossed the court well to the stand, she shot Tony and me hateful looks.

After the witness was sworn in, Vivian said, "Mrs. Wenderholm, are you the widow of Oscar Wenderholm?"

"Yes."

"How are you employed?"

"Oscar and I agreed that I would homeschool the children. We couldn't afford a private school after he lost his job at Lafayette Academy. Public schools are just too dangerous these days with all the drugs and guns. So, no, I am not employed outside the home."

"Mrs. Wenderholm, please tell us what you saw on the afternoon prior to your husband's murder."

"Oscar left for work as usual around 2:30 pm. He was working as a guard across the Bay. That's the only job he could get after what *he* said in court about Oscar." She shot a look at Tony. "Oscar worked swing shift, four to midnight and had to leave an hour and a half early to get to work because of the commute. I was doing the ironing in the kitchen when I noticed a mustard-colored Gremlin pull up in front of our house and park. I thought nothing of it at first. Then I heard arguing. I came out on the stoop and saw Anthony Paredes shouting at my husband."

"Are you sure the vehicle was a Gremlin?" Vivian asked.

Tony's car was a Gremlin.

"I had one in college," the widow said. "I was surprised there were any on the road anymore."

"Thank you, Mrs. Wenderholm. Now, for the record, would you please point out Mr. Paredes?"

Brita Wenderholm had sat behind her husband in the civil trial every day. She heard Tony testify about how Oscar had abused him. She listened as Oscar denied it on the stand. If anyone knew someone was lying, it would be a spouse. I believed Tony. Oscar was lying. How Brita continued to stand by her man was beyond me.

Mrs. Wenderholm extended her arm and aimed her forefinger directly at my client. "That's him. That's the man who killed my husband."

Judge Cranston held up a hand. "We need to let the jury decide that, Mrs. Wenderholm." He pointed to Vivian. "Continue."

"Would you please tell the judge what happened after you saw Mr. Paredes shouting at your husband?"

"I stayed on the stoop. I was afraid he might attack me."

Tony scoffed. I shushed him.

The widow continued. "I yelled. I said I'd called the police, and they were coming."

"Had you in fact called the police?" Vivian asked.

"No, I just said that to scare him off. What was the point of calling? They have accidents and shootings to deal with. They're not going to come running because of an argument, are they?"

Vivian made a check mark on her legal pad. "And what did Mr. Paredes do when you warned him that you had called the police?"

"He said, and I quote, 'I will kill you, Oscar. I will kill you.' Then he ran back up to his Gremlin and drove away."

"Are you in fear of Mr. Paredes for your personal safety?"

Judge Cranston and I exchanged looks. The question was leading. The judge would only get annoyed if I slowed down the hearing. He blinked at me, which I took to understand that he wasn't going to consider the answer and he was reminding me that he had given me a favor when he leaned on the DA to stipulate that the car trunk was broken. So, I didn't object. Better to keep the judge as close to my side as I can, or at least try not to irritate him, at this juncture. I had no idea if he would be the trial judge.

Mrs. Wenderholm shrieked her answer. "Of course, I'm afraid! He knows where I live. He's been to my house. He killed my husband. I'm a witness against him. I'm terrified that he'll come back. I have two children I need to protect. It's not like we're rich. With Oscar's paycheck, we were barely getting by. If it hadn't been for my brother, we would have lost the house. I don't know how we're going to survive now. I can't afford to move somewhere to keep my children safe. Are you going to put me into witness protection?"

Vivian was stunned. The truth was a routine murder case didn't warrant witness protection. This wasn't an organized crime prosecution that would lead to a cascade of convictions. Vivian couldn't announce to a full courtroom that the DA's office prioritized its cases. If she did, she could expect a social media onslaught accusing her of not caring about ordinary people.

Vivian ignored the widow's question and examined her notes. Mrs. Wenderholm correctly took that to be a "no, we're not putting you in a protection program." She turned to the judge. "Your Honor, I am begging you. Please don't let that man out of jail."

The judge denied bail on the grounds that Tony was charged with murder, had made threats to the victim before he was killed, and the widow was afraid for her safety.

After the bail hearing, I met with Tony in the secured conference room provided by the courthouse for attorneys to meet with clients.

He shook his hair out of his face. "She's lying. I never threatened to kill him. And I have no idea how that gun ended up in my car. It's not mine."

"Did you go to his house?"

"What if I did?"

"Tony, I can't help you if I don't know what the facts are. And I shouldn't have to pull the truth from you. Can we try this again?"

"Sorry," Tony said. "I've never been in a situation like this before. I don't know what to say."

"How did you find where he lived?"

"I followed him."

My skull felt like a steel band was tightening around it. I massaged my forehead.

"It was an accident," he said.

I looked up. "You accidentally followed him?"

"Noooo." He dragged out the word sarcastically. "I accidentally saw him at the game store in the Daly City mall. He came in with his kid. That's when I followed him to his house."

"When was that?"

"Months ago."

"How did you know what time he left for work?"

He looked at me like I was stupid.

I could make assumptions, but I needed facts. "In the months before Oscar Wender-holm was murdered, you followed him how many times?"

He struck a bored pose, bouncing a crossed leg. "I can't be sure."

"Did you follow him to his job?"

"To his job. Home from his job. To the barber. A bunch of places. Even saw him meeting Katsu. You remember Emerson Katsu, the Vice Principal at Lafayette Academy, the guy who found us together."

"You were stalking Oscar."

Tony jumped to his feet. "Whose side are you on?"

A guard knocked on the window and motioned Tony to sit down. He obeyed.

"Fine," I said. "Why were you *following* him?"

"This is going to sound dumb."

"Whenever you're ready, Tony."

"Because I wanted to make sure he wasn't hurting kids."

Chapter Five

Rick

THE FIRST THING EVERY morning, Rick worked out in his home gym. Sweated out impurities, burned calories, cleared his mind. He had been into fitness ever since high school, running at least a hundred miles a week. It was his vanguard against the heart disease that had killed his mother. But no amount of exercise would save him from being run over by a garbage truck, like his father had been.

He felt a little queasy from the night before as he pounded on the treadmill, but he knew it'd be gone soon. If not, he'd vomit when he started his gut-burning Pilates routine.

Sweat poured from him, but he didn't feel hair glued to his forehead because of the new haircut. Umberto had been right. It not only looked good, it felt good. He wiped the sweat from his brow with a thumb and flicked it onto the carpet.

The wall-mounted television blared local news. Foster Heiki leaving the Capital building after a vote. Foster Heiki meeting with the Governor. Foster Heiki leading the polls against an unknown candidate, Rick Stevens, local car salesman.

"Car dealership owner," Rick shouted at the screen.

Rick used to listen to pulse-racing hard rock when he ran or lifted, but Umberto said he needed to educate himself on the issues. Not that it mattered much. Rick wasn't allowed to speak his mind. Instead, Umberto taught him a series of crowd-pleasing noncommittal phrases, the kind of stuff anyone in the audience could believe if they wanted.

Oscar Wenderholm's picture flashed on the screen. It was the story about his murder and the man who'd been arrested for it. The photo of Oscar was cropped from what looked like a chess team portrait, given that beaming smile used when he posed for a camera. It had been taken years ago, Rick figured, when Oscar was working at that school. Pale, flabby round face. Nondescript hair parted and combed. Blazer and tie. He looked average. That was Oscar all over. Average. Not quite smart enough. Not quite talented enough.

To be fair, Oscar had made their high school chess team, but just barely. He was better than average, but he wasn't competition material. He never won when it mattered. He claimed he had performance anxiety.

Performance was never a problem for Rick. The more attention, the better.

In school, Oscar tried to hang around with Rick, and it got to be a full-time job ditching him. Oscar couldn't be trusted. He just couldn't keep his big mouth shut. Not then, not now – well, at least not until recently, because now he was dead.

Rick was hitting his stride when he saw a reflection cross the television screen. Someone had just come through the door behind him. He stumbled and nearly fell. "What the effin'!"

Umberto shouted over the machine and television. "We need to talk!"

It wasn't eight in the morning yet. "How did you get in?"

"Appollonia gave me keys."

She must have a thing for that guy. Why would he need his own keys? If Rick was at home, he could let him in. If Rick was gone, why would he need to come to the house? Maybe a late-night rendezvous with the good Mrs. Stevens, she lying in bed pretending to be asleep, waiting for Umberto to let himself in and come play some freaky little burglar game?

Umberto seemed to read his mind. "So, I can work when you're away."

"Give me an hour. I'm in the middle of my routine."

"Now." Umberto slipped the television remote from the treadmill caddy and pointed it at the screen. News gone. A grainy, gray-toned image from the security camera mounted over Rick's front door came on. He saw the lawn. The driveway. The wrought iron gate stood open.

"Why is the gate open?" Rick asked.

"They must have followed me in," Umberto said.

A Cadillac pulled into the driveway. Two guys got out. One tall, skinny, loose-limbed, with jail tats covering sinewy arm muscles wearing a Hawaiian shirt. The other, in sweatpants and a hoodie, was built like a halfback. Rick knew them. The skinny one was the mouth. The big one was a former football player, washed out his first year after a knee injury.

Rick's body went cold. He wound down the treadmill. When it was slow enough, he straddled the belt, one foot on either side of the frame, and took a big pull from his water bottle. He needed time to think.

Umberto paused the video. "Who are those guys?"

Even with the pixelation, Footballer's smashed nose made him easy to identify. "No idea," Rick lied.

"They seem to know you."

"Everyone does. I'm famous."

Before the campaign, Rick did his own car dealership commercials. Strolling around the showroom in a tailored Italian suit, the fabric draping across his lean frame, talking about how special his cars were. When he went into the clubs, the first thing someone mentioned was seeing his ad and how good he looked.

"They claim you owe money to a friend of theirs."

Rick rolled his eyes. "Everyone wants a piece of me." He didn't say *especially Herman Jules.*

"Do you owe money?"

If Rick told the truth, Umberto would be on the phone to Mr. Toussaint, the last person who needed to know about Rick's temporary financial difficulties. Mr. Toussaint had financed Rick's campaign. Would he back out if he knew Rick was broke? Worse than broke, really, since the accountants said he owed far more than he owned and could hope to earn. They kept going on about fair market value, leverage, points, blah, blah, blah. His only hope was winning the election and then selling the business and getting out from under the debt.

Rick gave Umberto a side-eye. "Are you interrogating me?"

Umberto ran the video. A man came out of the house, someone Rick had never seen before. He was so tall, the other two had to look up at him. That was mighty tall. Rick was eye-level with Skinny Guy, but Footballer was at least two inches taller than them both.

There was no audio. But Rick could see Skinny Guy talking, his arms swaying around like they could fall off any minute. Footballer said nothing but kept flexing those beefy hands hanging by his side. The guy who'd come out of Rick's house shifted his weight and when he did, the two visitors looked past him into the foyer.

Skinny Guy held up his hands. He and Footballer backed away, got into the Caddy, and peeled out.

Rick pointed at the screen. "Who's that?"

"Your friends?"

"They're not my friends, I told you that. The other guy, the one who came out of my house."

"There are two guys for security. It's a good thing I hired them. Some gangster thinks you owe him money."

Herman Jules wasn't a gangster, not like in the movies. Just a guy Rick knew who hung around the clubs. Quiet, nondescript. Didn't play cards. Didn't shoot pool. Didn't drink. Didn't play around. Cheap suit. Cheaper tie. If it weren't for the diamond-encrusted pinky ring, he would have looked like a churchgoer scouting for lost souls. One night, about a year ago, when Rick kept losing at the tables, Herman had loaned Rick a few thousand. Within a week, these two, Skinny Guy and Footballer, showed up to collect.

Rick had kept up with the interest payments for a while, but then he just didn't have the cash flow. He promised he'd get the money. He tried, but his credit cards were maxed. He couldn't even borrow money against his house equity. As it turns out the business owned that too and it had already sucked all the equity out.

"Bull," Rick said. "I have no idea what they're talking about."

AFTER HIS SHOWER, RICK changed into linen slacks and a shirt, ascertained that Appollonia had taken the Bentley into town for another all-day shopping trip, then made a protein shake and wandered into his home office. Umberto was resting his butt on Rick's desk while he scanned his phone. Two identical beach boys on steroids were sitting on Rick's couch. They were enormous, built like granite, with deep tans and white-blonde crewcuts, wearing black t-shirts and black jeans straining across their bulks. They could be iron-pumping versions of Tweedledum and Tweedledee. Neither of them got up.

"Meet your security team," Umberto said. "Martin and Thaddeus."

Rick extended his hand. "Hi, guys. What shall I call you? Marty and Todd?"

"Martin and Thaddeus will do," said the one on the right, who gripped Rick's hand and squeezed a little harder than he needed to, then held on, pulling Rick down awkwardly.

"Got it," Rick said. "Glad to meet you. I'm Rick."

The man let his hand go.

Rick shook the other guy's hand. "So, which of you is which? You look like twins."

"We are," the second one said. "Don't bother. Not even our mother can tell us apart."

Tweedledum and Tweedledee it is, then. Good thing they were on his side. Skinny Guy and Footballer would never get past them.

Umberto slipped his phone into his blazer pocket. "Let's get to work."

The rest of the morning was filled with reviewing the day's schedule, practicing sincere answers when Umberto pretended to be a reporter, and instructions on how to behave with a security team.

"Always tell the boys where you're going," Umberto said. "They will follow you in a black SUV – you can't miss it."

"Why do they get a full-size and I have to ride in that little crossover?"

"Because they're bigger than you," Umberto said. "They won't fit. When you arrive, the boys will get out of their car first, check out the location, then signal it's safe for you to get out. One of them will walk in front, the other behind. If either of them gives you a command, like 'hit the dirt,' do it. Don't ask questions. Don't look around, just do it."

This afternoon would be their first excursion with Dum and Dee in tow – a park dedication. Kids, balloons, cotton candy. Boring as shit. What could possibly go wrong?

UMBERTO DROVE THE MOMMY mobile while Rick watched the twins' SUV follow in the sideview mirror. He wished he had the kind of leg room the Dum Dee boys had. As it was, he had to fold himself up to fit into the passenger seat.

As planned, they pulled up to a derelict lot between two brick buildings in a "economically struggling" neighborhood. Rick wasn't allowed to use the word "poor." Umberto wrangled an invitation for Rick to break ground for the new park and playground. Although the land was cleared of broken beer bottles, crack pipes, and used condoms, the foundations of a burnt-out building remained, what was left after a failed business owner cashed in on the insurance policy. A shiny yellow bulldozer was parked in the back of the lot, ready to dig it up.

Twenty or so people milled around. Kids with balloons, just as Rick expected. An ice cream truck was parked on the lot, off to the side. Back at the house, Umberto had told Rick to meet and greet. Shake hands, smile, ask their name and how they're doing, then move on.

The SUV parked behind them. One twin got out and walked up and down the sidewalk, looked around slowly, then gave a nod to Umberto. Rick pried himself out of the car. He hoped his suit wasn't wrinkled, but he couldn't check in public. There would be reporters, and everyone was a cameraman with cell phones these days. The last thing he needed was a picture of him tugging the seat of his slacks.

A middle-aged woman with a clipboard strode towards them. Not Rick's type. "So glad you could make it!"

One of the twins stepped in front of her.

"Oh, hi," she said, looking up at the blond Goliath. "I work for the city council, kind of organizing this thing. We are so thrilled Mr. Stevens could join us today. The set-up is over there." She turned and pointed at the balloon-covered arch, then looked at her watch. "Almost time!"

Umberto stepped around the twin and motioned Rick forward. "And the next senator is thrilled to be here!"

Rick took her hand. When he spoke, he dropped his voice to his come-on baritone. "Thank you so much for inviting me. What's your name?"

"Sally."

"How's your day been so far, Sally?"

"Great, great." She began to blush. The mommy mobile wasn't a problem for her, but she wasn't – as the Hollywood types would say – in his personal target demographic. Yet, as Umberto told him multiple times a day, every vote counted. So, Rick held her hand gently until she looked away.

Umberto gave Rick's upper arm a squeeze, the signal to move on. "Where do you want us?"

Clipboard Sally led them to the arch where three men in suits were lined up. She introduced Rick to a local councilman, a community developer, and a builder, whose names Rick immediately forgot.

Silver shovels were handed to Rick and the three other men. As they posed for the cameras, he remembered Oscar's goofy picture smile. It wasn't the smile that was so goofy as the glassy look in Oscar's eyes. Rick made eye contact with Clipboard Sally, now standing in the back of the small crowd, and deepened his dimples just for her when he smiled.

On cue, Rick and the others stabbed their shovels into the baked earth. It was like concrete. He gave a little laugh, then stepped on his blade with enough force to drive the tip in. The others followed suit. They tossed their little clumps of dirt aside. Umberto was in the crowd, leading a cheer.

Reporters snapped more photos of the men shaking hands as Umberto led one young couple with a little boy in tow over to him. He spoke to them in Spanish, introducing Rick. Rick knew enough of the language to understand that much.

The couple wore matching gold wedding bands. The wife was petite and pretty. The husband was drop dead gorgeous. Rick's height. Dark skin and hair. Stocky. Fit. He carried himself with confidence. Sexy.

"Thank you so much for what you have done for our community," the husband said.

"Our children are our future," Rick said, again with the baritone. It was the slogan Rick himself came up with. Umberto said it was a cliché, but he hadn't come up with anything better. Besides, everyone likes a man who likes kids. That's why there's so many pictures of men with kids on social media and dating sites. Catfishers, they called them. People who scam money by promising love. Like love wasn't a scam already. Rick should know.

The boy tugged Rick's pant leg.

"No, Xavier," the husband said. Then to Rick, "I'm so sorry."

Rick held his arms out to the little boy and the boy climbed up him like he was a tree, planting his dirty little sandals on Rick's pantlegs.

"Beautiful," Umberto said. "This deserves a picture." He ushered the parents to Rick's side and motioned for a photographer to come over. Rick could feel the heat of the husband's body next to him. When he turned just so, Rick could see down his shirt. Dark curly hair, lots of it.

After the photographer took a few snaps, Umberto sidled up to them and said to the little boy. "How about some ice cream?" Then to the parents, "Is that alright with you, mama, papa?"

The boy squirmed out of Rick's arms. As Umberto led the boy and his parents to the picnic tables, he looked over his shoulder at Rick and mouthed the words, "absolutely not."

The cell phone in Rick's pocket buzzed. He took it out and looked at the caller ID. Skinny Guy. Rick hit the decline icon. He was about to thumb through his inbox when a texted photo popped up from Skinny Guy. It was a picture of Rick exactly where he was standing, staring at his phone. Rick looked up and saw Skinny Guy's Cadillac with Footballer in the passenger seat, double-parked in front of the mommy mobile. Footballer pointed at Rick, then laughed out loud. A threat. *We can find you and get you anytime we want.*

Rick couldn't believe it. Twice in one day. He hadn't seen these two for weeks before this. Granted, he'd been a very good boy. No parties. No clubs. But they had never come to his house before, much less followed him. Rick blinked to make sure he wasn't imagining what he saw. When he focused again, Footballer was still laughing. Skinny Guy gave Rick a wave and then pulled out into traffic.

Where the hell were the Dum Dee twins? Rick found one of them making time with Clipboard Sally. The other came out of an outhouse, shaking his jeans into place.

Umberto appeared again. "What's wrong?"

"Those two guys that came to my house this morning."

"Your friends?"

"Not my friends. I just saw them. They must have followed us."

"You're being paranoid, Rick. This event was publicized all week. It's on your campaign website. Anyone with internet could find out where you are."

"I have a campaign website?"

"Of course, you do. And your schedule is updated every day. That's why we have the security team. Look, if there's something you need to tell me, something you're afraid of, I'm here to help. Trust me, Rick. I'm here for you."

The election was months away. Every day his debt to Herman went unpaid, interest racked up. If the devil offered to buy his soul, he still couldn't pay Herman off. He needed money and he needed it now – just enough to get those two goons off his back for a while.

He'd just have to go old school.

Rick patted his jacket, pretending he was looking for his wallet. "Say, got any cash on you?"

"What do you need with cash?"

"Appollonia deserves something special. Flowers. I haven't paid enough attention to her lately."

"So put it on your credit card."

"Can't. Some screw-up with the bookkeeper. She called in sick, so the bill didn't get paid on time. The card's frozen – just temporarily. I'm sure she'll get it straightened out in a couple of days."

Umberto gave Rick a stony look.

"Come on, compadre, you know where I live."

"I told you not to call me that." Umberto pulled an expensive leather wallet out of his back pocket and slid out two one-hundred-dollar bills.

"Come on, man, there's more where that came from."

"How much could flowers cost?"

"Flowers and champagne. She deserves that much – she's a fantastic lady."

Umberto pulled out another three hundred dollars.

Rick slid the bills into his inside pocket. "Thanks, bud. I knew I could count on you."

RICK'S NIGHT STARTED OFF fantastically. Umberto left by dinner time, saying they'd worked enough. Dum and Dee followed Umberto out the driveway after Rick promised he'd spend the evening home watching television. Appollonia passed out early.

When his watch said it was eleven pm, he pulled on a pair of old jeans, running shoes, a zip-up hoody over a t-shirt, a baseball cap, and wraparound sunglasses. Just another guy roaming around town, no big deal. To be on the safe side, he took the mommy mobile. In case he was followed by Herman's goons or the Dum Dee twins, he parked in an underground hotel parking lot, jogged up the stairs to the lobby, scooted through the kitchen where his friend, the chef, was waiting for him with a line of coke, a hearty "have a great night, bro," and a slap on the rear. Then he headed out the backdoor to a waiting Uber.

Gassed up by the coke and with Umberto's five hundred dollars, he told the driver to take him to a place where he knew he'd find a card game. Within a few hours, he turned those five bills into fifteen thousand dollars – enough to satisfy Herman's goons.

That was the last thing he remembered. He could have sworn he had only one or two drinks, tops. But one of the waitresses kept circling the table, so it was possible she brought him a third drink. Or more. She was a pretty thing with a cute smile and bouncy blonde hair.

It was all a blur.

WHEN RICK CAME TO, he was naked and cold, his body covered in oily sweat. He groped for something to cover himself but all he could find was a sheet tangled around his legs. He gave up. His skull was too heavy to lift. Searing pain shot through his head. His eyeballs felt like they were going to rupture. The taste in his mouth was somewhere between rancid cesspool and turpentine. He tried opening his eyes, but blaring daylight was like a knife stabbing him straight into his brain. He decided to go back to sleep and try again later.

Something touched his nose. He brushed it away. It touched him again, three times. This time he batted the thing away. "What the fu—"

"Now, now, Rick, what did we say about language?" It was Umberto.

Where was this place? Why was Umberto here? What happened?

Rick opened one eye, just enough to see a sliver. An unfamiliar ceiling. Cheap motel furnishings. An old television bolted to the wall. The other side of the bed was trashed but no one was in the room, just Umberto, sitting cross-legged in a chair as if he was a guest on a late-night interview show waiting for the host to ask him a question.

"When did you get here?" Rick asked.

"Twenty minutes ago."

"How did you –"

"The door was unlocked."

Rick pushed himself up, found a nightstand covered in cigarette butts overflowing from a crushed beer can and an empty fifth of tequila. Rick only smoked when he was coked-up. He didn't remember smoking last night, and he'd only had that one little spoonful at the hotel. Then he saw a discarded straw and razer, and a small mirror on the nightstand, smeared with saliva where someone had licked it clean. He recognized that diesel aftertaste lurking in his sinuses.

Rick swung his feet to the floor and staggered a yard towards the bathroom. Not even a water glass in sight, this place had to be the seediest motel he'd ever been in. He turned on the faucet, cupped his hands beneath the water flow, and drank. At least it was cold. There probably wasn't any hot water, anyway.

The room began to spin. Rick braced himself against the wall as he shuffled back to the safety of the bed. When he tried to sit, his legs buckled, and he fell onto the mattress. The impact sent waves of pain and nausea through his body. He clenched his eyes shut until it passed. When Rick could open them again, he spotted Umberto calmly examining his own nails.

"How'd you find me?" Rick asked.

"We never lost you."

Rick frowned, confused. Who is "we?" Umberto wasn't there last night. Was he?

Umberto said, "The twins followed you. From your house to the hotel to the club – if that's what you want to call it – to the liquor store and then here. They were sitting outside that window all night." He nodded in the direction of drawn curtains. Rick registered the sounds of a nearby highway, the scream of thousands of tires speeding past, the growls of semi-trucks as they upshifted.

Did Umberto find someone with Rick? If he didn't, maybe it'd be better not to ask. It was rare for Rick to wake up alone after a night out. Debris on the nightstand on the opposite side of the bed suggested someone had been there. But he couldn't remember. The waitress maybe? The chef had planned to join them after the restaurant closed. It could have been him. Or both.

Screw it.

Rick waved a hand in the direction of the other side of the bed. "Where is?"

"Gone."

"Who was it?"

"The twins said a cute blonde and a skanky man."

The waitress and the chef.

The money. Last Rick remembered, he had over fifteen thousand dollars.

"Where's my wallet?"

"In your pants?" Umberto cut his eyes towards a pile on the floor.

"Could you?"

"I'm not your valet, Rick." Umberto stood and brushed his undertaker suit. "Get yourself cleaned up. The boys will take you home in fifteen minutes. And oh, by the way, you owe me five hundred dollars." With that, he left the room.

Rick slid off the bed and fell onto the carpet. Tiny bits of gravel ground into his palms and knees as he crawled to his clothes. He felt the bulk of his wallet in the jeans' back pocket, at once reassuring – he still had it – and alarming – it should be thicker. He couldn't make his fingers work right to pull it out, so he shook the pants until the wallet fell out. The money slit was bare.

He must have run into Herman's thugs, Skinny Guy and Footballer. They could be counted on to find him whenever he was winning, take his wallet away from him, and take everything he had. That was his plan, after all. Win a lot of money and give it to them so they'd leave him alone for a while.

Rick's cell phone buzzed. It had fallen out of his jeans and was a couple of feet away. He laid down to reach it. The caller ID said Skinny Guy.

Rick answered. "Did you get your money?"

"What money?"

Chapter Six

Maureen

LAFAYETTE ACADEMY WAS HOUSED in a former Catholic school, a block-long, white three-story Mission style building with a large archway entrance, arched windows, red tiled roof, and bell tower. Quinn and I cruised for half an hour before I found a parking place, even though I was driving Sunny, my yellow BMW, which was small enough that, at times, I had jockeyed into spots not technically designated as parking. It was late afternoon when we walked up to the red tile steps and pushed a security buzzer.

"How can we help you?" a female voice answered through the crackling intercom.

"We're here to see Emerson Katsu," I shouted into a rusty microphone.

"Do you have an appointment?"

"Tell him Maureen Gould is here."

"I'll check to see if he is available."

The wait was far more than one minute. Several cyclists sped by. A faint breeze rustled the trees. A jet passed overhead leaving contrails.

The voice came back on the speaker. "Mr. Katsu said that if you want to speak with him, you need to call his attorney."

"Or I could get a subpoena. Would he prefer that?"

"Just a moment."

The lens mounted on the wall over the speaker could have been a working camera, so I modeled professional lawyer behavior for Quinn, staring straight ahead, hand hooked on the shoulder strap of my briefcase, slightly bored. She imitated my stance.

The sound of heels clacking on polished floors grew louder as someone approached. I tried to look like I wasn't peering into the sidelight window even as I did so. A form materialized from the shadows. Metal scraped as the deadbolt was shunted aside. The door opened.

The woman who stood in front of me was at least six feet tall, built like a long shoreman, and dressed like a dorm mother from a 1950's situation comedy. She could have been any age from forty to seventy. Dark hair was pulled back into a severe bun. A mauve blouse was buttoned at her throat under a mauve sweater that had embroidered flowers decorating the neckline. The ensemble was completed with a matching mauve calf-length skirt, nude stockings, and thick-heeled nun shoes. Half-lens reading glasses hung at her neck from an imitation pearl and gold cord.

I felt the urge to curtsy, but I resisted.

"We are closing soon but Mr. Katsu can make a few minutes for you." Mauve Woman ushered us down a long shadowy hall, into an office reception area filled with hot, dead air and a large empty desk, presumably hers. After she knocked on a closed door, a man's voice called, "Come in." She opened the door. We entered. She left the door ajar as she departed and sat down behind the desk – within ear shot.

Emerson Katsu was a witness in the civil trial. He had been friends and played competitive chess with Oscar Wenderholm as an adolescent. Katsu obtained his education degree and rose through the ranks at Lafayette Academy. When he discovered Tony and Oscar in a supply closet, he was the vice-principal. Oscar was given a severance package, Tony was expelled, and Mr. Katsu was promoted to principal.

Katsu stood when we entered the room and gestured to the two visitor chairs. He was remarkable only in how unremarkable he was. Average height, average build, black hair, off-the-rack blue suit, blue shirt, blue striped tie.

The office was large enough to hold a square dance. There was a wall of glass-enclosed cabinets in which were displayed trophies. Another wall was devoted to photos of children's school teams, interspersed amongst them were framed newspaper clippings. Quinn strolled by those as Katsu and I took a seat.

"I don't feel entirely comfortable speaking to you without my attorney present," he said.

"That's fine, as I told your assistant. I can get a subpoena and we'll take your deposition if you prefer."

"Concerning what?"

"Oscar Wenderholm."

He squeezed his eyes shut. When they opened, his expression was that of tired resignation. He wasn't surprised to see me. He shouldn't have been. On the stand in the civil case, he testified for half a day about how he met Oscar in another school when they were students and he had never seen Oscar engage in any unseemly behavior before he caught Oscar with Tony. He had recommended Oscar for the job at Lafayette because he knew that Oscar was available, and the Board had decided to create a competitive chess team as a means of attracting students. The day he found them in a supply closet, Oscar was on his knees before Tony, pants around his ankles.

"You may have heard Mr. Wenderholm passed away."

He scoffed. "What I read was Tony Paredes shot him in front of his home and left his body there for his children to find."

The children hadn't discovered the body. The wife had. I didn't want to wrestle with Katsu over the facts. Anything I said would be repeated to the prosecutor, Vivian Thandi.

"Tony has been charged with homicide, that much is true, but the State's case isn't strong." I'd be happy if he reported that back to Vivian. "I don't need to repeat anything you said at the trial, I have that transcript. What I want to know is what happened after the verdict."

"Could you be more specific? I don't understand the question."

He clearly remembered his lawyer's instructions. Say as little as possible and only answer when you can't avoid it. I brought Quinn along not only to witness what Katsu said, but also to what he didn't say.

"Have you had any contact with Tony since the trial?"

"I have not."

"Have you had any contact with Oscar Wenderholm since the trial?"

He flinched. "How do you define 'contact'?"

Again, he was following his attorney's directions. Get as narrow a definition as possible so that later, if confronted with an inconsistency, you can state, "That's not what you asked me."

"No problem, Mr. Katsu. I'll break it down if you like. Did you receive any texts from Mr. Wenderholm?"

"I don't text." A twitch started beneath his left eye.

"Then you didn't receive any texts from him either, is that correct?"

"You may assume so."

"Did you have any telephone conversations with him?"

"Since the trial?"

"Since the trial," I confirmed.

He stared at the far wall, frowning, then he pretended to notice Quinn drifting along the picture display. "We're very proud of our student achievements here at Lafayette Academy." He directed his comment to her.

She nodded at him, then resumed her examination.

He turned to me. "What was the question? I'm sorry, I forgot." Another attorney's instruction: confound the questioner – maybe they'll give up.

"Did you talk to Mr. Wenderholm on the telephone since the trial?"

His eyes flickered. "I couldn't tell you. We're old friends, since childhood. We may have spoken." He smoothed his hands over his face. When he reappeared, he had composed his expression into a blank mask. "You were saying?"

"We have established that he didn't text you, you didn't text him, and you're not sure if you had a telephone conversation with him since the trial, but have you seen him?

He lifted the tail of his tie, studied it, scratched it with a thumbnail, then smoothed it into his blazer. "What do you mean by 'see'?"

"A face-to-face interaction. At his home, your home, perhaps. Met for coffee. Dinner or lunch in a restaurant. Go for a walk."

He tilted his head as he gave the appearance of trying to recollect. "Again, couldn't tell you. We were old friends, as I said."

"Then, just to be clear, Mr. Katsu, if a witness testifies that he had seen you with Mr. Wenderholm in, say, the past month, that testimony would not be true."

I was fishing. No one had made such a statement. I wanted to shake some information out of him, or at the very least, shut the door, preventing him from claiming later that Wenderholm talked about being afraid of Tony.

He leveled his eyes at me. "A statement like that would be unequivocally false."

"In the past year?"

He glanced at a Longine watch on his wrist. He wasn't wearing it during the trial. If he had been, I would have noticed. I recognized that model from when I had shopped for a gift for Jake. I bought the Rolex instead.

He stood. "Now, ladies, we're about to close the building so I must insist that we terminate this interview."

BACK INSIDE SUNNY, I asked Quinn, "Did you catch all that?"

"For sure."

"Take a few moments to write down everything he said." Recording witness interviews while they were still fresh in one's mind is vital. Details which might not seem important at the time can easily be forgotten.

Quinn pulled a tablet out of her scuzzy backpack and typed for a few minutes. In my rearview, I saw a parking enforcer's little cart pull up several car lengths behind me. I started the engine.

"Okay, got it," Quinn said.

"And did you make a note that he didn't answer my last question?"

"Yes, ma'am."

The cart moved up a few more yards. I slowly pulled out onto the street. The last thing I needed was to get into an accident while avoiding a parking ticket and have it witnessed by a law enforcement officer. In the long run, not a lot of recriminations, such as spending the rest of your life in prison, but the hassle wasn't worth it.

"What were your first impressions?" I asked Quinn.

"You make him nervous. He doesn't want to answer the questions because he's afraid he'll say the wrong thing. He *really* doesn't want to get involved. He's hiding something."

"Good, what else?"

"He still has a big crush on that Wenderholm guy."

"What makes you say that?"

"When you mentioned the name, his pupils dilated. Besides, there's the pictures on the wall."

"What did you see?"

"They weren't just Lafayette team photos. Some of them were older, from when Mr. Katsu was a student. The caption said they were a high school chess team and listed all the members, including Wenderholm."

"Did you notice the names of the other kids that played with Oscar?"

"I wrote them down." She patted her tablet.

"How can you remember all that?"

"Sorry, I didn't mention it before, but it just didn't come up. I have a photographic memory."

▼

THE SPEEDY TRIAL RULE in California says that a defendant has the right to go to trial within sixty days of his arraignment. That's not a lot of time to prepare a case but an eternity for a client sitting in jail. Tony insisted, and I agreed, that we wouldn't ask for a delay in the trial date which would be scheduled for September. That meant working on the case constantly until court.

Quinn and I rolled into the office the next morning, a Saturday, after stopping by the café down the street and picking up a raspberry mocha for me and an herbal tea for her. When we arrived, Yolanda was already there with files laid out in a mosaic pattern on the conference room table and a box of donuts open on the cabinet. I was amused that Quinn, despite her health-food fixation, picked up a chocolate glazed.

We took our plates to our usual seats. Me at the head of the table. Yolanda closest to the door, in case someone came in. Quinn opposite Yolanda, not knowing that was where Eli used to sit. She had never met him.

Eli Conroy had been my private investigator. He was tall, lanky, and sarcastic even when he was in a good mood. As Quinn settled in, Yolanda gave me a knowing look. We had spent many Saturdays at the office just like this, only with Eli. He always took two cake donuts, both smothered in frosting. He'd eat half the first in one bite, then see frosting on his fingers, then get up again to retrieve a small pile of napkins from the cabinet.

Eli had been murdered on the street in a drive-by shooting, directly beneath the conference room window. Just before he died, I learned he was feeding confidential information to the opposing attorney – who happened to be Francis E. Gould, my father. Frank's client hired a couple of thugs who were disappearing potential witnesses before I could interview them, having been led to them by Eli. When I refused to quit the case, the thugs came for me. Eli threw himself in front of me just before the gun fired.

Quinn took a nibble of her donut and flakes of the sugary crust floated to the table. Then, just like Eli, she got up to go over to the cabinet for napkins.

Yolanda patted my hand to get my attention. "How are you doing?"

She had often found me lost in thought in the weeks after Eli's murder.

"Fine," I lied.

Ironic, I thought, that I would continue to grieve his loss when he had betrayed me. But life, and feelings, are complicated. The camaraderie I had felt for him was real. Even if I was deluded into thinking that he felt the same.

After Quinn returned to her chair, hands wiped, she scrolled through her tablet. "I started a timeline. Last night, I found some articles on the internet about Wenderholm's chess competition. I was thinking a big picture on who Wenderholm was might lead us to other suspects."

"Great idea," I said. Eli had worked on Tony's case with us and had done similar research, but his notes were lost. After he died, his sister cleared out his apartment while I was busy in a trial. When I called the sister, she said she had tossed all the paperwork.

Yolanda flipped through a file to a page marked with a sticky. "Here's a list of our witnesses in the civil case with a summary of their testimony."

"Get the civil case transcribed," I said. Summaries are great information, but when a witness is on the stand and changing their story, you needed to hand them a written copy of their earlier testimony to confront them with the inconsistencies. Evidentiary rules required it. Better yet, juries loved the theatrics. Counsel asks for leave to approach the witness. The judge grants permission. Counsel stalks across the well with a document, then forces the witness to read it aloud. The next question was always some variation of "which is the truth, what you said then or what you're saying now?"

"You got it, girlfriend," Yolanda said as she wrote in a legal pad. "Did you talk to Emerson Katsu?

"We did. He's the principal now and sporting an expensive new watch. He was fuzzy about seeing Wenderholm after the trial, but Tony says he saw them together. And guess what! My little girl has a photographic memory. There were pictures on his office wall of Katsu and Wenderholm when they competed, listing the other team members. Tell Yolanda what you found."

Quinn scrolled through her screen. "The team included Constance Robertson. Looks like she quit competing after she graduated high school. She lives in Fair Oaks now. They have a couple of kids in the swim team. She's into Rotary Club, PTA, and the garden club. No arrests. No civil cases."

"You got all that just now?" Yolanda asked, impressed.

Quinn shrugged. "No big deal."

I had taken a bite of my sugar-covered donut and now washed it down quickly with my mocha so I could speak. "That sounds familiar. Eli gave her a call, but she had no information. Saw nothing. Heard nothing." Or that's what Eli had said. Towards the end, I got the feeling he claimed to do a lot more work than he had.

"Didn't she have a brother?" Yolanda asked. She was being generous. She knew what was in the file but was trying to look like she wasn't competing with Quinn.

Quinn looked up to see Yolanda taking notes. "I can just email you what I have."

"That'd be great," Yolanda said as she put pen to paper.

Quinn went back to her screen. "Constance's brother is Charles Robertson. He went to law school and is a personal injury attorney in San Jose. Married once for almost two years. No kids. No arrests. No civil cases. Looks like he dropped out of chess competition too."

Yolanda flipped through a file. "He was listed as one of Wenderholm's character witnesses in the civil case, but he was not called by the defense. I don't think Eli ever got a hold of him."

I licked donut sugar off my fingers. "Interesting. It seems like Wenderholm's attorneys looked into the old gang. Also, interesting that they didn't call Constance. Katsu testified because I subpoenaed him. It wasn't easy either. He suddenly went on a sabbatical before the trial. Remember that? We had to get a process server to track him down."

Yolanda half stood and reached across the table to grasp a file. "Tagged the guy on an archeological dig somewhere way out in Alaska. The process server had to take a jet, then a small airplane, then a boat to find him. He took a photo of Katsu for proof." She flipped the folder open. "Here, take a look at this."

There was a photo of Emerson Katsu wearing a fishing hat and a multi-pocketed outdoors vest. Sunburned, with a sparse beard and shaggy hair, he extended an arm to keep the photographer away, frowning, as his mouth rounded to the word "no!"

"But he testified, right?" Quinn asked. "He flew all the way back for the trial?"

"He had to," I said. "It would be contempt of court if he didn't."

"No wonder he doesn't like you." Quinn swiped her screen again. "You're going to want to know about this guy, Dakota Vaughn. It wasn't on Mr. Katsu's wall, but I found this picture online."

"Who's that?" Yolanda asked. Constance and Charles Howard had been listed in the civil case as potential character witnesses, but Dakota Vaughn was new.

Quinn passed the device to me which I looked at before I slid it over to Yolanda. The image showed teenagers, four boys and one girl, in shirtsleeves and ties, lined up behind a table full of trophies. A taller kid with an easy affable grin was in the middle with his arms around Wenderholm and Emerson Katsu.

"As soon as he turned eighteen," Quinn said. "He was convicted for driving while under the influence. He was represented by an expensive local firm and got a suspended imposition of sentence. No jail. Then he picked up a bunch of tickets for speeding, running stoplights, stuff like that. Eventually his license was suspended. He picked up a few more tickets near his parents' house in Palo Alto when he was in his early twenties. And then he went to prison."

"Where did you get all this?" Yolanda asked.

"Online. Newspaper articles, court records."

"I don't remember Eli digging up all this stuff."

Neither did I.

"He went to prison for bad driving?" Yolanda looked alarmed. "Can they do that?"

"His prison sentence was for child abuse," Quinn said. "It was, you know, um, sexual abuse. Like the thing Wenderholm did to Tony."

Yolanda's pen stopped.

"Where is this guy incarcerated?" I asked. "We need to find him."

At the same time, Yolanda said, "You got it, girlfriend," and Quinn said, "Will do."

Yolanda raised her pen. "Quinn, did you want to do this?" She had tracked down witnesses before and was good at it. When Eli was around, she would compete with him for work. She wasn't just a secretary, she reminded me after a dust-up, she was a paralegal too and she wanted more responsibility. But with Quinn, she was different, deferential even. It wasn't like Yolanda. We'd have to talk about it. Later.

"How about Quinn finds Dakota Vaughn," I said. "And Yolanda, you find the current whereabouts on the other two."

"I have all that," Quinn said, offering her device up as proof.

"Email that to Yolanda so she can confirm, just to be on the safe side. Online stuff isn't always up to date."

Quinn frowned while she typed. There would be a talk with Quinn about sensitivity and teamwork.

The mood was broken when Yolanda's desk phone began ringing.

"Who calls a law office on a Saturday?" Quinn asked.

"Someone who needs to talk to an attorney." Yolanda was already on her feet, and at her desk reaching for the phone. She answered, listened, then she held the phone aloft and mouthed, "Tony."

Chapter Seven

Maureen

GIVEN I HAD SHOWN up at jail in jeans, a sweatshirt, and running shoes, I had some difficulty convincing the guard at the front desk I really was a lawyer. Or maybe he was just giving me a hard time. He made me wait two hours.

Thirty minutes after I was finally situated in a visiting room, Tony was brought in. Now habituated to incarceration, Tony lifted his hands for the guard to unlock his cuffs without being told. When he turned to me, I instinctively covered my mouth.

The entire left side of his face was swollen and red. His mouth had seen the worst of the battle, maroon, lips swollen as fat as leeches, with a deep split showing tender violet tissue. Just beneath his eye was a cut that had been closed with a butterfly bandage. His entire eye socket was beginning to blacken. His glasses were gone.

When he sat down, he gently lifted his right hand onto the table using the other arm. I pointed to his hand. Two of his fingers were swollen.

"Can't move it."

"Because of pain or it just won't move."

"Bof." His lip was so swollen, he couldn't speak clearly.

"What's the doctor say?"

He snorted. "Doctor?"

"You did see someone, right?"

He answered slowly. "Some guy. Not a doctor. He said I sprained my fingers, said I should keep my hand elevated."

"Did they give you any pain meds?"

The less injured side of his face tried to smile which made him grimace. "Aspirin."

"Who did this to you?"

He shrugged. "Don't know names."

"More than one?"

"A bunch watched. Just one guy hit."

"What started it?"

He winced as he adjusted in his seat. "Money. Said I was a millionaire. He'd seen me on TV. If I pay him, he'll make sure I didn't get hurt. I told him I never got the money. He said I was lying. He pulled my glasses off. Then he slammed me into a wall. Don't remember much after that. It's a blur."

"Where were the guards?"

He rolled his eyes. "Around somewhere. Maureen, please. You got to get me out of here. They're going to kill me."

AFTER TONY WAS TAKEN back to his cell, I went directly to the guard on the desk, the same one who'd made me wait.

"I need to see whoever's in charge," I said.

"It's a Saturday. The captain has the weekends off."

"There must be someone in charge. What if there's a problem?"

He dug in his ear with a forefinger. "We don't usually have problems on weekends."

"We do now. And if I don't get to speak to someone in charge, I'm going over to court, and we'll get a judge and the DA involved." I pulled out a pen and legal pad from my briefcase. "I'll need your name for the record."

He pointed to his nameplate. "Jones."

"I can see that. First, middle, and badge number please."

Instead of giving me the information, Jones jerked his head at another guard who appeared to be standing around doing nothing. The second guard walked down a short hall and knocked on the door of an office with a window overlooking the lobby. A venetian blind was pulled up. Guard Two jerked a thumb in my direction. A small, square woman in a tan business suit peered at me. The blind dropped back into place.

Jones' console buzzed. He picked up the receiver, listened, said, "Yes, ma'am," then put the phone back down. "You're to go down the hall to the first door on the right."

I took the short walk. Guard Two moved out of the way so I could enter, then closed the door behind me with more force than necessary.

A woman was seated behind an army-style metal desk. One bookcase held manuals and binders. There were a few certificates on the wall.

"I'm Lieutenant Stacy," she said. "What can I do for you?"

She didn't invite me to sit but I took a visitor's chair anyway.

"My name is Maureen Gould. My client, Anthony Paredes, was beaten up by another prisoner."

She lifted her receiver and punched a button. "Is there an incident report concerning a prisoner named Anthony Paredes?" She covered the speaker and said to me, "When did this happen?"

"Last night."

She repeated the information into the phone, then said, "I'll hold." Her eyes wandered around the room, never meeting mine, for a few minutes. Then she said, "OK, got it," and hung up.

"Last evening at approximately 8:03 pm, one of the guards found Mr. Paredes in the common room, on the floor, crying. He claimed he had been assaulted. When the guard questioned the other prisoners, they denied having witnessed an assault. It was suggested that Mr. Paredes had slipped on some spilt coffee and fell into a wall. He was taken to the infirmary, looked over, and released to return to his cell."

"What about the video?"

"You'll need a court order. Prisoners who might be on the video have privacy rights, you understand. If I released it to you without a court order, I could get into trouble with some lawyer." She gave me a self-amused smile.

"You could look at it and tell me what you see."

"We can't access that on the weekend. Short staffed. I could pull it on Monday, but more likely it'd be Thursday or Friday before I'd get back to you. Tuesday and Wednesday are my weekend." She folded her hands on top of her desk.

"Look, I'm not trying to be difficult. I just want to make sure my client is safe. He's only been in this jail for a few days and look what happened. It's a protection racket. They think he has money and they're going to keep beating him up until he gives them some. But he doesn't have any money to give. Another four or five days is a long time to leave him in such a dangerous situation."

She nodded in an agreeable professional way she'd probably learned in some leadership seminar. "I understand completely. But as I said, there are no witnesses to the assault you allege. You need to understand my position. Prisoners will sometimes make up stories about other prisoners so they can be moved to a new module. They've also been known to injure themselves, hoping to get a bed in the infirmary or transferred to a hospital. This isn't a hotel. We can't cater to their whims. We have a discipline that must be enforced at all times. Mr. Paredes was returned to his cell. But I can see that you are concerned so I'll send a note to the guards to keep an eye on him."

I WENT TO THE office. Yolanda was working at her computer with a half-drunk iced latte sweating on her desk. She looked up long enough to nod at me then went back to work. I found Quinn in the conference room with a bottle of something murky and green that looked disgustingly healthy and the remains of a hummus wrap pushed aside. I suddenly realized I was hungry. Before I had a chance to ask, Yolanda called out, "There's a Cobb salad in the fridge for you."

I grabbed the salad, went back to my desk, and called the District Attorney's office from my land line. I wanted my caller ID to show up on their end. After an automated greeting, a menu of options, and a twenty-minute hold, Rupert, who had been the receptionist when I was at the office, came online.

"Miss Maureen, how's it hanging?"

"Not at all, thankfully." Jake had recently cued me in on what that greeting meant. For years, I had answered idiotically only to be greeted with quizzical looks from the men in the room.

"If you're looking for Mister Jake, he isn't here. Oops. Not sure I should have said that. Never mind. I'd be happy to take a message."

"Thanks, honey. He's playing basketball with some of the guys from the force this afternoon – no need to cover for him. I'm looking for Vivian Thandi."

"She's not in today, sorry. I have the strictest orders not to bother her, on pain of death, as if manning the phones on a Saturday isn't punishment enough. Don't mind me. If you like, I could put you through to the assistant on duty."

"Please."

A few minutes of hold were followed by, "District Attorney's Office, Assistant DA Travers speaking." The voice was young and female with a note of suspicion, the kind that came when you're afraid that someone is going to make you look stupid in your first real job. Any anecdote, fact or fiction, would follow her around the rest of her career, whispered in the backrooms by those who wanted to eliminate her as competition. It was hard enough for a woman to try to get ahead at the DA's office. I would not be the person who made her career more difficult.

"Rupert might have told you my name is Maureen Gould. I used to work in the DA's and I'm in private practice now. One of my clients is in jail and he's been given a significant beating. Looks to me like he has a couple of broken fingers in addition to facial injuries. Someone's trying to extort money out of him. I'm deeply concerned that he will be beaten again, perhaps more severely next time, because he doesn't have money to pay off the extortionist."

There was tapping on her end of the phone. Then she asked, "Was this reported?"

"It was. He was taken to the infirmary and seen. Also, I personally reported it to Lieutenant Stacyabout an hour ago."

"Do you want me to call you back or do you want to hold?"

"I'll hold."

I put my phone on mute and speaker and listened to static as I dug into the Cobb salad. I looked around for something to wash it down with, but I didn't want to leave the room to go to the kitchenette in case Ms. Travers came back online, which she did a few minutes later.

"Lieutenant Stacy read the report to me. She assured me that she has done everything she can do under the regulations."

"This is not reassuring, Ms. Travers. And that is the reason for my call. I believe he is in danger and that the guards are looking the other way."

"Did you report your concerns?"

She thought I was building a case to sue the City for Tony's injuries in jail. "It's not about documentation. It's about making sure my client lives long enough to go to trial."

"There is nothing else we can do. I suggest you call the jail on Monday. Ask for the captain." With that the line went dead.

I hung up the receiver and began typing an emergency motion for bail review.

Yolanda filed it first thing Monday morning but because the State was entitled to two business days' notice, the hearing was set for Thursday.

By that time, the prisoners found out that I had complained, so they cornered Tony with an extra-special message.

When the prison called to tell me that he had been transported to ER, hours after the assault, I sped over to the hospital to see him. The floor nurse let me into his room because I was his attorney. In addition to the broken fingers from the first beating, he had a shattered femur, fractured ribs, a bruised lung, and a brain injury, the extent of which could not be determined yet, and he was heavily sedated to prevent brain swelling.

I was so angry, I cried.

Then I took a photo.

BAIL REVIEWS WERE A cattle call. The gallery was stacked with lawyers, family and friends of the victims and defendants, and the jury box was filled with prisoners in chains. After their cases were dealt with, the gang was escorted out and a new one brought in. By the end of the afternoon, the jury box and the gallery were empty and there was only Vivian Thandi and me.

"Where is the accused?" Judge Cranston asked, looking first at Vivian and then at me.

I stood. "In San Francisco General Hospital in intensive care. If I may approach?"

The judge motioned me forward. I dropped a copy of the photo on Vivian's table as I strode across the well.

Judge Cranston winced when he saw the photo. After he had a chance to take in the tubes, bandages, and black eyes, I set Tony's medical records on his bench. He thumbed through them, and I returned to the lectern.

"When will the hospital release him?"

"There's no way of knowing, Your Honor. The doctors said that depending upon the extent of his brain injury, he may need months of in-patient rehabilitation."

The judge said to Vivian, "does the State object to the release of Mr. Paredes to such a facility?"

Vivian stood. "Given his health, the State feels that Mr. Paredes no longer poses a danger to the community and does not object to his continued hospitalization, subject, of course, to reevaluation."

"And the trial date?" Judge Cranston asked. "If Mr. Paredes is in a coma, he clearly cannot work with his attorney to prepare a defense. When he comes out of the coma, if he does, he may not be found competent to stand trial."

"The State asks the Court to continue the trial date, Your Honor."

"Ms. Gould, what is the defendant's position? I understand he isn't here to speak for himself, but for the matter at hand, you have the right to respond."

Tony wanted this case over. But he also wanted to win. So many questions come up during an investigation that only the client can answer. I couldn't prepare for trial without him. Besides, there may never be a trial. If he didn't recover from the coma or if the brain injury was severe, the State would drop the case. "No objection."

"Very well," the judge said. "We'll vacate the trial date and set a status hearing for thirty days hence. You are excused."

In the hallway outside the courtroom, Vivian was waiting for me. "I'm sorry, Maureen. I know you called over the weekend. The on duty assistant DA thought you were just laying the groundwork for a civil case against the jail. Even so, there was nothing we could do over the weekend."

"You could have put him in protective custody."

"That was Lieutenant Stacy's call. The DA's office has nothing to do with that."

"Does the State have a problem releasing the video to me, you know, just to back up that story that my client slipped on spilled coffee?"

Vivian frowned. "The jail claims the video was inadvertently wiped. Sorry."

"And the Sunday afternoon beating, the one that put him in the hospital?"

"Off camera, I'm afraid. And no witnesses."

By THE TIME I arrived home, Jake and Quinn had eaten. She was at the breakfast bar, her laptop open. He was on the couch watching television with Germaine Greer draped around his neck.

I stopped by the front hall table, dropped my briefcase on the floor, and thumbed through the mail. Bills and junk mail, but no hand addressed letters from a prison. It had been days since Frank had written. I wondered what his next trick would be.

Jake muted the television. "We saved you chili and cornbread. It's in the fridge."

Quinn got up. "I'll get it for you. Have a seat."

I fell into a bar stool. Quinn opened a bottle of Anchor Steam, poured it into a glass, and set it in front of me. I took a sip.

"How was court?" Jake asked.

"Trial date vacated. Vivian agreed to transfer Tony to rehab instead of back to jail when he gets better."

The microwave dinged. Quinn set in front of me a bistro bowl of chili, garnished with melting cheddar cheese, and a basket of warm cornbread. "What are you going to do about his case?"

Before I had a chance to answer, the Bakelite telephone on the hallway table rang. Quinn was startled. "What was that?"

"The phone," Jake said.

"The one on the table? I thought it was a decoration."

Apparently, she had missed it plugged into the wall.

The phone rang again. She ran over to it and lifted the receiver. "Hello?"

Her eyes widened and she held the receiver out to me. "It's a recording. A call from a correctional institute. Do I accept?"

Frank.

I found myself on my feet, taking the receiver from Quinn, and setting it back on the hook.

"Don't you want to know who it was?" Quinn asked.

"I don't need to know. The only person who had this number was my mother. She gave me the phone as a housewarming gift, a reminder to call home more often." The master of guilt, my mother, ironically. None of it was my fault. She could have stopped it. She had to have seen what was going on.

My mother was gone. Blaming a dead person felt like screaming into a void. Pointless and exhausting. I wondered when I could let it go.

"It had to be Frank," I said.

"Don't you want to know why he called?" Quinn asked.

"A ploy for attention, that's all I need to know."

My scars itched. I wanted to scratch them. But not in front of Jake and Quinn.

I picked up my bowl and bread, covered them and put them back in the fridge. I could feel Jake and Quinn's eyes on me. Quinn looked over at him, her posture one big question. He waved at her, signaling not to say anything.

I picked up the beer on my way to my bedroom. "Think I'll take a bath."

The tub was where I usually retreated to cut myself. It was the easiest way to get rid of the blood. I hadn't indulged in years. But every time something came up with Frank, I was a lonely teenager again. Living in a residential school with nuns and other girls who'd been rejected by their parents, I hid in the bathroom for privacy while I blotted out the searing ache in my heart and wondered what I'd done to deserve this.

While the bath filled, I finished my beer and wished for another, but I didn't want to go back into the living room and have Jake and Quinn see me being the fragile, damaged child that I was. I heard the bedroom door open and close, and then a light knock at the bathroom door.

"Can I come in?" It was Jake.

"You may."

He entered, carrying an opened bottle of beer. "Thought you might like another."

"Yes, thanks." I took the bottle from him and sipped.

"Look, Red, Frank isn't going to stop."

"If I outlive him, he will."

"That could be years. At some point, he's going to be released and then he'll be on our doorstep. Like it or not, you're all he has left."

"It's not just me. It's Quinn he's after."

"You don't think he's attracted to her, do you? Isn't she a little old for him?"

"As in she's not fourteen years old? Right. Remember what happened at the funeral?"

"I didn't exactly see anything. I just know he upset you."

After my mother's funeral mass and the burial, the mourners met at the O'Shaughnessy mansion, where my parents then lived. The house was full of people I'd known growing up, my parents' friends and my father's business acquaintances – only the legitimate ones as far as I knew. At one point, Jake had left me in the parlor overlooking the rose garden. It was a grey and moody day, even without burying my mother. My father appeared at my side and asked me to join him in his den. I followed him without thinking. Maybe it was because of the parental tone he used. Or maybe it was because I was exhausted from grief.

When we were alone, he made a pass at me. Now with my mother gone, he said I could be his little girl again. It wasn't my imagination. He was standing too close. His hand brushed against my breast. Jake walked in just as I threw my drink in Frank's face.

I couldn't look Jake in the eye. "He came on to me."

"You never said."

"What is there to say? He is what he is. Nothing's going to change that. And after what happened during the trial, I'm certain he wants Quinn. He wants to possess her. Defile her, the way he did me."

Shortly after Quinn reappeared in my life, I was in trial representing a young woman who had been sexually assaulted by the Hollywood producer she worked for. Frank defended him. Frank and I spent every day, all day long, sparring in court.

Close to the end of the trial, one of my witnesses didn't show up, so I drove across the bay to her apartment looking for her. On my way back, I called home and learned that Frank, who Quinn believed at the time was only her grandfather, had picked her up, claiming that he was taking her to dinner.

He had promised to tell her about her birth father.

When I found them, they were at the mansion. He was drunk and rambling. He hadn't revealed the truth to Quinn.

She was terrified, not knowing what to do with a drunk old man, or how to get out of the situation. When I ran inside to pull her out of there, I could see the look on his face, the desire he had. He hadn't touched her, but she seemed to sense the danger she was in.

Quinn looked exactly like me. In his mind, he owned her, even more than he owned me, because she was both his daughter and granddaughter. He believed he was entitled to her.

I had parked in front of the mansion. While I was arguing with Frank, my BMW was firebombed by his client's thugs, the same men who murdered Eli.

"You're right, Jake. He isn't going to quit. He's bankrupt. His prestige is gone. My mother is dead, and the mansion is mine. All he has left is us." I began scratching my scars furiously.

Jake pulled me into a hug. "And you have me. I swear, Maureen, he isn't going to hurt you or Quinn ever again."

It was sweet of him to say. But there was only one way to make sure Frank wouldn't hurt someone. Neither Jake, nor I, would cross that line.

Chapter Eight

Rick

By the time the Dum Dee twins brought Rick home, Appollonia had already left for her spa day. Umberto was sitting in the den, behind the desk, thumbing his phone when Rick walked by. "At your convenience," Umberto said, without looking up.

Rick went into the gleaming white kitchen, all air and light and Italian marble that made his eyes hurt, and mixed a Bloody Mary, then hauled himself upstairs for a shower.

Afterwards, in fresh clothes and with his cocktail drunk, he was just beginning to feel human again. On his way to the den, he stopped off in the kitchen for a second drink. Tomato juice, a healthy splash of Tabasco sauce, vodka, and the traditional swirling with a forefinger. He tasted it – perfect. When he turned around, Umberto had appeared, making him jump.

Umberto took the glass out of Rick's hands and poured it down the sink. He jammed a pod into the coffee machine, put a mug under the spout, and hit the button. A few seconds later, Umberto handed Rick the coffee. "Here, you can have this. No more booze."

"Ever?"

Umberto snorted. Rick hadn't meant to be funny.

"Until we finish work today. Do you think you can handle that?"

Umberto was getting just a little high-handed. "I really don't care for that tone, compadre. I'm the boss around here. You need to remember that."

"Guess again, Rick. I don't work for you. I work for Leon Toussaint. He's financing this campaign and he's the one who signs my paychecks."

"So, you're going to rat me out?"

"Mr. Toussaint trusts me to handle whatever comes up. Look, Rick, you are our man. Mr. Toussaint believes in you. Between now and the election, my job is to make you shine.

To tell the truth, I feel like you're sabotaging the effort. If something like last night went viral, I don't know if I can save you. So, I really, really need you to be on your best behavior. It's only for a few more months. That means lay off the drugs, cut back on the booze, and no more gambling, clubbing, partying."

"You make me sound like a derelict." Rick was not a bum. He was a hedonist, a term he had picked up at a party. He lived for pleasure. Most people didn't understand. They thought it was a psychological disorder. It was not a disease, but a philosophy of an artfully lived life. Rick had heard that at a party too.

"It's for your own good. Let's get to work." Umberto slapped Rick's upper arm, in a manly affectionate gesture that hurt. "We have that interview to prep for. Appollonia should be back soon, but we can work on your stuff until she shows up."

Umberto led Rick into the den where a video camera on a tripod and lights were set up, facing the couch. Umberto sat on a dining chair in the middle of the room, playing television interviewer. He directed Rick to the couch. Dum and Dee were dispatched to walk the grounds.

"First a little warm up," Umberto said as he shuffled through index cards. "Mr. Stevens, thank you for talking to me today. Our viewers would love to know more about your background. Where did you grow up? What was your life like before you announced your candidacy?"

Umberto had warned Rick daily that everyone was on the internet these days including amateur fact-checkers galore. Tell the truth but make it sound as good as you can.

"Thank you for having me," Rick said. "I grew up right here in San Francisco. My aunt and uncle raised me after my parents passed away. I was lucky I had family who took me in. Not all kids are so lucky. My father was killed in a car accident when I was a baby. My mother passed away from heart disease. I'd originally wanted to become a doctor so I could find a cure for her condition and maybe fewer kids would grow up orphaned. But that didn't work out."

He could have been a doctor. He was smart enough. But he couldn't afford college since his uncle had spent Rick's inheritance. The only reason his aunt and uncle took him in was because of the settlement from his dad's accident. Half of it went to his mother, who used it up before she died. The other half was in trust for Rick's care, administered by a court, but his uncle and aunt were allowed to recover living expenses which included his "room and board."

Besides, his high school grades weren't that great because he had to work in the dealership after school and on the weekends, so he had no time for homework. He wouldn't get into a decent college even if he could afford it. He was screwed from the minute David's body was found.

The Bentley sped past the window on its way to the garage. The back door banged open. Appollonia screamed, "You bastard!"

"She's home," Rick said brightly.

Appollonia stalked into the den, an envelope in her hand. She threw it at him. "You pervert! I knew there was something wrong with you. You never touch me. I tried so hard to please you. The gym. The diet. The clothes and hair. Look at me. I look like a model. I am sexy. Everyone tells me that. Now I know the reason you don't want me. You're disgusting. I want a divorce."

Umberto sidled up to Appollonia, slid an arm around her shoulder and spoke to her soothingly as he led her out of the room.

Rick opened the envelope. Inside were pictures. Of Rick. Rick and the cute waitress. Rick and the chef. Rick and the cute waitress and the chef. What's the big deal? They were all consenting adults.

A note fluttered onto his lap. "Time's up." It was signed, "Herman Jules."

A FEW DAYS LATER, Umberto escorted Rick into the Presidential Suite of the St. Francis Hotel. Built by a railroad magnate, the hotel survived the 1906 earthquake, and was host to movie stars, opera singers, war heroes, and presidents. Theodore Roosevelt, John F. Kennedy, Ronald Regan, as well as Queen Elizabeth II, had stayed in this very suite.

On this occasion, Leon "The Lion" Toussaint was in residence.

A butler admitted them, then disappeared through a side door. Rick was drawn to the windows overlooking Union Square. In the distance stood the Ferry Building clock tower, another structure that survived the '06 earthquake. The Bay Bridge disappeared into the Treasure Island tunnel. Out in the bay was Alcatraz, the island prison that once held Al Capone. They said it was inescapable.

What was Rick, an orphaned kid who hustled cars for a living, doing in the Presidential Suite of the St. Francis Hotel? It felt like a joke. At the same time, it felt magical, as if any moment now, his glorious destiny would reveal itself and he would step into the life that he deserved.

For the first time, someone other than Rick himself had recognized that he was something special. That person was Leon "The Lion" Toussaint.

Heir to a Texas oil dynasty and a graduate of the London School of Economics, The Lion talked like a down-home good old boy in television interviews, but his nickname and reputation had been earned. His friends were the lords of the savanna, his enemies were torn to pieces.

Rick was beginning to feel dizzy. The one Bloody Mary had worn off and he hadn't the stomach to eat. His body was screaming for more booze. He looked at his watch. "I thought you said the appointment was at two o'clock. It's nearly two thirty."

Umberto glanced up from his phone. "Mr. Toussaint is a busy man, Rick. You can wait."

Rick dropped onto a yellow leather sofa that faced the matching one where Umberto sat. A fan of magazines on the coffee table included Forbes, Conde Nast, and Architectural Digest. On the Forbes cover was a picture of Leon Toussaint.

A door opened and the man himself appeared. Tall and bulky with red, fleshy face and silver mane, he wore his trademark white linen suit and a chunky turquoise bolo tie that made his eyes look bluer and the whites of his eyes look redder. The butler followed him in.

Umberto stood and motioned for Rick to get up.

The Lion gave Umberto's hand one shake. "Good to see you, son."

"Good afternoon, sir. Let me introduce you to the next California state senator, Rick Stevens."

The Lion took Rick's hand into his big warm paw and held it. "I've been hearing some good things about you, boy."

"Yes, sir. Thank you, sir." Rick sounded servile even to himself, but he delivered the lines Umberto made him practice in the car. "Thank you so much for your support."

"Right." The Lion bared his teeth in a fake smile. "What are you boys drinking?"

"Nothing for us, thank you, sir," Umberto said before Rick could answer.

Toussaint turned to the butler. "Vodka tonic." Rick's favorite drink. The Lion settled into the couch that Rick had been on, spreading an arm across the backrest, angling his legs so when he crossed an ankle over knee, he took up half the space. "You boys take a seat."

Umberto sat back down, and Rick sat beside him. The butler handed The Lion a tall glass sweating with condensation, ice cubes tinkling, tonic fizzing. Rick really needed a drink. The Lion took a sip then set it on the coffee table between them. Rick couldn't take his eyes off it. He felt The Lion watching him, like a predator sizing up his prey.

"Umberto here tells me you've got yourself into some trouble, is that right, son?"

Slaughter it is. Why did Umberto bring him here? So much for "I have your best interests at heart."

Rick forced himself to look directly at The Lion. He wasn't sure how much Umberto had said. "Yes, sir."

"I thought we'd swept all the dirt under the carpet when that Wenderholm fella popped up with his book."

Umberto hadn't told Rick how to respond to this, so he said nothing.

The Lion went on. "Did you read it?"

"No, sir," Rick said truthfully.

"An unfortunate peccadillo, what happened when you were in school. Nothing they could prove, that's for sure. But it looked bad. It'd stuck to you like dung to a bull's rump. But I took care of it. We didn't want the press focusing on that – it's the issues that count, isn't that right, son?"

What issues? Rick wasn't allowed to talk about policy. "Yes, sir. I've given that some thought. I'd like to work on my platform – you know, tell the voters what my positions are."

"Don't you worry about that," The Lion said. "We got our pollsters taking the voter's temperature. When the time is right, we'll put something together for you. Right now, your job is to be the charming boy you are, show off that pretty wife of yours, and do what you do best."

"What's that?"

"Look good for the camera."

The Lion pulled a fat cigar from his blazer, and Umberto was out of his seat with a lighter just as The Lion jabbed it into his mouth.

After the big man puffed a few times and got the cigar going, he waved Umberto aside. "Now, as for the money thing, I get it. Boys will be boys. But you got to realize, son, I got a lot of money riding on you. I'd hate to see it go to waste."

Rick felt his destiny slipping out of his grasp. He needed to be good. For as long as it took. "Yes, sir. I understand."

"You know some fellas can sit down at the card table and walk away any time. And some fellas can't. I've seen more than my fair share of good men destroy themselves. Cards, horse races, it doesn't matter. They'd bet on anything. It's like a disease with them. So, this gambling thing's got to stop."

Umberto must have told Toussaint about the Herman Jules debt. Had he squealed about the pictures, too? "Yes, sir." Rick felt his head going up and down like a bobble toy on a hotrod dashboard.

"Do I have your word on that, son?"

"Absolutely, sir. No more gambling."

"And I believe you. Your Mr. Jules won't be bothering you again. He's taken care of."

Rick's destiny came into view again. He could almost see it on the other side of a gauzy curtain. "Thank you, sir. I don't know what to say. I won't let you down."

"Good boy. This is only the beginning, believe you me. California this year. DC down the road. I got big plans for you, son, but there's just one more thing."

"Sir?"

"A famous man once said the only way he'd lose an election was if he got caught with a dead girl or a live boy."

The pictures.

Umberto laughed. It was a weird sound, like a crow cawing. Rick had never heard it before.

The Lion stood. "So, we won't be seeing any dead girls or live boys, isn't that right, Rick?"

When Rick tried to laugh, he sounded like he was choking. "Yes, sir. Absolutely, sir."

The Lion stuck his hand out again. "We're going to win this election, aren't we, son?"

Rick took The Lion's hand and shook vigorously. He could be good. He had a reason to, now. This man was a king maker and he had picked Rick to be his next king. "Yes, sir, we are."

Chapter Nine

Maureen

I WAS IN MY office finishing up a call with the telephone company to have my condo landline disconnected so Frank couldn't invade my home anymore, when an incoming email pinged on my computer. It was from Vivian Thandi. The subject was "State vs. Paredes, witness statement." Attached to it was a pdf and a video file.

I opened the attachment. It was a witness statement that read:

> My name is Robert Morgan. I make this statement based upon my personal knowledge of the events described herein. I am the night manager of Acme Security where Oscar Wenderholm worked before his death. I was personally familiar with Mr. Wenderholm. I reviewed our security video.
>
>
> Two weeks before Mr. Wenderholm was murdered, a yellow-colored Gremlin followed Mr. Wenderholm's black SUV into the parking lot. After Mr. Wenderholm parked his SUV and got out, the man I now know to be the defendant, Anthony Paredes, stopped his car abruptly and got out too. The defendant, Anthony Paredes, confronted Mr. Wenderholm. They argued for several minutes. Mr. Paredes was very agitated. He waved his arms around. It appeared that he was crying. Mr. Wenderholm was not aggressive to him at all but appeared to be listening. After several minutes, Mr. Paredes got back into his car and drove off.

When Mr. Wenderholm failed to come into work, I telephoned his wife
and learned that he had been murdered. I watched the television news to
see if I could learn more about it. I saw the video of the man identified as
Anthony Paredes being transported to jail. That is when I found the video
that shows the events described herein. I turned a true and correct copy of
the video over to the District Attorney's Office. I execute this statement
of my own free will. Signed, Robert Morgan

I opened the video file. The image was night-time and grainy, but the parking lot lights
made it clear enough to see. Wenderholm's SUV pulled in, followed closely by Tony's
Gremlin. When Tony stopped the car, his trunk lid flew open. He got out and yelled at
Wenderholm for just under four minutes. Then he shut the trunk lid before he got back
into the car and sped off.

The witness's telephone number was on his statement. I called.

A man answered. "Acme Warehouse."

"May I speak to Robert Morgan?"

"You got him." He apparently spotted my name on the caller ID because he sounded
suspicious. "You're that defense lawyer, for the guy who killed Oscar. They told me you'd
call. Even told me when. What's it you want?"

It was routine for the DA's office to warn witnesses that they could expect a call. It was
also routine for the DA to tell them that if the witness was uncooperative, it would look
bad for them when they testified at the trial.

"I just want to review your statement, get some more details if I may."

"Yeah, okay, alright. What do you want to know?" Here was another witness who had
been instructed not to volunteer information, just to answer the questions put to him as
narrowly as possible.

"I'm curious about why it took you so long to review the surveillance video," I said.

I could hear him spit. While I waited, I imagined a man with a red handlebar mustache,
wiping his mouth with the back of his hand.

He answered, "How was I to know?"

"Know what?"

"I didn't know Oscar would get killed. The next two days after his murder were his
weekend. When he didn't come in on the third night, I called his wife. That's when I
found out."

"Did you immediately review the video?"

"Not then. A couple of days later, I made a condolence call to Oscar's wife because that's what decent people do. I even took over a casserole my mother made. Oscar's wife told me about this skinny guy in a Gremlin that was harassing Oscar and that's the guy who shot him. So that's when I remembered what Oscar said and I pulled the video. Good thing, too, Oscar parked his rig right in front of the camera. That SUV of his was so big there was nowhere else to park it."

"What did Oscar say to you?"

"Some crazy guy was stalking him and asked me to keep an eye out. I told him he should get a pistol for personal protection. Oscar said he didn't like guns. Besides, he didn't think the guy was that dangerous, just a nuisance."

"Did you type up your statement?"

"No, ma'am. Someone at the DA's office did that."

Interesting that the DA left off the statement that Oscar believed Tony was harmless. It was just because of these kinds of omissions that I always interviewed the witnesses myself.

Wenderholm's black SUV dwarfed the full-sized pick-up trucks around it. It was shiny, new, and impractical. Smaller cars made more sense zipping through traffic and trying to find a park place. It was pricey for someone who earned a little more than minimum wage as a security guard. "Don't know if you can tell me this, but how could he afford such an expensive vehicle?"

"Said his wife inherited some money and she bought it for him."

"Thank you for your time, Mr. Morgan. I appreciate your cooperation."

"Yeah, well, I'd say good luck, but I hope your boy fries." He hung up.

I yelled for Yolanda.

She appeared at my door. "There is an intercom, you know."

"But then I wouldn't get to see your smiling face, would I? Look, can you find out if Oscar Wenderholm's wife came into an inheritance? He told a witness that she bought him a new SUV."

"Where's Quinn? Isn't online research her thing?"

"Have a seat."

Yolanda dropped into a visitor's chair with the enthusiasm of a kid called into the principal's office.

"I hope you know how much I depend upon you. Since Eli has been gone, it's just been you and me."

She gave me a skeptical look. Eli wasn't that helpful as time went on.

"And even when he was around, you and I did most of the work," I added.

"All of the work," Yolanda said.

"Of course, you're right. He was useless." He did a good job at first, but I was trying to establish a rapport with Yolanda, so I agreed with her interpretation.

"Worse than useless, he sabotaged you."

"Yeah, I get it. I shouldn't have trusted him."

In the distance, a cable car clanged its bell over the din of street traffic. I searched for the words that would make a smooth transition from "I was wrong" to "help me" without sounding pathetic. I wanted to maintain my dignity. But despite being a trial attorney, I had never felt eloquent. The only real tool I had in my advocacy skill set was honesty.

Yolanda scooted towards the end of her seat. "Is that it?"

From the heart it would be, even if it sounded pathetic. "The thing is, I don't know what I'm doing with this motherhood stuff."

"No one does, Maureen. We just make it up as we go along."

"Yeah, but you have your mother and your aunts. I have no one." I didn't say that if my mother was still alive, I wouldn't have asked her anyway. She didn't protect me when I was young, and she dumped me in a boarding school when I needed her most.

Yolanda's face softened. "You have me."

"That's right, I do. All I know is I want Quinn in my life. I look for ways to make it easy for her to stick around. I was so excited when she said she wanted to go to law school, and then she was accepted. She's interested in our practice, so I hoped that if we found some things for her to do, it'd help with her studies and maybe make a career decision down the line. Which, of course, means since you were doing everything before, some of your tasks are going to shift over to her. But it's only temporary, just this summer. She starts class in the fall, and I don't want to distract her from studying. I hope you're okay with it."

"You hardly know her, Maureen. That's what worries me. She just wandered in here a few months ago out of nowhere. You take everything she says at face value. You don't know what her intentions are, if she's a good person, if she's honest or reliable. And you're giving her all this responsibility in a murder case of all things."

"You think I'm making the same mistake I made with Eli."

"I didn't say that."

"You painted the picture."

The street sounds seemed to disappear while Yolanda and I sat across from each other, locked in an invisible struggle.

"You're right," Yolanda said. "That's what I think. You trust her too much. You want things to be like a fairy tale, like Sleeping Beauty or something, but life isn't like that. All I'm saying is I want you to be careful."

I reached across the desk and took her hand. I had never done that before. "You're right, of course. How about this? How about I put her under your direct supervision? If you see anything you think I should know about, you tell me immediately."

That's when everything fell into place for me. Yolanda was the office mom. I needed to respect her authority.

She pretended to think for thirty seconds although it was obviously a performance. She let go of my hand and stood. "Okay, you won me over. So, what was it you called me in for?"

"Brita Wenderholm's inheritance?"

"You think he lied about where the money came from?"

"I think if she inherited a pile of money like that, why was he still working as a night watchman?"

"Maybe it was just enough to buy a new car."

"Maybe. Still, I'd like to know."

"I'll see what I can do."

A FEW DAYS LATER, the hospital called. Tony was out of the coma. When I arrived, I found a guard posted just outside the room and another one inside his room, sitting in a visitor's chair.

The first thing I noticed about Tony was his horn-rim glasses were gone. He looked naked without them.

There was a small hose that ran into both nostrils. He was still hooked up to an IV. There were less bandages, so his injuries were more obvious. His head had been shaved. Stitches closed a long cut across his skull. One of his legs was in a blue plastic splint.

A nurse stood at a computer station, inputting data. She reached across the bed and pulled up Tony's sheet to cover his bruised torso. "And you are?"

"My attorney," Tony said, his voice raspy. "She's okay."

He recognized me, a good sign.

To the guard, I said, "I need to speak with my client privately."

"What about the nurse?" he asked.

She said, "I was just leaving."

He glanced at his watch. "I'll be back in five minutes." He waited for her to leave, then he followed. She reached back in and closed the door.

I dragged a chair up to his bed, took a seat, and set my briefcase on the floor. "Hey, buddy, how are you doing?"

"Alive."

"Do you remember what happened?"

"They keep asking me that. My name is Anthony Paredes. I'm in San Francisco General Hospital. I got beaten up in jail. And I didn't kill Oscar Wenderholm."

I wasn't a psychiatrist, but to me, he sounded mentally fit for trial.

He grabbed my forearm with a surprisingly strong grip. "I can't go back to jail. Not ever. The doctors say I need surgery on my leg. Not sure when that's going to happen. They were waiting for me to wake up."

"The DA's office agreed you can go to rehab instead of jail."

He rolled his eyes. "I wouldn't be in the hospital if it weren't for them. What about the trial date?"

"It was vacated."

"Dammit."

"I'm sorry, but there was nothing I could do. We didn't know when you were going to wake up or if you would be fit to stand trial when you did."

I pulled out my laptop, hit the power button, and found the warehouse clip. I held it up for Tony to see. I hit play. "Take a look at this."

Tony squinted at the screen.

"What happened to your glasses?" I asked.

"Lost them when they beat me up. What's the video about? It's all blurry."

"Do you remember visiting Oscar at his work?"

He nodded.

"Can you tell me why you went to his workplace?"

"To talk to him. I told him to stay away from kids."

"How did you know where he worked?"

"I followed him from his house."

Not good. But I had to know the worst of it to be prepared. "You looked agitated in the video."

"I was upset. I didn't threaten him or anything. I just wanted him to leave kids alone. I didn't kill him. I swear to you. Someone's set me up. I'm the victim here. First, Oscar. Then those jurors. And then those guys at the jail. When is this going to stop?"

A nurse opened the door and stuck her head in. "That's enough. Time for you to go."

WHEN I WALKED INTO the office, Yolanda was on the phone. She made eye contact with me and said, "Just a minute, I'll check." She covered the mouthpiece with her hand, and mouthed to me, "Ian Napier."

He had been my father's law partner. The break-up of their firm had left Ian nearly bankrupt. He let go of most of his staff and moved into a smaller office on a lower floor in the same building.

I had known him from visiting my father's office when I was little and from the cocktail parties my parents hosted at the mansion. I don't know if he was there the night my father left the gathering and crept into my bedroom. I can't remember.

Despite being an intelligent man, he had been my father's stooge. When Frank's disbarment came up for hearing, Frank testified that he had not confided in Ian about the source of the money he had deposited in the firm's account or the nature of his clients' businesses. Ian seemed to think they were on retainer with several legitimate businessmen. The truth was his clients were human traffickers who distributed child pornography.

Ian had to be blind to not see that there was something wrong. He must have been mesmerized by my father's magnetism. He couldn't believe that my father was in league with very bad people – not even when my father was disbarred, pled guilty to money laundering, and went to prison.

I didn't trust Ian. Frank had written and telephoned in the past few days. As soon as I had the phone disconnected, here was Ian calling my office. Frank would have known he would never get past Yolanda. If he asked Ian to call on his behalf, Ian would.

"What's he want?" I mouthed.

She uncovered the mouthpiece. "May I ask what this is in regard to?" She listened, then punched the console hold button.

"Emerson Katsu."

"Put him through."

I let Ian wait as I grabbed a cup of coffee. I took off my blazer, draped it over a visitor's chair, unpacked my briefcase, took a deep breath, and picked up the receiver. "Good afternoon, Ian."

"Good afternoon, Maureen. I hope you're well."

He sounded sincere. But he would because he was a nice man. Nice stooges were the best stooges of all.

"I am, thank you. What can I help you with?"

"Emerson Katsu came to see me. I believe you interviewed him. He'd like to meet with you, and me, and clarify a few things for the record."

"When?"

"How about now?"

YOLANDA AND I CLOSED the office. I wanted her with me when Katsu talked – as a witness. If he later changed his story, I would put her on the stand to testify as to what he had said in this interview. Then I'd explore in very pointed questions why his testimony was different from his statement.

When we arrived at Ian's office, we were quickly led into a small conference room. I recognized the furniture, pared down from the partnership, and the art from the firm, an abstract painting of the Golden Gate bridge at sunset, hanging over the coffee cabinet. The view from the window was different than in the old office. Instead of a sweeping vista where the sky seemed to balance on the tops of high rises, with low-hanging clouds pierced by their pinnacles, we now looked at another building across an alleyway that was so tall that it blocked out the sun, throwing this room perpetually into shade. On the floor in a corner, a light-starved philodendron clung to its moss pole.

Ian entered with Emerson Katsu. He was dressed in a suit, as before. Ian wore a gray suit, white shirt, black and red striped tie, his graying hair neatly clipped. He looked thinner and more drawn than when I had last seen him at Frank's sentencing.

Pleasantries were exchanged. Coffee and tea were offered and declined.

I began the meeting. "Mr. Katsu, this is Yolanda Martinez, my paralegal. She will take your statement in shorthand and also record it on her phone. Is that alright with you?"

If I had the time, I would have called a court reporter, but I was afraid Katsu would get cold feet if I delayed even by one day.

Katsu looked at Ian, who nodded. Katsu nodded too.

Yolanda opened the voice recording app, set her phone in the middle of the table, and put pen to paper.

"So, Mr. Katsu, what did you want to talk to me about?"

"I wasn't entirely truthful with you before. You took me by surprise when you showed up at my office. I wasn't sure how much to tell you."

Generally, taking a witness by surprise will get you more information than if you wait for them to talk to an attorney. That's why I didn't call Katsu in advance of our visit. I was afraid he'd call the DA's office and tip them off that I was interested in him, and then stonewall me.

But that didn't mean Katsu's sudden show of cooperation now meant he was going to be truthful.

"I'm listening."

He smoothed his tie, exposing his expensive watch again. He caught me looking at it, as I intended. He said, "The watch was a gift from Oscar. He wanted to make amends for the trouble he caused me at the Academy."

I wasn't sure how much trouble Katsu had. Oscar lost his job. Tony was expelled. Katsu got a promotion.

"Go on," I said.

"He said his ship had come in."

Yolanda hadn't found anything in the court records regarding an estate that Mrs. Wenderholm would have benefited from. She also looked for obituaries that named the widow as a survivor but found none. "By that do you mean he received a large amount of money?"

"An 'advance,' he called it. He wrote a book about his experience in high school. I think he was trying to explain why he got involved with Anthony Paredes."

"Involved? Mr. Katsu, Oscar Wenderholm raped Tony."

Katsu recoiled. "This is difficult for me. You know what I mean. The thing is stuff like this happens all the time. Not that is an excuse, but an explanation. It happened to Oscar when we were in school. The chess coach, in fact. After your trial, Oscar did some online research. He realized that he was a victim, and that he had perpetuated the abuse he suffered as a means of dealing with it. He said that if he told his story, schools would be more careful about who they hired. He wanted to protect future generations of children."

Wenderholm claimed he wanted to protect children – and, coincidentally, make a lot of money doing it.

As skittish as Katsu was, I tried to be delicate with my next questions. "You were in that chess club in high school."

"I was."

"Were you victimized as well?"

"I wasn't. I'm not sure why the coach didn't target me. I had no idea what was going on until Oscar showed up a few months ago and told me."

Yolanda had checked the department of motor vehicle records. That was about the time Oscar bought the new SUV.

"How much money did he receive?"

"He was coy, said it was confidential, but it was enough to buy this watch and his new truck."

"Did he tell you the name of the publisher?"

"Sorry. He said that was confidential, too."

"When can we expect the book to be released?"

"There was some confusion about that. Oscar had hoped that it would be out in the next few months, so he could start earning royalties and go on book tours. He wanted to quit his job. The last time I saw him, he said that there was some hang-up, and he was starting to get worried. He said that if he'd known it would take this long, he would have found a different publisher."

THE IMMINENT DISCLOSURE OF scandal could be a motive for murder. I needed to talk to the remaining members of Oscar Wenderholm's high school chess team. Who of them would stand to lose if his book was published?

At dawn the next morning, I launched Sunny II from an onramp onto Interstate 80. One of the rare opportunities I had to legally push her was bringing her from city traffic pace to highway speeds. Her body squatted like a tiger about to strike as I shifted through the gears and the sheer power at my disposal thrilled me. I take my joys where I find them.

Traffic towards the Bay Bridge was light this early in the morning as most commuters were coming into San Francisco. But by the time I passed Fairfield, it slowed down to a crawl. An accident had occurred up ahead, judging by the sirens and flashing lights in the distance. Still, I pulled into my destination, an expensive, recently built Fair Oaks neighborhood an hour and one-half after I'd left my condo.

Sunny's GPS led me to a curved driveway leading to a two-story house with a stone façade that looked fake. The front garden was drought resistant, a combination of shrubs and artfully arranged rocks. A woman in skintight yoga pants, a sports bra, and gauzy shirt opened the driver's door to a big black SUV – identical to Oscar Wenderholm's rig. She tossed a rolled-up yoga mat into the passenger compartment as her expertly cut shoulder-length blonde hair swayed with her movements.

I parked on the street, blocking her exit, and scrambled out to meet her. "Excuse me, are you Constance Robertson?"

She took a step back. I would have too if I were hailed by a stranger who called my name. I halted to give her space.

"Who wants to know?" she asked.

"My name is Maureen Gould. I'm an attorney in San Francisco, working on a murder case involving Oscar Wenderholm. I believe he was a friend of yours?"

"You're that killer's attorney. I don't know how you people can live with yourselves."

"I'm searching for the truth, Mrs. Robertson. My client says he's innocent. If he didn't do it, then there is a murderer roaming the streets. It's in everyone's interests that we find out what the truth is."

"He'd say he was innocent, wouldn't he? The cops wouldn't have arrested him if they didn't have evidence."

"The DA's case is flimsy." She could call Vivian the minute I left and tell her I said that. She asked, "How did you find me?"

"It wasn't hard. Everything is on the internet these days. What can you tell me about Oscar Wenderholm?"

"I only have a few minutes, so let's make this quick. I knew him in high school but haven't seen him in years."

"What can you remember?"

"Oscar wasn't as bright as he thought he was. He wasn't popular. Kind of a hanger-on."

"Was there a specific group of people he hung around with?"

Her eyes cut to the distance, then she looked back at me.

"I just remember him from the chess club."

Constance Robertson owned a car dealership and had a car that was the twin of Wenderholm's. I took a leap of faith.

"You sold him an SUV recently."

"Who told you that?"

Bingo. "It's in the DMV records." It was, but I hadn't checked.

"So what?"

"Mr. Wenderholm was working as a night guard. How could he afford such an expensive vehicle?"

"You'd have to ask him."

I waited. I wasn't leaving. And my car wasn't going to move out of her way.

"My class starts in ten minutes," she said.

"I really need some answers to my questions, Ms. Robertson."

"Look, I felt sorry for the guy, okay? He was pitiful back then and even worse now. He could barely support his family after that trial. His reputation was ruined. He couldn't get a job around kids. That's your fault. His car was falling apart, so he came to me with big crocodile tears, and I sold him a new vehicle at cost."

"What do you know about the book he was writing?"

She barked a laugh. "A book? Oscar? What could he possibly write a book about?"

"A tell-all about high school. Did you know anything about that?"

She looked bewildered. "What did he say happened?"

I didn't want to let on how much I was told. Constance might tell quite a different story than Emerson Katsu had if she didn't know what he said.

"Something to do with your chess coach?"

"I have no idea what you're talking about. Now, I've answered your questions and if you don't move your car, I'm calling the police."

Chapter Ten

Rick

RICK STOOD TO ONE side in his den, trying to stay out of the way, while Umberto showed the television people where to set up. One guy snaked power cables across the room. Another assembled light stands. A woman, the interviewer, stood near a window as she touched up her face powder while two more women, both wearing headsets and consulting clipboards, conferred with her. One of the women was in jeans and looked bossy. Another woman was young and cute, wearing a little plaid skirt, tight t-shirt, and sneakers. To complete the schoolgirl look, she wore a ponytail.

The Lion said no dead girls or live boys. He didn't say anything about live girls.

Rick was bored. He wasn't allowed to drink because Umberto didn't want booze on his breath when he was interviewed. Appollonia was allowed to take a pill to calm her nerves. She was in the master suite, bonding with a make-up artist Umberto had hired.

"Do you mind?" It was the guy with the cables, gesturing that he needed to get past Rick, who was standing in front of an outlet.

Rick thought, *it's my house, I'll stand where I please.*

Rick said, "Yeah, no problem." He wandered out of his den down to the game room.

He was lining up a shot on the pool table when the schoolgirl came in, wearing a headset. Her sassy ponytail swished back and forth when she talked. "Excuse me, Mr. Stevens. I was sent to find you. You're not needed yet, but Mr. Salazar wanted you close by. We've been delayed for just a little bit. One of the microphones quit working, so we had to send for another."

Umberto must have noticed Rick watching her. Did he send her as a present, to keep Rick occupied?

"Don't you pack extras, just in case?"

"We did, but they weren't working either. Someone forgot to check the batteries." She began to blush.

He said, "Then you probably don't have much to do. Care for a game of pool?"

She looked over her shoulder into the hallway, uncertain of her instructions.

He leaned against the table, chalking his cue. "Come on. Tell the truth, you were sent to keep an eye on me."

She nodded. "But I don't know how to shoot pool."

Perfect. "I'll teach you."

He pulled a cue from the cabinet and handed it to her before he gently closed the door. He racked the balls in the center of the table and positioned the cue ball.

"Over here," he said. She obeyed. Good little girl.

He bent over, leaned on the table, then thrusted the stick through his fingers. With a loud crack, the cue ball demolished the neatly arranged balls and sent them skittering across the table. "Just like that. See?"

He racked the balls and positioned the cue ball again. "Now it's your turn."

She bent over, as he had, and placed her left hand on the table to brace the stick. Her t-shirt rode up and he could see a flowery tattoo on her lower back disappearing into the skirt waistband. He stood back, enjoying the view, while she took the shot. Her stick glanced off the cue ball and it drifted a few inches away. "See, I told you I don't know how to do this."

"Let me show you."

RICK WAS LOST IN the moment. The girl was sprawled across the table on her back, her t-shirt pulled up over a lacy bra. Rick's hand was sliding up her naked thigh when he heard the door open.

Umberto slammed the door shut and leaned against it.

If Rick had just three more minutes.

Umberto cleared his throat. "We're ready."

Rick pulled the girl's shirt down and helped her off the table. Without looking up, she straightened her skirt, and disappeared out of the room.

"What is wrong with you?" Umberto asked. "There's a house full of people. Your wife is upstairs. That girl was wearing a microphone on that headset. So is the producer. She heard everything."

Funny they didn't send someone to rescue her sooner, the filthy voyeurs.

"I was bored."

"Bored?"

Rick shouldn't have to explain himself. Appollonia didn't care what he did, despite the scene she threw the other day. What she cared about was that he didn't do it with her.

"I thought you sent the girl to me."

"Not for that!" Umberto waved a hand up and down in the direction of Rick's trousers. "After you've calmed down, come into the den. Let's get the interview done. We'll talk about this later."

THE INTERVIEW WAS A success. Rick was charming. Appollonia was adoring. The reporter cooed over the story of how Rick had wanted to become a doctor to cure people who had his mother's heart condition. Now that the crew had packed up, Umberto was pacing on the driveway, phone to his ear, as he waved goodbye to the television truck while Rick sprawled on the couch in his den, a vodka tonic in one hand, the television remote in another. He flicked on the news.

Umberto came into the room. He loosened his tie. "That went well."

"You sound surprised."

"Of course not, you're our boy."

Umberto didn't sound like he meant it. He pulled an ottoman up to the couch and sat on it, feet planted in a manly spread, elbows on knees, hands clasped. "Look, we need to talk."

Rick submerged an ice cube into his drink, then licked the booze off his finger. "You said it went well."

"It's not that. It's the other thing. The girl today. Not just her, but the others too. I can't keep putting fires out, Rick. I need to focus on the campaign. So, tell me, what's going on here because I don't get it. There's a beautiful woman upstairs. She's all yours. Anytime you want. Why all these –" Umberto searched for a word.

"Peccadilloes?" It sounded like a Victorian farce. Amusing. No harm done.

"If that's what you want to call them."

Everything Rick said to Umberto would go back to The Lion. He was sure of it. But they were committed to him. Rick had won the primary and there were less than three months until the general election. If they wanted to get rid of Foster Heiki, Rick was their only hope. They needed him.

A picture of Oscar flashed on the television screen, next to the picture of the guy accused of killing him. Rick turned up the volume. The reporter said, "...trial postponed."

"What's going on?" Rick said.

Umberto watched the story for a moment, then explained. "That guy who killed your friend is in the hospital. Don't you ever watch the news? He was attacked in jail."

"So does that mean the trial's off?" If there was no trial, no one would find out about Oscar's book.

It was like Umberto could hear Rick's thoughts. "Are you worried that someone would find out about the book?"

"Aren't you?"

"Wenderholm was the problem. He's gone now. The book will never be published. Problem solved. Now, about the –"

"Peccadilloes." Rick snorted. It was funnier every time he said the word.

Umberto took the remote away from Rick and muted the television. "Look, your best interest is my only concern. We want to get you elected. Part of my job is to make sure your needs are met. All your needs. Discreetly. So, talk to me, Rick. Let's see if we can come up with a solution."

I feel dead. That's what Rick wanted to say.

It came pouring out before he could stop. "I feel like this isn't my life, like I'm walking around in a stranger's clothes, living in a stranger's house. I'm a ghost. No one really sees me or hears me. I knew someone could walk in on me and that girl this afternoon. That's what made it exciting. The only time I feel alive is when there's a risk."

Umberto rocked back. "So, the other night in the motel?"

"Sometimes I need to blow off steam."

"What's your preference? Girls or boys?"

"Boys, but girls will do. But no hookers. They get paid, so there's no thrill." Rick had tried prostitutes, girls and boys. They were bored, had seen it all, done it all, didn't care. With other people, those who wanted to be with him, there was a delicious intimacy when doing something naughty. Just for a few hours, he was alive, seen and appreciated.

Then they went their separate ways. No needy phone calls afterwards. No messy scenes. No empty promises. Just clean sex.

Rick still had his eyes on the TV. He couldn't look at Umberto. He didn't want to see the same disgust that had been on Appollonia's face. They didn't understand him – only the hookups did. Appollonia didn't matter anymore, but Umberto did. He was the key to Rick's bright new future.

Another image flashed on the television screen. Two booking photos, one of Skinny Guy, the other Footballer. Rick scooped the remote out of Umberto's hand. He punched the volume button.

The announcer said, "... found dead in an empty lot, where construction of a child's playground was scheduled to begin. Both victims were known to the police. There is no official cause of death, but anonymous sources said it appeared to be a gangland execution. An investigation is underway."

Is that what The Lion meant when he said he handled the Herman Jules problem? Did he kill those goons?

Rick pulled himself upright. "Isn't that where we had the dedication?"

Umberto drifted towards the door. "Could have been. One empty lot looks like another."

"Who'd dump their bodies there out in the open for anyone to find?" *Just like Oscar's murder.*

Umberto shrugged.

Was it some kind of message? Who would the message have been for? Herman Jules? Or was it for Rick?

Umberto interrupted Rick's thoughts. "Looks like they offended the wrong person." He slipped his cellphone into his pocket. "You're in for the night, right? Promise me. Or do I need to send the twins over?"

Umberto's eyes were dead.

What did Umberto know? That the Lion killed those two guys as a message to Rick? When Umberto said that Oscar wasn't a problem anymore because he had been murdered, was he hinting The Lion was involved in that too? Or was he pretending to know something dangerous just to frighten Rick into behaving?

It didn't matter. Rick was scared.

"In for the night, promise," Rick said. He meant it.

Chapter Eleven

Maureen

VIVIAN THANDI AND I waited in court, seated in the first pew. We nodded to each other politely when she arrived after me and took her seat on her side of the room.

Judge Han was in the middle of a trial. She announced a short break to take up "another matter" – meaning our case. The jurors were ushered out. The lawyers at counsel tables closed their binders and flipped their legal pads over so we couldn't see what was written. They walked through the gate that separated the well from the audience, glancing at their watches. Before Judge Han left the room through her private door, she had warned them they had enough time to take a "rest break" – in other words, visit the restrooms – and they should come right back.

As soon as the departing lawyers passed us, we filed through the gate and took our positions standing behind our respective tables. There was no point in sitting down because when the judge returned, we'd only have to stand again.

"I see you still wear the pearls," Vivian said. "Your good luck charm, am I right?"

Vivian was trying to rock me back on my heels, suggesting that I knew I was no match for her and so needed a talisman. I touched the necklace that I always wore to court. Not just for good luck, but also as a tribute to Elizabeth O'Shaughnessy, who had been the only person who believed in me.

"They have sentimental value," I said.

The judge entered unexpectedly, and the clerk sprung to her feet. "All rise!"

As Judge Han settled back into her chair, she said, "Please be seated."

My chair was still warm from the last occupant's body heat. It felt strangely intimate.

The judge said, "I see Mr. Paredes is not present in the courtroom."

Vivian said, "We didn't have enough time to arrange transportation, Your Honor."

That wasn't true. They knew there would be a hearing days before I did, when they decided to file the motion. The truth was, he was still in the hospital, and they didn't want to go to the expense of moving him by ambulance with an armed guard.

"Is defense counsel willing to proceed in his absence?" Judge Han asked.

As an accused, Tony was entitled to be at every hearing in his case. But he just had leg surgery and was on heavy pain medication. He would have been useless. I was afraid that if we delayed the hearing, I wouldn't get what I'd wanted today. "Yes, Your Honor."

The judge said, "It is my understanding that the State is asking to return the defendant to jail as he has recovered sufficiently from his brain injury."

I stood. "Your Honor, I thought was had an agreement that he could go to rehabilitation after he was discharged from the hospital."

Vivian stood. "What we agreed to is that the defendant would be allowed to remain in the hospital, subject to further evaluation. There is now a change in circumstances. He has recovered from his brain injury sufficiently that the doctors feel he does not need in-patient rehabilitation. To the extent that he needs treatment, the therapists can visit him in jail."

"That's not exactly true," I said. "He doesn't need in-patient rehabilitation for his brain injury, but the doctors say he does need extensive rehabilitation for his physical injuries. His femur was shattered in the attack. He just recently had extensive surgery and will need weeks of rehab. I submitted a letter from his doctor stating that he spoke with the institution's medical staff and learned that they don't have the proper equipment or room to facilitate his therapy. In addition, the doctor stated in his letter that my client is too fragile to withstand another beating. His skull fractures are far from healed. Another trauma could collapse his skull and cause a life-threatening brain injury. Even an accidental fall could kill him."

Judge Han held up her hand. "But the defense agrees that Mr. Paredes is mentally competent to stand trial?"

There was no point in arguing. "We do."

"If I may, Your Honor," Vivian said. "We would be happy to allow Mr. Paredes to wear a helmet to protect his skull."

I spun towards Vivian. "You have got to be joking! You might as well pin a 'kick me' sign on his back."

Vivian wheeled in my direction, mouth open, ready for battle.

"Please address your comments to the court, both of you," Judge Han said. "Ms. Gould, how long until your client is well enough to return to jail?"

"Six months."

"Does the State agree that it will take six months for the skull fractures to heal fully?"

"Our doctor said it could be three to six months."

"And how long until Mr. Paredes is finished with physical therapy?"

"Twelve weeks," Vivian said.

"Twelve weeks until he is re-evaluated," I clarified. "He may need another twelve weeks after that."

"This is what I'm going to do," the judge said. "I'm ordering that Mr. Paredes is to be returned to jail thirteen weeks from now. That will give his doctors sufficient time to reevaluate him. If they feel he needs additional treatment that the jail cannot accommodate, Ms. Gould, you are to bring that to my attention."

"But that's not enough time for the skull fractures to heal," I said.

"I shall also order that he may be allowed to wear a helmet."

Brilliant.

Tony would be furious. He was terrified of going back inside and he had good reason to be. If a gang of inmates can beat him senseless with no one willing to admit they saw it, they could surely pull a helmet off his head next time.

"We request a trial date," I said. This was the reason why I wanted to go forward with the hearing today. My only hope to keep him out of jail was to get him acquitted by a jury before he had to go back in. I wanted the trial to start while he was still in the hospital.

The judge said, "Madam Clerk, please consult the criminal calendar."

The clerk appeared to scroll through a database. "The next opening is in five months."

I said, "That's too late, Your Honor. My client has a right to a speedy trial."

"The time he was in the hospital shouldn't be counted," Vivian said. "The State would agree to trial in five months."

Vivian was worried. That's why she was arguing that the hospitalization shouldn't count. She should be. If Tony was denied a speedy trial, I would ask for the charges to be dismissed. He would go free.

"Your Honor, the right to a speedy trial means sixty days from the date of charge. Even if the court determines that the hospitalization doesn't count, if he is remanded twelve weeks from now, the trial date is well beyond the time frame. However, it is unnecessary to make a ruling on that argument. The State essentially admitted that he is not incapacitated because he recovered sufficiently from his brain injury, so that time should begin running as of the date of the State's motion."

Eat that, Vivian. If Judge Han agreed with the prosecution and delayed the trial, I would file an immediate appeal. Judges hate being appealed. They especially hate being told by a higher court that they made a wrong decision. If Judge Han wanted to avoid that, she needed to agree with me.

She said, "For the record, Ms. Gould, is it your position that the defendant is not willing to waive his right to a speedy trial?"

To be absolutely clear, I said, "Anthony Paredes is not willing to waive his right to a speedy trial. On his behalf, I request that the trial date be set within sixty days of the State's motion."

"Very well," the judge said. "We will set trial for the third week in October."

"The State objects," Vivian said.

"So noted," Judge Han replied. "You are dismissed."

Vivian whisked out of the courtroom without saying goodbye.

When I arrived at the office, a stack of unopened mail was resting on Yolanda's desk. I picked up the envelopes and shuffled through them. Yolanda pulled the pack out of my hands.

She turned to Quinn who had just come into reception from the conference room, a cookie in hand. "The first rule of law office management is that you don't let the lawyer open the mail. They'll wander off with something important, put it down somewhere and forget where. Then they'll panic because they can't find it. So, I scan every document before handing them over."

Yolanda was speaking in general terms when she referred to "the lawyers," but since I was the only lawyer in the firm, she was talking about me. She was right. I tended to temporarily misplace documents when I was deep in thought.

Quinn covered her smile with one hand. It was nice to see them enjoy a joke together, even at my expense. Yolanda was re-establishing her position in the hierarchy since our little talk and Quinn had sensed the shift.

I gave them both a mock frown. "I don't always lose stuff."

"Only when it matters," Yolanda answered.

I rolled my eyes like a petulant teenager. "Maybe, sometimes."

"Moving on," Yolanda said. "What happened in court?"

"We're going to trial the third week in October. Tony will still be in the hospital, but he should be able to walk, or at least sit in a wheelchair by then. Let's sit down and figure out what needs to be done."

I led Yolanda and Quinn back to the conference room. On the wall were cabinet doors which, when opened, revealed a whiteboard. I dropped my briefcase into my chair and picked up a marker. Quinn skirted around to the seat that used to be Eli's but now was hers. Yolanda came in last, with a legal pad and pen. The files were on the table, with yellow stickies neatly protruding from the sheaves.

A plate of Yolanda's brightly colored sugar cookies, obviously not as full as it had once been, was near Quinn's chair. Apparently, Yolanda had brought cookies in to charm Quinn, not just her maternal instinct kicking in but again a subtle assertion of her authority. Basic animal instincts drive people to pay attention to where the food comes from. That's why they train dogs with treats.

I leaned across the conference table, grabbed a cookie, and took a large bite. I was as easily trained as any pooch. I can eat and write at the same time. I had two hands, after all.

They settled in and I opened with, "The big question is, who killed Oscar Wenderholm?"

They looked at me blankly.

"Who wanted him dead?" I asked.

Yolanda said, "Don't you always look at the wife first?" She watched a lot of television cop shows.

"Good one." I wrote "Brita Wenderholm" on the board. "Now, does she have the means, motive, and opportunity?"

"They didn't keep guns," Quinn said. "He was afraid of them."

I wrote "no gun" beside Brita's name.

"And what's her motive?" Yolanda asked. "Even if she hated him, she needed his income to support their kids."

I wrote "motive" with a question mark on the board. "Opportunity?"

"She was there," Quin said.

I wrote an "O" with a checkmark beside it.

"Who else?" I asked.

"Isaac Marjan," Quinn said.

Yolanda frowned.

"Interesting." I wrote his name on the board. "Means, motive, opportunity?"

"The gun was found in Tony's car. Isaac could have hidden it there. He might have killed Wenderholm to protect Tony, thinking if Wenderholm was dead, Tony could stop obsessing about him. He was home that night."

Yolanda raised her pen for attention. "But why would he plant the gun in Tony's car? If he's trying to protect Tony, why frame him for the murder."

Quinn stood her ground. "Maybe he didn't intend to frame Tony, only to get rid of the gun temporarily. Maybe he didn't expect they would search the car so quickly and he planned to move it later."

I wasn't sold on Isaac as a suspect, but this was a brainstorming session. To keep the creative juices flowing, everyone had to be considered. I drew a star by Isaac's name, then wrote "means" with a question mark, "motive" with a question mark, and the "O" with a check mark.

"The book," I said. "Oscar was writing a tell-all about his chess coach abusing him in high school. One thing we know is that pedophiles are opportunistic. If what Emerson Katsu told us is true, any one of those kids on that chess team could have been abused too and might not appreciate Oscar violating their privacy." I wrote Emerson Katsu's name on the board. "Quinn, who were the other members?"

As she recited them, I made a list. "Rick Stevens, the politician, Constance Robertson, who you saw in Fair Oaks, and Gerald Robertson, her brother. He's an attorney in San Jose now. The last one is Dakota Vaughn."

"I told you about him," Quinn said. "He's been in trouble since he was a teenager. Driving violations, driving under the influence, drug possession. He pled no contest to reduced charges and was sentenced to drug rehabilitation every time. Later on, he was charged with sexual assault twice. Both cases were dismissed. In the third case, sexual assault of a minor, he went to trial and lost. He's been in prison for years."

"His parents had money," Yolanda said.

"The driving charges occurred in Palo Alto. He was represented by retained counsel in every case except the last. That time he had a public defender."

"His parents must have gotten tired of bailing him out," Yolanda said.

"Oscar's attorneys wouldn't have listed him as a character witness," I said. "That wouldn't have looked good. That's why we didn't hear of him before."

I wrote a star by the name of Dakota Vaughn. "The thing is about prisoners, they're bored. They love visitors. And they love to talk."

"Do you think he'll talk to you?" Yolanda asked. "You're representing the man accused of killing his friend."

"There's only one way to find out."

THE NEXT DAY, QUINN and I were in my BMW snaking our way up into the foothills of the Sierra Madre mountains. We were on our way to California State Prison at Snowden. Yolanda didn't mind Quinn going on a prison visit with me. She said she had too much to do at the office, but I suspect being locked into a building filled with dangerous convicts wasn't appealing.

Quinn, however, was thrilled. She clasped my briefcase on her lap. It was filled with printouts of Dakota Vaughn's cases, a list of addresses he had lived in before he was incarcerated, and every other detail she could find on the internet the night before. I doubted I would need any of that, but I was pleased with her enthusiasm.

The prison was just outside the town of Snowden. In the nineteenth century, a silver ore discovery nearby attracted Welsh miners. A camp, then a town, sprung up. When the mine went bankrupt, the economy collapsed. There had been an effort to attract tourism, like Virginia City, but that had failed. Virginia City was near Reno, a popular gambling destination, and Lake Tahoe, known for summer water sports and winter skiing, whereas Snowden was at the end of a badly maintained two lane highway. Its only economy was prison related. The town consisted of small Sears mail-order kit houses for the guards and staff, a motel for those visiting prisoners, a gas station, a convenience store, and a diner.

Quinn had dozed off by the time I left the freeway and started winding up the mountain. As I slowed for a stop sign, she woke up, looked around, and said, "Depressing."

I agreed. The atmosphere spoke of the end of a road for prisoners and prison staff alike. There were no signs of children. No playground, no school.

When we checked into the prison, the guard asked who we were visiting. I said, "Dakota Vaughn."

"You came all this way just to see one inmate?" the guard asked.

"Just the one."

Quinn looked askance at me. She knew that Frank was in this prison. We hadn't spoken about him since the day she answered his phone call. I knew she was curious, but I didn't feel like explaining myself that day. I don't know if there would ever be a right time, but I wanted the right words when that time came.

We went through the routine of jail visiting. We stashed her backpack and my briefcase in a small locker. We were only allowed to bring in a legal pad, files, and a pencil. A guard ushered us through a series of locked corridors and then to a small room with a metal table bolted to the floor and mesh windows on two walls. We were locked in.

I pointed to the chairs against the wall. I didn't want our backs to the door when Dakota Vaughn entered the room. He didn't have any charges for violent assault but that didn't reassure me. We would be pinned behind the table if there was trouble, but the guards would be able to remove him more quickly if he was next to the door. When they showed up.

I wished I'd brushed up on the self-defense skills I'd learned in a class Jake made me take when we were first dating. He was a black belt in Brazilian Ju Jitsu but had quit working out when we were married. He couldn't believe any female – or male – wandering around San Francisco wasn't trained. As a former cop, he told every woman he met they should learn how to defend themselves.

When Dakota Vaughn was escorted into the room, I became less worried about a violent attack. Tall, lanky, broad-shouldered but not beefy, he had no tattoos, short brown hair, and a sparse brown mustache. If it weren't for the prison t-shirt and sweatpants, he would have looked like a salesman.

His light brown eyes were mischievous. He shouldn't have had any idea who we were or why we were there, but he was savoring the anticipation of amusement as if he was waiting for an opportunity to take control of the moment and spin it to please himself.

I suppressed a shudder.

Having read his record and learned of his propensity for abusing teenaged girls, I was not concerned for myself. But if he came across the table at my daughter, he'd run into an open palm to the chin. Then I'd follow up with whatever presented itself, probably a left hook since the table would be between us.

It had been a long time since I planned out my moves in the event of an attack. Since I'd left the DA's office, I wasn't in a courtroom every day with a crowd of people behind me that saw me as the enemy. I was surprised how quickly the moves came back to me as I rehearsed them in my mind.

The guard unlocked his cuffs and left us alone with the inmate. Dakota eased himself into the chair and waited.

"Mr. Vaughn, my name is Maureen Gould. I'm here to talk about Oscar Wenderholm." I intentionally didn't introduce Quinn. I didn't want him to know her name.

"You two look like sisters." He smiled, slowly, one side of his mouth reaching upwards before the other. This would be his seduction smile. I felt nauseous.

"You may not have heard that Mr. Wenderholm was murdered recently."

He shrugged. "It was on the news."

"You went to school with him, is that correct?"

He sneered. "Decades ago. What does that have to do with anything? You couldn't possibly be accusing me of his murder." He swirled his hand overhead, indicating the prison walls. "As you can see, I have an alibi." This time his smile was quick, darting.

He pushed his chair back so he could cross his legs and rested his hands in his lap in a manner that could be called elegant. It was as if he was imitating a television commercial for brandy, where a tuxedoed man was worshipped by gown-wearing women.

"I'm interested in background, Mr. Vaughn. What can you tell us about when you knew Mr. Wenderholm?"

He gazed into the distance, dragging the interview out. "It was high school. We played chess. He wasn't that good. He wasn't smart or handsome. Kind of annoying really. No one wanted to hang out with him, as I recall. Why, do you think one of them did it?"

"One of who?"

"The chess club, that's how I knew him. Um, there was Connie and Charlie. Quite the pair. And there was the little Japanese kid. He was a year behind us. Smart as hell, though."

Quinn wrote the names down. We'd known them already but what Dakota was willing to tell us, and willing to withhold, was significant too.

"Anyone else."

"No," he said dreamily. "That would be the lot."

He hadn't mentioned Rick Stevens.

"Have you had any contact with Mr. Wenderholm in the recent past?"

"You dad is here. Are you going to see him?"

So, he did know who I was. And there was every chance that anything I said would go back to Frank. There was also the chance that no matter what I said, Dakota would make something up, for his personal entertainment. I was getting the impression that he was a chaos agent, someone who churned up trouble to prove he had control.

"I'm here to speak with you about Mr. Wenderholm."

He took a long look at Quinn. "Wow, you do look just like sisters. Frank didn't say he had two daughters."

Creep.

"Mr. Vaughn, if you're not going to talk to us about Oscar Wenderholm, I'll call the guard."

An irritated frown flashed across his face. "Fine. Oscar. No, I haven't seen him. I don't get out much these days, as you might imagine. And he didn't come in for a visit."

"Did you know he wrote a book about being abused by your high school chess coach?"

His chin dropped as he locked eyes with me. "What book?"

"Were you aware that the chess coach had abused him, or anyone else, for that matter?"

He blinked once slowly, then pulled himself to a stand. "We're done here. Sorry I couldn't be more help to you."

With that he banged on the door. A guard appeared, cuffed him, and led him from the room.

Chapter Twelve

Maureen

IT WAS MY TURN to make dinner, and after a long day of driving I had no imagination, so I fell back on that old family favorite, pancakes. I was in the kitchen beating batter, with the bacon I'd just fried warming in the oven, when Germaine Greer sashayed towards the front door, purring loudly.

Quinn was at the breakfast bar, her laptop opened in front of her. "Jake's home."

I turned the burner gas on, moved a clean skillet over it, and dumped in a chunk of butter.

I heard the front door open and close, then something heavy hitting the floor – Jake's briefcase I assumed – and his voice. "Who's Daddy's good girl?"

I rolled my eyes.

He came into the room, Germaine Greer held to his chest as she rubbed her head along his neck.

I pointed my spatula at him. "She's shedding. You'll have to take that shirt to the cleaners. The tie, too."

"Jealous," he said.

Maybe he was right.

He kissed the top of my head while I poured batter into the pan. "Yum, pancakes. Again."

"You love my sourdough pancakes." When we were first married, that was the only thing I knew how to make. He said he loved them then. Unless he was prepared for a cutting cross-examination, he should admit that he still loved them. Besides, who doesn't love pancakes?

He opened the fridge and pulled out a bottle of beer with his free hand. "Anybody want one?"

"Sure," Quinn and I both said.

He pulled out two more bottles, deftly uncapped them while Germaine Greer clung to his shoulder, set mine on the counter and passed one to Quinn, then took a sip from his. "How was the trip?"

"What a creep!" Quinn said.

I breathed a sigh of relief. I was still getting to know my little girl and I was pleased that she showed the ability to judge character. So many women are victimized because they don't know how.

"Who's the creep?" This was Jake's delicate way of asking if I had visited Frank after all, something that had been the subject of a short, but tense, discussion as we went to bed the night before. He thought I should take command of the situation. I told him I wasn't ready.

I shot him a frown.

Quinn chimed in, "Dakota Vaughn, of course. The guy we went to see. Mom told me to pay careful attention to what he said and what he left out. Guess what he didn't say. Just guess."

"Beats me," Jake said.

"He never mentioned Rick Stevens. The only one from their clique to get rich. The only one who is running for senate and is on television every night. But he admitted he saw that Wenderholm had been murdered on the news, so he had to have seen his old friend Rick Stevens, too. Don't you think that's strange?"

Jake set Germaine Greer onto the floor and pulled a can of cat food out of the cupboard while she wound herself around his ankles. "Yeah, actually, I do. Got any theories?"

"I'm not so sure," Quinn said. "But maybe it has something to do with this."

Jake went around the counter to see Quinn's laptop screen. "What am I looking at?"

"A scan of the yearbook from when Rick Stevens, Dakota Vaughn, and Oscar Wenderholm were in high school together. I found it online."

"And?"

She pointed to the screen. "See this. It says, 'In memoriam of David Shroeder, beloved teacher and chess coach'."

I turned from the stove. "What? The chess coach died?"

"Looks like it."

"During the school year?"

"Yup. Found his obit. They were at a chess match in Las Vegas."

"The same chess coach that Oscar Wenderholm said abused him?"

"Has to be. He was the only chess coach at the school."

Jake examined Quinn's screen. "The pancakes are burning," he said without looking up. Over the years, he'd developed a heightened sense for blackened dinner. We used to joke that my pancakes were Cajun-style.

I flipped the three in the pan. They were only a little charred around the edges.

I turned back to them. "So, Katsu was happy to tell us about a book that Oscar is writing about being abused by their coach, most likely this Shroeder person. Connie Robertson was on the chess team and didn't know anything about the book or abuse, but she recently sold Oscar a car – just as he received the advance for the book. And, Dakota Vaughn, who is in prison for abusing teenaged girls, pretended he didn't know Rick Stevens and walked out of the interview when I asked about the chess coach abusing anyone."

Jake looked up from the screen, his expression serious. "There's something going on here, Red."

IT WAS QUINN'S NIGHT to wash up. I'd eaten the slightly burnt pancakes and served the following perfect batches to Jake and Quinn. The bacon was crisp and not burnt at all. As Quinn cleared the table, Jake picked up his beer bottle and mine, took my hand and led me to the couch.

"What's up?" I asked.

"I got a call at the office today."

I couldn't imagine why he would receive a call at his office that he needed to inform me about. He rarely talked about his cases at home because, he said, he wanted to leave his work at the office.

"From Snowden Prison?"

He took my hand. "Don't get mad, yet. Hear me out."

I threw myself backwards into the cushions.

"You need to hear this, Red. He called after you'd left Snowden. He knew you had been there to see Vaughn."

"So, you knew when you walked in the door that I hadn't seen him, yet you pretended not to know."

"I only knew what he told me. I wasn't sure what the truth was."

"Fine. What did he say?"

"He says he has information about Dakota Vaughn that is relevant to your case. He doesn't want to send it out in a letter because the guards would read the mail. He doesn't want to tell you over the phone – even if you'd take his calls – because the guards would eavesdrop."

"He wants me to come in to see him."

The scars on my arms suddenly stung as if I'd been attacked by a bee swarm. "No way."

"If he's telling the truth, it could be important. It might help Tony's defense."

"Since when has Frances Eugene Gould told the truth?" He had led a secret life, that of a pedophile. He had squandered my mother's inheritance. He had laundered money for his kiddie porn friends. He told my mother that I had gotten pregnant by a boy I knew. She should have known the truth, but his accusation was enough for her to pretend that she didn't.

I began rubbing my arms. I really wanted to scratch.

"Is something wrong?" It was Quinn. She'd come out of the kitchen.

I couldn't tell her, not yet. Ironic when I was so furious at my parents for lying.

"It's carpel tunnel syndrome from all the typing I do." I had no idea if carpal tunnel would cause pain in my forearms, but it's all I could think of on short notice. I'd heard about it from a secretary at the DA's office who wore braces on her arms.

Quinn went back into the kitchen and came back a few minutes later with two dish towels wrapped around crushed ice. She knelt before me and pressed the packs around each arm. The coolness helped calm the burning. I felt horrible for lying, but I wanted to protect her from the horrible truth that my father was her father too for as long as I could. All I could come up with was, "Thank you, sweetie. It feels much better now."

Jake had sneaked out of the room while Quinn was administering to me. When he returned, he brought a lumpy package wrapped in brown paper with "recycled" stamped all over it and tied up with twine – our new school gift. I hadn't seen it yet. He picked it up on his lunch break after polling the DA's junior staff about environmentally conscious backpack products.

"Happy first day in law school!" we said as he offered her the gift.

"Oh, wow, guys," she said as she tore into the wrapping revealing an eggplant-colored laptop bag with zippers on every side and shoulder straps. She found the tag and read it, nodding agreeably. Jake had done his homework. She unzipped and zipped the pockets and peered into the depths of the bag. "Totally awesome. Thank you so much."

"Are you ready for your first day?" Jake asked Quinn.

She ran over to her old bag and pulled out a small beaten-up paperback entitled "Legal Maxims."

"Go ahead," she said. "Ask me anything."

Jake took the book and thumbed through it. "Here you go. *Ipso Facto.*"

"Easy one. It means 'by the very fact'."

"Give us an example."

"The beer bottle is empty *ipso facto* someone drank the beer."

"Someone could have poured it out," Jake said. "Always keep your mind open. How about this one? *Post hoc, ergo propter hoc.*"

"Um. I remember this. Give me a minute."

Jake set the timer on his watch. I elbowed him in the ribs.

"After this so before this?" Quinn guessed.

"Close," Jake said. "After this, because of this before."

"Gotchya. And what does that mean?"

"It's called the *post hoc* fallacy, meaning faulty logic. If an argument is *post hoc, ergo propter hoc*, it's unsound because it assumes that because one thing happened before, it caused the next thing to happen. For instance, the argument that the sun went down so the moon came up would be *post hoc, ergo propter hoc*. The truth is the moon is going around all the time, but we can't see it when the sun is out too."

"Ok, you guys," I said. "Quinn and I have an early morning, *ergo* it's off to bed we go."

As we walked to our room, Jake said into my ear. "Are we going to talk in Latin from now on?"

"All I know is legalese," I said. "But if that's what rocks your boat."

"Are you kidding? I was reading from her book. I never heard of *post hoc, ergo propter hoc* before tonight. Don't tell Quinn!"

EARLY THE NEXT DAY, Quinn and I took Jake's Blazer out on the freeway and headed down to San Jose. Quinn held her new bag on her lap. When we climbed in and got a whiff of that old Blazer smell, she said she'd rather hold it than risk getting it stained by something that might have been on the floorboard.

We were on our way to see Charles Robertson, the only member of the chess team we hadn't interviewed. His sister, Constance, had seen Sunny and would have warned her brother about the pushy lawyer in the bright yellow BMW. Since I planned to beat him to his office and surprise him after he arrived, I wanted to remain *in cognito*.

We arrived at a strip mall, not yet open. We cruised to a café, went in to get coffee for me and tea for Quinn plus a couple of bagels, and visited the ladies' room. Then I parked the Blazer nose out like a bank robber so we could see Robertson's office, but far enough away that it didn't look like we were waiting for him. Just two women having their breakfast in a parking lot. For all anyone knew, we were waiting for the quilt shop to open.

About fifteen minutes later, a dingy older pick-up truck pulled up and let out a woman wearing a bright flowery summer dress and heels. She unlocked the office door, went inside, and flicked on the lights. When the pick-up drove away, it passed close enough that I could see the driver, a bearded, shaggy-haired man in his late twenties or early thirties, in a t-shirt. He lit a cigarette with his right hand while steering with a tanned left arm propped in the open window. Her boyfriend, I figured.

"That has to be the secretary," Quinn said of the woman who had just opened the office. "How long until you think the lawyer shows up?"

Just then, an enormous black SUV, just like the one belonging to Constance Robertson, and the one she sold to Oscar Wenderholm, lumbered past and pulled into a spot marked "Law Office of Charles Robertson - Employee Parking Only." A besuited man, stocky with neatly trimmed thinning sandy hair, stepped out and strode into the office.

"Show time!" I checked in the visor mirror for crumbs on my face. Quinn did the same.

I grabbed my briefcase, not that I needed it, but it leant gravitas. Anyone in the legal business would recognize that I was a lawyer on a mission.

We entered a small reception room that led to a short hall with two doors, both open. The room at the far end was full of filing cabinets. The other door led behind the reception area so I couldn't see into it, but a shaft of light from that room cut across the hallway, so I knew the door was open. That would be Robertson's office.

The woman in the flowery dress was now seated behind a desk. From a distance, I had clocked her to be in her thirties, but up close, the lines in her face said she was more like mid to late forties. She was made up like a fashion model. Foundation, blush, lipstick, false eyelashes, eyeliner, and two shades of eyeshadow. Gaudy earrings matched her dress. Her home-dyed auburn hair was cut into a bob.

When you have naturally red hair, you notice who doesn't, because you spend so much time telling people that your color is real.

"Do you have an appointment?" she asked, an edge to her voice.

She would have known we didn't. That was her job.

"My name is Maureen Gould. This is my assistant, Quinn Brennan. We're here to see Charles Robertson."

"I'm not sure he's in."

"He just walked through that door." I pointed behind me.

Her face tightened. "I'll check to see if he is available. What is this regarding?"

"Oscar Wenderholm."

Robertson stepped into the hallway. Clearly, he had been eavesdropping. "It's alright, Marsha. I'll see them."

We followed him into his tidy office. The desk, cabinet and bookcase were strictly office supply store functional with faux wood laminated veneer. The books were old, leatherbound, gold-lettered California caselaw digests that no one used anymore because online legal research was so much more efficient, but they were pretty and would impress clients.

On his ego wall was a Santa Clara Law School degree and a Supreme Court of California certificate showing that he had passed the bar plus various photos of him with happy clients and big, fake checks.

He said, "I don't have a lot of time. What can I help you with?"

"I'm defending Anthony Paredes. He's accused of the murder of Oscar Wenderholm."

He blinked slowly. He already knew Tony was my client. Trial lawyers love gossip. If he hadn't seen the stories on TV, he would have heard about the case from other attorneys as they hung around the courthouse waiting to go on record.

He nervously thumped a finger on the glass-covered desktop. "I'm not sure what I can tell you."

Circumspect. That comes with years in the legal business.

"You can tell me about Rick Stevens."

The finger thumped rapidly, then he hid his hands beneath the desktop. "I thought you were here about Oscar."

"Rick Stevens was a member of your chess club, right?"

He sneered. "You can't possibly be trying to pin Oscar's murder on one of us! After all these years, why would we?"

"Your chess coach, David Schroeder, died during a meet in Las Vegas."

His face hardened. "That's right."

"Were you at the meet?"

"I was. I found him, in fact. Or to be more accurate, I was with the group that found him."

"How did that come about?"

"We had checked into the hotel the night before. We were supposed to meet for break-fast before going to the competition. He didn't show up, so we went to the registration desk and told them we were worried and would they please check on him. We followed the clerk to his room and when he opened the door, there was Mr. Shroeder. On the floor. Dead."

"What was the cause of death?"

He shrugged. "How should I know? I was just a kid."

"Was Rick Stevens with the group that found him?"

"The entire team was there."

I'd slept lightly the night before, too wound up in Tony's case to relax. Instead, I laid in bed while Jake, deeply asleep, snored and snuffled, and I pondered Dakota Vaughn's interview. He had failed to mention Rick Stevens. And he had clammed up when we asked about David Schoeder. Were the two linked?

"What was Rick Stevens's relationship with Mr. Shroeder?"

He frowned. "Relationship? What do you mean by 'relationship'?"

"Outside of the chess team."

He squinted at me. "Are you suggesting that something was going on between them?" He laughed. "That's ridiculous."

"Was something going on between Mr. Shroeder and Oscar Wenderholm?"

"I never saw anything."

Not a denial.

"Were you aware of Mr. Shroeder engaging in sexual activity with any of the students?"

"Again, I never saw it."

Again, not a denial.

"Oscar Wenderholm wrote a book about being abused by Mr. Shroeder."

"Is that a question?"

Here was a man who had sat through hundreds of depositions, who had coached hundreds of clients on how not to answer questions, and who had been stonewalled by hundreds of opponents.

The only reason to avoid a question is because you don't want to tell the truth. We both knew it. I smiled. "Did Mr. Wenderholm tell you that he wrote a book about being abused by David Shroeder?"

A big sigh. "Counselor, you know as well as I do that attorney-client privilege survives the death of the client."

Oscar had told him about the book.

"Mr. Robertson, why would Oscar Wenderholm consult you as an attorney about the book he had written?"

"I can't answer that. I'd lose my license. Now, if you don't have any more questions, I need to get to work."

IT WAS BARELY TEN a.m. when Robertson threw us out of his office. We had plenty of time to drive back to San Francisco before Quinn's law school orientation started.

As we approached University of San Francisco, I slowed down, cruising for a parking place.

"You can just drop me off anywhere," Quinn said.

"No way! I want to get a picture."

"On my first day of school, like I'm a little kid?"

My eyes stung. I didn't get her first day of school picture for kindergarten or any other year. I wasn't at her high school or college graduation. I didn't kiss her on the cheek when she trotted off with her posse to go to the prom. Someone else got to do all those things.

"I'm sorry," Quinn said, having seen my expression. "There's a garage." She pointed the way.

We parked the car and took the stairs to the ground floor in silence. I had no words. Quinn shouldn't need to apologize for having been brought up by adopted parents. It's me who should say I was sorry, but I didn't want to stir up deep feelings for either of us on her big day. She was starting on a new path, one that would lead her into a career that could be anything she wanted it to be. Today, she would begin making lasting friendships. I didn't want her to begin her new life in tears.

We stepped out of the garage onto a lush green lawn circled with palm trees.

"How about over there?" She led me to the shade. I pulled out my phone and snapped a few photos of her beaming and wearing her new laptop bag like she was modeling for an ad.

I handed my cell to her because she was better at selfies than I was. After I slipped in behind her, she held the phone up. We smiled and she clicked. We examined the screen and agreed that they had turned out.

A flood of students poured out of the garage on their way to the buildings.

"Got to go," Quinn said.

"Be a good girl," I said. "And remember to say, 'yes ma'am and no sir'."

Quinn rolled her eyes in mockery and kissed me on the cheek. Quietly she said, "I love you."

"Love you too. Go! Don't be late for class."

After she trotted off, I sent Jake a text of the best photo of Quinn and me.

He texted back. "Are you OK?"

"*Ipso facto!*" I answered, adding a happy face emoji.

When I got back to the Blazer, I cried. I don't know why. Maybe Yolanda could tell me.

Chapter Thirteen

Rick

RICK SAT NEXT TO Oscar's widow in the first pew of a small chapel. Appollonia, dressed in a fitted black suit, sat on his other side. On the widow's far side were Oscar's kids, a doughy teenaged boy, the spitting image of Oscar, and a mousy twelve-year old girl. Rick had already forgotten their names, but Umberto had forced him to rehearse a greeting to the widow so many times in the car, he couldn't forget it. Brita.

When they had arrived, Umberto dropped them off at the door and drove the Lincoln to the funeral home's parking lot where he would remain. The Dum Dee twins had followed in their black SUV and parked beside the Lincoln. The only reason Umberto allowed Rick to take the Lincoln instead of the mommy mobile was that it was black, and they were going to a funeral.

When Rick ushered Appollonia into the chapel, the widow was standing by the door greeting mourners.

"I am so, so sorry for your loss, Mrs. Wenderholm," Rick had said. "May I call you Brita?"

"If you must." Her face was an angry mask. Dumpy, with thin graying blonde hair and blue eyes, she wore a navy-blue dress with rhinestone buttons that looked like a thrift store find.

Brittle Brita. Rick would be careful not to say that aloud.

A minister approached, glad-handed Rick, thanked him for the generous flower arrangements, gave Appollonia a shy smile, then turned to Brittle Brita. "It's time."

Rick and Appollonia followed the widow and preacher into the chapel, Rick careful to make eye contact and nod to the few people scattered in the pews. Connie, without her husband and kids, thank heaven, was seated next to her brother Charlie. Emerson Katsu was across the aisle. There were a handful of people Rick didn't recognize. The widow's friends or family, he figured.

There were two huge white flower arrangements on tall stands on either side of the altar. Those would have been the ones Umberto had sent. On the altar was a large arrangement of lilies, probably from Connie and Charlie, and two grocery-store bunches of white carnations. In the middle of the altar was a small white box containing the departed's ashes.

Oscar's kids were already in the front row. The boy was playing with a little plastic dragon action figure. As his mother sat down, she took it away from him and dropped it in her purse. He gave her an open-mouthed offended expression. She faced the pulpit, her stony mask unchanged. The boy crossed his arms and slumped. The sister shot him a judgmental look.

Get used to it, dude, women will judge you for the rest of your life.

The pew opposite the family's was empty, but the minister gestured to the space next to the widow. "Your company would be such a comfort, Mr. Stevens."

When Rick slid in next to her, the widow continued her fixed stare. She didn't look comforted to him.

He leaned into Appollonia for her attention. She gave him a side-eye, then subtly changed position so they weren't so close.

Rick turned around to locate Connie. He raised his eyebrows in their "can you meet me later" sign. She blinked her "yes" response. At least someone was talking to him. Good old Connie.

The preacher stepped up to the pulpit and started talking.

THE SERVICE LASTED PRECISELY fifty-four minutes. When it was over, the minister thanked them for coming. Recorded organ music began, and the mourners began to move around. Just as Rick turned to Brittle Brita for a few final words, she turned her back to him, most definitely not comforted by his presence.

That was one vote he would not count on, but as he escorted Appollonia to the exit, he smiled warmly at the strangers – just in case.

The old school gang collected under an oak tree.

"Would you like to meet my friends?" Rick asked his wife. She snorted at him and stalked across the tarmac to the Lincoln, where Umberto was leaning against a fender, like a chauffeur. She must have said something to him because Umberto's face slid into a sarcastic smile, then he opened the back door for her. Rick watched his wife and campaign manager enjoy their joke, the butt of which was probably him.

Umberto shut the door behind her, then approached Rick, who was still on the sidewalk. "I've arranged for a dinner for you and your friends at the Hotel Blanc in the penthouse suite, which you have for the night. My good friend, Dimitri, will see to your needs." Umberto slipped a pack of cigarettes into Rick's pocket. Rick only smoked when he used coke, Umberto knew that. Umberto winked. "*All* your needs. Dimitri is discreet. You'll like him. I'll take Appollonia home. She'll be fine. Go off with your friends."

"They don't party."

Umberto patted Rick on the back. "Take them to the hotel for a few drinks and a nice dinner. After they leave, you stay behind. Enjoy yourself. Everything will be fine, I promise you." Again, the hand on the heart.

"What about the twins?" Rick asked, referring to his bodyguards, sitting in the darkened SUV parked next to the Lincoln.

"They'll take the night off. No worries."

And no witnesses.

At first, Rick felt like he was being dismissed. That feeling evaporated. He was free. Free to do and be whatever he wanted. Umberto made that happen for him. He was a true friend, even if he was probably screwing Rick's wife. Someone should.

"Thank you, Umberto."

"Don't mention it."

RICK HAD NEVER BEEN to the Hotel Blanc, the newest hotspot in The City. A few blocks off Union Square, the old-San Francisco Beaux Arts exterior had been preserved by the conglomerate that had purchased and remodeled it.

As soon as Rick stepped out of Connie's SUV, a doorman in a high-collared black Nehru jacket recognized him. Before Rick ran for office, when he was recognized, it was with a smirk, like he was some kind of flim-flam man. Now it was with respect.

"Good evening, Mr. Stevens, we have been expecting you. Dimitri will be your host."

A valet took Connie's keys while the most beautiful man Rick had ever seen appeared in the foyer. He was slender and very pretty, wearing a tailored black suit with thin lapels, a narrow waist, and broad shoulders. His eyelids were naturally dark along his lashes, as if he wore liner. The jade green eyes were stunning next to his bronze face and curly dark brown hair. His skin was smooth as an altar boy's. No mustache, no beard, no sideburns, no stubble, not even a hint of five o'clock shadow. Rick wanted to touch him. He considered a handshake to satisfy his desire, but Umberto would not have approved of Rick treating the staff like peers when there were witnesses.

"Good evening, Mr. Stevens. My name is Dimitri. If there is anything you desire – anything at all – please do not hesitate to ask." His voice hinted of a foreign accent Rick couldn't place.

Dimitri swept his arm towards the interior, inviting them in. Rick touched a hand to Connie's elbow and followed a half step behind her.

Oblivious as ever, Connie announced, "What in the world! It's mausoleum chic," referring to the décor. Clean lines, dark wood, gray upholstery.

A model-thin woman with a heavy curtain of black chin-length hair glanced up from her desk, nodded at Dimitri, smiled cooly at Rick and Connie, then returned to her work.

Dimitri led them through the lobby and down a hallway that ended at a secure elevator. He waved an electronic key card across the screen and the door slid open.

"We're expecting two more guests," Connie said.

"Mr. Katsu and Mr. Robertson," Dimitri replied. "They will join you as soon as they arrive."

On the top floor, the elevator opened onto a room that looked westward over the rolling hills of San Francisco. The interior was decorated like the lobby, dark and gray, which contrasted dramatically with the ribbons of sunset colors descending in the sky. Beneath a chandelier was a table for four, set with linen, crystal, and chinaware.

"Welcome to the penthouse," Dimitri said.

It wasn't as big as the presidential suite in the St. Francis, where The Lion had stayed, but it was just as swanky. Rick could get used to living like this.

As Dimitri touched a dial on the wall, the chandelier began to glow. His curls appeared to glitter under the soft light. He was standing close enough that Rick could smell his cologne, a favorite of Rick's, an expensive brand that had been a gift from a past lover.

Rick was surprised that someone in the hospitality industry would wear fragrance. Once, he had worn it to a meet and greet, and Umberto told him in no uncertain terms to never wear it in public. Many people were allergic to perfumes and Rick didn't want to lose a vote because of his vanity.

Dimitri asked, "While you wait for your guests, would you care for drink?"

"Champagne," Rick said. He was feeling festive.

Connie shot a judgmental look at him. Just like that kid at the memorial, Rick had been admonished for his bad behavior by a woman. She didn't know what Umberto had planned for Rick's evening and she would never find out.

To Dimitri, she said, "A glass of white wine, please."

Dimitri lifted a wall-mounted telephone and placed their orders. Several minutes later, the drinks arrived. They were served by another beautiful young man who left the bottles and a plate of hor d'oeuvres on the bar.

Connie stood at the window, a glass in her hand, with her back to them. Rick was suddenly bashful, a feeling that he hadn't experienced since he first met David. He was fifteen years old then. David was in his late twenties, but there was a coolness to him that made him appear both unapproachable and enticing. At that age, Rick already knew that he was attracted to boys, but his efforts hadn't gone beyond fumbling, and he had never been with a man. Their confidence frightened him. He was unsure of his ability to read the signs and he was terrified that David would be repelled. The situation was so much more delicate because David was his math teacher and the chess team coach.

Rick was forced to wait for David to make the first move. It soon came. David invited him to join the chess team. The following week, David began tutoring him in chess. Not long afterwards, David showed him so much more. It suddenly occurred to Rick how similar his story was to Oscar's seduction of that boy.

Rick hadn't thought of that first time with David in years. It must have been Oscar's memorial and seeing the old gang that dredged up the memory.

Rick pulled himself out of his reverie to find Dimitri watching him. He gave Dimitri a sad smile. Let him think Rick was mourning Oscar. Dimitri returned the smile, then reached into his pocket, and pulled out a slim cell phone which he glanced at. "Your guests have arrived. They will be up momentarily."

Connie looked over her shoulder, nodded, then returned to the view.

In a quiet voice directed only to Rick, Dimitri said, "I'll check on you periodically through the evening." He nodded in the direction of the wall-mounted telephone. "Please, if there is anything you need, anything at all, don't hesitate to call."

The air between them felt charged. He and Dimitri were suspended in that moment, eyes locked upon one another. Rick was not imagining this.

The elevator doors opened. Competitive as ever, Charlie Robertson and Emerson Katsu squeezed out of the lift, shoulder to shoulder, each not wanting to be the second man off the carriage. Dimitri stepped back, leaving Rick to greet the newcomers. "Welcome, boys, there's wine and champagne."

Charlie scanned the room and nodded his approval. Emerson's face went slack. He blinked rapidly before he regained his composure. Dimitri stepped into the elevator, gave Rick one last hint of a conspiratorial smile, before the door slid closed.

An incredible evening was ahead of Rick as soon as he got rid of his guests.

CHARLIE EXPLORED THE BAR and helped himself to beer. Connie, who'd always played the mother role, called in their dinner orders. The food arrived promptly. Steak for Rick and Charlie, crab for Emerson, and Alaska salmon for Connie. Every time the pretty waiter boy silently appeared with more food or to clear the table, he opened and poured fresh bottles of wine. Rick's belly was full, and his head swimming.

The group moved to a sitting area with a square Art Deco-style settee and two matching chairs upholstered in gray. Emerson sipped on tonic water, his choice of beverage. He didn't drink – never had. Connie switched to tea because she was driving. Charlie was getting hammered while Rick nursed a scotch. He had chosen one of his less favorite liquors so he would drink slowly before the real party began.

Outside, the shameless colors of sunset faded into deep blue and then black above the glittering lights of San Francisco. The mood shifted to a mixture of exhaustion and elation.

"To Oscar!" Charlie held up his beer.

The others raised their glasses, repeated his toast, and drank. Rick loosened his tie and put his feet on the coffee table.

"You know who's missing, don't you?" Charlie asked.

Connie answered, "Oscar, duh."

Charlie pointed at Connie. "Always the bright one. No, I was thinking of Dakota Vaughn. He used to be a lot of fun."

Fun wasn't how Rick would put it. Dakota was their drug supplier. Coke and pot. But the boys, Charlie and Rick, had kept the drugs away from Oscar, Connie, and Emerson. They couldn't be trusted.

"Whatever happened to him?" Connie asked.

"He's in prison," Rick volunteered.

Connie asked, "How do you know?"

"When I decided to run for office, one of my backers did a background check. He found out and told me."

Connie lowered her wine glass. "You mean they investigated all of us?"

"Of course, they did. We can't have an old scandal coming out during the campaign." He pinched Connie's cheek and shook it. "Don't worry, babe. You came out smelling like a rose."

She jerked away from him.

Rick held up a hand. "Sorry, sorry. I've had a little too much to drink. Long day. Oscar and all. It's been stressful." *When will they leave?*

She glared at Rick until Emerson spoke, breaking the mood. "You've come a long way, Rick."

"Thanks, bro." If only he knew.

An awkward silence descended.

Connie asked, "Do you think he did it?"

Rick answered, "Who did what?"

"The guy they arrested. Do you think he killed Oscar?"

Emerson asked, "Why would they arrest an innocent man?"

Connie answered, "It's just that his lawyer came to see me. She seems to think someone else did it."

Rick snorted.

She gave Rick another disapproving look. "One of us."

"No way." Rick spoke a little too loudly. Briefly, he had thought The Lion might have been involved with Oscar's death, but he since convinced himself it was nonsense. Politics was business to the great man. He wasn't a thug. If he had a problem, he'd throw money at it. But what about Skinny Guy and Footballer? Who killed them if it wasn't The Lion? No way. Not The Lion. But maybe someone working for him?

Emerson cleared his throat. "I'm afraid that might be my fault."

Connie hissed, "What did you say to her?"

"Look, Connie, I don't want to get into trouble for hiding the truth," Emerson said. "That's obstruction of justice, right?"

They turned to Charlie, who was at the bar, popping open another bottle of beer. "If you lie to the police, it might be obstruction," he said.

Connie repeated slowly and a little more loudly, "Emerson, what did you say to her?"

"I told her the truth. That Oscar had written a book. He got a lot of money for it, and he was supposed to get more after it hit the bookstores. But there was some holdup, and it wasn't getting released, and he wanted to get his rights back so he could find another publisher. All the money they gave him was spent, and he needed more. He wanted to quit that crappy job and go on a book tour and do television interviews."

"Television?" Connie shrieked. "What made him think his little book would get him on TV?"

Emerson answered. "Oscar thought it was newsworthy. He said that David had abused him, you know, sexually, when David was tutoring him for the chess team. He said that he'd researched online and learned that he was recreating his trauma when he did the same thing to that boy."

Rick's David? He knew that they weren't exclusive, but Oscar?

Connie cackled. "What! That's ridiculous. I never saw anything going on between David and Oscar. Did you?"

Emerson shook his head.

Connie hadn't seen anything between David and Rick either, even though she was supposed to be Rick's girlfriend. And she was his girlfriend in every sense of the word. But as far as he was concerned, their relationship was part curiosity and part smokescreen. He had made out with her. They'd even gone all the way a few times. But for him, sex with her was just a release of pent-up energy – a carnal thing, like bulls and cows in a field. Nothing special. No magic.

It was different with David. Angel choirs, tympani drums, canon explosions. When Rick was with David, it felt like their souls transmuted into one being. He was David and David was him.

Rick had been afraid to tell David he loved him. Afterwards, when they laid in bed, David would say what they had was special. Rick settled for that. Special was good, it could turn into love someday. And when Connie asked Rick if he loved her, he gave her the same line. She settled too.

"Oscar and David?" Rick said. "No way."

That last night, David had asked Rick to invite all the boys to his room. Oscar, Dakota, Charlie, and Emerson. Connie had a separate room at the hotel. She would never know.

Rick went to Dakota's room to pick up the coke. While he waited for Dakota to hand over the slip, he said David wanted all the boys at the party. Dakota snorted. "What, like an orgy or something?"

"What makes you say that?" Rick asked.

"Come on, I got eyes. Thanks for the offer, but not into it. Girls are my thing."

Had David been sleeping with all of them?

When Rick returned with the drugs, David was seated at a table, snorting a line. At the time, Rick wondered why, if David already had drugs, he had sent Rick out for coke. But he didn't dare ask.

David threw back his head, blocked his nostrils, and sucked until he needed air. He asked when the boys were coming. Rick lied and said he couldn't find them. In truth, he hadn't tried. "Besides, I thought it'd be just the two of us."

David scowled then brutally grabbed Rick's crotch. "Ever heard of poppers?" He pulled a small vile from his jeans pocket, opened it, and held it under Rick's nose. Rick instantly felt light-headed. He had to sit on the bed to keep from falling. David was on top of him in an instant.

That was when Rick realized what he had felt was an illusion. David had been using him.

As the years passed, Rick suppressed this knowledge. But the truth was back now, crushing his chest so hard, he couldn't breathe. There was no such thing as love.

Connie's voice invaded the memory. "Oscar was just trying to cash in, that's all. Make a few bucks off his little sob story. What a loser. Who knows if it's even true? Besides, how could Oscar get his rights back anyway?"

Emerson answered, "Don't ask me. I'm not a lawyer."

They all turned to Charlie again. He was slumped in one of the chairs, his face red and bloated from booze, a shirt tail protruding from his open fly. "What?"

Connie scooted forward in her chair. "Did Oscar talk to you about getting his book rights back?"

Charlie shook his head, then turned to stare out the window.

"Charlie!"

He flinched. "I can't talk about it."

"I'm your sister, and they're your friends. If this is about us, we have a right to know."

Charlie's head lolled as he tried to reel towards Connie. "It wasn't about you. It was about Oscar and David."

There was no such thing as love.

Connie persisted. "Why didn't the publisher release the book?"

"No idea."

"Who was the publisher?"

Charlie shrugged.

"Lone Star," Emerson volunteered. "Oscar said Rick got him the book deal."

This time they all turned on Rick.

"I just introduced him to someone, that's all." He had handed Oscar's call off to Umberto who in turn put Oscar in touch with The Lion's people.

Connie jabbed Rick in the leg with a boney finger. "So why didn't they publish the book?"

To protect Rick, of course. Rick was The Lion's boy.

That last night, in the Las Vegas hotel room, after he and David had finished David's drugs and snorted the cocaine Rick brought, David fell onto the floor, one hand clawing at his chest. He thrashed, then twitched, then stopped moving. Rick ran back to the room he shared with Oscar. He crawled into bed fully clothed, too high and frightened to sleep.

Oscar heard him come in. "Where have you been?" he asked, ever ready to collect secrets worthy of betrayal.

"With Connie, not that it's any of your effin' business."

Oscar responded with a leering snicker, then rolled back over, and started snoring.

Connie poked Rick again, harder this time. "Answer me! Why didn't they publish Oscar's book?"

"How the hell should I know?"

Chapter Fourteen

Rick

AFTER DAVID'S BODY WAS found, the hotel called the Las Vegas police. The clerk told them they had to go back to their rooms, but they wanted to be together. Connie, ever stoic, herded the boys to her room. Emerson was near tears. Charlie, shocked. Oscar wanted to know if they could call room service.

As they turned down a hallway, Dakota disappeared. Rick assumed he was flushing his stash. They never saw Dakota again.

Pizza and pop were delivered to the room. Oscar flicked on the television. He sat at the edge of a twin bed, a slice of pizza in hand, watching an old western. Emerson, seated at the table, slipped into a hypnotic state. Charlie had Connie's laptop open and was absorbed in what he found there. Rick and Connie sat on the other twin bed, leaning against the headboard, his arm around her shoulders, to appear that he was giving her comfort.

A rap at the door startled them. When Connie opened it, a policeman and policewoman came in. They looked around. The man said, "I thought there were six of you."

Connie said, "There are."

"Who's missing?"

"Dakota."

"Is he in his room?"

"How the hell should I know?" It was the catchphrase amongst their group to indicate the speaker knew but wasn't telling. Oscar looked up, a devious smile on his face. Rick would have kicked him if he could. It appeared the cop didn't notice.

"Why are you keeping us here?" Connie asked.

"Mr. Shroeder died under suspicious circumstances."

"Like someone killed him?" she asked.

Rick wanted to throw up.

The cop didn't answer her question. "When your parents arrive, we'll start the interviews. Then you'll be free to go home."

"Why can't we just go home now? Rick has a driver's license. He can take us back in the van."

"We're keeping the van for the time being. Don't worry, young lady, you'll all be safe and sound in your own beds tonight. Meanwhile, stay put." With that, the police left.

Connie turned to her brother, Charlie, whose ambition was to go to law school. "What does he mean by suspicious circumstances? We all saw the drug paraphernalia in David's room. He must have died of an overdose. That's like an accident or suicide, right?"

Charlie answered. "In the state of Nevada, someone who delivers a controlled substance to another resulting in a death is culpable of manslaughter."

"English, please," Connie said.

"If David died of an overdose, whoever gave him the drugs is guilty of murder."

Rick lunged into the bathroom just in time. He threw the toilet seat open, fell to his knees, and began heaving.

Connie followed and closed the door. She spoke quietly as she rubbed his back. "I know you two were close. I am so sorry, Rick."

He was crying by then. "You don't understand."

She kneeled beside him. "You're right. I don't understand. You lost your parents. And David was like a father to you, and he's gone now. I have no way of imagining what this is like."

He sobbed in her arms for a long time. She was right, up to a point. But he couldn't tell her the whole truth. What if she told?

"Look, Connie, I need to ask you a favor."

She brushed the sweat-soaked hair from his forehead and kissed it. "Whatever you need." In those days, she probably really loved him. By then, he had been cooling towards her. He didn't want to hurt her. He was hoping that by graduation, they would go their separate ways and that would be the end of it. Then he and David could be together, and it would be alright because Rick would be an adult by then.

"I don't have an alibi," he said.

"Why would you need one?"

"They're going to want to know where we were when David died and who gave him the drugs."

Connie wiped his brow with a washcloth. "It was Dakota, of course."

"Yes, but, see here's my problem. I wasn't in my room last night. And when I got back, I told Oscar I was with you."

"Where were you?" she asked, a jealous note in her voice. She had busted him using her as a cover before. He knew she suspected he was with another girl, but she kept hanging on.

"I was in the casino, playing the slot machines. I had my fake ID, just in case. I didn't want Oscar to know because I was afraid he'd tell." It was partly true. Rick had sneaked into the casino for a few minutes before he went to David's room.

"Oscar can't be trusted," Connie said. They had often talked about Oscar's jealousy of Rick. Rick was good-looking, charming, smart, and a great chess player. Oscar was none of those things. And he liked to snitch people out. It was a power trip, the kid no one liked could ruin them – to the extent that someone could be ruined when the teacher found out his girlfriend did his homework.

"And now, they'll think I had something to do with David. I'm screwed. The only alibi I have is underaged gambling. I could go to juvenile hall. And that's if they believe me."

Connie rocked him until he was spent. "Don't worry, I'll tell them you were here with me."

Later, they were taken away one by one for interviews. When Rick's turn came, he was led into a hotel conference room. Seated at the table were two male detectives and his uncle and aunt. He with the pencil-mustache and short-sleeved button-down shirt, she of the bleached bouffant hairdo and polka-dot shirtwaist dress, their faces pinched like they had just drunk pickle juice. They were an embarrassment, especially now. The cops would suspect Rick just because his family was weird.

One detective did the talking. After Rick explained that he had sneaked into his girlfriend's room for most of the evening before going back to the room he shared with Oscar, the cop asked, "What can you tell us about Dakota Vaughn?"

Rick shrugged. "Fair chess player, good enough to get on the team."

"Are you friends?"

"Not really."

"Were you aware that he possessed illegal drugs?" Rick wanted to cry. His voice was shaky when he answered. "No, sir."

"We suspect that he was the source of the cocaine that killed Mr. Shroeder."

"I couldn't tell you. I was with Connie."

The talking detective gave Rick a hard look, like he knew Rick was lying. The other detective looked up from his notepad.

"Is Dakota in trouble?" Rick asked.

"He's been arrested."

Auntie stiffened. "We had no idea there were drugs in that school."

"I'm sure you didn't, ma'am," the detective said.

Dakota was smart. His uncle was a biker, in and out of trouble, and Dakota was raised streetwise. He wouldn't confess. He'd rather plead guilty to the possession charge. If he didn't confess, there was nothing to link Rick to David's death.

Rick was allowed to leave with his uncle and aunt, who had driven from Daly City. It was almost dawn when they returned. They hadn't spoken the entire trip. As Rick headed to bed, Uncle ordered him into the living room.

Uncle had never liked Rick. Auntie was his father's sister. They'd acted as if they took him in because he was family, but the truth was they wanted Rick's inheritance. Uncle pretended he made a lot of money, but he didn't. He was a car salesman. He didn't even own the dealership. He didn't even have his own car. His boss let him drive around a new car as a means of advertising.

"We've spent hard-earned cash to get you into the best school we could find. And this is what happens? Drugs," Uncle said. Auntie sat by his side, wringing her hands, looking guilty. Uncle blamed her for having a dead brother and an orphaned nephew.

"It's not your money," Rick said.

"I feed you. I clothe you. I pay for everything the trust doesn't cover."

"I had nothing to do with drugs."

"Don't waste your breath. Your word means nothing around here."

They'd busted Rick sneaking out a few times and Auntie had found some pot in his jeans when she did the laundry. No matter how polite he was, how hard he worked around the dealership, doing janitorial and washing cars, they never forgave him.

"You're lazy and deceitful," Uncle went on. That's when he dropped the bomb. "You're just like your parents, your druggie father and your boozer mother."

"My dad died in a car accident."

"Your dad died on the way home from an all-night drug party. It was only dumb luck that he got run over by that garbage truck."

Auntie winced.

"That can't be true, Auntie."

"Tell him," Uncle said.

"We wanted to protect you. What good would it do for you to know?"

"And my mother?"

She took a deep breath. "She died of alcoholism."

Uncle knocked on his head like it was a door. "In case you're too stupid to get that, your mother drank herself to death."

Uncle said mean things just to hurt Rick. But Auntie never had. She had said that his mother died of cardiomyopathy. That's why Rick wanted to go to Standford University, to get a medical degree and get into research. He wanted to save other mothers from dying and save other children from living with opportunistic bastards like his uncle. That's why he wanted to go to the private school, so he could take the right classes that would get him accepted by Stanford.

"You said she died of heart disease."

"Caused by her drinking," Uncle said. "First thing Monday, we are enrolling you in the public high school. Maybe we'll get some of the tuition money back. You can work in the dealership after school and on the weekends. And when you turn eighteen, you're out of here."

Rick called Connie using his secret pay-as-you-go cellphone and told her the bad news. She cried. She told him she loved him. He said he loved her too. It was a kindness. It's not like they'd ever see each other again. Charlie had told them there was no statute of limitations on murder in Nevada. As long as he lived, he needed her to keep his secret. After that, they kept up a telephone romance for years even when she went away to college, right up until she found someone to marry. He told her he understood – that she would always be his best friend.

As it turned out, Rick could sell cars, even when he partied all weekend. Why shouldn't he have fun? He wasn't going to be a doctor. He wasn't going to save other children's mothers. His own mother drank herself to death rather than raise him. His father got himself killed because he was out getting high when he should have been home with Rick and his mom. Rick had no one depending on him, no one to disappoint, and no one who would feel abandoned, so he was free to party the way his parents did.

He worked his way up at various dealerships until he owned a franchise. He made Connie his business partner. She ran the dealership in Fair Oaks and was making money. He ran the one in San Francisco. If she ever told his secret, and he went to prison, she could expect to lose her business. Her devotion to him might have kept her quiet in the early days, but Rick liked the added insurance of Connie's greed, because there was no such thing as love. If there was, his parents would have chosen to live and be with him.

IT WAS ALMOST MIDNIGHT when Emerson stood and announced he was leaving. Connie asked Emerson to help her with Charlie, who had been snoring. She would drive them both to his home in Milpitas.

Rick thought about offering to get them rooms for the night, but he was afraid if he did, Connie would want to stay with him. He could beg off, say he was going home, but what if he ran into her in the morning when they were leaving? She would be hurt. Hell hath no fury like a woman scorned. She could ruin him.

Rick helped them get Charlie into the elevator.

"Coming?" Connie asked.

"I have to settle the bill. Won't take long. Drive safe!" He waved as the elevator door slid shut. He went over to the bar, poured another whiskey, and picked up the hotel phone.

"They're gone. And we're out of champagne."

When the elevator opened again, Dimitri, with his covert smile, stepped out and held the door open. At first glance, it looked like Mae West, Marlene Dietrich, and Marilyn Monroe poured out with the pretty waiter boy in tow. But the movie stars' hips were too slim and their shoulders too broad to be women.

Mae West sidled up to him, threw a muscly arm around Rick's waist and gave him a rib-crushing squeeze. "Hello, big boy! Ready for some fun?"

Dimitri went over to the bar, produced a baggie and a razor blade from a pocket, and began chopping up rocks of cocaine. Mae West draped a feather boa around Rick's neck, pulled him to Dimitri's side, and handed him a straw.

Rick bent over and snorted a line. The diesel flavor flashed up his nose and set fire to his brain.

He felt alive.

Rick stood upright and threw back his head. "You betchya, baby!"

WHEN RICK WOKE THE next morning, he was filled with guilt, dread, shame, and remorse. He knew it was just the hangover, something chemical going on in his brain, but it felt real. It'd go away as soon as he could have another drink.

He was alone, sprawled naked and face down on an oversized king bed. Through the window was a clear blue sky. He wondered where he was, then he noticed the chic gray décor.

Where had Dimitri gone? Last night, it felt like Rick had made a real connection with another human being. The others were fun, but Dimitri understood him.

There was a noise. Rick rolled over to see what had caused it. The feather boa still wrapped around his neck tightened. He pulled it free. When his vision cleared, he found Umberto seated comfortably in a bedside chair. On the side table was a platter with what appeared to be a large Bloody Mary.

The scene reminded him of when Umberto had busted him in that seedy hotel, except now the cigarettes butts were in a crystal ashtray and there were empty champagne flutes instead of crushed beer cans.

Umberto looked smug. "Did we enjoy our evening?"

Flashes of the night came back. Rick on Mae West's lap. Snorting coke off the six packed torso of the pretty waiter boy, then licking off the dust that remained. Bodies on the bed, arms and legs entangled, laughing, groaning. The things he had done. The things that had been done to him.

The only face he saw was Dimitri's, with his dark curls and jade green eyes. Rick had been delighted to find an elaborate angel's wing tattoo on Dimitri's shoulder. Would it be silly to think Dimitri was heaven sent? Rick could still smell his cologne on the pillow, reminding him of their fingers interlinked during moments of ecstasy.

The bad feelings faded away. "We enjoyed our evening very much."

"Didn't I tell you? Old Uncle Umberto has your best interests at heart."

"It was the best night of my life." Rick covered his face to hide his schoolgirl blush. Then, in attempt to sound casual, he asked, "Where's Dimitri?"

A salacious grin split across Umberto's face. "You liked him?"

"We had some fun."

"The poor boy must work for a living, Rick. I'm sure you could see him again if you wish."

"Is that what he said?"

"He said he enjoyed the evening very much."

"Did he say anything about me?"

"You gave him a night to remember." Umberto handed the Bloody Mary to Rick. "Hair of the dog. Drink up."

The first sip was a salty, wet coolness that Rick didn't know he craved. He gulped down half the glass.

"Careful," Umberto said, as he patted Rick's thigh. "We have a long day ahead of us."

The night before, Connie had poked the same thigh when she was digging for the truth.

"Umberto?"

"Yes, Rick."

"That book that Oscar wrote. It's never going to come out, is it?"

"Never."

"Did you read it?"

"I did."

"Did he talk about how David Schroeder died?"

"He said that your teacher died of a combination of cocaine and amyl nitrate."

The night he died, David was snorting poppers, little blasts of amyl nitrate inhaled from a small bottle. Rick had never seen them before but had seen them at parties in the years since David died.

Umberto went on. "The police speculated that he had company. They charged one of your classmates with cocaine possession but were not able to prove that he delivered the drugs that killed your teacher, so he got off with a light sentence."

"What did Oscar say about me?"

"That you spent the evening with your girlfriend, and she corroborated your alibi. Why do you ask?"

"I'm just worried, you know, that if someone got their hands on the book and they nosed around, I could get into trouble."

"What kind of trouble?"

"Whoever gave those drugs to David could be guilty of murder, right?"

"Was it you?"

Could Rick trust Umberto?

"No, of course not. I was just a kid. Where would I get cocaine?"

From his good buddy, Dakota, obviously.

A mask fell across Umberto's face. Rick's protestation had been too quick and too loud to be believable. "Mr. Toussaint promised no one would get their hands on that book. You're too important to him to let ancient gossip destroy your future."

"The guy who they arrested for killing Oscar, he has an attorney snooping around. If she finds out about the book and what it said, she might think one of us killed Oscar. And then everyone will know about the book and what it said because it'll be evidence, right?"

"What would you have me do, Rick?"

The Lion had bought Oscar's book to make sure it wouldn't be published. He had big plans for Rick, Sacramento and then DC.

Truth could be bought as cheaply as one man's dreams. Oscar wanted enough money to never work again. The fact that anyone would publish his book was a dream come true. All it took was a little flattery to convince him that when his book was published, he would be a rich man. So, Oscar let himself be bought off with an advance and a promise of royalties when the book was released. What a sucker.

When Rick was feeling paranoid, he suspected The Lion had killed Skinny Guy and Footballer, but if he did, he might have killed Oscar too. Rick kept telling himself that he was just being paranoid. Maybe his suspicions were part of that chemical shame that came with hangovers.

Rick drank the rest of the Bloody Mary.

He was too frightened to ask Umberto if The Lion was responsible for those deaths. If he was wrong, confronting The Lion would make an enemy of him. If he was right, knowing about it could only pull him into a conspiracy if the police found out. Or worse, make him a threat to The Lion. It was safer not knowing.

Rick asked, "Can't you make the trial go away?"

Chapter Fifteen

Maureen

WHEN I ARRIVED AT Tony's hospital room, he was on his feet, shuffling across the small room, guided by a physical therapist. A sympathetic pain shot down my body as I saw the strain on Tony's face. Isaac was in the visitor's chair, staring at the floor, his arms crossed tightly in front of his chest. The guard was seated next to Isaac, reading a newspaper.

I scooted out of the way and put the daisies I'd bought in the hospital gift shop into an empty plastic vase on the window ledge.

The PT helped Tony into bed, plumped his pillow, and tucked him into bed. "That's enough for today, Tony. You did great. I'll see you again tomorrow."

As soon as he was gone, Tony asked, "Where are those nurses? I need my meds."

"I'll go find them," Isaac said, and he left.

I looked at the guard. "Can you give us some privacy for an attorney-client conference?"

He tucked the newspaper under his arm and left the room, leaving the door open. I closed it.

"Is there any news?" Tony asked.

"Vivian Thandi called with a plea offer. She's offering manslaughter with an agreed sentence of no more than three years."

"Back to prison? No way. They'll kill me."

He was in pain and agitated. I needed to give him the bad news in tiny bites, so he understood exactly what risks he was taking by going to trial.

"There's something else, Tony. A new witness."

"Now? Who?"

"A jailhouse snitch."

I had told Tony time and again not to talk to anyone. It didn't matter what he said. What mattered is that talking to someone at all gave them an opportunity to fabricate statements. The truth was, Tony had little impulse control. If he spoke to anyone, it would be about how much he hated Oscar, which the DA was going to argue was his motive.

Tony said, "I didn't say anything to anyone."

"This guy claims he brought your meals to you when you first were arrested and were in lockdown. And he claims that you told him how much you hated Oscar, about what he did to you, that he ruined your life, that he was living in a nice house and driving a brand-new SUV while you drove an old Gremlin, and that you weren't sorry he was dead."

Everything in the snitch's statement was something that either Tony had told me himself or I knew from the evidence. The snitch could have seen the story about Oscar's assault of Tony on TV. The news stories following his arrest ran an old interview – that I had advised against – taken by a reporter on the sidewalk in front of his apartment building in which Tony said Oscar had ruined his life. So that bit was in public access. But I couldn't easily rationalize how the snitch would know that Oscar was living in a nice house and driving a brand-new SUV and that Tony owned a Gremlin. None of that information was in the public arena.

Tony repeated, "I never said a word to anyone, I swear. He's lying. I'm being set up. Can't you see that? You're my attorney. You're supposed to believe me."

"I'm supposed to critically evaluate the evidence and advise you on the risks, Tony. I'm doing my job."

Isaac returned. "The nurse is on her way."

Tony began crying.

"What's wrong?" Isaac asked.

"She wants me to plead guilty."

Here was a perfect example of Tony's lack of impulse control. "Look, Tony, it's really important that we maintain attorney-client confidentiality. I'm afraid we can't include anyone else in our conversations. The DA could call Isaac as a witness against you."

Tony slammed his hand on the mattress. "I'm telling the truth! Let the bitch call him! He's my only friend, and I want him here with me."

"Guilty to what?" Isaac asked.

"Tell him," Tony said.

"Manslaughter with a maximum of three years in prison."

Isaac looked like he was going to faint. He braced himself against the wall as he moved to the visitor's chair.

I needed a break from the tension. I grabbed the vase of flowers, took them to the small sink in the room, and filled them with water.

"But why?" Isaac asked.

Tony answered. "She says there's a snitch who's going to say I confessed to killing Oscar."

"I don't understand," Isaac said.

"Explain it to him."

I put the flowers back on the window ledge. "First off, I didn't say I wanted Tony to plead guilty. But I am ethically obligated to extend any offer made by the prosecution. They would accept a no contest plea."

"Is that better?"

"It's not an admission. Theoretically, it prevents the victim's family from using the conviction as evidence in the event they sued Tony for wrongful death."

"Now they're going to sue me?"

This was getting way out of hand. "I'm just explaining the difference. No one said they're going to sue you. I would be surprised if they did because you don't have any money."

"But they called me 'The Millionaire' in jail. How does Oscar's wife know I'm broke?"

"Her attorney would have told her. Let's focus, okay? There's a plea offer and a new witness, a jailhouse snitch. He didn't say exactly that you confessed to killing Oscar."

"But he said I hated him and that I was glad he was dead, so that's pretty much the same thing, right?"

"I'm concerned the jury would see it that way."

"He's lying."

Isaac took Tony's hand, and they exchanged looks. Tony calmed. That was the first time I'd seen them display affection. Had their relationship developed to the next step? Or had they always been together and only now, were willing to let me in?

Isaac asked, "What's the possibilities, if he doesn't take this deal?"

"We go to trial. If we win, Tony goes free. If we lose, Tony could be convicted of first-degree, or second-degree murder, or a lesser crime. Depending on the verdict, he could spend twenty-five years in prison."

"Can't we counteroffer?"

I shook my head. "The prosecutor assured me that this was her last, best offer. She isn't known for bargaining." I didn't tell them that Vivian only offered a deal when she thought there was a chance she might lose. She might think the jury would sympathize with Tony and acquit him even if she had proven his guilt. Or she might think that her circumstantial evidence case was too shaky. Her reasons were too speculative for Tony to base his decision upon.

Isaac said to Tony, "I don't want you to go back to prison. Not even for one day." They were still holding hands. Isaac turned back to me. "What can we do?"

"Go to trial as soon as possible while Tony's still in the hospital and fight for an acquittal."

Isaac asked, "Can we have a moment?"

"Sure," I said. "I'll go down to the cafeteria and grab a coffee. Do you want anything?"

Tony said, "Tell the nurse to hurry up."

"Will do."

I delivered the message at the nurse's station and then took the stairs to burn off my adrenaline. When I returned, I found a nurse coming out of his room.

"Is he asleep?"

"Not yet. But in twenty minutes or so, he will be."

When I walked back into the room, Tony and Isaac were still holding hands. They had both been crying.

Before I had a chance to speak, Tony said, "Tell the bitch we'll see her in court."

AFTER VEGETARIAN PIZZA FOR dinner – it was Quinn's night to cook – we settled in front of the television to watch the news. In the senate race, pollsters had Rick Stevens and Foster Heiki tied. Stevens' campaign was everywhere: on billboards, television, radio, and social media.

"No one knew who this Stevens guy was a few months ago," Jake said. "Someone's spending a fortune to get him elected. Why isn't Heiki fighting back?"

"He doesn't have as much money," Quinn said, as she knelt in front of me. "He'll swamp the media with his ads a few days before the election." She took my right hand in both of hers and began massaging my palms.

The pressure felt good. "What are you doing?"

"It's for your carpal tunnel syndrome. I researched therapies."

Carpal tunnel syndrome, what was she talking about? Then I remembered. She had witnessed me scratching at my scars and I lied to her about why my arms itched. Being a loving daughter, she wanted to relieve my discomfort. Tangled web, indeed. I felt sick, betraying my daughter's trust while trying to protect her.

Jake gave me a look. He'd witnessed me lying to her.

I let her continue until she wanted to pull up my sleeves and work on my forearms. "Not tonight. I'm feeling a little sore. But thank you." I gave her a kiss on the top of the head.

"Would you like an icepack?" she asked.

"That sounds nice."

She went into the kitchen and came out with a fluffy purple pack that had been chilling in the freezer.

"That's new."

"I found it at the pharmacy this afternoon."

So, she had been shopping for my fictional carpal tunnel syndrome as well as researching. She was thoughtful and kind and I was a fraud. I didn't deserve her. I certainly hadn't earned her affection.

That night, as Jake and I prepared to brush our teeth, he looked at my reflection in the bathroom mirror. "You have to tell her sometime. The longer you wait, the worse it'll be."

"You don't know that," I said to his reflection. I stuck the toothbrush in my mouth and scrubbed furiously.

"You're throwing that wall up again."

My self-protection had nearly cost our marriage. At first, I just wanted to hide the truth of what had happened to me when I was fourteen. To do that, I lied. Then I had to cover up one lie with another one. I then became defensive and hostile. Before I knew it, we could barely speak to each other without getting into an argument.

I rinsed my mouth and spat into the sink. "She's so sweet. So good. I want to protect her."

"Remember what you said in closing argument in the Navarre case? Secrets bind the shamed to the guilty. And only truth can set them free. Those were wise words, Red."

Chapter Sixteen

Rick

"WHY DID YOU MARRY her?" Umberto asked. They were sitting on the couch in Rick's den, drinks in hand, their feet up on ottomans. Umberto had loosened his tie. Rick had pulled his off. They both had vodka tonics in their hands. The Dum Dee twins were gone for the night.

It was the end of a long day, a Rotary Club lunch, and a photoshoot in a rented hall where Rick pretended to make a speech. The pollsters said he had finally passed Heiki, if only by a few points. It felt like they could finally relax.

Since the night at the Hotel Blanc, Rick's perception of Umberto shifted. He used to be like an evil stepmother, finding fault at every opportunity. But now he was the fairy godmother, magically rearranging the world for Rick's happiness.

Rick answered, "I had just taken over my first dealership when I brought a few of the top salesmen down to Cabo for a long weekend. I was a young buck then, driving flashy cars, with beautiful women on my arm everywhere I went. I liked the attention. The envy. By then, I knew I liked men, but I dated women too because I didn't want to commit to a choice. There's no coming back from 'hey, world! I'm gay!'"

"The guys and I were seated around a table on the lanai when this exotic creature came out of the bar, hips swinging, to take our drink order. Appollonia. The guys were tongue-tied, she was so gorgeous. I felt it too. And I thought, this woman can make a straight man out of me if anyone can."

Umberto glanced up at Rick. "Did she?"

"At first, sure, it was amazing. When she got off shift, I took her back to my room. We finally fell asleep after dawn."

"Then what happened?" Umberto asked.

"We got married. And it wasn't fun anymore."

"Did she turn into her mother?"

"It wasn't her fault. It's me." Rick polished off his drink. "More?" he asked Umberto.

"I'm good."

Rick dragged himself to the liquor cabinet, mixed another gin and tonic, then worked up the courage to ask. "Have you heard from Dimitri?"

"I have."

"Has he said anything about me?"

"He asked how you are."

"Like casually, or like he really meant it?"

Umberto snorted. "You have a crush."

Rick sat on the couch, facing Umberto. "I felt like we really connected, you know. I'd like to see him again."

"We need to be careful, Rick. Gay politicians have an uphill battle. Philandering politicians, who get caught, lose points. Put those two things together and if people find out, I'm not sure you can win this election."

Before Rick had met Dimitri, he was convinced there was no such thing as love. That one night changed Rick's mind. Dimitri made him feel alive. "This isn't just a fling. I mean, I know I only spent one night with him, but it felt real. Like we could put something together. I'd like to see where it takes us."

Rick had fantasized about a love nest. He could rent Dimitri a condo somewhere secluded and visit him whenever he wanted. As time went on, Rick would get a divorce and then he could be with Dimitri every day forever.

"Okay but you need to be discreet," Umberto said. "Understand me? Tell no one."

"Who would I tell?" Rick said. "You're my best friend."

Chapter Seventeen

Maureen

I NEVER SLEEP WELL the night before a trial. At 4:30 am, I gave up trying and got up to make coffee. Quinn was at the dinner table, with stacks of paper neatly surrounding her open laptop.

"Have you been up all night?" I asked.

"Fell down a rabbit hole."

"Shouldn't you be studying?"

"Done."

"Your studies come first. I don't want you neglecting class to work on the case."

"I know." She looked up from the computer. "Mom."

I was being patronized. I could live with it. I didn't know how to act like a mother, so I was probably heavy handed, now and then. "Do you have class tomorrow?"

"It's a Monday. We only have lectures on Tuesday and Thursday."

"And you're prepared for class?"

"Absolutely, Mom."

"So do you want to come to jury selection tomorrow?"

"Try and keep me from it." She went back to the computer.

That's my girl.

I flipped on the electric kettle and put an herbal teabag into a mug for Quinn, then slipped a pod into the coffee maker for me, positioned another mug underneath that, and pushed a button. The kettle gurgled and the coffee machine sputtered to life. "Find anything?"

"Tons," she said. "Did you look at the witness statements?"

Of course, I did – the minute they arrived. It was her awkward way of introducing a topic and it was too early in the day, the week, and the trial to let out my inner grouch. "Find anything interesting?"

"Did you notice that when Brita Wenderholm made her statement to the police, she brought her own lawyer?"

"I did."

"A divorce lawyer."

That, I had missed. I looked up the guy online and saw he practiced personal injury law, car accidents, and medical malpractice. I figured Mrs. Wenderholm was exploring whether she could file a lawsuit against Tony and once the attorney figured out Tony had no money, he dropped her case.

I poured the hot water into the tea mug and brought Quinn's tea and my coffee out to the dining room. "I thought he did personal injury."

"And divorce."

"Leading to the inference that?"

When Quinn started law school, she learned the professors discussed how evidence leads to inferences, rather than stating "this proves that" so I kept up with the lingo. I wanted to show her respect as due to a peer, even one who was new to the study of law.

Quinn leaned back in her chair and folded her arms. "She was thinking about a divorce before her husband was killed."

"Maybe. Or she was thinking about suing Tony. Or he's a friend of the family. But it's worth asking her about. Make a note of that in her witness file."

"Is she going to testify?" Quinn asked.

"Without a doubt. The prosecution wants to humanize the victim. They need to garner the jury's sympathy. Loving husband and father. Besides, she found the body and she's the witness to Tony's visit to her house the night before Oscar died. She pulls the whole case together."

"That's not all," Quinn said. "Connie Robertson, the lady in Fair Oaks with the car dealership. She's partners with Rick Stevens."

"Not a huge surprise. They went to school together."

"And Rick Stevens owns the warehouse that Oscar was working at, so he's the boss of the guy who said he saw Tony threaten Oscar."

"There was surveillance video too."

"Okay, Mom, I get that. But, what about this? Why was Oscar Wenderholm working in a warehouse owned by Rick Stevens, and he bought a car from a dealership owned by Rick Stevens, after he wrote a book about going to school with Rick Stevens?"

Because they were close personal friends and Rick Stevens wanted to support Oscar after his downfall?

Or did Rick Stevens want to buy Oscar's silence?

"That's a really good question."

THE NEXT MORNING, YOLANDA, Quinn, and I arrived early for the first day of trial to find the courtroom locked. We huddled nearby with paper cups, coffee for Yolanda and me, tea for Quinn, waiting for the clerk to open the doors. Down the hall, an elevator whooshed open, and I heard the clatter of wheeled bags. Vivian Thandi came into view. At her elbow was a young male assistant DA who carried a thin, expensive briefcase and a thirtyish female paralegal dragging the two file cases on wheels. Typical. It might be the twenty-first century, but young male lawyers were admonished by older men not to lower themselves to women's work if they had ambition. In law, that meant all the heavy lifting was left to women.

Vivian and I exchanged polite nods. Her team turned their backs on me.

I wasn't surprised by the cold shoulder. Employees of the District Attorney's Office are true believers. Their mission is a holy crusade to rid the streets of crime and restore order. When someone leaves the DA's office to start their own practice, like me, they are a traitor to the cause. Worse yet, they are money-grubbing sharks who use their prosecutorial training for their own personal gain. That's how I got the nickname "Mo Gould" meaning "more gold" when I left the DA's. Funny, but they don't hold my escape against Jake. He was a former cop, and as such beyond reproach – despite his poor choice in marriage.

I left the DA's office because putting away bad guys did very little to help their victims. Once the case was over, the DA abandoned them and moved on to the next case.

I wanted to make a difference by helping victims build a new life. That meant suing the wrongdoer, winning large judgment for my clients, and shepherding them to a brighter future. Every time I interacted with them, I needed to be positive and supportive emotionally. Trust, and the lack of it, was a major problem for my clients. And with reason.

They had been exploited intimately by someone they had trusted. To be of service to them, I needed to be counselor and confidante as well as their lawyer.

I was musing how the prosecutors' snub hardly stung anymore when the courtroom doors opened. Vivian and her team entered. We followed, with Quinn and Yolanda each pulling a wheeled suitcase. I usually brought in one of the bags, but Quinn insisted. She and Yolanda were falling into a routine of their own, Quinn anticipating Yolanda's needs and Yolanda motherly nurturing of Quinn.

Tony was currently a patient in a rehabilitation unit. Every morning, court security would pick him up in a van and wheel him into the courtroom before the jury arrived. Judge Han suggested that he could remain seated when the jury entered and exited, but he wanted to stand. He was worried that if he was the only person sitting, the jurors would feel slighted by him. I agreed.

I settled at the defense table and unpacked my briefcase. Two legal pads for me and one for Tony. A gaggle of pens. Ever since law school, I was deeply concerned about running out of ink at a crucial time. Quinn and Yolanda unpacked the files which included copies of the indictment, motions, and orders, a binder with sections for every witness, and binders for the evidence that the prosecution had produced pretrial, and separate binders for the evidence we had found. During the trial, Yolanda would hand me whatever I needed so she arranged the files to her liking. I wasn't allowed to touch them.

When there was nothing left for me to arrange, for what was probably the tenth time that morning, I touched my throat to make sure I was wearing the O'Shaughnessy pearls. The back door opened, and a guard pushed Tony into the courtroom. He was wearing a navy-blue sweater over a white button-up shirt and navy tie and black slacks that Isaac had bought for court. He had a new pair of black horn-rim glasses. Thinner and paler than when he had been arrested, his hair had grown enough to cover the scar across his scalp.

I had met with Isaac a couple of weeks prior to discuss Tony's court attire. A suit would look like he was trying, and failing, at the appearance of authority, much like that young assistant DA at Vivian's elbow whose neck swam in his shirt collar. Young men, even young male lawyers who wear suits every day, look like they are playing dress up in their father's clothes. Besides, even suits off the rack are expensive. A necktie was sufficient to show Tony respected the arena. A sweater softened him and would keep him from playing with his tie nervously.

As the guard locked the wheelchair for Tony to stand, Isaac came through the main door, having followed the van to the courthouse. He would have gone to the rehab unit early to help Tony dress. Isaac was dressed similarly to Tony, in navy sweater, tie, and slacks.

I helped Tony into his chair. We didn't speak as the guard would hear everything we said and would report it back to the prosecution. Isaac leaned across the rail and reached for Tony's hand.

The guard stepped forward to get between the two. "No touching."

Everyone at the prosecution table stopped, turned, and watched us.

Isaac pulled back his hand as if it had been burned. Tony turned on the guard. "Really?"

I leaned into Tony. "He's just doing his job."

He reeled on me. "But!"

I shook my head. "It's not about you. There are procedures in place and it's for everyone's safety. They can't make exceptions."

That earned a nod from the guard. He stepped back.

I laid my arm across the back of Tony's chair and spoke directly into his ear so no one would hear us. "We have a long day ahead of us. Let's pick our battles."

The clerk announced, "All rise!"

I helped Tony to a stand as the door directly behind the judge's bench opened. Judge Han stepped into view. "Please be seated."

Jury selection began.

Logic suggests that out of eighty people, more than a few would admit they had heard about Wenderholm's murder and Tony's arrest on the news, but that wasn't the case. A few years ago, everyone watched the evening news. Now, not so much, it seemed. Most people claimed they didn't read the papers and didn't subscribe to network television and the only news they read was on social media. Those who thought they might have heard about the case stated under oath that they had not formed an opinion and could be fair.

The panel that was selected consisted of twelve jurors and two alternates. The fourteen included four retired people, three white-haired women and one man, and two college students, a young woman, and a man. She was a wide-eyed nineteen-year-old, a recent high school graduate. He was older and earnest. Having taken a payoff to leave his investment banking job, he went back to school at thirty-five to obtain a master's degree in Catholic education leadership.

We called him the Sweater Man. He was about six foot two inches and lean. Like Tony and Isaac, he wore a sweater over a shirt and tie. And I realized that I had inadvertently dressed my client in a Catholic school boy uniform.

Tony didn't like him. He was worried that the Church sex scandal and the multi-million-dollar settlements would prevent Sweater Man from being fair. During jury selection, Tony had insisted that Sweater Man wouldn't support the Church if he accepted its role in enabling the abuse of children. I asked Judge Han for the opportunity to question the juror privately. The judge turned on a white noise machine for the courtroom and ushered Sweater Man, Vivian, and me into the hallway where the judge held a microphone to record our questions and responses in the event of an appeal.

I looked up at Sweater Man when I said, "Sir, this case involves sensitive evidence, some of which may be difficult for jurors to listen to. Specifically, my client was sexually abused by Oscar Wenderholm when he was a student."

Vivian lifted onto her toes to object. I gave her a frown. The abuse was an established fact decided by a jury. It was admissible. She settled back onto her heels.

"My client sued Mr. Wenderholm and won a large verdict."

Sweater Man studied me closely. "I see."

"We are concerned that given your allegiance to the Church, and its payment of large settlements arising from similar claims, you would have difficulty being fair to my client."

Sweater Man clasped his hands together in a priestly gesture. "Let me put your mind at rest. It is because of the Church's mishandling of the claims, and its failure to police its own, that I was drawn to the field of Catholic education. I want to help reorganize the system so that children are not put at risk again."

Worked for me.

But not for Vivian. She said, "Excuse me, sir. I don't want to pry but we need to establish that you can be fair to both sides. I wonder if you, or anyone you know, was abused by a priest."

"I wasn't. I'm not sure if my classmates were. But there was one priest who handed candy out to girls on the playground. It was rumored that when they were old enough, which was third grade, they could come visit him in his office. I resented that boys weren't given candy, but I was too young to understand the implications. A few years ago, I saw his name on a list of abusers. It made me think."

Vivian asked, "Do you have strong feelings about what you observed?"

"I only have suspicions. I'm not certain what happened."

The judge intervened. "Is there anything about your experiences that would make you unable to be fair in a case involving the murder of an established child abuser?"

"No, ma'am."

I was convinced that Sweater Man was thoughtful and not likely to jump to conclusions. I explained to Tony what I had learned and that we could excuse him from the jury but that would mean his seat would be filled by someone we didn't know. He surveyed the prospective jurors sitting behind us. There were a few that gave him filthy looks. He agreed to leave Sweater Man on the jury. Sweater Man took the first seat in the front row of the jury box, the closest to our table.

The jury also consisted of a young woman, Amber Haley, who worked as a dog walker and looked like she was going to cry. She was most troubled about being in a courtroom with a judge and lawyers who she'd only seen on television before she came to court. But she promised she would be fair. There was a legal secretary, a mature woman, who followed everything closely, and a librarian in her sixties. The Librarian wore a shawl. A pair of reading glasses hung on a faux pearl studded chain around her neck. I guessed the jury would elect the Librarian as foreperson because she was authoritative. During her questioning, she stated that no case was as it appeared in the beginning, and only after all the evidence is in, can someone decide what was right or fair.

The other jurors included a male certified nursing assistant who appeared in court in scrubs on the first day, explaining he had just gotten off shift. There was a female social worker in her mid-fifties who was happy to be of service and a grizzled disabled man in his seventies shifted uncomfortably in his chair several times an hour. Judge Han told him he could get up and stand next to the jury box when he needed to, if he could hear the testimony and see the witnesses. And there were two long-time unemployed young men, both looking for work, one in restaurant, the other in anything, but neither had job interviews coming up.

After the jury was selected, the courtroom emptied so my team could have its first postmortem. It was important for Tony to synthesize what had happened and to prepare him for tomorrow's events. In my role as counselor and confidante, I wanted him to feel heard. It was his case and his life, not mine. He was entitled to the opportunity to express his feelings. In working with him in the civil case, I learned that giving him a structured time to do so calmed his anxiety.

The guard left the room as well because this was an attorney-client meeting and confidential. As soon as the door closed behind him, I vacated my chair and motioned for Isaac to take it. He had been sitting quietly in the front row beside Quinn all day. He moved into my seat and his hand and Tony's hand disappeared under the table.

"Are you okay?" Isaac asked Tony.

"A little sore, but yeah, I'll live."

I had asked Tony to lay off his pain medication as much as possible so he would be coherent. He looked more than a little sore, so I wanted him to return to the rehab unit as quickly as possible to rest and get some medication.

I asked him, "How do you feel about the jury selection?"

"Good. I was worried about Sweater Man, but from what you said, he's seen both sides so he should be alright. What's happening tomorrow?"

"Opening statements. The first thing you're going to hear is why the state thinks you're guilty. In your civil trial, because we were the plaintiff, we went first. But this is a criminal trial, so the prosecution gets the first shot at the jury. It's going to be rough to hear, so prepare yourself."

"But we get to tell them our side of the story, right?"

The best defense is someone else did it. But I didn't have a suspect. I only had a smattering of innuendo and suspicion. The weakest defense, in my opinion, was to harp on the state's obligation to prove its case.

"We will get the chance to tell them our side of the story. And we will, Tony. Trust me."

Chapter Eighteen

Maureen

THE NEXT MORNING, VIVIAN stood at a podium which had been moved to the courtroom well, facing the jurors. She was surrounded by flimsy metal easels, upon which were set large board-mounted photographs and diagrams.

"Good morning, ladies and gentlemen. On behalf of the State of California, I want to thank you for your jury service. We know how much of an imposition it is. Keeping that in mind, we will present our case as straightforward as possible."

She was pandering to the jury. The jurors were the most important part of this process, and they were entitled to have their sacrifice acknowledged. But it could sound like groveling if overdone. Sweater Man listened politely. The Librarian chewed on the stem of her reading glasses. Grizzled Man pushed himself half off the chair, twisted his torso, then settled back down again.

Vivian continued. "The facts are simple and clear. The evidence will show that Anthony Paredes, now seated at the defense table, shot and killed Oscar Wenderholm."

A few of the jurors shyly peeked in our direction. Amber Haley, the dog walker, chewed her lip. The Social Worker looked at Tony with compassion in her gaze. She was prepared to believe he had a good reason to murder Oscar, but she might convict him anyway.

Tony gripped his armrest, his knuckles white. I rested my pen on my legal pad, implying I'd take notes if, and when, Vivian said something important.

"The accused was not a stranger to the decedent, Oscar Wenderholm."

She was forced to refer to Oscar as "the decedent" because of a protective order I had won. To call him "the victim" would be a subtle attempt to stir pity. The judge had instructed the jurors not to be swayed by their sympathies, but instead they were to decide the case on cold, hard evidence.

"In fact, Anthony Paredes had known Mr. Wenderholm for a very long time. When Mr. Paredes was attending Lafayette Academy, a private high school, Oscar Wenderholm was the coach of his chess team. Years later, Mr. Paredes accused Mr. Wenderholm of sexually assaulting him during that time. He filed a lawsuit which went to trial, and he won a multi-million-dollar judgment against Mr. Wenderholm and the school."

In her motions, Vivian had routinely referred to *Paredes v Wenderholm* as the "#metoo" case. She argued that the moniker was needed so she could distinguish the civil action from our criminal trial. I argued that the term "#metoo" had become so politically charged that using it was prejudicial. The term suggested that my client was trying to cash in on allegations of ancient events that were never witnessed, couldn't be corroborated, and didn't merit complaint at the time – if they even happened. In short, she accused Tony of adjusting the truth to make money.

The judge agreed with me. Vivian was forced to refer to the prior case by either "the civil litigation," or by its name, *Paredes v Wenderholm.*

Winning these small skirmishes was no reason for me to be cocky. It was not a good sign when the judge agrees with the defense on every pretrial matter. It can mean the judge thinks the case will result in a conviction and she doesn't want to give the defendant any grounds for appeal.

Vivian spent forty-five minutes discussing the evidence. Tony's testimony of what Oscar had done to him in school. The huge verdict that was later set aside. Tony's visit to Oscar's home the day before the murder in a highly emotional state. His threat to kill Oscar witnessed by the widow. His visit to Oscar's workplace the week before when he screamed at Oscar. The untraceable murder weapon found in his car. The statement to another inmate following his arrest that he was glad that Oscar was dead.

She showed photos of the autopsy, the murder scene, the search of Tony's car, the gun, and a diagram showing bullet entrance and exit wounds.

The jurors paid attention. Amber Haley chewed her lip. Grizzled Man with the bad back and hip fidgeted throughout. The male nurse watched Grizzled Man, more concerned with a nearby person in pain than a story being told to him.

Vivian thanked the jury then returned to her table. Judge Han announced a break before the trial continued. The jury filed out.

I leaned in Vivian's direction. "Can I have a few minutes privately with my client?"

She said a few words to her team, and they left the room. The guard left as well. The only people in the courtroom were Tony, Quinn, Yolanda, Isaac, and me. I wanted to speak with Tony before we continued. He had arrived so late before the trial day began that I had not had the chance earlier.

Tony watched the door behind the guard close, then turned to me. "What are you going to say?"

"Nothing. I'm going to reserve our opening statement until after the close of the prosecution's case."

"What?"

The current philosophy is that the defense should make its opening as soon as possible, right after the prosecution's statement, to disrupt the bond that the district attorney had built with the jurors, and to plant questions into the jurors' minds that would keep them from accepting the State's case at face value.

Historically, it was more common for the defense to reserve its opening until after the prosecution finished its case. There were good reasons for that.

"Look, Tony, if I give our statement now, all I can say is that we don't see the evidence the way Vivian sees it. That's a weak start. When I do stand up to make your opening, I want to hit them with something hard and then follow it up with irrefutable evidence. I want to completely blow up the prosecution's case."

Isaac had scooted around the railing, and he was holding Tony's hand. "Does that mean you don't have any evidence?"

"What about all those other kids Oscar raped?" Tony asked.

"We looked at that. We can't put any of them in the area at the time of the murder."

"Yeah, but there were no eyewitnesses," Tony said. "The gun was planted in my car. I didn't have any gun powder on my hands when they tested. They can't prove I did it."

"I get that, Tony. It's a circumstantial case. But for a dramatic effect, something that's really going to grab the jurors, I need more. And that's the problem with rushing to trial." I held up my hand as Tony opened his mouth to launch an argument. "I completely understand the importance of getting to trial before the State had a chance to remand you back to jail where you were so badly beaten and might be killed the next time. I agree with you, and I support you. But that means we're still investigating."

The clerk entered the room. "Are we ready?"

"Fine," Tony said petulantly with a shoulder wag.

"We're ready," I said.

Isaac went back to his seat. Quinn left the courtroom to let Vivian know we were going back on record. The guard appeared, followed by the judge and the jury.

When everyone had settled, Judge Han asked, "Ms. Gould?"

I stood, touched my pearls, and spoke loud enough for everyone to hear me. "The defense reserves the right to make its opening statement."

The jurors looked around the room, confused.

"Ladies and gentleman," Judge Han said. "The defense has the right to reserve its opening statement until after the conclusion of the prosecution's case. You are not to draw any inferences from this reservation. Now, Ms. Thandi, you may begin your case."

Vivian stood. "The State calls Mrs. Brita Wenderholm."

THE PROSECUTION'S PARALEGAL ROSE from her chair at counsel table, walked down the aisle, and opened the door. I did not turn to watch the widow's entrance. Instead, I quickly scanned the jurors for their response as I heard her clomping to the front of the room. They were engaged, interested, curious.

The gate behind me swung open with a small thunk as the hinges resisted. Vivian was at the podium. She turned to greet the witness and gestured towards the witness box.

The judge said, "Please step forward, Mrs. Wenderholm."

The widow crossed the well, stepped up into the box and remained on her feet. She was wearing a plain knee-length black dress, gathered at the waist, with a narrow leather belt. Her pumps were black and well worn.

She shot a frightened look at me as she waited for further instructions. No surprise there. Witnesses are generally afraid of opposing counsel, having watched television courtroom dramas. They expected to be confronted by someone who was smarter than them and who would tear them apart while dozens of people witnessed their humiliation.

I had no intention of being aggressive with her. There is nothing to be gained by dissecting a grieving widow. The jury would hate me for it.

The clerk swore her in.

"Please be seated," the judge said. "You'll need to attach the little microphone in front of you on the witness stand to your dress."

Vivian began her examination of the witness. "Mrs. Wenderholm, are you the widow of Oscar Wenderholm?"

"I am."

"Do you have any children?"

"Two kids. I homeschool them."

"Mrs. Wenderholm, would you please tell the jurors about the events that brought us to court today?"

The objection to be made to this question was that it called for a narrative. Witnesses were not supposed to wander through their stories on the stand in case they sneak in inadmissible evidence such as a hearsay statement or speculation. They are supposed to respond to carefully tailored questions designed to elicit only admissible evidence.

But Vivian knew I wouldn't interrupt. It would be seen as an attack on a grieving widow.

Mrs. Wenderholm scanned the room one last time, then answered.

"I was in the kitchen ironing when I heard Oscar announce that he was leaving for work. I heard the door slam, then out of the corner of my eye, I saw his back as he went down the stairs. That was the last time I saw him alive."

She reached for the tissue box that was routinely kept on the stand and pulled a single sheet.

"It was around 2:30 pm. Oscar worked swing shift, four to midnight, and had to leave an hour and a half early to get to work because of the commute. I went back to my ironing, and then I saw a mustard-colored Gremlin pull up in front of our house real quick, like it was in a hurry, and then it parked."

"Are you sure the vehicle was a Gremlin?" Vivian asked.

"I had one in college. I was surprised there were any on the road anymore. Then I saw him get out."

Vivian bent to the lectern microphone. "By 'him,' who do you mean?"

"Anthony Paredes."

"Can you point Mr. Paredes out in the courtroom?"

"Him!" The widow thrusted her arm at Tony so violently, he jerked in response. All fourteen heads in the jury box turned in our direction. It was their opportunity to stare. Vivian's question had invited them to do so.

I patted his arm underneath the table to calm him. He gave my hand a squeeze.

"Should I go on?" Mrs. Wenderholm asked.

Vivian waited for the jurors to return their attention to the witness, then said, "Please continue."

"I heard arguing. So, I came out on the stoop to see what was going on. That's when I saw Anthony Paredes shouting at my husband."

At this point in her testimony during the bail hearing, Mrs. Wenderholm accused Tony of killing her husband and had been admonished by the judge. This time, she put her hands in her lap and waited for the next question.

"Would you please tell the jury what happened after you saw Mr. Paredes shouting at your husband?"

"I yelled at him. I said I'd called the police, and they were coming."

"Had you in fact called the police?" Vivian asked.

"No, I just said that to scare him off."

Sweater Man made a note in his legal pad, as did the Librarian, who was frowning. She didn't like the witness making an empty threat.

Vivian gave a small nod. "And what did Mr. Paredes do when you warned him that you had called the police?"

"He said, and I quote, 'I will kill you, Oscar. I will kill you.' Then he ran back to his car and drove away. The next morning, I woke up and realized Oscar hadn't come home. He didn't answer his phone. So, I went out to see if his truck was in the driveway. That's when I found my husband."

Vivian asked, "How did he appear?"

"Dead. That's how he appeared. He was dead."

Mrs. Wenderholm lifted a plastic cup half-filled with water that the clerk had put on the stand before court that morning. The witness' hand was trembling, and the water sloshed violently. It was because witnesses were nervous that the cup had been half full. Mrs. Wenderholm paused as if she was contemplating whether she would put it down again or try to drink. She brought up her other hand to stabilize the water, put it to her lips briefly, then slowly lowered the cup to the desktop.

The jury was riveted to her. The young female student and Amber Haley, the dog walker, seemed embarrassed by her difficulty with the cup and looked down at their own hands. Grizzled Man pushed himself to a stand and took a position in the back of the jury box. A few glanced over at Tony, then turned towards Vivian, waiting for the next question.

"Thank you, Mrs. Wenderholm. I just have a few more questions."

The widow nodded.

"Was this your first encounter with Anthony Paredes?"

"Hardly."

"When did you first became aware of the accused?"

"When he sued Oscar."

Every juror leaned towards the witness stand.

"Can you tell the jurors about the lawsuit?"

This was the second time Vivian had cued the witness to address the jury. The first time, when she began her testimony, Mrs. Wenderholm missed the cue and had fixed her attention on Vivian, which turned the jurors into an audience as if they were watching a play. Every trial lawyer wants the witness to establish a rapport with the jurors. That meant eye contact.

This time, the widow picked up on the cue. She shifted in the witness stand so she could face the jury box.

"Oscar used to teach at the Lafayette Academy. He also coached the chess club. Oscar had been a chess champion when he was younger. The Academy sought him out because they wanted a big-name player to draw students who wanted to compete. It was trying to build up its profile so it could take in large donations and raise the tuition."

From everyone I spoke to, Oscar had not been a champion. He barely made the team. I could have objected on the grounds of relevancy but that would have only antagonized the jury and the judge. Better to let the witness get through her story.

"After a few years, the school decided to go in a different direction. They weren't going to have a chess team anymore. They wanted to cut Oscar's pay because he wouldn't be coaching. He was teaching social studies and they offered him just the teacher's salary. Oscar refused and quit."

Again, that wasn't what I heard. But it well may have been what he had told her.

"The Academy gave him a letter of recommendation but, as it turned out, there isn't a market for chess coaches in the Bay area. We couldn't live on a teacher's salary, so Oscar got various jobs and coached chess on the side. Sometimes, he had to work two jobs at a time so we could make ends meet. He worked at a game store at the mall. He managed a school daycare program. He tutored high school students who were preparing for college exams."

All jobs where Oscar could access children.

Sweater Man glanced at Vivian, then at me. He got it. He recognized the typical pattern of a pedophile, short-term low-paying jobs around children where he could move on to another field easily when trouble arose.

But it remained to be seen how Sweater Man's comprehension of who Oscar was would impact his verdict. Would he be willing to accept another person could have reason to kill Oscar? Or, even if there were multiple suspects, would Sweater Man conclude that Tony had the most motive, so he was most likely guilty?

The widow continued. "Years after Oscar left the Academy, *he* sued."

"Do you mean the defendant, Anthony Paredes?" Vivian asked.

"The defendant, yes." Sputtering, the widow said, "He claimed Oscar abused him." Her eyes locked on Vivian's, she vibrated with anger.

"What was the outcome of the civil trial?"

Some attorneys object to every question their opponent poses in order to break up the testimony. Their theory is that fractured evidence will be harder for the jury to piece together.

I'm not one of those attorneys. I save my objections for when I have a fighting chance of winning. I wouldn't win a relevancy objection on this line of questioning. The judge would rule Oscar's abuse of Tony and the civil trial was relevant to Tony's motive to murder Oscar. Revenge.

I'd warned Tony this would be difficult testimony to hear. His knuckles were white as he gripped his armrest. Reliving the abuse had to be painful for him. I should know. Further, being reminded of the civil trial disaster would stoke his understandable fear that the judicial system could fail him again.

I laid a hand on top of Tony's. He relaxed a little.

Mrs. Wenderholm said, "The jury gave him an outrageous verdict, but the judge saw through it and, what do you call it, he set it aside. But by then, the damage was done. Our lives were ruined."

"Do you know why the judge set aside the verdict?"

"It was a miscarriage of justice, that's why!"

Sweater Man raised his eyebrows, surprised by the outburst. The Librarian scowled and pulled up her shawl. Amber Haley pinched her lower lip with her thumb and forefinger.

Brita Wenderholm's explanation was inaccurate, but deeply felt. The truth was, the defense uncovered jury misconduct during deliberations. A juror had researched Oscar online and discovered that he had been accused of sexual abuse years before he met Tony. That evidence had been ruled inadmissible because the Lafayette Academy was unaware of the prior accusations when it hired Oscar. So, as to the case against Lafayette Academy, this evidence was irrelevant.

As to case against Oscar, the prior abuses were considered character evidence and inadmissible. A party is not allowed to shore up their case with the argument that their opponent is a bad guy.

I might have gotten a new trial after the verdict was vacated if it hadn't been for what Tony did next.

"When you say your lives were ruined, what do you mean?"

"He." She pointed at Tony again. "Went on television and told the world that my husband was a serial child rapist."

During the civil trial, Tony had been outraged that the evidence of prior misconduct had not been admitted. I'd warned him about giving television interviews. He had heeded my advice until the defense filed their motion to set aside the verdict. Then he went on camera, standing on the sidewalk in front of his apartment, and told the reporter that Oscar indeed had abused children in schools before. The story went viral. When I tried to get a new trial, the judge ruled that the jury pool was tainted – the defense couldn't obtain a fair trial anywhere in California.

Most of the jurors glanced at Tony. Grizzled Man was standing alongside the jury box now, twisting his back this way and that. The frown he wore when he looked at the widow suggested he wasn't impressed by her distress. He was in real, physical pain.

The widow continued. "No one would hire Oscar to work with children after that. He ended up getting a job as a security guard. If it hadn't been for my brother helping us out, we would have been on the streets."

Vivian closed her notebook dramatically. "The State passes the witness."

Judge Han raised her head from her notetaking. "Ms. Gould?" She knew as well as I did that dissecting the outraged, grieving widow would win me no friends on the jury.

I stood. "The defense has no questions for the witness."

Chapter Nineteen

Maureen

THE JUDGE ANNOUNCED THE mid-day break. The jury was led back to the jury room where the take-out that had been ordered that morning would be served. The courtroom cleared except for the guard who waited to take Tony back to a holding cell. He moved to the exit door to give us some privacy.

I leaned into Tony. "Are you okay?"

He nodded and pulled a handful of tissues from a box which the clerk had provided to both counsel tables. He scraped his eyes, tilting his head back in a failed effort to staunch the tears. "I am so screwed."

I wanted to tell him he wasn't – that we'd win the trial and he'd go free. But I just didn't know. "It's early yet, Tony. Hang in there."

The guard pointed to the clock. He needed to get Tony down to the holding cells, get him fed, let him attend to his physical needs, and then back up to the courtroom in less than ninety minutes.

"I can't sit here any longer." Tony called to the guard, "Let's go."

YOLANDA PACKED OUR FILES to keep probing eyes from looking through them while we were on break.

Isaac was waiting in the hallway. "She was lying! How can you let her get away with it? Aren't you supposed to do something, like object?"

"I get you're worried, Isaac. But listen to me. This is a sensitive case. Just like you, Mrs. Wenderholm has strong feelings. Truth isn't black and white. It's more like a diamond, multi-faceted. So, while you're looking at one part of the gem, she's looking at another part. The truth, as we know it to be, is a harsh thing for her. Everyone – I mean everyone – rewrites their history to some degree. They reject what doesn't fit into their theory and focus on what does."

"Yeah, but –"

"What you need to understand – and this is very important – is that Mrs. Wenderholm's truth is not necessarily the jury's truth. Her world has been upended. She needs to think her life was happy and that Oscar was a good family provider before things changed for her. She blames that change on Tony, not Oscar. She needs to, for whatever reasons, to make herself feel better. I'm not going to convince the jury at this point that she's lying or delusional by aggressive cross-examination. And I'm not going to win points with the jury by beating up on a frightened woman."

"You're sure not going to win points with them by being nice to her."

"I may not, but so far, I haven't offended anyone."

Isaac jammed his fists into his pockets. "Fine. You're the expert."

"Thanks, I appreciate the vote of confidence. Now if you want to see Tony before we go back on record this afternoon, you should scoot down to the basement."

YOLANDA AND I MET Quinn at the office. She had left early to pick up our lunches: a veggie wrap for her, a turkey sandwich for Yolanda, and a protein shake for me. I had told Quinn that morning my stomach was too touchy to digest anything more solid.

"How do you feel?" Yolanda asked as we sat around the conference table, unpacking our meals.

"The first day is always the worst for the defense," I said. "Vivian knows how to put on a drama and she's coming through."

"Who's next?" Quinn asked.

"She'll put on the cops, the forensics, and the medical examiner."

Quinn asked, "What about the jailhouse snitch?"

"That will be her big dramatic final witness. Start big, end big, put the boring stuff in the middle."

"Did they teach you that in law school?" Yolanda looked skeptical.

"Trial advocacy, as a matter of fact. It's the primacy-recency effect. People tend to remember best what they heard first and last. The rest of it becomes a blur."

I sipped the smoothy. It tasted earthy. When I pulled off the lid, I saw that it was brown. Quinn had ordered it. I gave her a look.

"Carob," she said brightly. "It's antioxidant with inflammation reduction properties. Great for your carpal tunnel syndrome."

"Yum," I said. I had asked for chocolate.

Yolanda's oversized step counting watch buzzed. She pressed it, killing the noise. "Time to go back!"

Quinn gathered the lunch detritus and took it to the kitchen while Yolanda whispered to me, "Carpal tunnel syndrome?"

I whisked my fingers at her in a shooing gesture. "Later."

VIVIAN CALLED A HOMICIDE detective as her next witness, Detective Zimmerman. He was a friend of Jake's and gave me an apologetic look before his testimony began. I had no reason to resent him. He was doing his job.

He testified about arriving at the scene shortly after Mrs. Wenderholm called 911. Vivian had him identify photos. A long shot of the house from the street. The front door open. An ironing board visible in the kitchen window. Oscar's body on the lawn. He explained the blood splatter evidence was inconclusive as by the time the police arrived, a pair of paramedics had entered and traveled around the immediate area and destroyed what evidence there was.

The detective explained police diagrams. Tony's Gremlin parked on the street. Oscar standing on the lawn near the driveway. Tony standing on the sidewalk. Another diagram showed the bullet entry and exit with an arrow drawn to demonstrate the angle had been downwards as Oscar stood below Tony when the bullet was fired.

He testified Mrs. Wenderholm told her that she believed Tony had killed her husband and had told them about Tony's visit to the house the day before. They found Tony's Gremlin parked behind his apartment building, secured it while they waited for a search warrant which was quickly issued. When they asked Tony for the keys to the car, he told them it was open. He never locked his car, and the trunk lock was broken. Inside, they found the gun wrapped in Tony's sweatshirt in the hatch. They arrested Tony. He had no powder stains on his hands or any other clothes. The lack of powder stains could be explained. He might have worn gloves and other clothing which he had disposed of somewhere between Oscar's house and his apartment.

Tony was a night delivery driver. The police theory was that he had gone to Oscar's house in his delivery truck and shot him when Oscar arrived home from work. The deed took so little time that Tony finished his deliveries and returned his truck without anyone noticing a delay. Only one little old man down the street who had been up to visit the bathroom remembered hearing something like a gunshot in the early hours of the morning. Given the neighborhood, it was a common occurrence. The witness thought nothing of the noise and went back to bed.

Vivian's next witness was the medical examiner. He testified that the bullet had nicked the aorta causing the decedent to bleed out. Blow-ups of the autopsy were set up on easels in front of the jury. With a laser pointer, he directed the juror's attention to the entry and exit wounds.

The jury was enraptured by both the cop and the medical examiner. They leaned in as they testified. The notetakers wrote furiously in the legal pads balanced on their laps.

It was late in the day when the medical examiner was finished. Vivian didn't want to start another witness, only to have to break for the evening, so the judge let the jury go early.

After the room had cleared, I asked Tony how he felt. He said he was tired and in pain and wanted to go back to the hospital.

▼

THE NEXT DAY, VIVIAN put Robert Morgan, the night manager from Oscar's warehouse, on the stand. His testimony followed his affidavit exactly. Vivian ran the entire video once so that the jury could see the whole story then rewound it so that she could have him comment on particular events.

The first clip was Tony following Oscar into the parking lot when he stopped the Gremlin abruptly and the hatchback flew open.

"What does this footage show?"

"Oscar comes in driving his SUV, then right on his heels is this yellow Gremlin. I can't read the license plate number. Sorry, ma'am."

"How do you know that the SUV belonged to Oscar Wenderholm?"

"Cause he got out of it."

The jury snickered at Vivian's expense. I didn't. The problem with law is that you have to plug all the holes. Even if the question sounded stupid, the answer was important for the record.

She ran the video a few more seconds. "What happens here?"

"A man gets out of the Gremlin and starts screaming at Oscar."

"Was there audio?"

"No."

"How do you know he was screaming?"

"His arms are flying everywhere, and it looked like he was crying, so I just assumed."

"Can you identify that man for the jurors?"

Morgan jabbed his finger at Tony. "Him, that's him."

I glanced at my client. His head was bowed. He was picking at his cuticles.

Vivian advanced the film. "And how did Mr. Wenderholm respond to Mr. Paredes?"

"He was calm. Just kind of stood there and took it. You can see for yourself."

The video then showed Tony slamming his hatch lid, then jumping back into his Gremlin and speeding away.

When Vivian was finished with her direct cross examination, I told the court that we waived cross examination. I could hear Isaac rustling behind me. The judge shot him a frown. He settled down.

The judge dismissed the jury at just after 12:30 pm. The afternoon session would be out of the presence of the jury, just the judge, Vivian, and me reviewing jury instructions.

The guard was anxious to move Tony quickly. If we were going to take testimony in the afternoon, the judge would have dismissed everyone earlier, giving the guard plenty of time to transfer Tony to a holding cell and get his own lunch before the afternoon session. But as it was, the long morning disrupted the guard's schedules. He wasn't being petty. Guarding prisoners well is dependent upon routine. Every disruption is another opportunity for an escape or an attack or a suicide.

Before the door swung close behind the last juror, the guard approached us. I held up a finger to stay his advance as I leaned towards Tony. "Are you okay?"

He nodded. When he came in that morning, he was unusually subdued. To me, he looked depressed.

I said, "it's not over until the fat lady sings. Remember that."

He snorted. "What fat lady?"

"Ma'am?" the guard said.

I patted Tony's arm. "We'll talk later."

As the guard rolled Tony out of the room, Isaac, who had lingered, turned on me.

"Why aren't you doing something? Object, or ask questions, or something?"

"What would you have me do, Isaac? The prosecutor is playing it safe. She's putting on absolutely solid evidence. There was no point in cross-examining the witnesses. If I bored the jury because they already heard everything, they will resent me, and in turn Tony, for wasting their time."

The second reason not to cross a witness is that would engrave that evidence into the juror's minds.

I didn't want to explain the second reason to Isaac. If I mentioned it, he would ask for a recitation of every fact and then he'd want to argue the significance of each or the proof or the counterproof. I knew my case. I didn't need to walk through it in minute detail with Isaac.

But Isaac had a valid concern. As people learn the facts of a new story, they need to organize it somehow. At first, their theories are flexible. But at certain point, each person begins rejecting evidence that doesn't fit. It's human nature.

The trick was to get your facts into their heads before their minds are made up. That's why most defense attorneys give an opening statement at the beginning of the trial. That's why effective cross-examination can help shape their opinions.

And that is why I was feeling insecure at this point in the trial. I had nothing to give to the jurors. If we were going to win, I'd have to come up with a giant surprise, something that would blow Vivian's case completely out of the water.

It was Tuesday. The jury deliberations would begin early next week. I had five or six days to come up with that bombshell.

No problem.

It was my night to cook, so I gave Quinn my credit card and asked her to pick up something. She brought home with Mexican food and a six-pack of Dos Equis.

When I came out of my bedroom, showered, and changed into fresh sweatpants and t-shirt, Jake handed me a beer, poured into a lager glass in keeping with Quinn's sensibilities. If it had been him and me, we would have picnicked in front of the television, drinking beer from the bottle.

"Dinner is served!" Quinn called as she brought out two plates of enchiladas, rice, and beans, and placed them on the table. A bowl of taco chips was already set out alongside salsa and guacamole.

Jake and I took our seats while Quinn returned with the third plate and her own glass of beer.

Dinner smelled fantastic, savory, spicy, and warm. I was starving. Because of the short lunch hour before I had to go back to the courtroom for jury instruction review, I'd picked up the last tray of dried-out California rolls in the basement canteen and gobbled them down along with a cup of rank and lukewarm institutional coffee, while sitting on a wobbly chair at a sticky table. It filled my stomach but only just.

We dug into the Mexican food. It was delicious.

"Where'd you get this?" Jake asked.

"Soy Vegano, the new restaurant down the street," Quinn said.

"Vegano?" I asked.

"It means 'vegan' in Spanish."

Jake and I exchanged looks. Quinn was trying to improve our eating habits. I was happy with the way I ate, and Jake was a steak and potatoes man. But we could adapt. Inviting a new person into the family meant adjustments.

"I like it," I said. "We should observe meatless Monday."

Jake frowned at me.

"We'll keep taco Tuesday and pizza Friday and Italian Sunday. One day a week won't hurt us. It'll expand our horizons."

Quinn added, "Vegan is good for you. A veggie diet has anti-inflammatory properties that will help with your wrists."

Jake's frown deepened. Not only was Quinn trying to make us healthier, but it was because I'd lied to her about having carpal tunnel syndrome. I felt guilty enough for deceiving the child who cared so deeply for me so Jake's objection to being force-fed refried beans wasn't as impressive as he'd hoped.

"You polished off that enchilada pretty fast, Jake," I observed. "Quinn, is there any more?"

While she carried his plate into the kitchen for a refill, I mouthed to him "Suck it up." He mouthed back, "You owe me."

I was raised Irish and Catholic and as far as I was concerned, anyone who wasn't Irish Catholic was a rank amateur at the guilt game. I signed the tiny violin gesture in mock sympathy as Quinn was returning with Jake's second helping.

Since I got out of cooking dinner, I volunteered to clean the kitchen, which meant trashing the carryout boxes, and storing what little was leftover. By the time I was finished, Quinn had spread the trial notebook out on the dinner table and opened her laptop. We were preparing for the testimony of the jailhouse snitch, a man named Javier Fuentes.

I set a cup of herbal tea next to Quinn, then sat and placed my cup of coffee far enough away that I wouldn't accidentally knock it over and soak the files.

The trial notebook, a three-ring binder Yolanda had assembled, was open to the tab marked "Javier Fuentes." The first document was the witness' typed statement which was signed in a childlike signature. It read:

> My name is Javier Fuentes-Salazar. I make this statement from my personal knowledge. I met Anthony Paredes when we were both in jail. He had just been arrested. I brought his lunch to his cell. He asked me if I had seen the news on TV. I asked him, what news. He said about him getting busted for killing a guy named Oscar. I said no, I didn't see it. He told me that he hated this Oscar guy and he (Anthony Paredes) was glad Oscar was dead.

Next was a copy of Mr. Fuentes-Salazar's current charges, a parole violation. His parole officer had searched his apartment and found a gun and a modest amount of marijuana. The gun was the big problem. Javier was previously convicted of drug dealing so he wasn't allowed to own firearms. He had a hearing coming up in three weeks on the parole violation.

"Are you in the court database?" I asked Quinn.

"I just pulled up Javier's cases."

"How many?"

Her eyes widened. "Lots." She consulted the legal pad where she'd written Javier's full name, social security number, and date of birth. "He got traffic tickets almost constantly since he was eighteen years old plus a couple of assaults, two reckless driving, one DUI, and the one drug charge."

Lots of traffic tickets means that the cops were keeping an eye on him. It could mean they suspected him of illegal activity and were hoping to see something in his car that would justify a search. Or there could have been another reason.

"Check the dates of these tickets," I said.

Quinn ran her eyes down the screen. "It was like once a month."

Jake came out of the kitchen with another beer on his way to watch television. "He's an informant."

Quinn looked up. "How can you tell?"

"That's how cops keep tabs on their snitches, by pulling them over. It gives the cop an opportunity to talk to him. If anyone sees it, he can claim he's just getting hassled, but because he's so smart, he didn't get busted. Builds his street cred."

"But he got charged with drug dealing."

"He probably got caught dead to rights in a big bust with several co-defendants. If he was let off scot-free, the others would know that he's a snitch. So, he had to go down for something. Bet the prosecution gave him a nice deal too but not so nice that his buddies would suspect."

Jake kissed me on the top of the head, then walked down to our bedroom where he could watch TV without disturbing us. Germaine Greer trotted in front of him, anticipating some private time with her favorite human.

Quinn asked, "Do you think they planted Javier in the jail to get a confession from Tony?"

"Nah. Tony's small fry. I think it was just convenient for Javier to meet Tony and then he saw an opportunity he could exploit."

"Can you get him to admit he's a snitch?"

"Unlikely. He needs to save face. If the other prisoners found out that he's been cooperating, they'd kill him."

"How would they find out?"

"The guards gossip. Sooner or later, the information would get back to a crooked prison guard, someone who's on a gang's payroll. Fuentes won't admit he's a snitch, but I can paint a picture for the jury that would suggest he's lying."

Human nature makes people suspicious of a story that is sold. Whether it's sold for money or traded for concessions, people wonder why – if the story is true – it's only given up in an exchange. Shouldn't the truth be free to everyone? When a story is sold, there is an incentive to lie to increase the story's value. The more money given, the greater the incentive. The greater the incentive, the more false the lie.

It was good stuff, but it wouldn't devastate the prosecution's case.

In the world of criminal defense, there are only a few strategies. One strategy is "death by a thousand cuts" when the defense attorney attacks every iota of evidence as inaccurate or taken out of context or a flat-out lie. So far, all the testimony Vivian had put on was solid so I couldn't run this defense.

Another defense strategy is "the other dude did it," commonly referred to as "ODDI." That's effective when there are two suspects. Even though Tony insisted he didn't do it, we didn't have someone else to offer up.

At this point in the trial, our defense was "it wasn't me" which is best used when there is a strong alibi. And, we didn't have that.

I needed that bombshell.

Chapter Twenty

Maureen

On Wednesday morning, Javier Fuentes-Salazar wore chinos, a white button-down shirt, canvas deck shoes, and sweat socks, no doubt supplied by the State of California, as he stood to be sworn in by the clerk. He was small and skinny. His black hair was buzz cut. He would have blended into a crowd if it weren't for the fading jailhouse tats on his fingers.

He knew his way around the courtroom, evident in how comfortably he rose from the pew when his name was called, casually opened that gate without being told to come forward, strutted across the well and posed by the witness stand with his right hand raised. For all the jury knew, he could be just another witness, if it wasn't for the extra guard at the back door and two new guards by the front door. When an unshackled prisoner is wandering around a courtroom, anything could – and has – happened. The prisoner may make a break for freedom or assault someone if he gets close enough.

As Fuentes held up his hand, Tony hissed in my ear, "I've never seen him before in my life." Sweater Man must have overheard; he turned his head towards us. Judge Han caught the movement and shot me a cautionary look. I pointed to the legal pad in front of Tony. He wrote, "I don't know this guy. Never seen him."

After Javier was sworn in, sat down, and clipped on his microphone, Vivian opened her direct examination. "Mr. Fuentes, were you recently incarcerated in the San Francisco jail?"

"Yes, ma'am." Fuentes voice was quiet. His chin was lowered in a submissive gesture, the effect of which made his brown eyes appear large and sincere as he focused on Vivian.

Several of the jurors pushed back in their seats, trying to get as far away from him as possible.

"On what charges were you incarcerated?"

"Parole violation."

"Do you know the defendant, Anthony Paredes?"

"I don't really know him, ma'am, but I met him once when I was serving lunch to the prisoners in their cells."

"Did you have a conversation with Mr. Paredes?"

"Yeah. He asked me if I'd seen him on TV I was like, oh big man, why would you be on TV? He said he'd gotten busted for killing some guy named Oscar and it should be all over the news. I hadn't seen it, so I told him so. Then he said, out of nowhere, I'm glad he's dead. He said Oscar was a baby rapist and the world was a better place without him."

Sweater Man frowned at the witness and made a few notes. The Librarian appeared to be taking his testimony down verbatim. Amber Haley had pulled her long hair across her face, like a curtain, and had slouched down in her seat.

I could hear Isaac moving around in the row behind me. He'd want me to do something. I could have objected on the grounds that the statements didn't constitute an explicit confession and therefore were inadmissible. Then Vivian and I would get into an argument about whether they were an implied confession. Meanwhile the jury would know that I was afraid of this evidence, and they would pay extra attention to it. And I'd lose the argument and the statements would go in.

So, I ignored Isaac.

"Did you report this conversation to anyone?" Vivian asked.

"Yes, ma'am. I called my lawyer."

"Then what happened?"

"Some cops pulled me into an interview room. My lawyer was there. And I told them what Mr. Paredes said."

"Were you honest?"

"Yes, ma'am. Absolutely."

"Did you tell them everything Mr. Paredes said?"

"Every word."

"Did you make any of these statements up?"

Javier lifted his head. "Like did I lie?"

"Exactly. Did you lie?"

He scoffed. "No, ma'am."

Tony picked up the pen and scratched "LIAR" in big heavy letters. Sweater Man glanced in our direction.

Vivian asked, "Were you promised anything in exchange for your testimony here today?"

Javier squinted at Vivian when he said, "Like what?"

"Like leniency in sentencing?"

"Absolutely not. No, ma'am."

"Do you currently have a plea agreement to any outstanding charges?"

"Not that I know of. You'd have to ask my lawyer."

"Thank you. The State passes the witness."

I rose as Vivian cleared her papers off the lectern. Tony tugged at my sleeve while at the same time stabbing the legal pad where he had written "LIAR." I made eye contact with him and nodded my understanding.

Funnily enough, opening with a question like "isn't it true you're a liar?" doesn't often elicit a confession.

I spread my notes across the lectern, touched the O'Shaughnessy pearl necklace for good luck, and said, "Good morning, Mr. Fuentes."

Hostile witnesses hate being nice to the lawyer cross-examining them. You can tell a lot about how they react. If they're polite, they'll greet me in return. If they feel like the greeting is a power move, which it is, they'll try to take the upper hand.

Fuentes was one of the latter. "I'm sitting in a witness box. Don't know what so good about that." He smirked and scanned the jurors to see if they appreciated his humor. I'm sure back in prison, he'd get a few back slaps and guffaws, but here, the jurors' faces had set up like stone.

"Mr. Fuentes, would you please describe for the jury the reason why you are in jail?'

The witness turned to Vivian, who was now seated, his eyebrows lifted in a "do I have to?" expression. Sweater Man caught the meaning and watched Vivian for a response. She nodded.

Fuentes answered, "Parole violation, like I said."

"And you were on parole for what conviction?"

"Conspiracy to distribute a controlled substance."

"In plain English, that would be drug dealing. Is that right?"

"If you say so."

"What drugs were involved?"

"Meth."

I flipped through my binder and found the exact drugs he was caught with. "Actually, it was methamphetamine, oxycodone, and fentanyl, is that correct?"

"Whatever."

Sweater Man had crossed his ankle over his knee and leaned back as he took notes. He had settled into his role as a juror.

"What quantity of drugs were involved in the conspiracy?"

Fuentes looked at Vivian again. "Do I have to answer that?"

She nodded.

Not satisfied, Fuentes looked up at the judge. "Really, do I have to answer? Don't I have like a right against self-incrimination?"

Judge Han said, "Mr. Fuentes, Ms. Gould is merely asking you what you were convicted of, not what you did. Yes, you need to answer her question."

"It doesn't seem right. I thought I was here to talk about him," Javier said, jerking his head at Tony.

"Please answer the question, Mr. Fuentes," Judge Han said.

The witness pushed himself back into a corner on the witness stand, bracing himself against the desk, cocked his head at an angle, and then said, "Three ounces of meth, an ounce of oxy, and an ounce of fentanyl. Happy now?"

I asked, "Were there other individuals named in the conspiracy?"

He jerked his chin upwards. "I'm guessing you know the answer to that."

I did. Quinn had printed out the indictment and it was on the lectern in front of me.

"We need your testimony. How about this? Instead of naming these people, would you confirm for me –," here I tapped the indictment eight times for each name listed, "there were eight other individuals indicted with you."

"If you say so."

"And all of these other individuals were sentenced in federal court whereas you were sentenced in state court, is that right?"

Fuentes' eyes narrowed. "So what?"

"You received a considerably lighter sentence than any of your co-conspirators because you were sentenced in the state system instead of the federal system, is that right?"

"You'd have to talk to my lawyer."

"Did you go to trial?"

"Lady, my life is one long trial." Another smirk, another short glance at the jurors for validation. They weren't amused.

I repeated the question. "Before you were convicted, did you go to trial?"

Fuentes said something garbled.

"I'm sorry, we need an audible response for the recording."

He shot another look at the judge. By now, he had given up on Vivian rescuing him.

"No." He spat out the word. "I pled up."

"So, let me get this straight. You were indicted with eight other people, all of whom received substantially more severe sentences than you, longer jail time with larger fines, because you were prosecuted in state court instead of federal court and because you pled up. Is that right?"

"Yeah, like so what? That's how things are done."

"Mr. Fuentes, were you given this sweetheart deal because of your lengthy history as an informant?"

Fuentes shot to his feet. "I don't have to answer that."

Amber Haley recoiled. The Social Worker was sitting next to her and reached across her protectively. The male nurse, who now wore jeans and a quarter-zip sweater, sat up, suddenly alert.

Fuentes ripped off the microphone and strode across the courtroom to the prosecution's table. He jabbed a finger in Vivian's face, shouting, "That wasn't the deal."

Tony pushed away from our table, pinning his chair against a railing. He was curled up in a ball. I moved in front of him in case Fuentes went for him next.

Two guards, one on each side, grabbed Fuentes, spun him around, and flattened him on the carpet.

Judge Han was on her feet. "This court stands in recess. Bailiff, remove the jury."

Sweater Man raised his eyebrows at me in a "surprised/not surprised" look. Amber Haley teared up. The Librarian looked like she had just smelled something foul. The group rose and filed out of the room.

Judge Han said, "Guards, remove Mr. Fuentes from my courtroom. Counsel, we will meet again in fifteen minutes outside the presence of the jury." With that, she swept out of the door behind the bench.

Vivian stalked out of the room with her associate and paralegal in her wake. I assumed she was on her way to the holding cells to have a heart-to-heart talk with Mr. Fuentes.

"What just happened?" I heard Isaac, sitting behind me, ask.

"Can we have a moment?" I said to the one remaining guard.

His neck was stiff from the adrenalin rush following Fuentes' outburst. "Sorry, ma'am, I need to be where I can see him."

I spun Tony's chair around so he could see Isaac. Tony was trembling and pale.

I held up a finger, reminding my team not to speak. Very quietly, I said, "When Quinn researched Mr. Fuentes, she found a history that suggests he's a snitch, and has been for years. It's admissible because it goes to his character for truthfulness insomuch as he has an incentive for currying favor with the prosecution, because they have him in prison which means he's more likely to lie or embellish to save his own skin."

I'd fallen into legalese because I was stressed. "Sorry, guys, did you understand all that?" They nodded.

I looked over my shoulder. The guard watched us from the far corner.

I continued. "In order for his testimony to be admitted, he must submit to cross examination. The prosecutor knows this. If he doesn't answer my questions, his testimony will be stricken from the record. He's her star witness. They had a case before he popped up, but it was strictly circumstantial. Now, they're worse off than if they hadn't put him on, because if the judge instructs the jury to ignore his testimony, it looks like the prosecution got caught playing dirty."

"They did," Isaac said. "That's exactly what they're doing."

From the defendant's point-of-view, using snitches is dirty dealing. But the prosecution figures they'll use what they have and leave it to the defense attorney to prove there's something wrong with the evidence.

"What happens next?" Tony asked, his voice cracking. He shuddered, on the verge of tears. Yolanda's hand came forward with a small package of tissues, which he accepted. He pulled all of them out in one clump and spread them across his eyes as he began to sob.

"Let's see if Fuentes will get back on the stand," I said.

Chapter Twenty-One

Maureen

"Mr. Fuentes refuses to continue." Vivian told Judge Han.

That was unexpected. I figured Vivian would have convinced Fuentes that it was in his best interests to cooperate in order to salvage whatever deal was hanging over his head.

Judge Han blinked twice. "Very well. Will the defense make an application?"

Usually, a defense attorney would ask the judge to strike the witness' testimony because it would leave less evidence in the record if the case went up on appeal. But what good would that do? The jury had already heard it. And there would only be an appeal if Tony was convicted, which means he'd go back to jail, and it was unlikely he'd live long enough to see his conviction reversed.

"I need to discuss this with my client, Your Honor. We didn't have our lunch break. If the court would give us another hour to grab something and meet, I hope to give you a response this afternoon."

"Very well. One hour. I'll expect your application at that time and then we'll proceed with the state's evidence. Court is adjourned."

Vivian and her crew left the courtroom while I arranged with the guard to have Tony put into an attorney-client meeting room. As he was wheeled out, I turned to Yolanda and Quinn. "Please pick up the usual for Tony, get me whatever you can find, and get yourselves something. See you downstairs in fifteen minutes." Tony's usual was egg salad sandwich. He had eaten those every day of our first trial when we sued Oscar Wenderholm for the assault. It seemed so long ago.

To Isaac, I said, "we'll get your lunch too. Let Yolanda know what you want. But I can't let you in the meeting room with us. It's a work session. I'm sorry."

Twenty minutes later, we were unpacking our lunches at a small table in the conference room. As was his habit, Tony crumpled a napkin in his right fist to use while he was eating.

"Egg salad, you remembered." Tony smiled when he looked up at Yolanda.

She made a pretense of handing him napkins in case the guard outside the window was watching and patted him on the hand.

I opened my wrapper. Hummus filled pita bread with lots of sprouts. Quinn must have ordered. I hope Tony enjoyed garlic breath. Quinn handed me a plastic juice bottle that contained something green. The label read "wheatgrass." I broke off the cap and took a swig. It burned. When I looked over at my daughter, she was beaming.

"I don't get it," Tony said. "What happened?"

"Fuentes won't continue with the cross-examination, so we need to decide how to handle that. I asked the judge for more time so we could talk about it. It's your case and your life so you should make the decision."

"Here are your choices, Tony. We can ask to have Fuentes' testimony stricken from the record and the judge will give an instruction to the jury to ignore it. Or we can let the testimony stand and ask the judge for an instruction that it could take into consideration his refusal to complete his testimony as evidence of his lack of trustworthiness."

"Will she tell them he was lying?"

"She won't say that. It's the jury's purview to decide who is telling the truth."

"So, what good does it do to leave it in?"

"If we leave it in, it gives me the chance to argue in closing that he is a liar. The judge can't say that, but I can."

"The jury already heard what he said. They can't unhear it. I don't see the point in getting it taken out. What would you do if you were me?"

"To tell you the truth, Tony, it's a difficult decision. A lawyer playing it safe would ask to have the testimony stricken. A standard argument on appeal is that the prosecution introduced insufficient evidence to support a guilty verdict. If Fuentes' testimony is stricken, all they have is the gun in your car and your behavior in the days leading up to Oscar's death."

"But I didn't have any gunpowder on my hands."

"I know that."

"And the gun didn't have my fingerprints on it."

"I know that too. We'll point all of this out to the jury in closing."

"What's this about my behavior?"

"Some people might conclude you were stalking Oscar because you showed up at his house and workplace."

"Only because I wanted to talk to him, to tell him to stay away from kids."

"I get that, Tony."

"I never talked to Fuentes. I never said that to him, that I was glad Oscar was dead. I want to tell the jury what really happened."

My ears started buzzing, a sign my blood pressure had just shot up. I touched the O'Shaughnessy pearls and took a swig of the wheatgrass, just to slow down the conversation. When I had composed myself, everyone was staring at me.

"Are you saying you want to testify?" I asked.

"Absolutely. It's my life and my story. You keep saying that. And I want the jurors to hear my story from me."

"Let's take a minute and talk about that, okay?"

Tony's eyes narrowed. "Fine."

"Vivian will have a ton of cross-examination for you. It will be painful. She's going to bait you. She'll try to make you angry, to show the jury that you lose self-control. If you fall for it, it won't look good."

"How bad could it be?" Tony's voice was rising. "Any worse than being raped by a grown man? Worse than being expelled? Worse than being treated like low life by your own parents? How about going to court and telling your story and having it plastered all over the media and then losing the case? Then getting arrested in my own home? Worse than nearly getting beaten to death?" He was sputtering, breadcrumbs spewing from his mouth.

A guard strolled past the window.

I wiped the spit-soaked crumbs from my face with a napkin. "Just like that, Tony. If you behave like that on the stand, the jury could take it the wrong way. Do you want to risk it?"

"My life. My story. You said I get to decide."

"That's right."

"I'll get to tell the jury I never met that Fuentes guy, right?"

"Yes. But just so you understand, if you are convicted, the appeals court will never overturn the verdict because of insufficiency of evidence. The jury has the right to decide who's lying and who is telling the truth. If you testify, they could decide it's you who lied and convict you. The combination of your testimony and Fuentes' testimony would be more than sufficient to support their verdict."

Tony threw a crumpled napkin down on the table. "Maureen, if I'm convicted, it won't matter. They're going to kill me."

WE WERE BACK IN the courtroom with Tony at my side. Isaac, Quinn, and Yolanda behind us, Vivian and her crew at their table, the judge on the bench and the jury box empty.

Judge Han said, "Before I bring back the jury, we need to hear from defense counsel regarding Mr. Fuentes' refusal to complete his examination."

I stood. "Your Honor, my client requests the court to give a midtrial instruction to the jury regarding witness credibility."

"That's it?" Judge Han was surprised.

"To be clear, Your Honor, we are not asking for the testimony to be stricken from the record."

The judge took a long look at Tony. He returned her gaze.

"Ms. Thandi, the State's response?"

Vivian stood. "The State has no objection."

"Very well. Madam Clerk, call the jury back."

As the jurors filed in, they scanned the room. The last thing they saw before they left was two guards smashing Javier Fuentes into the carpet. He was gone and the witness stand was empty. They had left during high drama and returned to a quiet courtroom. They had been cooped up in the jury room for hours with strict instructions not to discuss the case. They weren't allowed access to their cell phones or television. They must have been bored out of their minds and curious as to what had happened.

Judge Han sensed their mood. After they settled in their chairs, she said, "Ladies and gentlemen, you were kept for an unusually long period of time and for that I apologize. But it couldn't be helped. Sometimes during a trial, unexpected events occur which must be dealt with outside the presence of the jury. This was one of those occasions. We are back on record now and you will see that Mr. Fuentes is no longer in the courtroom. He will not be returning. I will now give you an instruction on witness credibility."

Judge Han flipped open a binder and began reading aloud. "You alone must judge the credibility or believability of the witnesses. In deciding whether testimony is true and accurate, use your common sense and experience. You must judge the testimony of each witness by the same standards, setting aside any bias or prejudice you may have. You may believe all, part, or none of any witness's testimony.

"Consider the testimony of each witness and decide how much of it you believe. In evaluating a witness's testimony, you may consider anything that reasonably tends to prove or disprove the truth or accuracy of that testimony. Among the factors that you may consider are: What was the witness's behavior while testifying? Was the witness's testimony influenced by a factor such as bias or prejudice, a personal relationship with someone involved in the case, or a personal interest in how the case is decided? What was the witness's attitude about the case or about testifying? Has the witness been convicted of a felony? Has the witness engaged in other conduct that reflects on his or her believability? Was the witness promised immunity or leniency in exchange for his or her testimony?"

I watched the jurors as they listened. Amber Haley hid behind her curtain of hair. It was difficult to see if she was taking anything in. Sweater Man leaned forward slightly, his pen poised on paper to take notes, but he was so absorbed that he didn't. The Librarian sat in a formal pose, knees together, legs crossed at the ankle, but she was more relaxed than some of the others. Her job must provide great opportunities for people watching, during which time, she would have quietly developed her own theories about human behavior.

The judge closed her notebook. "We will now resume with taking of the evidence. Ms. Thandi, please call your next witness."

Vivian stood. "Your Honor, the State of California rests its case."

Irritation settled on Judge Han's face, her muscles tight, her nostrils flaring slightly. The jury was going to get sent out again after only five minutes in the courtroom. The State had promised at the beginning of the trial it would take the entire day with its case but apparently Fuentes was its last witness.

Instead of ending big, Vivian ended with a sputter, but I'd been around long enough not to try to divine whether the jury would convict or acquit based upon one moment. Hopefulness or paranoia can lead to mistakes.

Judge Han composed herself before she turned back to the jury. "As you have heard, the State has rested its case. At this point in the trial, the court must entertain motions from the attorneys. I'm afraid I must return you to the jury room."

There was an audible groan from Grizzled Man, who walked with an obvious limp. Getting up out of his chair was an ordeal every time. The Librarian looked resigned.

Amber Haley's head whipped back and forth to the older jurors. When they rose, she stood too. The bailiff opened the back door, and they filed out again.

It's protocol for the defense to move to dismiss the case at the end of the prosecution's presentation. When the door was firmly closed, Judge Han said, "Ms. Gould?"

I stood. "Your Honor, the defense moves the court for judgment of acquittal. The prosecution's case is flimsy at best. There is no evidence connecting Mr. Paredes to the scene, or any evidence putting him in the vicinity at the time of Mr. Wenderholm's death. His fingerprints were not found on the gun. There were no fingerprints at all on the weapon, which suggests that someone wiped the gun before planting it in Mr. Paredes' vehicle. There was no evidence of gun powder on his hands when he was arrested. All the State has is evidence of Mr. Paredes' understandable dislike for the decedent and a gun, which it can't tie to him."

Behind me, I could hear Isaac stirring again. Out of the corner of my eye, I could see Tony locked onto my every word. I hadn't anticipated that Vivian would rest early, so I hadn't had a chance to talk to Tony about making the motion for acquittal. If I had the chance, I would have warned him not to get his hopes up.

Judge Han said, "Motion denied."

"But –." It was Tony.

Judge Han interrupted. "Mr. Paredes, please allow your attorney to speak on your behalf. Ms. Gould, you reserved opening statement. I realize events moved more quickly than we had anticipated, but are you prepared to go forward today?"

Judge Han was worried about wasting the jury's time. But I needed to reorganize after this day's events. And because this was a criminal trial with my client's liberty, and life, on the line, his need for adequate representation outweighed the juror's convenience.

"I'm sorry, Your Honor, we are not."

"Very well. Madam Clerk, please send the jury home for the day. We will resume in the morning."

Chapter Twenty-Two

Rick

UMBERTO PROVIDED HIS OWN apartment for Rick's dates with Dimitri. If anyone spotted Rick, it could be explained that he was visiting his campaign manager. Every time Rick arrived, Dimitri was always there waiting for him, with a warm, cooked dinner, something French or Greek

On their first date, they didn't eat until midnight.

As Rick got to know Dimitri, he fell more deeply in love. Dimitri had been an orphan, too. He had immigrated from Greece to live with family, but he didn't fit in. He had worked in their restaurant, learned to cook, just as Rick had worked in a dealership and learned to sell cars. Dimitri worked his way through college, getting a degree in hospitality, which is how he got his job at the Hotel Blanc.

He was a fan of the old horror and sci-fi movies that were Rick's favorites. After their lovemaking, they'd lounge in front of the television watching shows like *King Kong* or *The Creature from the Black Lagoon*.

Soon, Dimitri began to anticipate Rick's needs. He made Rick's favorite drinks. He cooked meals to cater to Rick's favorite foods. He knew when Rick wanted to be loved.

They fit together. More and more, Rick pictured a future with Dimitri by his side.

RICK ENTERED THE STAGE, holding hands with Appollonia, as Foster Heiki and his slick lawyer wife entered from the opposite wing, and the audience cheered. Rick pulled Appollonia to him in an embrace as they waved to the crowd. She wrapped her arm around his waist and gave him a kiss on the cheek. Out of the corner of his eye, he could see Heiki and his wife waving too.

Appollonia had done everything that was asked of her. She had gone to teas with women's groups. She had read books to the patients in children's hospital wings. She had stood by his side and played the loving wife at every event. It felt wrong, plotting to get rid of her after the election, but his new life with Dimitri awaited him. Rick would make sure that she had plenty of money for her future. It was only fair.

The moderator, Ned O'Brien, a public television news commentator in an off-the-rack suit with barber shop clipped graying hair, walked onto center stage, and palmed the air to quiet the audience.

"Ladies and gentlemen, allow me to welcome you to a very exciting evening. This will be the only debate that takes place for the eleventh district senate race. Please hold your applause as I introduce, Foster Heiki, the incumbent, and his challenger, Rick Stevens."

The crowd didn't hold their applause. Heiki's name was met with polite clapping, but when Rick was announced, his fans hooted and clapped for so long that O'Brien had to signal them again to quiet down. Rick glanced off stage to see Umberto applaud as he clasped his cell phone under his elbow. He looked pleased and gave Rick a nod. One of the Dum Dee twins was by Umberto's side. The other was standing in the back of the auditorium, like an usher on steroids. Both twins wore earpieces.

Dimitri wasn't in the building, but he promised to watch the debate on television. Rick wanted him there, but Umberto was adamant. He said that if Rick left Appollonia after the election, amateur fact checkers would examine every online photo looking for Dimitri and Rick together so they could spread smutty stories of marital infidelity. Rick responded that it was not *if* he left Appollonia, but when. Rick deserved happiness like every other person.

The house lights dimmed, the stage lights brightened, and three little red lights burned in the darkened auditorium as television cameras went online.

O'Brien thanked Mrs. Heiki and Mrs. Stevens for joining the candidates on stage and wished them goodbye for now. He gestured for the candidates to come forward.

O'Brien read from a card. "On my left is the incumbent, Foster Heiki. Senator Heiki has been in office for two terms and was one of the youngest senators to have been elected. He has two master's degrees, one in public management and one in business. Before his election, he was on staff with his predecessor, Senator Avril Bergeron—"

The audience on Heiki's side of the auditorium clapped with enthusiasm. Avril Bergeron had been in office for decades before California enacted term limits. Often in the news, he was praised for how much government money he brought back home to San Francisco.

Heiki came to life with the mention of Bergeron's name. He clapped along with his supporters and smiled genuinely. In photos, Heiki looked like a boring intellectual. But when he smiled and adjusted his retro gold wire rimmed glasses, his shoulders swayed just enough that suggested confidence. He was sexier than Rick had given him credit for. Not as sexy as Dimitri, but Heiki would appeal to many.

"And now for our challenger," O'Brien announced as the applause died down. "Richard Stevens, born and raised in the Bay Area, successful businessman, has thrown his hat into the ring. Give him a big round of applause."

Rick didn't have any degrees. Umberto had planted stories about the sad circumstances of Rick's orphaning, the tragic garbage truck accident that killed his father, the heart disease that took his mother, and how Rick had pulled himself up by the bootstraps, starting as a car detailer and working his way up to own a franchise of dealerships.

Heiki's fans went silent while Stevens's made noise like they were at a hockey game. It was embarrassing. Rick wished his followers were intellectual and well-behaved, but a vote was a vote, and these people were, according to Umberto, "Rick's base."

O'Brien announced, "Gentleman, to your podiums."

When they were in position, O'Brien said, "The first question will be answered by Senator Heiki, then Mr. Stevens will have an opportunity to respond. Senator, San Francisco's infrastructure is in an alarming state of decay. How do you see your role in obtaining funds for improvements?"

Heiki adjusted his retro glasses. "Thanks, Ned. That's an excellent question. First, my record speaks for itself. I co-sponsored every bill last session to appropriate funds for infrastructure. Second, it's a difficult topic to address, but San Francisco must take responsibility for how it handles money. There is waste. The city has spent money on ill-considered projects, awarded contracts to irresponsible vendors, and more than one department is under investigation. This mishandling of money must come to a stop."

Heiki's fans applauded politely.

O'Brien said, "Mr. Stevens, what is your response?"

Rick and Umberto had rehearsed this answer for a week.

"First, allow me to thank you for hosting this event, Ned. The state of our great city is a critical priority. Not just the roads, and the bridges – they're important – but the schools, the libraries, daycare for working parents, solutions for homelessness, the cost of living, and job opportunities are issues I will address when I am elected to the senate."

Rick's fans cheered. You'd think they were paid by the decibel.

He continued, "San Francisco has problems, that much is true. But these problems can be solved. With the help of the best advisors available, I will work with the legislature and write bills that will make our fair city glorious again." He smiled, consciously deepening his dimples, and his fans roared.

And so, the debate went on. Rick talked about the beauty and uniqueness of San Francisco. Heiki talked about policies and budgets and belt-tightening. Rick's followers were boisterous. Heiki's were polite but their clapping grew increasingly loud. One of them even hooted once, but it sounded like he didn't know how. Rick's audience laughed at him.

When it was over, the wives joined the husbands on stage for more waving and applause. Rick caught Umberto's eye, who gave him a thumbs-up.

There was an after-party with Rick's top contributors in the Hotel Blanc ballroom. Prettily arranged appetizers were offered, but few celebrants ate. Champagne poured freely. A bar provided hard liquor as well.

Rick made the rounds, shook hands, patted backs, thanked his supporters, winked at their blushing wives, and posed for selfies. Appollonia stayed for the first hour, then left quietly. It was time for her sleeping pill. Rick wondered if she should combine booze with her medication. Could she overdose? That would certainly solve his problems, unless, of course, she lived. Then he would be forced to play the dutiful husband for the next several decades to a brain-damaged woman. Would Dimitri stay with him if he did?

When the last of the partiers left, Rick made his way to the presidential suite. Dimitri was waiting for him, dressed only in a ruby silk robe that draped open from the neck to the belt, revealing smooth pectorals. Rick worshipped every contour of that chest.

"You were brilliant. I watched the whole thing," Dimitri said. He handed Rick a champagne flute and held his own aloft. "To Senator Richard Stevens."

Rick liked the sound of that, Senator Rick Stevens, spoken by the beautiful Dimitri in his soft European accent.

"And to my love, Dimitri Angelis."

Chapter Twenty-Three

Maureen

JUDGE HAN WAS ON the bench. Vivian Thandi and her crew were seated at their table. Isaac, Yolanda, and Quinn were in the first pew. I was seated next to Tony.

Judge Han said, "Ms. Gould will now make her opening statement."

I squeezed Tony's hand, and he squeezed back.

This was the most important trial of my career because a man's life was at stake. When I touched the O'Shaughnessy pearls, I heard Granny's voice. "You're as smart as any of them and smarter than most." She had believed in me. It was her words that carried me through the worst times. I wished Quinn had met her.

I stood, walked into the well, and faced the jury. "Good morning, ladies and gentlemen."

Sweater Man nodded at me. The Librarian gave me a deadpan stare. She was skeptical. It was nothing personal. Amber Haley blurted out "good morning" in response, then covered her mouth with her hand, embarrassed when she realized she was the only one who had spoken. I gave her a small smile to let her know it was okay. The Social Worker next to her patted her hand.

"I won't show you pictures, charts, or diagrams this morning as Ms. Thandi did in her opening. There is one reason for that, and one reason only." I swept my arms through the space around me. "That is because there is no evidence."

This was the theme of my case, the one that I wanted the jurors to recite to themselves and each other when they went back into the jury room to deliberate. There was no evidence.

"There is no one who testified that he saw Anthony Paredes shoot Oscar Wenderholm."

I let that sink in.

"There is no evidence that Anthony Paredes owned the gun. There is no evidence that he handled the gun used to kill Oscar Wenderholm. His fingerprints weren't on it. There were no powder stains on his person when he was arrested a few hours after the murder. The evidence shows that the real murderer planted the gun in Anthony Paredes' car."

I took a sip of water while the jurors absorbed my last statement.

"There is no confession. The witness you heard, Javier Fuentes, is a longtime police informant, a snitch. He exchanges information for deals. Shortly after his arrest on a parole violation, he came up with the story that he had spoken to my client. Anthony Paredes will explain to you that it never happened. Javier Fuentes lied. When I confronted him with the truth, you saw how he reacted."

I stepped out of the space that Fuentes crossed when he leapt from the stand and where he was subdued by court security. I pointed out his path as I spoke.

"Mr. Fuentes ripped off his microphone. He lunged from the witness stand. He flew at Ms. Thandi. And he was thrown to the floor by court security and subdued. When you were escorted from the courtroom, two guards were holding him down.

"Javier Fuentes didn't want to answer my questions. He didn't want to admit to the truth – that he made up a lie about my client in order to cut a deal for himself."

Sweater Man was with me. He nodded with every sentence I said. The Librarian was willing to accept Fuentes was a snitch and trying to cut a deal, but she wasn't convinced that he was lying. She needed more. Amber Haley was shaking again. The reminder of Fuentes' violence triggered a visceral reaction in her. I suspected she had once endured or witnessed something awful. That didn't mean she would naturally feel sorry for Tony. Instead, her sympathy could attach to the last person who suffered from violence in this story, Oscar, or his widow.

"Thank you for your time, ladies and gentlemen." I returned to our table, standing behind my chair.

Judge Han said, "Ms. Gould, you may call your first witness."

"The defense calls Anthony Paredes."

▼

TONY HAD PRACTICED WALKING short distances for this very moment. He didn't want to use a wheelchair or crutches which would make him appear fragile to the jury.

He pushed his chair back unaided, stood, and stepped slowly across the well to the witness stand. Trapped behind the lectern, I felt helpless. The judge watched him closely. If he fell, I would be accused of courtroom dramatics as an appeal to the jury's compassion.

When he sat down in the witness box, the judge's shoulders relaxed. Mine did not. The metallic taste that came from adrenaline coated my tongue. I touched Granny's pearls, silently praying to her for a blessing. Please let this day not blow up in my face.

Tony attached the microphone to his tie and raised his hand. The clerk swore him in. Then he looked at me, waiting for my first question.

"Mr. Paredes, did you murder Oscar Wenderholm?"

"Absolutely not." His voice was strong and clear. The jury was focused entirely on him.

"Did you know Mr. Wenderholm?"

"I'm sorry to say that I did."

"Please explain to the jury how you came to know him."

Vivian stood. "Objection, calls for a narrative."

What a petty objection! She was trying to break up his testimony. I had asked only three questions and already, she was afraid the jury was starting to like him. I didn't look at Vivian. To do so would give the appearance that I deferred to her. That is what she wanted.

Judge Han didn't want to appear like she was siding with Vivian and against us. Her job was to be an impartial decider of admissibility, not to guide the jury's verdict one way or another with subtle hints. "Can you rephrase your question, Ms. Gould?"

I said, "Mr. Paredes, please tell the jury how you met Oscar Wenderholm."

Tony was a seasoned witness. In the civil case, he had testified at trial for two days. When I asked him to speak to the jury, he caught my cue. He turned towards them. "It was when I was a student at Lafayette Academy. I'd won a scholarship to play on their chess team. My parents hoped I would be the next Bobby Fischer."

The older jurors nodded in recognition of Bobby Fischer's name. The younger ones looked lost. Tony noticed.

"He was a big deal because he was an American world chess champion. Usually they're Russian." Tony shrugged modestly. "I don't think I'm as talented as he was, but I was good. I liked chess. Loved it, really. And I wanted to make my parents proud."

Vivian was on her feet, poised for another objection.

Tony saw, but ignored, her. "That's when I met Oscar Wenderholm. He was my chess coach."

Vivian sat down.

I asked, "When he was your coach, what kind of interaction did you have with him?

Vivian folded her hands as she watched Tony. Her paralegal was taking notes furiously.

"At first, it was just in chess club after school. The club met a couple of times a week. On Tuesday afternoon, we learned something new, usually a strategy or some history. On Fridays, we played."

"You said 'at first.' Did your interactions change over time?"

"Yes." Tony lifted his hornrims and rubbed his eyes, then composed himself. "Things changed." His voice was quieter.

"How did they change?"

Tony faced me now. This part of the story was difficult, no matter how many times he had shared it. Looking into the faces of fourteen strangers as he exposed his darkest shame would have been harrowing. But he could tell me.

"He told my parents that I was a special talent and that with tutoring, he could help me become a champion. That was what they wanted to hear." He gave a wry smile. "He said he would work with me privately after the Friday club meeting and that he would bring me home so they wouldn't have to pick me up."

He stopped talking. He knew that if he went on too long, Vivian would be on her feet.

I asked, "Did Mr. Wenderholm begin tutoring you?"

"Every Friday afternoon."

"Did something unusual happen in these sessions?"

"At first, kind of, but not really." A frown crossed Tony's face briefly. "I guess you would call it grooming, but I didn't understand it at the time. He was more handsy, you know? In the beginning, it was just friendly stuff. He patted my back. Squeezed my shoulder. Grabbed my hand and held it in the air like I was a champion. Then he started hugging me, the way men do. Bro hugs, you know?"

Tony's voice was thick. He took a sip of water from the plastic cup on the stand.

When he was ready, I asked, "This went on for how long?"

"A few weeks. I'm not exactly sure. And then the other stuff started happening."

I lowered my voice a fraction. Not for a dramatic effect, but because we were talking about something intimate, so my questions shouldn't be shouted across a courtroom.

"Could you describe for us what happened?"

"One afternoon, after we had finished playing, he told me to put the chess board away in the supply closet like always. I did and when I turned around, he was right behind me. He kissed me. On the lips."

I heard rustling behind me. The jurors heard it too. They turned to see what was going on. By the time I looked over my shoulder, Isaac was almost at the door. He pushed it open and disappeared.

I cleared my throat for attention. When the jurors were facing me, I asked, "Mr. Paredes, how old were you?"

The jurors looked at Tony.

"Fourteen."

"How old was he?"

"Late twenties, maybe early thirties."

"How did you react?"

"I didn't. I was shocked. I mean, he was a man. A teacher at the school. My chess coach. My entire future was in his hands. My parents loved him. He was going to make me into a champion. I was just a kid. I didn't know what to do."

"Did you tell anyone?"

"I didn't. Like I said, I didn't know what to do."

"Did it happen again?"

"The very next Friday. He followed me into the supply cabinet and closed the door. More kissing. Some groping."

"Did you tell anyone then?"

He took off his glasses once more and wiped his eyes. "No."

I waited until he put the glasses back on, then asked, "Did anything else happen after that?"

"It was the third Friday. He followed me into the supply cabinet again. He told me how much he cared for me and that he wanted to make me happy."

"And then what?"

Tony tried to sound clinical, but a scarlet color crept up his throat as he answered. "The next thing I know, he was on his knees in front of me, my jeans were unzipped, and he, you know, he performed oral sex on me."

A small cry came from Amber Haley, the juror who had so much trouble with Fuentes' violence. The clerk came out from behind her desk with a box of tissues and held it out to her. She took a few. The Social Worker next to her accepted the box and kept it on her lap. The clerk returned to her desk.

"Ms. Gould, is this a good time for a break?" It was Judge Han. She was concerned that Amber Haley's strong emotional reaction was distracting the panel from the testimony, so the judge wanted to give the juror a few moments to collect herself. I was worried too.

"Yes, Your Honor," I said. "This would be a good time for a break."

"We'll reconvene in fifteen minutes."

The jury was led out while Tony remained on the stand. Judge Han left as did Vivian and her crew. When we were alone except for my team and the ever-present guard, I walked over to Tony. "Are you okay?"

He nodded. "Where's Isaac?"

Yolanda heard. "I'll go see." She left the courtroom and Quinn followed her.

I asked Tony, "Do you want the guard to take you to the men's room?"

"No, I'm fine."

The door opened. Yolanda came in with Isaac, Quinn following.

Isaac stopped at the railing. "Can I?"

"It's okay," I said.

Isaac pushed open the gate and crossed the well tentatively like a hamster who had escaped his cage and was afraid someone would step on him.

"It's okay," I said again. I moved out of the way so Isaac could stand next to Tony.

The guard, still on high alert from Fuentes' outburst the day before, shifted so he could watch both Tony and Isaac. "No touching."

Isaac looked at the guard and then leaned towards Tony so close that he was almost touching, but not quite. "I'm sorry. I just can't."

"That's fine. I get it. I just wanted to know if you're alright."

"It's not about me. It's about you. Are you alright?"

"I have to do this," Tony told Isaac.

"I know."

Tony said, "But you don't have to. Really, I wish you didn't. It'd be easier for me if you weren't here. Maureen, how long is this going to last?"

I said, "All day, probably."

Tony said to Isaac, "Go home. I'll call you when it's over."

"Are you sure?" Isaac asked.

"I'm sure."

The clerk's door opened and she half-stepped into the room. "The judge wants to know if you're ready."

THE PLAYERS WERE IN their places: Judge Han on the bench, the jury in the box, Vivian and her crew at their table, Tony in the witness stand, and me at the lectern.

I said, "Before the break, we were talking about how Oscar Wenderholm abused you in a supply closet at Lafayette Academy when you were fourteen years old."

I heard a wheel squeak as Vivian must have pushed back her chair, preparing to stand for an objection, not that she had any, but she wanted to break up his testimony. Again, Sweater Man glanced at her. The judge shot her a warning look. The wheel squeaked again as the chair was rolled back to the desk.

I continued. "How long did this abuse go on?"

"I couldn't tell you. Weeks, months maybe."

"And then what happened?"

"Mr. Katsu caught us in the supply closet."

"Did the abuse stop then?"

"Then and there. Mr. Katsu hauled me to his office and called my parents to come get me. I never went back to the Academy after that. The next week, my parents went to a meeting. He told them that I would be happier somewhere else and, given what had happened, I was no longer enrolled."

"They expelled you?"

"Whatever you call it. I wasn't allowed to come back."

"And what happened to Oscar Wenderholm?"

"I didn't know at the time. It was years later before I found out."

I asked, "What did you find out?"

"Objection, hearsay!" Vivian shouted so loudly that several jurors were startled.

"It's reputation evidence, Your Honor," I said. "A classic and time-honored exception to the hearsay rule."

"Objection denied. You may continue, Ms. Gould."

An old war horse litigator once told me to punish opposing counsel when they break up your evidence with bogus objections. The way to do that was by repeating everything that had been said so the jury would hear it a second time. Sooner or later, the other attorney would give up.

I asked again, "What happened to Oscar Wenderholm after Mr. Katsu caught him abusing you and you were expelled?"

"He was given a severance check and a letter of recommendation."

"Was he fired?"

"Not fired. They called it a workforce reduction. I saw the letter. We got it in the civil case."

Sweater Man was leaning towards Tony. The Librarian nodded sagely. A couple of the younger jurors looked confused. They needed to understand that Lafayette Academy was covering up a crime.

"Did the school report the assault to the police?"

"They didn't."

"Do you know whether the school was legally required to report the abuse?"

I heard movement at the prosecution table. Tony glanced in that direction, then before Vivian had time to object, he quickly said, "That is my understanding."

"But as far as you know, the school never reported the abuse."

"That's right. We got the complete file from the school in the civil case. There wasn't a report."

Vivian stood. "Your Honor, I fail to see what this has to do with the events leading up to the murder of Oscar Wenderholm."

I'd ground the point in as much as I could, that Oscar had gotten away with abusing kids. Villainizing the decedent wasn't the point, instead, the point was explaining Tony's hypervigilance. No one had stopped Oscar, so Tony felt like he was the only one who cared about the harm Oscar could do to children.

"Counsel?" Judge Han asked for my response.

"I'm finished with this line."

Vivian sat down.

I asked Tony, "How did your parents react to all of this?"

"My father came home from the meeting and called me a 'faggot.' He wouldn't be in the same room with me ever again. My mother cried a lot until she didn't. Then, she barely spoke to me."

"Did you continue to pursue chess?"

"I never played again. I went to public high school until I was old enough to drop out and then I got a job in a music store at the mall. So much for the next Bobby Fischer. As soon as I made enough money, I moved out."

"At some point, you filed suit against Lafayette Academy and Oscar Wenderholm."

"Is that a question?" It was Vivian. She hadn't bothered to stand. She knew perfectly well that a statement which calls for an explanation is legally a question. Her objection would be denied. The only reason she made it was to break up the testimony again. She was worried.

"Please continue," Judge Han said.

Vivian wasn't learning, so I repeated the statement. "Please tell the jury about the lawsuit you filed."

Tony faced them. "I went to therapy. I had to. I was suicidal. I took a bottle of aspirin and my friend, Isaac, found me and called an ambulance. If he hadn't, I probably would have died. After a few years in therapy, I realized that I had been victimized. I didn't get it at the time. Sounds stupid, but I was in shock when it was going on. I just didn't understand. How would I? No one warned me. And then we got caught, and suddenly I lost my dreams, my parents hated me, and my life was ruined. All that time, I felt like I had done something wrong to make all this bad stuff happen. In therapy, I realized it wasn't my fault, so I went to the police station and gave them a statement. They said they couldn't prosecute because too much time had passed. That's when I filed the lawsuit."

The scars on my arms felt like they were alive and crawling across my skin. I wanted to scratch them until I tore them off. My realization that Frank's abuse of me wasn't my fault wasn't sudden like Tony's. It came to me in bits and pieces. The shame I had dragged around for years appeared as anger most of the time. But there were some days, even now, when I felt like I was drowning in humiliation.

Tony was so very brave to say all these things out loud in a room full of strangers.

I rubbed my arms, satisfying the itch, then took a moment for a sip of water, to collect myself before I continued.

"Please tell us what happened with the civil case."

"We went to court, to trial, just like this. I told the jury my story. They believed me."

Vivian stirred. Judge Han held a hand up to quiet her.

Tony ignored them. "They gave me millions of dollars. It was great. I felt like they understood. And then it all went to hell. It wasn't about the money. It never was. It was about getting the truth out there. The school had swept it under the rug, the police did nothing, so going to court was the only way I knew how to tell people what happened."

Sweater Man was nearly on the edge of his seat. The Librarian took notes furiously.

I said, "Please explain what happened after the verdict came in."

"The day after, the defense attorney found out that a juror had gone online and got all kinds of stuff about Oscar that wasn't admitted in the trial. Oscar had abused children before he came to San Francisco. He had gotten jobs at schools or volunteered with kids' groups where he could get at children. So, the judge said the verdict was illegal because inadmissible evidence was leaked to the jury and my attorney, you, asked for a new trial. But I screwed up."

We discovered Wenderholm had abused children only after we filed suit because when our case hit the news, other victims came forward. The judge kept the evidence of prior abuse out because Lafayette Academy had no way of knowing about it before they hired him and because it was inadmissible character evidence as to Wenderholm. He was to be judged on whether he abused Tony, not whether he was a serial pedophile.

Tony went on without a question. "I was angry. I wanted everyone to know that what I said was true and that Oscar was dangerous to kids. So, I gave an interview to a news reporter and told her everything I knew about his past. The story went viral. The judge said I violated a gag order, that the defense couldn't get a fair trial now and I should have known better, so there would be no new trial. That was it. Case over. I went back to my job at the mall with everyone knowing what happened. I could see it in the way they looked at me. I couldn't handle it anymore, so I quit and got a night job driving a delivery truck so I wouldn't have to see anyone."

The Social Worker had a careworn expression on her face. She had seen stories like this many times in her career, and, no doubt, had felt helpless to stop the wave of child exploitation.

I said, "You heard Javier Fuentes testify that you had a conversation with him."

Tony answered, "I heard him say that, but it isn't true."

"Could you explain?"

"I never met him. And I never said I was happy Oscar was dead to him or to anyone."

I was ready to sum up. I asked, "Did you stalk Oscar Wenderholm?"

Tony looked at the jury when he answered. "I did not."

"Did you murder Oscar Wenderholm?"

"I did not."

I closed my notebook. "Thank you, Mr. Paredes. Your Honor, I have no further questions at this time."

Chapter Twenty-Four

Maureen

After a break, Vivian spread her notes across the lectern. Her first question was, "Mr. Paredes, are you happy Oscar Wenderholm is dead?"

There's a strict rule in trial advocacy. Never ask a question you don't know the answer to.

Tony said, "No, ma'am."

That wasn't the answer she was expecting. "Oh, come on, Mr. Paredes. You're in a court of law. You took an oath to tell the truth. You said Oscar Wenderholm abused you, that you lost your dream of becoming the next Bobby Fischer because of it. You were thrown out of school. Your parents rejected you. Your life was ruined. Mr. Wenderholm suffered no consequences for his actions. Yet, you expect the jury to believe that you aren't happy he's dead?"

I felt my shoulders tense. She was trying to trigger Tony into an emotional outburst.

"I'm not," Tony said, uncharacteristically composed. "I think it's terribly sad that his children lost their father and that his wife lost her husband."

"But it's not your fault, is that right?"

"I didn't kill him."

Still calm, Tony was holding his own against Vivian.

"In fact, nothing that happened was your fault."

I was surprised that Vivian, the experienced trial attorney with a 72-1 win/loss record, had asked that question. She must have felt like she was losing and hoped that she could goad Tony. Her gamble failed.

Tony adjusted his glasses, then looked directly at her. "Do you mean the abuse? I was a child. He was a grown man with a history of grooming and abusing children. No, that was not my fault."

"Very well," she said in a tone that meant to convey she didn't believe him. "Explain to me how you knew where Mr. Wenderholm worked."

"I followed him."

She pretended to look shocked, a shade dramatically for the benefit of the jury. "You were stalking him?"

Sweater Man shifted in his chair for a better view of the witness stand.

Tony hid his hands beneath the desk. From his arm movement, he appeared to be picking at his cuticles. "No ma'am, I was not stalking him. I didn't intend any harm. I just wanted to talk."

Vivian reached for the plastic water cup on her table, took a sip, and put it back down. She was stalling.

"You followed Mr. Wenderholm to his work from where?"

"His house."

"So, you admit to visiting Mr. Wenderholm's house."

"I was there. Again, not stalking. I just wanted to talk. And I never threatened him."

"Are you saying Mrs. Wenderholm lied when she testified that you threatened her husband?"

"I can't tell you want she thinks or what she believes. But I can tell you it never happened. I just wanted to talk to him."

"How did you know where he lived?"

"I followed him."

"Just to talk."

"That's right."

"You followed him from where?"

Vivian had taken the bait.

"I followed him from a gaming arcade at the mall. He went there regularly on Saturday afternoons with a boy, I guess it was his son. While the boy played, he'd walk around talking to other kids, played games with them, gave them tokens so they could play longer, bought them drinks and food. He was grooming them. I could tell. He planned to do something to them."

Vivian realized she had been led into this line of questioning. She wanted out - quickly. "But you have no way of knowing that. It's speculation on your part, isn't that true, Mr. Paredes?"

"Why would a grown man spend his Saturday afternoons in a gaming arcade playing with kids who weren't his children and weren't his children's friends? These kids were total strangers to him. Why would he do that?"

"Your Honor, the State moves to strike Mr. Paredes' testimony as speculation."

Tony looked at me, worried. He must have thought he had done something wrong. I tried to psychically convey that he had not while I could feel Sweater Man watching me.

If the jury caught me smiling at Tony, it might be misconstrued as smugness. I didn't want them to think it was a contest between Vivian and me, although it was. I wanted them to understand the trial was about finding the truth.

Before I could respond, Judge Han ruled. "You asked the question, Ms. Thandi, you can live with the answer."

Tony relaxed.

Vivian gathered her notes. "I have nothing further for this witness."

Judge Han looked at me. "Redirect?"

The Social Worker looked relieved. Amber Haley was pulling at her lip. The look she gave me suggested she didn't want me to ask any more questions. But the jury needed to understand what was going on in Tony's mind.

I slid behind the lectern as Vivian vacated it. "Mr. Paredes, what did you say to Mr. Wenderholm when you went to speak with him?"

Tony took in a deep shuddering breath. "I told him how much he had hurt me and that I didn't want him hurting any more kids. That's all. I didn't threaten to kill him. I wanted him to know that I saw what he was doing. I didn't kill him."

Tony's voice was breaking. He took off his glasses and wiped his eyes with tissue.

"I have no further questions."

Judge Han called for a recess.

As the jury filed out, I silently thanked Granny Shaughnessy for seeing us through Tony's testimony. After the jury's door closed behind them, I pulled his wheelchair out of the closet, helped him get into it, then wheeled him back to the counsel table. He was shaking with emotion and exhaustion. He crossed his arms on the table and laid his head down.

Quinn and Yolanda went to the restroom. When they returned a few minutes later, Yolanda said, "Jake wants you to call him."

As I left, Yolanda replaced me at the counsel table. She poured a glass of water and touched Tony on the elbow. The guard didn't challenge her. Few would dare to take her on, fierce mother-woman that she was. Tony sat up and accepted the glass.

In the hallway, I powered up my cell phone. There was one text from Jake, all in caps: "CALL ME!"

I hit the speed dial. He picked up on the first ring. "Give me a moment." I heard him go into a quiet room which I assumed was his office. I pictured him standing against the door, preventing anyone from coming in.

He said, "Frank called me."

"Jake, I'm in the middle of a trial."

"He knows that. He said he had information for you but couldn't get through to the houseline."

"I had it disconnected."

"What? When did you do that?"

"Nevermind. I don't have time to talk. We're on a quick break."

"I told him not to say anything to me because, technically, my office is prosecuting your client. Conflict of interest."

"Jake." I said, hinting that I was about to lose my temper.

"He says he has information about your case, and he needs to talk to you in person – not on the phone – as soon as possible. Tonight, if you can. Tomorrow at the latest. And whatever you do, he said, don't rest your case until after you talked with him."

The bastard. The last person I wanted to see was Francis E. Gould – ever, much less when I was in the middle of a murder trial. It was just like him, pulling a stunt for attention when I was at my most stressed.

Jake said, "He claimed he has information vital to your case."

"Of course, he did."

"He might have. Red, you have to go see him."

If I didn't investigate a suggestion of evidence that could exonerate my client, I would have failed in my duty to Tony. Ethically and morally.

Quinn came out of the courtroom. "The judge wants the parties assembled. Now."

▼

JUDGE HAN WAS BACK on the bench. Vivian and her crew were at their table. Tony was sitting beside me, less shaken, but visibly exhausted.

The judge said, "We have a note from one of the jurors."

The clerk came out from behind her desk and handed Vivian and me each a piece of paper. It read, "Please excuse me from this trial. Personal reasons." It was signed by Amber Haley, who was so emotional during the testimony.

We had selected fourteen jurors, twelve to serve and two alternates in case one of the twelve didn't finish the trial. To maintain their attention, the alternates are not told who they are until the end of testimony at which time they are thanked and excused.

The judge would prefer that we agree to excuse a juror if a problem arose. Otherwise, she would have to make a ruling and that ruling could be grounds for appeal. Judge Han asked, "Ms. Thandi, what is the State's position?"

"The State requests the Court to bring Ms. Haley in for *in camera* review."

In camera meant privately. Vivian's request was standard operating procedure. The parties were entitled to know why this juror believed she could no longer be fair. Once either of us invoked the request, it would be granted. It was unnecessary for me to respond.

"Madam Clerk," Judge Han said. "Please bring in Ms. Haley."

The clerk disappeared through the back door and returned a few minutes later, ushering in the young woman. She scanned the room quickly, then lowered her face, her curtain of hair hiding her eyes.

Judge Han said, "Ms. Haley, if you would take a seat in the jury box."

The juror took the seat she had occupied during the trial. The clerk handed the young woman a microphone, then returned to her console.

Judge Han said, "I received a note stating that you want to be excused from this trial."

Amber Haley nodded. Her knuckles were white with strain as she gripped the microphone.

"Is that yes?" the judge asked.

The juror's voice was barely audible. "Yes."

"Can you explain to us why you don't want to serve anymore?"

Ms. Haley stared at the judge. "It's private."

"I understand. Would you feel more comfortable speaking just to the attorneys and me?"

"Yes, ma'am. I mean, Your Honor."

"Very well. We'll recess to chambers. It will take a few minutes for Madam Clerk to set up the recording equipment. She'll bring you in when we're ready."

A FEW MINUTES AFTER the judge and clerk left, the clerk returned to the courtroom and spoke quietly to Ms. Haley, then motioned for us to follow as she ushered the juror out. Vivian strode across the well so she would be next in line. Of course, she did. She was competitive to the bone.

"What's going on?" Tony whispered.

"I'm not sure. This juror wants off the case and we're going into a private session to find out why."

"Aren't I entitled to be there?"

"You could insist, but I will be there for you. It's obvious this young woman has something going on and she doesn't want to talk in front of a lot of people. I think it would be better to find out what she has to say and then take it from there. Is that okay with you?"

He relented. He knew pain when he saw it.

I hurried to the judge's chambers, an office behind the courtroom, and arrived just as Judge Han, still in her robe, motioned for Ms. Haley to take the visitor's chair. "Counsel may sit over there," the judge said as she indicated a small sofa with ornate Oriental carving and upholstered in red velvet which was shoved against the wall.

Vivian sat first. When I sat beside her, the sofa was so small that our elbows brushed. She didn't acknowledge that I was there. That was okay with me. It was her game face, the powerful woman in control of the situation, deferring to no one unless she had to.

Judge Han said, "Ms. Haley, I want to talk to you a bit about your request. When I'm finished, the attorneys may have questions. I understand that this matter is a private one for you, but we have certain rules in criminal trials that must be followed."

"I understand," Amber Haley said.

"Very well. Would you explain to us why you want to be excused from this case?"

"I'm sorry. It's just that I thought I could handle it. But I can't." She began fanning her face and was quiet for a few moments. The clerk typed rapidly, taking down as much as she could. When she finished, she looked up from her task. In the distance a ferry blew its horn.

Ms. Haley spoke. "Something happened when I was a little girl. It didn't happen to me. It happened to my older sister. I didn't even know about it at the time. So, I didn't think it mattered."

In jury selection, Judge Han had asked the jurors whether they had any experiences with abuse and whether their experiences would affect their abilities to be fair jurors. Amber Haley had said nothing.

"It was my mother's boyfriend. When she found out, she kicked him out of the house and called the cops. I give her credit for that. He went to prison for a while."

We waited.

"I was so little; I don't even remember him. But what happened to my sister couldn't be fixed. When she hit high school, she started drinking and drugging. I was a little older by then and I knew what she was doing, but I didn't want her to get into trouble. I idolized her. So, I didn't say anything. And then, one day, she walked in front of a muni bus. The driver didn't have time to stop."

Vivian was holding her breath. I was too.

Judge Han handed Amber Haley a box of tissues. She took one single tissue and wiped her nose. "I feel so guilty. I should have said something. When my mom found out that I knew about the partying, she blamed me. But I didn't know that my sister had been abused. If I had, I would have understood that she wasn't just trying to be cool, she was hurting. They tried to protect me by not telling me, but if I had known the truth, maybe I could have done something."

I could feel Vivian relax, just a bit. This juror was going to be excused. There was nothing she or I could do about it, not that we would want to keep her. It was clear the trial was dredging up her trauma. I didn't want to cause her more pain. I'm sure Vivian didn't either. Nor was it fair to the State or Tony to have a distracted juror. She might not hear the evidence. She could arrive at a verdict based upon her emotional state. And she could be easily manipulated by other jurors.

Judge Han turned to us. "Counsel, positions?"

Vivian spoke first. "The State has no objection to excusing this juror."

Then I said, "Mr. Paredes has no objection to excusing Ms. Haley." Tony would understand. I wasn't worried.

"Very well. Ms. Haley, the court thanks you and excuses you from service on this trial. You may go."

Chapter Twenty-Five

Maureen

BEFORE THE JUDGE AND jury returned, I explained to Tony about Ms. Haley's situation, and he agreed with my decision. When we were back in the courtroom and on record, Judge Han instructed the jury that Ms. Haley had been excused and they were not to speculate as to the reason.

Judge Han said, "Ms. Gould, your next witness."

"Your Honor, we request a recess until Monday morning."

Vivian threw her pen down.

I continued. "The State promised it would take the entire week for its case at the beginning of the trial. When it rested early, the only witness I had available was Mr. Paredes. My witnesses will not be available until Monday at the earliest."

Technically true. I had submitted a witness list that included everyone I had spoken to during our investigation in case something in the prosecution's case triggered a reason to call them. But when the trial started, I didn't have a defense theory other than "prove it," so I had no justification to call any of the witnesses I'd listed. If, in the highly unlikely event that Frank had something valuable, I needed to keep my case open until the following week.

Judge Han stabbed me with a look. Judges are never happy when there is any kind of delay. I opened my mouth to begin an argument about fairness, and the defendant's entitlement to his day in court, and his right to compel witnesses.

But Judge Han knew the law. "Motion granted. This court will stand in recess until Monday morning. Ladies and gentlemen of the jury, enjoy your weekend."

A FEW MINUTES LATER, we were alone in the courtroom except for one impatient guard, when Tony whispered, "What witnesses?"

"I have some work to do. I'll come by Sunday, and we'll catch up."

"But –"

"That's all I can say right now. Promise, I'll visit Sunday." I motioned the guard forward.

Yolanda and Quinn packed the case files. I would have helped if Yolanda allowed, but she did not because she said I'd screw up her system. When we emerged from the building with the handcarts, fat drops of rain had begun to splatter on the sidewalk. The air was heavy with the smells of ozone and moist dust. We loaded the files as quickly as we could into Yolanda's cherry red Ford Explorer, not very practical for city parking, but a great vehicle for a single mother with four kids. I pulled myself up into the passenger's seat as Quinn climbed into the back.

Yolanda started the engine, and the wipers began to slap across the windshield. She asked. "What witnesses?"

"Frank called Jake," I answered. "Said he has something for our case."

Yolanda jerked the truck's nose into traffic, her eyes locked on the sideview mirror. Someone honked, annoyed. She waved at them pleasantly, then chanced an eyeroll at me. "You have got to be kidding."

"And he doesn't want to give me the information over the phone."

"Does he know you're in trial?"

"He would have seen it on TV."

Yolanda changed the subject. "That poor Amber Hayes girl. Why was she excused?"

It wasn't my place to tell Amber's story, even if I told it to my team and our discussion was confidential. "Family stuff," I said.

Yolanda nodded. She was seasoned enough to draw basic conclusions that were correct.

But Quinn was not. She asked, "What kind of family stuff?"

"Just family stuff," I said. My entire left forearm suddenly felt like it was stung by a mosquito that had worked its way from my wrist to my elbow. I began scratching it violently.

Yolanda covered my forearm with her hand and held on until I relaxed.

I could feel Quinn withdraw. I looked at my sideview mirror and saw her staring out. Her face was obscured by the darkened glass and the rivulets of rain that trailed down the window, but I could see a frown on her face.

I was keeping a secret from her, and she knew it. A secret that Yolanda was in on, and Jake too.

I thought about the juror, Amber Haley, wracked with guilt because she hadn't saved her sister, thinking that if she knew the truth, she could have done something. Maybe she could have. I thought about Amber's mother, who tried to protect Amber by keeping the ugly story from her. She would have been protecting the older sister too, who may not have wanted Amber to know. And she was protecting herself from revealing her guilt and shame because she had allowed her older daughter to be abused.

I thought about my own mother, whom I had blamed for abandoning me when I became pregnant. During the plane ride back east to the girls' school, she had barely looked at me. She was vibrating with anger. I didn't know I was pregnant yet. The doctor told her, but not me, because I was only fourteen years old. I guess he trusted her to tell me, but she never did. That unhappy duty fell upon one of the nuns at the school.

After the plane had landed, when we were waiting for a cab, she said only one thing to me, "It's for your own good."

I didn't understand what she meant, but I was afraid to ask.

After Quinn was born and taken from me, I'd concluded that my mother hiding me away to have my baby in secret and then putting her up for adoption was the "it" that was good for me. She didn't want people to know I had a baby. I concluded, as any child would, that she was ashamed of me and angry at me for what had happened.

But what if that "it" she spoke about was keeping me away from my father?

I remembered glimpses of my mother intruding on my father and me, long before the rape. In his den, when I was little, coloring while he worked, she would open the door and come into the room with what seemed to be a pretext. Did my father want rice or potatoes with dinner? Or, she had suddenly decided we needed to go shopping because I had outgrown my shoes. My father would be annoyed, and I could feel tension between them. Then she would hustle me out of there.

The night that it happened was during a cocktail party. My father had sneaked into my room to wish me goodnight, he said. Much of what happened was blocked from my memory. But I recall that hours later, after the guests had left, my mother stood over my bed, staring down at me, stiff with rage. I'd assumed she was angry at me.

Maybe it wasn't me she was angry with, but my father, and herself.

In the Navarre trial, I had argued to the jury that secrets bind the shamed to the guilty. Later, I gave a television interview about having been abused by a trusted family member, whom I refused to identify. The people who mattered knew who I meant. That is, all the people that mattered except Quinn.

At the time, I could not face her and tell her the ugly truth of her paternity. She was so beautiful, fresh, open, loving. How could I curse her with the knowledge that her very beginning was the result of a monstrous act? Would she see herself differently? I didn't want to risk it.

Yet, this secret had become my prison. I clung to my shame, afraid that if I shared it, it would taint her. She was free from the ugly truth, but she was confused and hurt because she felt locked out.

I didn't realize until now that my mother had tried to protect me, but she had failed. She blamed herself, as any mother would do. My mother died several months ago, so it was too late to tell her that I understood.

Jake was right.

I had to tell Quinn the truth.

Chapter Twenty-Six

Maureen

I HELPED YOLANDA HAUL the files upstairs to my office, while Quinn took the BMW to law school to attend a lecture. This was the first chance I had alone with Yolanda to ask her about being a mother.

"The other day, when I dropped Quinn off for her first day of law school, I cried."

"Of course, you did. Children break your heart. With every step they take, they're walking away from you, and you can't protect them anymore. It's terrifying."

Fear? I had never been afraid of anything in my life. Maybe it was because I had never cared about anyone or anything as much as I cared about Quinn. Before she came back, I didn't have anything to lose except a trial. And that was really someone else's life, it wasn't mine. When Tony's civil verdict was lost, I went home like every other night and I got up the next day, like every other day.

The first time I felt real fear was when Frank lured Quinn to the mansion. I was afraid he'd hurt her, the way that he had hurt me. When I found out she was there, I drove like a madwoman from East Bay across the Bay Bridge to rescue her. I don't know what I would have done if something had happened to her.

"That's it," I said. "Fear. So how do you deal with it?"

"Me? I pray," Yolanda said. "You? You're going to have to figure that out for yourself."

I got it. The reason I hadn't told Quinn about her father was fear. She had a right to know. I needed to stop protecting her. If she hated me, I would live with it. If she wanted to establish a relationship with him, I'd think about that later. But now was the time. She was entitled to know.

After Yolanda gave me a lift home, I took a long hot bath while I struggled for the right words.

When I finally came out of my bedroom, Quinn had come home and gone into her room. Her door was closed. I grabbed an Anchor Steam beer from the fridge, pried the cap loose, and took it into the living room where I settled on the couch. Germaine Greer leapt up next to me and daintily lounged across my lap. She had never done that before.

I stroked the cat until she suddenly flew across me on her way to the door. The bonding moment was nice while it lasted. The knob turned and Jake came inside. "Hello, gorgeous," he said as he dropped his briefcase and picked up the traitor. Then he saw me sprawled across the couch. "Oh, and, you too."

"Cheers, "I said, knowing I wasn't gorgeous. My hair was wet. I had no make-up on. Inside, I felt wretched.

He came over, carrying the loudly purring cat, and gave me a kiss. "Have you thought about dinner?"

Dinner. I forgot. He could see it in my face.

"No worries. You had a long week. How about I grab some pizza?"

Quinn appeared. "Veggie, right?"

Jake said, "One veggie and one meat lover coming up. We'll have leftovers tomorrow. Nothing better than cold pizza for breakfast."

"Are you serious?" Quinn asked.

"He is," I answered. "Get yourself a brew. We need to talk."

Jake sensed that the time had come for me to tell Quinn the truth. He squeezed my shoulder and kissed the top of my head. "Will forty-five minutes give you enough time?"

"Hurry back." I wanted privacy with Quinn. But I wanted Jake close by to comfort me afterwards.

He left. At the sound of Quinn opening a can, Germaine Greer drifted into the kitchen. Quinn put the cat dish on the floor, then returned to the living area with two bottles of beer, one for her and one for me. She looked afraid.

I patted the couch next to me.

She sat.

"I have something to tell you," I said.

"You're pregnant."

"Good God, no!" I didn't mean to shout. I was just surprised.

"You want me to move out?"

Just like any kid, she assumed whenever bad happened, it was her fault.

I took her hand. "No, baby, not at all."

"Then what?"

"I need to tell you about your father."

BY THE TIME JAKE returned with two pizzas and two six-packs of beer, I had told Quinn the full story of how she was conceived. We cried. She wrapped her arms around me and held me as I wished my mother would have done, but never did.

Then I talked about shame and about cutting myself. I showed her my scars. I apologized for lying to her about why I scratched my arms. I thanked her for caring and trying to make me healthier with the detox teas and green drinks, which I hated, but I didn't say that.

Then we cried again.

When Jake arrived, Quinn went into her bathroom to wash her face.

"Everything okay?" he asked, handing me a fresh bottle of beer. My third. I didn't often get drunk, but if there was a night for it, this was it.

I couldn't make my voice work. So, I took his fingers and kissed them.

"I'm starved," he announced. "Who's eating?"

"I am." Quinn appeared.

"Me too," I said.

Jake set the table quickly and we sat down to eat. I was famished and wolfed down two slices of the meat lover. Quinn forced herself to eat one veggie pizza slice, one small bite at a time. Jake caught me watching her. He mouthed to me, "She's okay."

We watched an old Marx Brothers movie after dinner, breaking the tension. Afterwards, Quinn said she was exhausted, said good night, and went to bed. While Jake held me, Germaine Greer settled on his lap. That was a first too. Generally, she pouted when he and I snuggled.

"How did it go?" he asked.

"The pieces fell into place for her. She knew I got weird every time Frank was mentioned. She was surprised that I lied about the scars. I expected her to be angry at me for not telling her sooner, but instead, she seemed hurt. Now that she knows, it feels like things between us are different."

"They're bound to be. It'll take time, Red. Quinn loves you, and she's a good kid. Things will be okay. You'll see."

"But things will never be the same again. I can't undo it."

"They'll be better. Just you wait and see." He pulled himself away and appraised my condition, which was more than a little drunk and halfway to sleep. "So, you're driving up to the prison tomorrow?"

I nodded.

"Then it's time for you to get to bed." He took the beer bottle out of my hand. I'm not sure how many I'd had because I lost count at three. When he pulled me to my feet, the room spun, and I fell against him. I felt as fluid as Germaine Greer looked.

"Make me," I said, smiling into his sweatshirt.

The next thing I knew, I was floating. Jake had swept me up. He cradled me in his arms like I was a small child while he carried me to our bedroom.

"I love you, my brave girl," Jake said as he tucked me into bed.

"Love you, too." I usually corrected him when he called me, or anyone else, a "girl," but I decided to let it slide. I'd fought enough fights for one day.

Despite my hangover, the drive to Snowden went by more quickly than our last trip. I didn't think Quinn should come along, but she had insisted. I still wanted to protect her, even though she knew the truth.

Sunglasses shielded my eyes from the overly bright sun, but pain needled at my temple. My mouth was dry despite the two giant glasses of water and double shot of espresso I'd downed before we left. No sooner than we were on the highway, I had to pull off, ostensibly to buy coffee, but, in reality, to relieve myself.

Back on the highway, caffeinated and comfortable, I broke the speed limit by ten miles per hour. I wanted this visit over.

Quinn didn't nod off on this drive, like she had last time. Instead, she shuffled through my CD collection. The first disc she slotted in was bubblegum music, irritatingly cheerful. I shook my head. She exchanged that for cello adagios, far too depressing. She pulled that disc out before I could comment. Next, she inserted New Orleans Jazz. Heartbreak and murder with an energetic tempo. Just right.

We didn't speak during the trip. Everything I thought of was frivolous, given the circumstances. Since she had come to live with me, she asked about her father from time to time but I had ditched the question. She had met Frank but that was when she believed he was only her grandfather. Now she would look into his face, knowing who he truly was to her – and to me.

For me, this meeting was a reckoning. It would be the first time we would be together, each of us knowing the truth.

And I needed to know what the hell he thought was so important to drag me up here in the middle of a murder trial. This had better not be one of his little stunts for attention. If it was, it would be the last time he'd see me.

Quinn and I, along with a group of other visitors, were escorted by a guard to a multi-purpose room. Folding tables were set up in rows, some empty, and some had families seated already. The prisoners sitting alone watched the door hopefully. The other visitors drifted towards their inmates while I searched for Frank.

The men all looked alike. Some were younger, some older. I was accustomed to picking Frank out of groups of lawyers and businessmen, he in a bespoke suit with hair styled, holding court, a drink in one hand, oblivious to anyone and anything other than the attention he was soaking up.

On my third scan, I found him in the far corner, watching us. No longer the suave successful attorney with the beautiful heiress wife, he was thinner, paler, and his thick silver hair had been shorn by a prison barber. He had the same hopeful expression that the other waiting prisoners had.

We made our way across the room. Frank stood as we approached, ever the gentleman. What a laugh. He looked at me first, then Quinn. When his eyes returned to me, his usual mischievous glint was replaced with resignation. He could see that I wasn't there to play happy families.

"Thank you for coming," he said, as he gestured towards the chairs opposite him.

"You said you have something for me," I answered. Quinn and I sat down.

He sat too. "Right down to business. That's my girl."

"First off, I am not your girl. Second, I'm in the middle of a murder trial. This better be important."

Frank clasped his hands on the tabletop, leaning forward as if he was sitting behind his law office desk about to give bad news to a client. Now that I was closer, I could see that his hair was thinning, and his scalp was pink from sunburn.

"How could you?" Quinn asked quietly.

Frank blinked, then he frowned at me. There was pain in his eyes. Actual pain. As if I had betrayed him.

"How could you?" Quinn said, a little more forcefully. "Your own daughter. Fourteen years old. You sick bastard."

I was shocked. I didn't know what to say, or if I should say anything. In my family, we never talked about bad or hurtful things, especially to each other. Somehow, I had expected that Quinn wouldn't either. But she had been raised by other people, a couple I came to regard as her healthy and loving parents. She had been lucky to grow up with them.

Frank reached across the table to take her hand. She jerked it away. She was pale and hyperventilating. I was afraid she was going to faint, so I massaged her ice-cold hands the way she had done for me when she thought I had carpal tunnel syndrome.

She began to cry. We weren't allowed to have our purses, lest we smuggle drugs or weapons to the prisoners, so we had no tissues. She wiped her eyes with the heels of her palms.

"I'm going to be sick." She stood so quickly that her chair toppled, and she ran to the guard. I followed. She told him she needed to go to the restroom urgently.

He said, "You can't come back in if you leave, miss."

"I don't want to." She turned to me. "I'll wait in the lobby for you. Don't worry about me. Get what you need." She gave me a quick peck on the cheek and went out the door.

When I returned to Frank, he was crumpled, leaning against the chairback, holding on to the table with both hands as if he was afraid that he might slip out of the seat. "You told her."

"She had a right to know."

He eyed me. It was the "our little secret" look that he gave me from time to time when he thought no one was looking. It was a look of intimacy, threat, and invitation, all in one. It made me sick every time he did that. My stomach soured.

I wanted to go home. "You told Jake you had information for me."

"She's right, you know. I'm a sick bastard."

"It's not about you. This is not your chance to be the center of attention. Nothing is going to fix what you did to us."

"What I did is unforgiveable. Saying that I'm sorry seems trivial. If I ever get a chance, I'll do my best to make amends."

Right. How many times when I was an assistant district attorney would I hear those words coming from a suddenly remorseful defendant standing in front of a judge and about to be sentenced? More than I could count. The judge, the prosecutor, and the victims all knew their lawyers told them to say they were sorry.

"Last chance. Do you have information for me?" I asked. "If not, I'm leaving right now."

"It's about Dakota Vaughn. Before you came to see him, he consulted me about a case. The inmates know that I've been disbarred, but there isn't much the State of California can do to me now. So, I'm happy to give advice. In prison, it's good to have friends. Especially when you're aging."

"Not about you," I reminded him.

"Dakota wanted to know if he could get some money out of Wenderholm's book deal. He figured he would be featured prominently in it."

"Not concerned about attorney-client confidentiality?"

He smirked. "I'm not a lawyer anymore, remember? He also wanted to know if he could get into trouble if the book was published."

"That's a bit inconsistent, trying to make a buck off it but worried he'd get into trouble."

"He was assessing his alternatives."

Right. Frank had found his tribe.

"So, why would he get into trouble?" I asked.

"I'm not sure how much you know, but when Dakota Vaughn and Wenderholm were in high school, one of their teachers died on a trip to Vegas. He was chaperoning a group of kids."

"I knew."

"He died of an overdose, a combination of cocaine and amyl nitrate, a drug used to enhance sexual experiences."

I had been a sex offenses prosecutor. I knew what amyl nitrate was. I felt dirty and manipulated, like Frank had managed to bring the topic around to his disgusting fascination with sex and me, again.

This visit wasn't about me either. It was about saving Tony.

We had known the teacher died on the trip. We didn't know that he had overdosed.

"Book, dead teacher," I said. "Tie it together."

"Wenderholm was writing a book about being seduced by this teacher. He'd seen how much attention you got when you sued him. He figured there was money to be made, telling his tale of exploitation."

"What does that have to do with my murder trial?"

"Dakota Vaughn was afraid that if the book was published, people would find out he supplied the cocaine. There is no statute of limitations on homicide. I told him not to worry, because he wasn't at this little orgy. Someone else delivered the coke, someone he had given it to."

"And that was?"

"Rick Stevens, the car salesman turned politician."

Frank watched me do the calculations. If Rick Stevens gave the teacher the drugs that killed him, he could be charged with homicide. His career would be over. He'd go to prison. Did he know Oscar Wenderholm had written a book that would expose him? All their friends knew. Dakota Vaughn, Emerson Katsu, Constance Robertson, and Charles Robertson. Stevens had to have known. They would have warned him.

There had been a problem with getting the book published. Did Stevens kill it?

When Wenderholm realized the book wasn't being published, he wanted to do something about it. He went to Charles Robertson, for legal advice. Stevens had to know Wenderholm was trying to get his rights back so he could publish the book. Then, a few days after Wenderholm consulted Robertson, he was murdered.

Oscar Wenderholm was murdered because of the book he had written. Finally, Tony had a defense. It wasn't the bombshell that I had been hoping for, yet, but it was something.

When I stood to leave, Frank grabbed my wrist. "I just wanted to say, she's as beautiful as you were at that age."

I twisted out of his hold the way Jake had taught me, wrenching Frank's arm so much that I nearly pulled him out of his chair. "Hear this, old man. If you ever contact my daughter again, I will cut your heart out."

It felt good to say. Afterwards, I told myself that I had only spoken metaphorically.

ON THE WAY BACK from the prison, I called Yolanda to tell her that we needed subpoenas. She got them issued late on Friday and, judging by how much my office cell phone was blowing up, they were being served through the weekend. She had been driving her boyfriend, Gerry, a former cop, and a friend of Jake's, around San Francisco, tagging witnesses with their subpoenas. I put the ring tone on silent but watched for texts from her. She would let me know if there was a problem. Late Sunday morning, my cell phone buzzed with a text from her. "Done," is all it said.

Meanwhile, Quinn and I had spent the weekend at the dining room table, reviewing the exhibits, and preparing my examinations of the witnesses. Sunday morning, we went to bed around two a.m. and woke up just before noon to the intoxicating aroma of frying waffles. Jake was a good man.

Sunday afternoon, I went to the rehabilitation center to visit Tony. I brought four cups of coffee in a paper tray, one for both guards, and one each for Tony and me. The guard inside the room left without being asked and closed the door behind him. I dropped into the visitor's chair, not realizing until that moment how tired I was.

Tony asked, "what witnesses?"

"I don't want to get your hopes up, Tony. But I think we have enough evidence to support reasonable doubt – if the jury believes it."

"Then I can go home? I'll be free?"

"Not so fast. All I'm saying is that we have a theory, and we have some evidence. The jury could go either way. They may not believe it."

Tony was losing his patience. "What evidence?"

"In high school, Rick Stevens provided cocaine that killed one of their teachers. He could be charged with homicide. Oscar knew that and wrote about it in his book."

Tony's eyes went wide. "Are you saying he killed Oscar?"

"I'm saying he had a good reason too."

I filled Tony in on my plan.

When I finished, he looked frightened. Hope can be a terrible thing. When a client glimpses a chance to win, they are suddenly afraid they'll lose. It's easier to deal with despair than it is to believe your dream may come true, but you have no control over the outcome.

Chapter Twenty-Seven

Rick

SUNDAY MORNING, UMBERTO DROVE Rick home in Umberto's jet-black sports car.

Rick had spent the night at Umberto's apartment with Dimitri. That morning, Dimitri, ever shirtless, made omelets with tomatoes, artichokes, spinach, garlic, and feta cheese while croissants baked in the oven. As Dimitri beat the eggs, Rick mixed mimosas.

They were the happy young couple in love, just like on TV, gliding around each other in the kitchen space as they worked. Rick could see him living like this with Dimitri for the rest of his life. Yet when he mentioned their future, Dimitri was coy. Did he think he was just a plaything to Rick?

Rick couldn't bear the thought that Dimitri would doubt his devotion. He never had the nerve to tell David he loved him. He was glad that he hadn't because now Dimitri would be the first man Rick pledged his love to.

As they perched on stools at the breakfast bar, Rick pushed his food around with a fork. The moment had come. Playing house had grown stale, and Rick wanted more.

"Eat," Dimitri said. "You will hurt my feelings if you refuse my food."

"Can we talk?" Rick asked.

"Sure." Dimitri shrugged, dismissively. He reached for the mimosa pitcher and refilled Rick's flute.

"Look at me," Rick said.

Dimitri stood and threw his linen napkin onto the counter. "The big kiss-off, is it?"

Rick knew Dimitri had been hurt before. In quiet moments, he had shared how men had been infatuated with his beauty – he was confident about his looks – and how they would shower him with gifts and attention, until they became bored and moved on, having discovered that he was human like everyone else. He said he couldn't trust anyone again.

But Rick truly loved this man, the godlike and the human. Rick loved his foul breath in the morning. His off-key singing. His ridiculous laugh. How he sucked his teeth after dinner. These things made Dimitri real. It was the genuine Dimitri, vulnerable and vain, who made Rick feel safe because Rick was flawed as well. With Dimitri, he didn't need to pretend he was perfect. "I want to talk about us, our future."

"Rick," Dimitri slid into the kitchen and busied himself with cleaning up.

"Please, stop," Rick said.

Dimitri halted, pivoted in Rick's direction, with one fist on his hip, the irritated housewife.

"I love you." The words fell out of Rick's mouth before he had a chance to think about what he was saying.

Dimitri rolled his eyes and returned to his tasks. "Right."

Rick went into the kitchen where Dimitri stood at the sink, running hot water. Rick wrapped an arm around Dimitri's waist and kissed the angel wing tattoo on his shoulder. "Truly. I love you."

Dimitri's body was stiff. Rick stayed with him, his arms around Dimitri, not in a sexual way, but affectionately. He rested his cheek on Dimitri's shoulder. He savored the garlicy aroma of Dimitri's skin and soaked in the warmth of his body. After several moments, Dimitri relaxed and melted into him.

Dimitri then took Rick's hand and led him back into the bedroom.

Much later, a phone call from Umberto woke them.

On their way back to Rick's house, Umberto's car wound through the San Francisco streets as it was followed by the Dum Dee twins in their black SUV. At stop lights, people would point at Rick, having recognized him, and wave. Rick rolled down his window and gave them the thumbs up sign.

When they pulled onto Van Ness Boulevard, Rick said, "I'm divorcing Appollonia when this is over. I'm going to be with Dimitri."

"Does he know this?"

"I told him, in so many words."

"Let's deal with this after the election, shall we, Senator? Your numbers are good, but anything can change between now and election day. We've talked about this before – we can't afford a scandal. The election is next week. And then you'll be free to do whatever you want."

"I want Dimitri."

They had just pulled into Rick's driveway, when a third car, a red Ford Explorer, slipped in before the gate closed.

"What's going on?" Rick asked.

"Stay there." Umberto climbed out of the sports car and walked back to the Explorer as a man nearly as large as the Dum Dee twins got out and approached. He wore a plaid flannel shirt, jeans, and work boots, like a lumberjack. He even had a beard.

One of the twins got out of his SUV, but the lumberjack marched by so forcefully that the twin stepped back to give him room.

Words were exchanged. Umberto came back to the sports car, the big man following. Umberto motioned for Rick to step out of the car. When he did, the stranger said, "Are you Richard Stevens?"

Well, duh, he was. His picture was plastered all over every billboard, newspaper, and social media outlet.

"What's this about?"

Was he going to be arrested? This man didn't look like a cop. He didn't have a gun or badge or handcuffs.

The big man pushed a folded paper into Rick's chest with so much force that Rick instinctively reached for it as he stepped back to maintain his balance.

"You've been served," the big man said.

Rick turned to Umberto for explanation as the stranger stalked back to the red Explorer.

Umberto grabbed Rick's arm and steered him into the house. To the twins Umberto said, "you stay here. And try not to let anyone else in. Do you think you can handle that?"

"I don't understand," Rick said. "What's going on?"

"That man was a process server," Umberto said as he pulled the paper from Rick's hand.

"Someone's suing me?" This was insane. What had he done that would get him sued?

Rick fell onto the couch while Umberto stood over him, studying the document. "You know that murder trial that's going on? The defense attorney subpoenaed you to testify."

"About what? I don't know anything. You need to do something, Umberto. Make it go away."

Umberto reached into his pocket for his cell phone. "Get yourself a drink. I have some calls to make."

Chapter Twenty-Eight

Maureen

YOLANDA, QUINN, AND I arrived a half hour early on Monday morning. I'd expected trouble after the subpoenas were served. I was right.

I held the elevator door open as Yolanda and Quinn dragged the hand trucks stacked with bankers' boxers off the car, careful not to topple their loads as they crossed the metal floor trim, when I heard a voice behind me.

"Are you Maureen Gould?" I turned to find a besuited young woman, hair expensively cut, who I had never seen before.

"I am."

"This is for you." She handed me a stapled packet of papers. The top page was captioned "State of California versus Anthony Paredes." The document was entitled "Motion to Quash Subpoena of Richard Stevens." The attorney's name and address identified an expensive business law firm, one of my father's competitors, which I had never seen enter a criminal case before.

"What's this?" Yolanda asked.

I held the document up for her to see. Quinn peeked over her shoulder, then looked around to see if anyone was within ear shot. The young woman was now far down the hall, conferring with a young man. When they caught us looking at them, they turned their backs for privacy.

The firm had sent their junior staff to handle the matter. As the daughter of a business lawyer, I knew there was rarely anything pressing on the senior partner's desk first thing on a Monday morning that would prevent him from attending court. It was more likely that the senior partners didn't think the matter was worth their attention.

I couldn't help but note the female was tasked with the errand of serving me while the male hung back. There could have been a good explanation. She could have been his paralegal. She could have been a brand-new associate. But the look of it, the man giving orders, the woman carrying them out, rankled me.

Or maybe he was just shy, and I was overly sensitive to subtly expressed gender bias in the legal field.

Right.

"Is that bad?" Quinn whispered.

I shook my head. "You never know until it's over. Come on. Let's go do this thing."

I gave the heavy courtroom door a jerk and dragged it open, holding it as Yolanda and Quinn rolled the files in. While they unpacked, I read the motion and affidavit.

Rick Steven's attorney argued that I had violated the court rules by serving the subpoena less than forty-eight hours before he was expected to testify. Mr. Stevens was a busy and important man as he was the CEO of a multi-million-dollar car dealership and running for state office. Requiring him to appear on such short notice imposed substantial hardship upon him, the exact nature of which wasn't explained.

Vivian and her crew arrived fifteen minutes before the trial was scheduled to begin. She held a similar pack of documents in her hand. And she immediately went back out as her team unpacked their files. I assumed she was conferring with the expensive young lawyers.

The clerk stuck her head in, saw Vivian's chair was empty, and said, "The judge wants to know if we're ready to go on record."

Vivian's paralegal walked briskly out without answering. The clerk waited, half inside the door propped open with a shoulder.

The paralegal returned with Vivian and the two suits.

"We have a preliminary matter," Vivian told the clerk.

The clerk left, and the door drifting closed behind her. A few minutes later, the judge's door opened, and Judge Han swept in, as the clerk returned and slipped behind her station.

We all stood.

"Please be seated," Judge Han said. "Where's Mr. Paredes?"

I said, "He usually arrives shortly before we go on record."

Just then, the door behind the jury box used to escort prisoners opened and a guard pushed in Tony's wheelchair. He appeared more rested than he had been most mornings. Perhaps he was becoming accustomed to the stress of trial. Most likely, it was because he had told his story. He noticed the judge and the two new suits, then looked at me quizzically. He had expected to see Rick Stevens this morning.

The guard swung the wheelchair into place at counsel bench, then locked the wheels. Tony pushed himself up and side-stepped into his chair.

Judge Han said, "We have a motion to quash a subpoena. Is a Mr. Eberling in the courtroom?"

The young male attorney, who was now seated behind Vivian, raised his hand as if a teacher had called upon him in school.

"Mr. Eberling, have you served the parties with your motion?"

"Yes, ma'am."

The female next to him whispered in his ear and tried to inconspicuously point upwards.

He rose. "Yes, Your Honor."

"What is the State's position?"

Vivian stood. "The State objects to the calling of Mr. Stevens. He was not named on the defendant's witness list, so we have not prepared for his testimony. The State of California, like any party in a proceeding, is entitled to due process of law and a fair hearing. This is nothing less than trial by ambush. We ask the court to quash the subpoena."

Judge Han said, "Ms. Gould, what is your position?" She glanced at young Eberling who was still on his feet. "You may be seated."

I stood. "I apologize for the late notice of this new witness, Your Honor. I only learned this weekend that Mr. Stevens has information that is vital to my client's defense. As soon as I became aware of it, I emailed Ms. Thandi a revised witness list and served the subpoena. If the State prefers, we will stipulate to continue the trial. Say, a week?"

"But that's the election," young Eberling said. "He can't come in the middle of the election."

"You'll have the opportunity to speak when it's your turn, Mr. Eberling," Judge Han said.

Judge Han knew I would make the offer to continue the trial, and she didn't like it. Judges hate sending a jury home and then asking them to return days or weeks later. It causes a cascade of rescheduling problems for the subsequent trials. Also, all the jurors may not turn up. Then there is a mistrial, and the case must be restarted with a new jury. Or, during the continuance, the jurors may be exposed to information about the case. Again, mistrial and new jury.

Prosecutors also hated continuances in the middle of a trial. As time passes, the State's case seeps from the jury's memory. When the jurors deliberate, the freshest evidence they will remember is the defense case.

Judge Han said, "Mr. Eberling, what is the nature of the 'substantial hardship' that would be worked upon Mr. Stevens if he came to court today?"

Young Eberling stood. "He's preparing for the election."

"I understand. Does he have any public appearances today?"

Eberling looked at the woman next to him. She shook her head.

He said, "No appearances, Your Honor."

Judge Han said, "Then why can't he appear today?"

"He hasn't had the opportunity to meet with his attorney."

A scowl crossed the judge's face. "He had enough time to hire you, have you file this motion, and appear this morning."

"Yes, ma'am."

To Vivian, Judge Han said, "What is the State's position regarding a continuance?"

Vivian stared at her desk as if she was weighing the options for a few moments before she answered. "The state will agree to allow Mr. Stevens to testify if it has the opportunity to prepare before he goes on the stand."

"Mr. Eberling," the judge said. "What is Mr. Stevens' schedule like tomorrow?"

"Um, I don't know."

"Find out. This is your client's choice, Mr. Eberling. Mr. Stevens attends the trial tomorrow or he attends next week." Judge Han stood. "We'll be in recess. Five minutes."

As the judge left through the back door, Eberling's companion was walking out the front door with her cell phone in her hand.

Six minutes later, the judge was on the bench. "What will it be, Mr. Eberling? Tomorrow or next week."

He stood. "Tomorrow, Your Honor."

"Very well. Madam Clerk, bring in the jury. Ms. Gould, call your next witness."

I HAD ANTICIPATED STEVENS would complain about appearing on Monday, so I had also subpoenaed two other witnesses to appear. The jury filed in and took their seats as Quinn went out into the hallway and she returned a few minutes later, ushering the witness.

I stood. "The defense calls Emerson Katsu."

Ian Napier, his attorney, followed behind Quinn and Mr. Katsu. When Quinn opened the railing gate, the witness hung back a moment while Ian whispered in his ear. Then he noticed that everyone in the room was watching.

"Sorry," Ian said quietly. Then he drifted into the second pew behind my table, taking a seat where he would have an unblocked view of the witness stand.

"Please come forward, Mr. Katsu," Judge Han said as she gestured towards the witness stand. "And remain standing while the clerk administers the oath."

He did so, raising his right hand. When the oath was completed, Judge Han said, "Please be seated."

The clerk instructed him to clip the microphone to his suit lapel. He fussed with it a bit, then settled into his chair, and looked around the room.

"Good morning, Mr. Katsu," I said.

"Good morning," he answered.

"The following questions may sound awkward to you, but we need to establish how you became involved in this case."

He nodded.

"Do you know my client, Anthony Paredes?"

"I do. He was a student at the school where I work."

"That would be Lafeyette Academy?"

"Yes, ma'am."

"Did you know a man named Oscar Wenderholm?"

Mr. Katsu looked over at Ian for a moment and apparently received the signal that he was looking for. "I did."

"Please explain to the jury how you came to know him."

The witness faced me when he said, "we were students together in high school."

"Is that all?"

"We were on the same chess team."

"How was it that Mr. Wenderholm came to work at your high school?"

"The school wanted to develop a competitive chess program. I knew Oscar was available, so I recommended him."

Vivian was sitting erect in her chair, poised to stand for an objection.

I continued. "Were you involved in Mr. Wenderholm's dismissal from Lafayette Academy?"

Vivian jumped to her feet. "Objection!"

Judge Han said, "State your grounds, Ms. Thandi."

"May we approach the bench?" Vivian asked.

I suspected I knew what she was going to argue. If she said it in front of the jury, they would hear the evidence that she was trying to keep out.

Judge Han waived us forward. When we were both pressed against the bench wall, she pushed a button to engage the white noise machine.

"Ms. Thandi, your objection?"

"The decedent's character is not relevant to this case. This line of questioning is a mere attempt to demonize him in order to sway the jury's sympathy."

"Ms. Gould?"

"Your Honor, Mr. Paredes has already testified about the abuse he suffered from Mr. Wenderholm. In fact, it is an element of the State's case against him to establish motive."

"Very well," Judge Han said. "Ms. Thandi, you opened the door to this testimony. Objection denied." She flicked her hand as if to brush us away.

We returned to our positions, me at the lectern, Vivian in her chair.

I repeated my question. "Mr. Katsu, were you involved in Mr. Wenderholm's dismissal from Lafayette Academy?"

The jury seemed to lean into the witness, eager to soak up the information Vivian wanted to keep from them.

"I was."

"Please explain the circumstances."

"I was the one that found them together." Katsu fidgeted. "This is awkward for me."

The jury held its collective breath.

"Go on," Judge Han said.

"They were engaged in a sexual act."

The jury pulled back. They'd heard it before and didn't need a detailed retelling of the sordid story.

"Let's move on," I said.

The jury relaxed fractionally.

"Were you surprised at what you saw?" I asked.

"I had no idea Oscar would do that to a student. None. I promptly reported it to the principal. The boy, Anthony, was sent home. Oscar was suspended that afternoon. An emergency meeting of the Board took place that night. The Board decided to let Oscar go."

"Was a letter of recommendation provided by the school for Mr. Wenderholm?"

"I don't know. I wasn't involved in that decision. All I know is that he was let go."

"And Tony, what happened to him?"

"The Board felt that his continued enrollment in the school would be a distraction so it would be better for him and the student body if he withdrew."

Out of the corner of my eye, I saw Tony shaking his head. He didn't feel like the decision to expel him had been for his own good. He felt like it was punishment.

"Mr. Katsu, did you maintain contact with Mr. Wenderholm following his termination?"

He shook his head. "We weren't friends, at least not anymore. I nearly lost my job over what he did."

"Did he contact you?"

"I hadn't heard from him in years, and then he called out of the blue. Just a few months ago. He wanted to meet, he said. To make amends."

"Did you meet?"

"We did."

"What occurred in this meeting?"

"He told me that he had learned that what happened with Tony was the result of his own trauma."

The Social Worker nodded. It was a pattern she would have seen before. Sweater Man rested his head on his fist, absorbing a story he was all too familiar with.

"What was Mr. Wenderholm talking about?"

"He said that our high school chess coach, Mr. Shroeder, had abused him. Oscar, that is. And that he had never recovered from the abuse, so he felt compelled to recreate his trauma so that he could deal with it. I had no idea when we were in school that anything like that was going on."

"Was this teacher the same Mr. Shroeder who died during a student excursion to Las Vegas?"

Katsu's attention skittered to Ian Napier, then back to me. He wasn't expecting this question. "Why, yes. How did you know about that?"

"Were you on that trip?"

"I was."

"Do you know what Mr. Shroeder died of?"

"A heart attack. At least, that's what the school told us."

I shifted my weight to signal a change in direction.

"So, Oscar Wenderholm told you that he abused Anthony Paredes so he could make himself feel better?"

"Not in those words. It was all subconscious, he said."

"How did he come to this conclusion? Did he go to therapy?"

"He read about it online. How pedophilia is passed on from abuser to victim and then the victim becomes an abuser."

"You said he wanted to make amends. That was to you, I assume."

He nodded. "Yes."

The Social Worker looked over at Tony for a reaction. He stiffened. There were no amends from Oscar Wenderholm to Tony – only to Emerson Katsu.

"Did he apologize to you?"

"Not in so many words. He gave me a watch, a rather expensive one. He had bought one for himself too."

Katsu wasn't wearing the watch today. I pointedly glanced at his wrist. He covered it with his other hand and began to blush. He was ashamed of it, as he should be. "I don't wear it anymore."

"Mr. Wenderholm worked as a security guard. How could he afford two expensive watches?"

"He said he wrote a book, and a publisher gave him a lot of money for an advance."

This was news to the jurors. I could practically hear electricity crackle from them. Their heads turned in every direction, gauging the reactions of Judge Han, Vivian, Tony, me, and each other.

"Do you know what the book was about?"

"Vaguely. I gathered he had written about what happened to him in school."

"Was the book published?"

"As far as I know, it hasn't been. When I last talked to Oscar, he said there was some kind of delay. He was frustrated because he wanted to quit his job. He was hoping the royalties would be more than enough to support his family."

Tony's shoulders were hitched up. Wenderholm planned to cash in on his story after ruining Tony's life. I heard Yolanda come through the gate and take my chair. The guard started. He wasn't sure if she was allowed across the railing while the court was in session. The judge discreetly waved him back.

Yolanda poured a glass of water. She scooted the chair closer to him so he could feel her warmth. She was such a great mother. I could learn from her. Would she threaten to cut someone's heart out if they hurt her child?

I continued the questioning. "Mr. Katsu, did Oscar Wenderholm explain what caused the delay in publication?"

"He did not. But he said if it went on any longer, he was going to find a new publisher."

"When did he say this to you?"

"A couple of weeks before he died."

"So, you're saying that two weeks after Oscar Wenderholm told you he was going to get his book published, he was murdered?"

Vivian half-rose out of her chair but Mr. Katsu answered before she could make an objection.

"I guess that's what happened."

"Thank you, Mr. Katsu. I pass the witness."

The jury collectively took a deep breath and exhaled slowly. They were forming a group identity. It happened in every trial.

I gathered my notes slowly to give Yolanda time to vacate my chair and return to the pew behind the railing. When I took my seat, it was still positioned close to Tony. After all the time we'd spent in court, he knew not to speak in front of the jury. I looked at him. I wanted to know if he was happy with the questioning. He nodded, then focused again on Katsu.

The jury turned its attention to Vivian, waiting.

She flipped through the legal pad where she had recorded her notes, then stood. "The State has no questions for this witness."

Judge Han looked at the clock. It was nearly eleven thirty a.m. "Ladies and gentlemen of the jury, we will take an early lunch break."

Everyone stood as the jury filed out. When the door was closed, Judge Han, still on her feet, asked. "Ms. Gould, are you prepared to go forward with your next witness?"

"Yes, Your Honor."

"Very well. We shall reconvene at one this afternoon."

Chapter Twenty-Nine

Maureen

"The defense calls Charles Robertson." I was back at the lectern with the judge, jury, Vivian, and Tony all in their places.

Quinn stood by the back door, waiting for her cue. She slipped out and quickly returned. I watched Robertson's entrance, emphasizing for the jury that this was a witness they should pay attention to. He strode up the aisle, wearing an expensive navy-blue suit and midnight blue tie. When he was half-way to the railing, I could see the whites of his eyes were stained yellow, something I hadn't noticed before. My father's eyes had been the same. It was caused by heavy drinking.

Before Robertson swung open the gate, I smelled day-old alcohol seeping from him. As he passed, he took the opportunity to slide a side-eye at me. He wasn't happy to be here.

Tony wasn't happy to be here either, escorted by guards, still injured from a brutal beating, and in fear that the result of this trial could be a death sentence for him.

Charles Robertson could tolerate the inconvenience.

The witness was sworn in. He clipped the microphone to his lapel and turned to me, his face stony.

"Mr. Robertson, what is 'catch and kill'?"

"What?"

"Catch and kill. Please explain to the jury the meaning of that term."

"I don't understand." He was stalling, hoping Vivian would interrupt.

Witnesses are coached to say they don't understand the question. The counter is to suggest they are ignorant. They usually rise to the bait.

"Are you testifying you don't understand the term 'catch and kill'?"

Robertson didn't fall for the trap. "It's not really my field. I don't understand why you are asking me this question."

Vivian had been thumbing through her notes, distracted. She looked up and saw the witness begging her for help with his stare.

Robertson said, "Could you repeat the question?"

"Please explain to the jury the meaning of the term 'catch and kill'."

"Objection!" Vivian was on her feet. "This witness was not called as an expert. We don't see the relevance of this line of questioning."

Judge Han looked at me.

Never let an objection go unpunished.

"The relevance," I said deliberately, "is that Oscar Wenderholm was murdered because of 'catch and kill'."

Vivian's mouth hung open, her hands in the air.

The judge hadn't ruled so I kept talking. "Oscar Wenderholm wrote a book and sold it to a publisher. When the book wasn't released, he said he was going to demand his rights back so that he could find a new publisher. He was killed shortly after this decision."

Vivian's head whipped towards me and then to the judge. If she went on objecting, I would continue to deliver what was essentially my closing argument. She didn't want Robertson to answer the question, but she didn't want me arguing any more either.

Judge Han asked, "Ms. Gould, how is Mr. Robertson's testimony relevant on this point?"

Robertson leaned back in his chair with a smile on his face, showing that he approved of Judge Han's question. She shot him a look which conveyed she didn't care what he approved of.

I answered, "It is our belief that Oscar Wenderholm consulted Mr. Robertson about getting his book rights back."

Judge Han said, "If so, wouldn't that communication be covered by attorney-client privilege?"

Robertson's eyebrows lifted in an amused expression.

"I am not asking Mr. Robertson to tell us what was communicated to him. I am merely asking him to explain 'catch and kill' to the jury. Your Honor, this testimony dovetails with that of Mr. Katsu, who told us Oscar Wenderholm intended to get his rights back."

Judge Han said, "On this narrow point, I will allow testimony." She turned to the witness. "Mr. Robertson, please explain to us the concept of 'catch and kill'."

He filled the witness stand with his presence, then turned to the jury. "'Catch and kill' is when a publisher buys a story with no intent of publishing it for the purpose of preventing its release."

The Librarian and Social Worker wrote in their legal pads. Sweater Man, who had been facing the witness, turned his chair just enough to watch me.

Judge Han said, "Ms. Gould, do you have any more questions of this witness?"

"No, Your Honor."

"Ms. Thandi, cross-examination?"

"The State has no questions for this witness."

"Thank you. Mr. Robertson, you are excused."

Sweater Man leaned back in his chair, relaxed for the first time in the trial. The Social Worker, too, looked comfortable. They each had formulated a theory. From here on out, they would accept testimony that validated their stories and reject that which did not. It would take a mountain of evidence to change their minds.

I hoped they believed Tony was innocent.

Court recessed after Robertson's testimony as the judge had given Rick Stevens until the next day to testify. I asked the guard to give us a few moments to confer before he took Tony back to the holding cells.

Tony and I turned our chairs around so we could talk to Yolanda and Quinn, seated in the front pew. Back in the days when I prosecuted, I'd see clients lose confidence with their attorneys because the lawyer would interact with his team only, leaving the client on the sidelines.

This was Tony's life on the line. He had every right to be included in every discussion.

"How are you feeling?" I asked.

"Better," he said. "But do the jurors get it? Do they understand?"

Quinn had proven her keen observation skills in our last trial. Even though she was young, she picked up on subtle hints. She said, "Sweater Man and the Social Worker get it. The Librarian follows closely. She can see that you're going somewhere, but she wants more to convince her. Grizzled Man, the disabled older gentleman, appears a little bewildered and he's intrigued when Ms. Thandi objects."

Yolanda chimed in. "He's the kind of guy to expect a conspiracy. The harder Thandi fights you, the more likely he is to be on your side."

Or the more likely he was to believe that I was the conspirator and Vivian was the champion of truth. You could never tell. But I didn't say that in front of Tony – there was no reason to alarm him.

"The retirees, how are they taking it?" I asked.

"They're following but they aren't leaning in either direction."

Tony asked, "Do you think we're winning?"

"Oh, sweetie," Yolanda gripped his hand. Ever the mother, she sensed his fear and wanted to comfort him. I wished I'd had a mother like that. Even if the things that happened hadn't, my mother would never have been the warm, loving type.

The guard didn't challenge her. I glanced around and saw that he was pretending to be distracted by his thoughts.

I answered Tony's question as compassionately as I could. "You never know, Tony. Winning or losing is something we don't think about during trial. Because if we do, we can become complacent or anxious and miss something important. We'll just keep marching through this, doing the next right thing. Agreed?"

Yolanda looked over my shoulder. The guard must have decided it was time to go.

"Agreed," Tony said.

Chapter Thirty

Maureen

THE FOLLOWING DAY, I called Rick Stevens to the stand. He entered the courtroom with a silver-haired man in a gray pin-striped suit at his elbow – no doubt the senior partner. I'd never seen him before.

The man slipped into the pew behind Vivian and exchanged a hushed greeting with her as the prosecution paralegal opened the gate for the witness.

The jury sat a little straighter as Stevens crossed the well towards the stand, wearing an expensive blue suit that set off his eyes. When asked to recite his name, he gave the famous smile, perfect white teeth, deeply dimpled cheeks, amused that he would have to introduce himself. Several of the jurors smiled as well.

I didn't like how quickly they were being charmed by him.

"Mr. Stevens," I said. "Could you please explain to the jury the nature of your relationship with Oscar Wenderholm?"

He dipped one shoulder as he twisted to face them, posing. "We were in high school together."

"And since high school?"

"I've had very little contact with him," he told the jury.

"What do you know about the book he had written?"

He turned to me and feigned a confused frown. His eyes twinkled the same way Frank's did when he was confronted with a lie, thrilled with the cat and mouse game. "A book?"

"Yes, Mr. Stevens. Oscar Wenderholm's book."

"I don't know anything about a book."

The night before Quinn stayed up late, researching online. She woke me a little after midnight to show me her discovery. I flipped my trial notebook to the printout.

"Are you familiar with Lone Star Publishing?"

"Can't say that I am."

"Then you would not be aware that Lone Star Publishing has never released a book, is that right?"

He shrugged. "Never heard of them. How could I know?"

"Were you aware that Lone Star Publishing had purchased the rights to publish Oscar Wenderholm's book?"

The smile faltered. Stevens peered into the courtroom, locked onto his attorney, his head jutted forward, and he frowned.

I turned to see the attorney mouthing the words "if you know."

"If you know" is a cue attorneys give to their clients in depositions, telling them to dummy up, pretend they don't have any knowledge relevant to the question. It's witness tampering, but they get away with it in depositions because a judge isn't watching.

I was on my feet. "Your Honor, Mr. Stevens' attorney is coaching the witness!"

Judge Han said, "Ladies and gentlemen of the jury, we will take a short recess. The bailiff will escort you to the jury room now."

When they rose, Sweater Man gave me a knowing look before dropping his legal pad face down on his chair.

Judge Han waited for the door to click shut, then addressed Stevens' attorney. "Sir, please identify yourself for the record."

He stood. "Henry Northrup, counsel to Richard Stevens."

"Mr. Northrup, just before Ms. Gould made her objection, I observed you mouthing words."

Northrup said nothing.

"It appeared that you were trying to convey a message to Mr. Stevens."

Still Northrup said nothing. His face seemed to swell as his neck began to bulge above his collar.

Judge Han went on. "I don't claim to be a lip-reader, but it appeared to me that the message you were attempting to convey to Mr. Stevens was 'if you know.' I must agree with Ms. Gould's interpretation. You are clearly trying to influence the witness' testimony. I'm inclined to have you removed from the courtroom."

"Your Honor, I was just mumbling to myself, a nasty habit I've had for years. I apologize if it's caused any confusion. But the law is clear that Mr. Stevens is entitled to counsel of his choice."

Stevens was indeed entitled to whatever attorney he wanted. But why would he want an attorney with him unless he was worried that he might get into trouble?

Judge Han said, "I'm not confused whatsoever, Mr. Northrup. I must caution you that witness tampering is a serious offense as well as contempt of court. You should probably not say anything further in your own defense. If I see your lips move again, I will charge you with contempt. Do you understand?"

Northrup's face was now florid.

"Can I say something?" It was Rick Stevens talking.

Judge Han swung towards the witness stand. "Sure, Mr. Stevens, what do you have to say?"

"It's okay if Henry goes. I'll be fine on my own."

"Mr. Stevens," Northrup said with a warning in his voice.

"No, really. I'll be fine. Let's get this over with."

NORTHRUP LEFT THE COURTROOM, and the jury was led back.

Judge Han said, "Ms. Gould, you may continue."

"Before our break, I had asked you if you were aware that Lone Star Publishing had purchased the rights to Oscar Wenderholm's book."

"I was not aware. Like I said, I didn't know about a book, and I don't know who Lone Star Publishing is."

"Lone Star Publishing has the same business address as the political action committee that backs your candidacy. It's a post office box in Burlingame."

Stevens tried a quick smile, then shrugged. "Sorry, can't help you."

"You said you had little contact with Oscar Wenderholm after school, is that right?"

"Yes."

"But he was working at your warehouse."

"I don't see what that has to do with anything."

"How did it happen that he got a job working at your warehouse?"

Stevens snapped his fingers. "Now I remember! He came into the dealership a few years ago, looking for a job. He said he was having trouble finding work. I didn't get into the details with him, but he was an old acquaintance so I felt like I should help out. I didn't have anything for him on site, so I sent him to the warehouse."

"When you were in school with Oscar, did you go on a student excursion to Las Vegas?"

"Maybe. I'd have to think about it."

"This was a particularly noteworthy trip. One of your teachers died."

He blinked rapidly. "Of course. Poor Mr. Shroeder."

"We have had testimony that the book Mr. Wenderholm had written was about abuse he had suffered from Mr. Shroeder."

"Like I said, I didn't know that. I don't know anything about abuse."

"Do you know what Mr. Shroeder died of?"

He stared into the distance for a moment before answering thoughtfully. "I don't think anyone told me."

"It was a drug overdose."

Vivian leapt to her feet. "Your Honor!"

The judge looked at me.

"I have a good faith basis for asking this question." I was signaling to the judge that I had evidence, but I was careful not to detail it before the jury as it had not been introduced yet and I didn't want to cause a mistrial by discussing unadmitted evidence.

She said, "I'll give you some flexibility, but wrap it up."

I waited for the jury's full attention.

"Mr. Stevens, if Mr. Wenderholm's book revealed the truth about your teacher's overdose, then those responsible for giving him the drugs would be exposed to criminal prosecution."

Stevens fumbled with his tie. "I don't know what you mean."

"I'll explain it. If that person who delivered the drugs to Mr. Shroeder was you, Mr. Stevens, your political career would be destroyed, and you could go to prison. So, you would have a very good motive for wanting that book stopped. Don't you agree?"

"Objection!"

"Sustained!" The judge didn't give me a chance to argue. Since I had just accused Rick Stevens of having a motive to murder, I didn't expect Judge Han would let him answer the question. She wasn't going to allow Stevens to lie, inviting a perjury charge, or tell the truth in violation of his Fifth Amendment right to remain silent.

That's why I saved that question for last. I wanted that question emblazoned on the juror's minds. I looked at the jury box. The Librarian and Sweater Man were writing in their legal pads. The Social Worker looked like she had made her mind up. Grizzled

Man appeared confused. A couple of the other jurors looked as if they had just smelled something disgusting.

"Ms. Gould, do you have any further questions for this witness?'

"No, Your Honor."

"Ms. Thandi?"

"The State has no cross-examination."

Judge Han dismissed Rick Stevens and recessed court for the day.

Chapter Thirty-One

Rick

RICK COULDN'T GET OUT of that courtroom fast enough. He banged through both sets of doors. In the hallway, Henry Northrup, his so-called attorney, was nowhere to be found. This was all his fault. If Northrup had prepared him properly, he wouldn't have fallen into the lawyer-bitch's trap. Where does Umberto find these people? As soon as he was safely home, Rick would make sure Umberto fired that guy and put someone else on retainer, someone who didn't look like he was going to drop dead of a heart attack any minute.

That lawyer-bitch was clever, but everyone saw what she was doing. She was making Rick out to be the scapegoat. She as much as accused him of killing Oscar. Good thing there were no reporters in the courtroom.

The Dum Dee twins had dropped Rick off at the courthouse that morning. Umberto told him to text when he was ready to leave and then to be outside the courthouse twenty minutes later. Rick thumbed the words "pick me up" to Umberto, then slipped his phone back in his pocket.

The courtroom doors opened. The prosecutor came out with a couple of assistants behind her.

"How could you let that happen?" Rick asked.

She held up a hand. "Mr. Stevens, I'm not your attorney. I caution you not to speak to me."

"Yeah, but –."

"Don't say another word." She shouldered past him on her way to the elevator bank. Her assistants gathered behind her, forming a wall.

"So much for public servants!" Stevens shouted after her.

The courtroom door opened again. That lawyer-bitch came out, with two women behind her.

The men's room was the safest place to be while Rick waited for his ride. That bitch might have balls, but she wasn't going to follow him in there.

In the men's room, Rick tried calling Dimitri. His phone rolled over to voicemail. Rick didn't text because Umberto had cautioned him that any messages could be discovered some day, and they may not look good. At least Dimitri would have seen that he called, and he'd know that Rick was thinking about him. All Rick wanted was to go to his own home with his lover and drink Mimosas in the hot tub.

It wouldn't be long now before that dream would come true.

Rick checked his watch. It was eighteen minutes after he had texted Umberto. He took the elevator downstairs, passed by the courthouse security, and pushed open the heavy glass door.

"Mr. Stevens!"

Rick didn't recognize the voice. When he looked in the direction it came from, a mob of people ran towards him. Some held microphones pointed in his direction. Behind them were men and women with television cameras hoisted onto their shoulders.

The passenger loading zone in front of the courthouse was empty. Rick scanned the street. The twins' SUV wasn't parked anywhere. And it wasn't coming down the street.

"Mr. Stevens," a woman's voice called out. "Do you have any comments?"

Uh, no! He was just accused of murdering Oscar. But they didn't know that.

"Just doing my civil duty," he said. "Like any good citizen."

Rick raised his arm to ward off the reporters as he pulled out his cell phone. He hit the speed dial for Umberto. It rang over to voicemail.

A barrage of voices hit him, so many Rick couldn't make out what they were saying.

Where were the twins? Why wasn't Umberto answering his phone? Rick searched the street again.

A reporter held up a photograph in front of his face. Two people in bed. The one on the bottom, his face visible, was Rick. The other's back was to the camera, but Rick knew who it was. An angel wing tattoo was on his shoulder. Dimitri.

Someone had betrayed them. Their secret was out. Rick felt like he was going to throw up. When he ran across the street to escape the reporters, horns blared while cars screeched to avoid hitting him. He flagged a passing cab and dived in.

Who would have done this to him? Why?

Chapter Thirty-Two

Maureen

By THE TIME WE unloaded the files at the office, the story of the Rick Stevens scandal had gone viral. Someone had sent salacious photographs to the San Francisco news outlets. The images weren't published – no doubt the media was worried about a lawsuit – but they were described in various ways, depending on the tone of each site.

A few called them "intimate," while some said they were "lewd," and others used the word, "pornographic." Yet their theme was consistent. Rick Stevens had been photographed in bed with another man. That in itself would not be a problem in San Francisco, unless the person photographed was a populist candidate for office who held himself out to be happily married to a woman.

Rick Stevens' political career was over.

Yolanda, Quinn, and I stood in the reception area of my office, each of us scrolling through our phones reading the news, while the bankers' boxes, and my briefcase were on the floor where we had dropped them.

Yolanda looked at her watch. "Quinn, aren't you supposed to be in class?"

I was so wound up in the trial, I had forgotten about Quinn's schedule. Some mother.

"The prof excused me. I told him we had an important witness."

"Attendance counts," I said.

"My friends are taking notes for me. The prof said that just this once, it'll be okay."

"Just this once, then," I said.

Yolanda gave me a recriminating look. She did not approve of cutting class. "Where does this Rick Stevens thing leave us?"

I had no idea. "The jury isn't supposed to see the news."

"Does it matter if there's a scandal just as you put him on the stand?" Quinn asked.

"It shouldn't," I said, more in speculation than in confidence.

"You proved he could have killed Oscar," Quinn said.

"I suggested he had a motive. Means isn't a problem. Anyone can get a gun. But I can't see how Stevens had an opportunity."

"He didn't claim he had an alibi," Quinn pointed out. "He could have done it. Just drove up to Oscar's house, bang, and drove off. That's the prosecution's theory about Tony, right? They don't have any evidence he was actually there when Oscar got shot."

Quinn was correct. The prosecution had not placed Tony at the murder scene.

More importantly to me, its theory as to Tony's motive didn't ring true. Why, after all these years, would Tony kill? But Rick Stevens had a much more pressing motive to get rid of Oscar. If the book Oscar was trying to publish linked Stevens to the death of David Shroeder, Stevens could be prosecuted for that homicide.

I said, "Technically, we have enough evidence to establish reasonable doubt, but it's thin. I wish we had more."

Quinn asked, "Why don't you bring Dakota Vaugh in to testify?"

"He'd refuse to go on the stand. That guy is a savvy criminal. If what Frank said was true, then he supplied the drugs to Rick Stevens that ended up killing Shroeder. Dakota knows that he would be equally culpable for murder. There's no way he's going to admit to that unless he gets immunity, and I don't have the power to give it to him."

"That leaves Mrs. Wenderholm," Yolanda said. "She's your last witness. And she goes on first thing in the morning." Yolanda jingled her keys. She was ready to go home and feed her brood.

I looked at my watch. Traffic would be brutal at this hour, but Yolanda wasn't going to get home any faster unless she left now. "Yolanda, I'm so sorry. Get out of here. We'll see you tomorrow."

"Are you sure?"

"Quinn and I will take the files home. We've got this. Love to the kids."

LUCKILY, IT WAS JAKE'S night to cook, which meant that we had warm, nutritious food. He made what he called his "Manly Man Mac Supreme" which had three kinds of cheese and just enough pepper to give it some heat. Quinn and I had one Anchor Steam beer each with dinner because we had work to do. Before he retired to the bedroom to watch TV, Jake brewed a large pot of coffee for us.

Not that I needed a stimulant. Tomorrow was my last chance to save Tony's life.

We spread the files out across the dining room table. Quinn set up her laptop on the breakfast bar while I moved my chair to the middle of the table and set up my laptop there. I started with the crime scene photos.

Oscar Wenderholm's body was sprawled next to his truck, half on the driveway, half on the lawn. It appeared he had exited the vehicle and walked around the back of it on his way to the front door when he had been shot.

The prosecution's theory was that Tony had driven up in his delivery truck, jumped out, crossed the lawn to approach Oscar, shot him, and then driven away.

It was impossible from the physical evidence to challenge that theory. The bullet was a .22. When it entered Oscar's skull, it bounced around inside, causing extensive damage, and didn't exit. There was no way of calculating the angle of the trajectory.

The autopsy photos showed a mark on his hip that the medical examiner was unable to explain, however, he speculated that or when Oscar was shot, his body slammed into the truck before it fell. The report concluded that he was standing a few feet away from the vehicle when he was shot, but the exact spot could not be precisely determined.

The entry wound proved that Oscar was facing his killer. The prosecution theorized Tony approached him from the street, but in this theory, Rick Stevens could have just as easily shot the gun.

Or Oscar could have been facing the house when he was shot.

I grabbed the Brita Wenderholm file. Inside it was a transcript of her testimony during Tony's bail review. Something she had said bothered me at the time. I sensed that it was important but didn't know why. I read each sentence, one at a time, until I came upon it: "If it hadn't been for my brother, we would have lost the house."

"Quinn, what do we know about Brita Wenderholm's brother?"

"She has a brother?" Quinn didn't know about him because she wasn't at the bail review, so she didn't hear the testimony, and the brother wasn't mentioned anywhere in the file.

"A brother who helps her out. Do a full background search on her. Find her maiden name and people who she's lived with. From there, you should be able to identify him. Then get everything you can on him."

"Why?"

"I have a feeling, that's all."

It was difficult to focus on anything while Quinn searched for the brother, so I began typing up a timeline:

1993: Oscar Wenderholm, Dakota Vaughn, and Rick Stevens were in Las Vegas on a school trip when their chaperone, David Shroeder died of an overdose.

Shroeder's death wasn't the first thing that happened. I moved it down the page to insert above it:

1993: David Shroeder, a chess coach, sexually abused Oscar Wenderholm when he was a student.

Then came Shroeder's drug overdose.

2003: Oscar sexually abused Tony. Tony was expelled. Oscar was let go with a letter of recommendation.

2015: Tony sued Oscar. Wins millions of dollars. Judgment is set aside because of jury misconduct.

2018: Tony spotted Oscar talking to kids in a gaming arcade. Tony is worried that Oscar is grooming and will abuse them.

About the same time, Oscar concluded that his victimization of Tony was the result of his past trauma. He believed that he could profit from his story, so he wrote a book.

Oscar sold the rights to Lone Star Publishing. Lone Star has a relationship with the political action committee backing Rick Stevens. Stevens denies it. *Note: Stevens denies knowledge of the book. We need to link Stevens to Lone Star Publishing. Does Brita have information re publisher?*

June 2018: Oscar told Emerson Katsu that Lone Star isn't going forward with his book. He wanted to get his rights back so he could get it published.

June 2018: Oscar consulted Charles Robertson about getting his rights back. *Note: Robertson asserted attorney-client privilege. We need to show that Oscar consulted him about the book. Does Brita have information re attempt to get rights back?*

July 9, 2018: Oscar was murdered.

Quinn threw her arms up in victory. "I've got him."

She punched her keyboard twice, making the printer in her room wheeze and crunch to life. She ran down the hall and came back with paper, which she handed to me.

"Benjamin Hugois the brother's name. He owns an antique shop in San Jose. He travels around California and Nevada going to shows where he buys and sells stuff." She brought her laptop to me. "Take a look at his website."

The monitor displayed a home page template that looked like it was built years ago by an amateur. There was no menu. The home page was the entire website. On the left side was a list of wares he claimed to sell, including estate auctions, jewelry, and electronics. On the right was a column of photographs, long shots of his store taken at different angles. It didn't look like any of the antique shops my mother dragged me to in Napa when I was little. It looked like a pawn shop. The physical address was in San Jose.

The photos were filled to the brim with stuff and overwhelmed me. "Eek gad, what am I looking at?"

Quinn bent over my shoulder and touched the screen with two fingers, expanding one of the photos.

"This," she said.

I had the facts in the right order, but the thing that had come before was not the thing that had caused the murder.

Post hoc, ergo propter hoc.

Chapter Thirty-Three

Maureen

"The defense calls Brita Wenderholm to the stand."

I ran my fingers across the O'Shaughnessy pearl necklace for good luck while Quinn brought the witness into the courtroom. I didn't watch her, as I had watched Charles Robertson. She was the kind of person who sucked attention from others to stoke her fury. Using ever-escalating outrage, she controlled others around her.

I wasn't going to give her the chance.

I would look at her as little as possible. Instead, I would have eye contact with the dominant jurors, Sweater Man, the Librarian, the Social Worker, Grizzled Man, as much as I could to keep them from fueling her.

I feigned looking at my notes as she passed behind me, crossed the well, took the witness stand, and was sworn in.

Judge Han said, "Ms. Gould, you may begin."

Focusing on the list of questions I'd scripted the night before, I asked, "Mrs. Wenderholm, how are you employed?"

"I'm not. I homeschool my kids."

I checked off the question.

"Why is that?"

She answered, "Because the schools are too dangerous with all the drugs and guns."

Check.

"And, as their mother, you would do everything you could to protect them?"

"Absolutely." Her voice, clear and loud.

Check.

I looked at Sweater Man, then asked, "Mrs. Wenderholm, were you aware that your husband had gone to school with Rick Stevens?"

"He talked about it all the time."

Check.

"What did he say about Mr. Stevens?"

Her voice was growing incrementally louder with each answer. "That he knew this bigshot, the car salesman who was running for senate, and what a good friend Rick Stevens was to him, giving him a job when no one else would."

She was fighting for control of our conversation. I paused, to show her who really was in control. I flipped the page of my notebook, then asked, "That was the job at the warehouse?"

"It was the only job he could get after what your client said about him."

Check.

"By that you mean, what he said in the television interview."

"Everyone saw it."

"You saw it too."

"It was all over the news. I couldn't help but see it."

Big check.

Before court, Yolanda has set up a large monitor in the courtroom well. I picked up the remote she had left on the lectern and keyed it. The screen sprang to life.

I swept my eyes from the jurors to the screen, directing their attention, and took the opportunity to glimpse the witness. She wore a navy-blue dress with rhinestone buttons. Her graying hair had been recently styled and colored to a pale blonde. She was seated forward, locked on me, both hands gripping the desk in front of her.

The video image showed Tony standing on the sidewalk in front of a café. Behind him was the Alhambra Theatre marquee, a San Francisco landmark with a distinct Moorish Revival design. The interview had taken place across the street from the apartment he shared with Isaac.

I hit play.

Tony began speaking to a reporter who was out of frame but apparently standing next to the camera.

"Oscar Wenderholm is a monster," Tony said. "Everyone needs to know so they can protect their children."

Vivian pushed to her feet. "Objection. Hearsay."

Judge Han looked at me for a response.

"Your Honor, as I said before, the prosecution's theory is that Mr. Paredes was motivated by hatred of Mr. Wenderholm. The State opened the door to this evidence."

"Objection denied," the judge said. "You may continue, Ms. Gould."

Vivian had an air of resignation when she lowered herself into her chair.

I pointed to the screen. "Is this the video that you saw, Mrs. Wenderholm?"

"That's the one."

Check.

"When did you see it?"

"Right after the trial." She gestured at Tony. "That's why the judge canceled the verdict, because of what he said on TV."

"Is it your belief that the judge vacated the verdict because what Mr. Paredes said in this interview was the truth?"

The witness shrieked. "How dare you!"

Vivian kept her head down, giving the appearance that she was taking notes. I imagined that she didn't want the witness sucking energy from her either.

Judge Han said, "Mrs. Wenderholm, please control yourself."

There was a pause. I glanced up from my notebook to see the witness grabbing a handful of tissues which she pressed to her eyes. She took several gasping breaths, then took the wad away from her face.

I stepped back from the lectern. I wanted her to know that I was prepared to take as long as I needed to ask my questions. The jurors settled back into their chairs. Some glanced at their legal pads. Grizzled Man fidgeted. The Librarian and Social Worker exchanged looks. Sweater Man watched me.

"Mrs. Wenderholm, are you ready to continue?" I asked.

"What does this have to do with your client murdering my husband?"

I stepped back to the lectern and flipped a page in my notebook. "Mrs. Wenderholm, do you own a car?"

"What?"

"Do you own a car?"

"I have an old Ford Focus."

Check.

I clicked on the remote again. The next image that was shown was from the crime scene. The house was in the background. Police vehicles were parked on the street. Crime scene tape cordoned off the lawn and driveway. The body wasn't visible because an ambulance was in the way, but Oscar's SUV was in the driveway.

"Is this a photograph of your home?"

"After the police came."

"Where is your Ford Focus?"

"I didn't leave it in the driveway. What's this got to do with anything?"

"Where did you park it?"

"Out on the street."

"Why is that? There seems to be plenty of room for both cars."

"Because my brother came the afternoon before to pick up the kids to take them to Disneyland for the weekend. I moved my car out of the driveway so it would be easier for them to load their suitcases. I'm only thankful they weren't home to see their father like that."

"That would be your brother, Benjamin Hugo?"

She paused, then answered in a suspicious tone. "He's been a wonderful support to me through all this."

"He's an antique dealer in San Jose, is that correct?"

"So?"

I clicked the remote. "Is this his website?"

"I set it up for him."

"In that case, did you upload these images?"

"I took the photographs, got them scanned, and put them up on the website. What does this have to do with anything?"

Check.

I clicked the remote again. Up came a still image from the video of Tony's visit to the warehouse where Oscar worked. Tony was out of his vehicle, confronting Oscar. The Gremlin trunk was open.

"Mrs. Wenderholm, can you identify this scene?"

"That's where Oscar worked."

"Who are these people?"

"That's my husband, Oscar, and the other one is your client."

"Is that yellow car near Mr. Paredes the same car that he drove to your house?"

"That's the one. I don't see what this has to do with anything."

"When he came to your house, did his trunk lid come open?"

"I had the same problem with my Gremlin. The trunk lock was broken. Every time you stop the car, it flies open, and you have to close the –,"

She hesitated.

I looked at her. "When you stop the car, the trunk lid flies open, and you have to close it?"

"I can't remember now if it happened when he came to the house. He might have gotten it fixed."

I went back to my notes. "Would you be surprised to learn that Detective Zimmerman testified that the trunk lock was broken when they searched the vehicle the morning after Mr. Wenderholm's murder?"

"I wasn't here. I don't know what he said."

"Were you happily married, Mrs. Wenderholm?"

"Is anyone?" Her answer was rank with self-pity.

"Did you retain a divorce lawyer?"

"So what? I wanted to find out what my rights were."

"Did you file for a divorce?"

"I couldn't afford to. If I threw Oscar out, I'd only get child support. I can't get a good job because I haven't worked in years because I've been home, teaching my children, and keeping the house. We'd end up on welfare. I was stuck – for better or worse. I had to think about my kids."

"Your children are very important to you, aren't they, Mrs. Wenderholm."

"I live for my children."

"And you would do whatever it took to provide for them."

"Any mother would."

Check.

"Your husband had a brand-new SUV, is that right?"

"What's that got to do with anything?"

"You testified in the bail review that the family was barely getting by on his wages as a security guard. How could he afford such an expensive vehicle?"

"He got an advance from his publisher."

"By that do you mean a publisher paid him money for the rights to a book he had written?"

"Exactly."

"Has the book been released?"

"No."

"Do you know why?"

"All Oscar said was that he was going to get his rights back and take it to someone else. If it was published, he thought he could make enough money in royalties to quit his job."

"Did he consult an attorney named Charles Robertson about getting the rights back?"

"He said he was going to."

Vivian slid towards the edge of her chair, prepared to stand for an objection. I wasn't going to give her a reason. "I don't want you to tell me what was said between your husband and Mr. Robertson."

"I wasn't there, anyway. I don't know what they talked about."

"But he did go to the appointment," I said.

"He said he did."

"Mrs. Wenderholm, what was the book about?"

The witness didn't answer. When I chanced a look at her, she was staring into the mid-distance.

I asked again, "Mrs. Wenderholm, please tell us what the book was about."

She looked at Vivian. "Do I have to answer that?"

Vivian stood. "Objection, cumulative. We've had testimony already about the book's subject."

I responded. "Not from this witness, Your Honor."

I wanted the witness to say that she read the book, which is different evidence than whether there was a book.

The judge understood. "Objection denied. Please answer the question."

"Oscar said he had been assaulted in school by one of his teachers."

"You read the book."

"Enough of it."

Check.

Sweater Man was locked onto the witness. Mrs. Wenderholm stared at me. I looked down at my notes.

"In the book, did he discuss his history with abusing children?"

"He was the real victim, according to him. What he did wasn't his fault. It was like he was programmed to do things to children. It was all about him, like always."

Check.

"This must have been difficult for you," I said.

"For years, he told me the accusations were all lies. And I believed him. So, yes, Ms. Gould, it was difficult for me."

I flipped through my notes to find the exact quote. "And you would do anything to protect your children, as any mother would."

"Of course."

Checkmate.

"Is that why you murdered your husband?"

A gasp came from the jury box. It was the Social Worker.

Vivian flew to her feet. "Your Honor! The State strenuously objects to this question and furthermore seeks an immediate mistrial."

Judge Han held up a hand. "Not another word from anyone until the jury returns to its room."

Chapter Thirty-Four

Maureen

AFTER THE DOOR CLOSED behind the jurors, Judge Han turned to me, rigid with anger. "Ms. Gould, what is your good faith basis for asking the last question?" She was on the verge of holding me in contempt and might declare a mistrial if I couldn't show that I had evidence to support the question.

"Your Honor, the witness admitted she had motive, means, and opportunity to murder her husband.

"Motive: She knew her husband admitted to being a pedophile, however he refused to accept responsibility for his behavior. We can infer she believed he posed a threat of abusing his own children who she pledged to 'do anything' to protect.

"Means: She personally took the photographs displayed on the website she designed for her brother. If the court examines the exhibit, you will see that the photographs include a display of handguns under a glass countertop.

"Opportunity: She was home when the murder was committed.

"In addition, she saw Tony Paredes' Gremlin in front of her home. In the bail review, she testified that she saw him pull up and stop. The warehouse video shows that when he stopped his car, the trunk lid popped open. She admitted that she knew that vehicle had a broken trunk lock. She also testified that she had seen the television interview. That interview was filmed across the street from Mr. Paredes' apartment building. In the background was the distinctive Alhambra Theatre marquee, so she would have known the vicinity of his apartment. It would not have been difficult for her to find the Gremlin.

"We believe that after Mrs. Wenderholm read the book, she decided she had to protect her children from their father and came up with the plan to murder him and frame my client. She obtained a gun from her brother, who cooperated with her when he took her children away for the weekend. She met her husband when he came home from work and shot him. She had parked her car in front of the house so it would be easily accessible without disturbing the murder scene. She then drove to Mr. Paredes' apartment complex, found his distinctive mustard-colored Gremlin, and wrapped the gun in his sweatshirt. You will recall that there were no fingerprints on the gun – it had been wiped – and that there were no powder stains on Mr. Paredes.

"In short, Your Honor, the evidence shows that Brita Wenderholm planned and carried out the execution of her husband, Oscar Wenderholm."

When I was finished talking, the judge rocked back in her chair. She lifted an eyebrow ever so slightly, then brought her chair back down.

"The question will stand, but not the answer." She turned to the widow. "Mrs. Wenderholm, you have the right not to incriminate yourself. I suggest you speak to an attorney as soon as possible."

To me, the judge said, "I assume that was your last question."

"Yes, Your Honor."

To Vivian, Judge Han asked, "Will there be any follow-up?"

Vivian carefully laid her pen down. "No, Your Honor."

THE JURY DELIBERATED FOR three hours.

Upon the news that a verdict had been reached, everyone was called back to the courtroom. I held Tony's hand while the judge said, "Madam Foreperson, please pass the verdict form to Madam Clerk."

I was surprised. I could have sworn the jury would have picked Sweater Man for the foreperson, but they had elected the Librarian instead.

The clerk walked across the room, took a document from the foreperson, then carried it to the bench. The judge read the verdict silently.

"Very well," she said. "Mr. Paredes, please rise."

We stood.

The judge read, "We, the jury in the case of State versus Anthony Paredes, find the defendant not guilty of all counts."

Tony shuddered. I nearly fainted.

All the jurors smiled at us, even Grizzled Man.

Chapter Thirty-Five

Umberto

UMBERTO MET FOSTER HEIKI at the hotel suite door. "Good afternoon, Senator. Mr. Toussiant is waiting for you."

The Lion greeted the senator and wrapped an arm around his shoulders. "Congratulations, Foster. You ran a fine campaign. Come on in. Let's talk about our future."

Umberto followed them into the living area. The Lion swept his arm as he gazed out over San Francisco. "She's a beautiful city, your Frisco. Hope you won't miss her too much. We got big plans for you, my boy. Big plans."

"I have to be honest," Heiki said. "I was worried for a while. Stevens had some good numbers."

"He never stood a chance," the Lion said.

The plan was not to get Rick Stevens elected. It never was. The plan was to re-elect Foster Heiki.

Leon Toussiant was a multi-millionaire. He could buy anything he wanted, even a candidate.

Umberto had worked for The Lion since he was a teenager. He'd started as a lawn boy back in Texas. Then he became the limo driver. Over the years he proved his loyalty, and the Lion was impressed with his resourcefulness. That's why he gave Umberto the Rick Stevens job.

Catch and kill.

Umberto's focus was to keep Stevens from imploding long enough to eliminate his competitors in the primary. When it was too late to replace him, they would destroy his campaign and clinch the general election for Foster Heiki.

The book deal fell into Umberto's lap. Steven's friend, Wenderholm, called looking for help. Umberto set up the publishing company and gave Wenderholm an advance for the rights. Stevens was terrified of the book getting published. It turns out he had some hand in a teacher's overdose but that wasn't in the book. Instead, Wenderholm wrote about drug-fueled orgies during which he claimed he had been victimized. If only Umberto had known about the teacher, he could have worked that angle too.

The press would have a field day when the book was leaked at the eleventh hour before the election. Stevens wouldn't have enough time to beg for privacy and go to rehab. That was the plan. He'd lose and Heiki would win.

Then Wenderholm got himself killed. So, the plan changed.

When Anthony Paredes' attorney started snooping around, they were afraid the book would get leaked too early, so Umberto arranged for his cousin to be arrested, knowing he'd be sent to the same jail as Paredes. Umberto paid Javier to say Paredes had confessed. He figured the lawyer would give up and cut a plea deal. No such luck.

But Umberto had a back-up plan. He always had one because he didn't like to disappoint the Lion.

Stevens was a lonely man. Umberto cultivated his trust and found out what his weaknesses were. The Lion had known Stevens was a partier and a gambler and hopelessly overextended financially. He was also handsome and charming. That's why the Lion picked him for their stooge. What they didn't know was that Stevens was looking for love. After the orgy Umberto had arranged, the poor sap was as giddy over Dimitri as a teenaged girl.

So, Umberto enlisted Dimitri for a honey trap and set them up in his own apartment where he installed hidden cameras. When the time came, he sent the images anonymously to the press corp. With one news cycle, Stevens' candidacy fell apart.

The Lion always said, "You can't buy the truth. But you can bury it under a heap of lies."

Chapter Thirty-Six

Rick

THE EMPTY GIN BOTTLE slipped out of Rick's hand onto the patio. It shattered with a satisfying shriek of glass meeting concrete. He'd like to smash every piece of glass in the house, but he didn't have the energy to get out of the hot tub.

It would be so easy to slip beneath the water and be done. He lowered his body and dipped his chin. The oily water's surface slithered up his face. He sank to the bottom, leaving only his nose and eyes above water. Thin clouds drifted across the blue sky. A seagull soared low over the house, not knowing or caring he was being watched.

No one would find Rick for days. He was alone in the big house. Appollonia was gone. When he came home from court that day, she threw dishes at his head and screamed in Spanish. Some reporter had shown up at the house with the photographs while Rick was at court, looking for a comment. After a couple of hours, she packed several suitcases, dragged them out to the Bentley, and drove away.

He couldn't blame her. He married her thinking she would fix his life and when she hadn't, he ignored her. She had every right to be angry.

That morning, a process server had taped a copy of her divorce complaint on his front door. She was asking for half of his property. If he was dead, she'd have it all, but there was nothing to have. The business owned the house and cars. The lenders owned the business. Rick was broke.

Maybe she'd find a rich man to marry. She was still young and good looking and deserved to be happy.

Rick hadn't seen the Dum Dee twins since they dropped him off for court. It was just as well. He could tell they didn't like him. But without them, people were banging on the door all the time, reporters with questions, process servers with lawsuits, even a couple of guys that looked like they might be detectives.

He wasn't worried about the police. No one could prove that he gave David Shroeder the cocaine that killed him. The only person who knew was Dakota Vaughn and he sure as hell wasn't going to tell.

But the rest of Rick's life was in shambles.

Umberto never returned Rick's calls. After a couple of days, Rick quit trying. What would he say? Umberto had set him up. The pictures were taken on a hidden camera planted in Umberto's apartment.

Why would Umberto betray him like that? The Lion must have told him to. They plotted it all along. But why Rick?

Rick hated Umberto for what he did. And knowing that Dimitri must have been in on it, Rick's heart ached. What he felt was real love. Dimitri must have felt it too. Memories of their times together dominated his daytime thoughts and swirled abstractly in his dreams. Once when they were watching an old movie, Dimitri caught Rick staring at his handsome face, and Dimitri winked at him. He remembered the special meals Dimitri made and how he catered to Rick's whims. But then there was the time on that last day together when Dimitri wouldn't look him in the eye. Which was true? He loved me or he loved me not.

Everyone had abandoned Rick his entire life. His mother who'd rather drink herself to death than be his parent. His father, killed in a car accident, when he was out partying instead of staying home with his family. His aunt and uncle turned their backs on him. He had no one.

Who was Richard Stevens? An empty shell. All his life, he played whatever role was given him, ever the people pleaser. An imposter. With Dimitri, he felt seen and alive. Without Dimitri, he was nothing again.

But ending it all didn't make sense. Why had he lived so long through all that stuff unless there was a reason?

He was exhausted from years of hustling cars, looking good, oozing charm, trying to outrun creditors. It was all gambling, in one form or another. Rick realized he hadn't thrown dice or played cards since The Lion got Herman Jules off his back. He hadn't even thought about it.

Rick looked around for his gin. Then he remembered dropping the bottle. He pulled himself up and looked over the tub wall. It was in a million pieces, glittering under the sun.

He didn't feel drunk. No matter how much he had, he couldn't get high. Booze wasn't working for him anymore.

He needed to take a leak. He climbed out of the tub and dragged himself upstairs to the master bath.

When he looked in the mirror, he saw that his beard stubble was red with flecks of white. If he grew it, no one would recognize him. He could grow out his hair too and pull it back into a manbun. Or if he could shave the hair and leave the beard, he'd look like a Viking. No one would know who he was.

If no one knew who he was, he wouldn't have to meet their expectations.

He could start a new life. A new him, whoever that is. He could go to Mexico, get a job somewhere. Something low key, like renting paddleboard to tourists. Or he could go to Europe.

Maybe he could find Dimitri and they could start over.

Chapter Thirty-Seven

Maureen

QUINN AND I MADE dinner. As it turns out, she will eat seafood.

She chopped the veggies. I cut up the fish. We made bouillabaisse and served it with warm sourdough bread slathered in garlic butter. Tony and Isaac brought white wine. Yolanda and her boyfriend, Gerry, brought a box of gourmet cookies made by her niece.

We ate and laughed and talked about everything except law. Quinn had suggested it since we had guests who weren't lawyers. It wasn't easy because I'm not good at talking about anything except law, but I tried.

Gerry told a story about Jake and him when they were cops together. The punchline was that Jake had tripped and fallen while chasing a suspect who Gerry caught. Gerry got a commendation and Jake got a titanium rod in his leg, took early retirement, and went to law school.

Yolanda talked about her niece, an entrepreneur selling her Mexican-inspired gourmet cookies in pop-up shops. We all agreed her cookies were excellent.

I mentioned the weather was unseasonably warm. Everyone agreed politely.

"How about those Forty-Niners?" I asked.

I didn't follow the team, but most people did. All you had to do to get a conversation started is say "how about those Forty-Niners" and sit back. That kept everyone talking long enough for Quinn and me to clear dinner, make coffee, and serve it.

We were sitting around the table and the conversation had slowed, the coffee was gone, with the cookies just crumbs, when Quinn said, "I know we're not supposed to talk about law, but I can't take it anymore. What's going to happen to Brita Wenderholm? Are they prosecuting her?"

"Doesn't look like it," Jake said. "No witnesses. No forensics that point at her. At the very least, they would need to show she had possession of the gun. But she's clammed up and the brother isn't talking."

"So, she just gets away with it?"

"She has to live with the truth for the rest of her life," I said. "That's a prison of its own."

"She could have divorced him," Quinn said.

"Agreed," I said. "She should have. But she felt trapped. Lots of women feel like that. When she read that book, she must have snapped."

Jake gave me a side-eye. Brita had plotted the murder. She obtained a gun. She sent her children away for the weekend so they wouldn't see it. She framed Tony by planting the weapon in his car, knowing that the hatch didn't lock and where he parked it. She had left her car on the street so she could easily drive to Tony's house and plant the gun before she claimed to have discovered her husband's body. That wasn't just snapping.

Brita murdered her husband to protect her children, just as my mother had sent me away for my own good. The mother of the juror, Amber Hayes, had tried to shield her from an awful truth. And I had kept my secret, first out of shame and then to protect my own daughter. We do whatever we can for our children.

I wondered if telling Quinn that Frank was her father was a mistake. Or if keeping the secret from her for so long was the wrong decision. Would I ever be sure that I made the right choice?

Tony said, "I thought Rick Stevens killed Oscar to save himself. Maureen, how did you figure out it was Mrs. Wenderholm?"

"At first, I thought the murderer was Stevens or someone working for him. He had a lot to lose if the book was published. But when Quinn showed me the antique shop website that belonged to Brita's brother, full of guns, it all clicked."

"*Post hoc, ergo propter hoc*," Jake said.

"In English, please," Tony responded.

Quinn answered, with an air of authority. "It's a logical fallacy to believe that something that happened before caused something that happened later."

When I saw that website image, my memory flashed to that time in the prison when Frank grabbed my hand and commented on Quinn's looks. On impulse, I had threatened to cut his heart out, triggered by an overwhelming terror that he would hurt her. It was the same panic I felt while I drove from the East Bay to the mansion to rescue her. I don't know what I would have done that night if Frank had hurt Quinn.

There were times when I thought my life would be easier if Frank wasn't alive, Quinn would be safe, and I could finally relax.

"The logical fallacy was to believe Oscar was murdered because he wanted to publish his book. The truth was, Oscar was murdered because his wife had read it."

There was one thing I did right. That was turning the mansion into the Elizabeth O'Shaughnessy Foundation for Abused Women and Children. We had sold every stick of furniture and art, including a Diego Rivera painting, to fund it. I never regretted it. We gave women options better than murder. We gave them a safe place to live, food to eat, vocational training, and childcare, so they could get on their feet. Granny would have been proud.

Tony stood. "I need to say something."

Jake was stroking Germaine Greer, now curled up in his lap. He answered quietly, so as not to disturb her. "You have our attention."

"I want to say, I was a real pain in the ass. And I'm sorry for that. If I had taken your advice, Maureen, things would have been different. But the first case, the civil case, was never about the money. It was about telling the truth. When the verdict was set aside, I needed to get the truth out there.

"You saved my life. And I can never repay you. Not even in a million years. I don't even know how big the bill is, but I'm going to start sending you some money as soon as we get settled."

I hadn't kept track of my hours because I hadn't expected him to pay. For me, this case wasn't about fees, it was about justice. "Don't worry about it, Tony."

"No, I do worry about it. It's time I took some responsibility." He reached down and took Isaac's hand. "I wanted you to know I'm not running out, but we've decided to leave San Francisco. We're moving up to Oregon. Isaac's family has a bee farm and we're going to help, maybe become partners in the business if everything works out."

When I first met Tony and Isaac, Tony referred to Isaac as his roommate. That didn't change throughout the first trial. After Tony was arrested, it was apparent they were closer than just roommates, but they didn't bring up the topic and I hadn't asked because it didn't matter to me who Tony loved.

It was good to see him planning a future with a loving partner. Tony deserved that.

"Congratulations, guys." I got up and gave Tony a hug. Isaac smiled up at me from his chair. He wasn't going to accept a hug from me, and I was okay with that. Things had been difficult between us, because we both cared about Tony but had different approaches.

"Bee farming. That is so cool," Quinn said. She gave Tony a big, unselfconscious hug.

"I'm very happy for you," Yolanda said. She wrapped her arms around Tony. Then she pulled Isaac to his feet. There was no refusing a Yolanda Martinez hug.

Gerry punched Jake in the shoulder. "There's great fishing in Oregon. We should go up and check it out."

"Come visit us, anytime," Tony said. "All of you. Our house is your house."

Goodbyes were said. Hugs and kisses exchanged. Gerry and Jake traded friendly punches. Tony pulled me into a second hug and whispered in my ear. "You're my hero."

I whispered back, "And you're mine."

It was true. Tony was braver than I could imagine. He told the truth about Oscar's abuse in a public trial, long before I was able to tell my daughter privately. When I was terrified that he would be convicted, he refused to be bullied into taking a plea deal. He had put his life back together time and again. There was unfathomable strength deep inside of him.

Anthony Paredes stood for truth, no matter the consequences. I hoped to be just like him.

THE END

Hope You Enjoyed The Millionaire!

Author's Note

I began *Implied Consent* during lockdown. Originally it had two story lines, that of Josephine Navarre, and Tony's story. And the book was far too long. So, I cut Tony's story out and developed it for *The Millionaire*.

In this book, I wanted to explore why people go to court. After forty years of practicing law, I've learned there are many reasons. The widely held conception that plaintiffs are looking to make a quick buck is sometimes true. But, in my experience, plaintiffs with this motivation don't go the distance. Litigation is grueling. Living with uncertainty for a year or more is nerve wracking. Having your word doubted and challenged feels like the personal attack that it is.

The plaintiffs who survive the gauntlet are those who want to get their story out. They want justice. They want to make sure that the responsible party is held liable.

It has been my honor and privilege to represent people of this caliber many, many times.

To the Tonys of this world, I dedicate this book.

Keenan Powell

Anchorage, Alaska

11 January 2024

About the Author

Keenan Powell is the Agatha, Lefty, and Silver Falchion nominated author of the Maeve Malloy Mystery series.

Despite being one of original Dungeons and Dragons illustrators, art seemed an impractical pursuit – not an heiress, wouldn't marry well, hated teaching – so she went to law school. The day after graduation, she moved to Alaska.

She is the author of the Maureen Gould Legal Thrillers, Maeve Malloy Legal Thrillers, the Liam Barrett Gilded Age Novels, and numerous short stories. She is a member of Mystery Writers of America, Sisters in Crime, and International Thriller Writers. You can find her blogposts on Miss Demeanors.

When not writing or practicing law, Keenan can be found embroidering or studying the Irish language.

For newsletter sign-up: Home - Keenan Powell (keenanpowellauthor.com)

Acknowledgements

Bringing this book forth could not have been done without the kind and gentle support of my cherished friends Bruce Robert Coffin, James L'Etoile, Jenni Legate, Jean Clarkin, Debbie Burke, Cari Davis, Efrem Seeger, Sandy Maning, Susan Wolfe, and Randal Jackson. Thank you.

A huge thanks is due to my daughter, Rory Bryant, and son-in-law, Hardy Bryant, who suffer with compassion and grace through my prattling when I'm lost in the pages.

And what a cool cover designed for me by Mila Book Covers! I love it.

Also By

The Maureen Gould Legal Thrillers

Implied Consent (Three Hooligans Press, 2023)

The Millionaire (Three Hooligans Press, 2024)

The Maeve Malloy Legal Thrillers

Deadly Solution (Three Hooligans Press, 2023)

Hell and High Water (Three Holligans Press, 2024)

Hemlock Needle (Three Holligans Press, 2024)

The Liam Barrett Gilded Age Novels

The Sorrowful Girl (Three Hooligans Press, 2023)

Short Stories

The Liam Barrett Short Stories: Gilded Age Stories (Three Hooligans Press, 2023)

The Hen Who Crowed (Three Hooligans Press, 2024)

The Pied Piper

Prologue

When the security buzzer hummed its ugly little tone, everyone seated around the conference table turned to look, hoping the witness had finally arrived. He was twenty-five minutes late.

I was at the head of the table closest to the door, symbolically controlling who entered and left the room. I had been flipping through my scripted questions, occasionally making a scribbled note, ignoring the other attorney. When the buzzer alerted us to the new arrival, I picked up my coffee cup, noticed that it was nearly empty, and wondered if I should make a bathroom run before we started the proceeding.

Paul Lewis, the witness's attorney, had selected a chair as far away from me as possible, and was angled away from the table, ankle on knee, occupying as much space as he could, tapping a pen on his legal pad. When the buzzer sounded, he twisted around to see if his client had arrived.

At the far end of the table, was the court reporter. When the buzzer sounded, she put down the phone she was playing with and punched her keyboard, bringing her sleeping laptop alive.

My client, Esme Castillo, was next to me, dressed in a conservative suit of navy blue, her only jewelry an Our Lady of Guadalupe medal, and her thick black hair pulled back into a low ponytail. She was subdued, her hands clutched so tightly her knuckles were white, head bowed. Praying, perhaps. Behind her, the windows overlooked the historical

Jackson Square neighborhood where my office was, the view full of charming nineteenth century brick buildings on tree lined streets under a blindingly bright sky where seagulls wheeled overhead, cawing.

When the buzzer sounded, Esme's head jerked up.

On Esme's far side was Quinn, my daughter, who worked part-time with me while she went to law school. She appeared very grown up, in a gray suit that accentuated her gray eyes, the color of which she had inherited from her father. While we waited, she had been scrolling through her open laptop. That morning before anyone arrived, I told her to look occupied, and give minimal attention to witness and his lawyer. As Quinn was the image of me, tall, athletic, with unruly red hair, the effect would be to have two Maureens refusing to give them power. When the buzzer sounded, she glanced at the door, then looked over at me, waiting to see what I would do.

The man we were all waiting for was Alfred Tanzini, the plaintiff in this case, who had swindled Esme out of her business, and then sued to prevent her from opening a competing enterprise. My goal was to win back her company, which meant far more to her than simply a job. It was her heritage, her legacy, and her identity. I would show Tanzini no mercy. He didn't deserve it. In this deposition, I would expose how he had defrauded her.

When the buzzer sounded, my paralegal/office mom, Yolanda Martinez, was seated behind her desk on the other side of the glass wall that separated the reception from the conference room. She studied her monitor, the screen of which I couldn't see from where I sat. The buzzer sounded again, longer this time. She gave me a frown and quick shrug, then pushed herself out of her chair and crossed the few feet to the entry door, which remained locked during business hours due to recent events.

Yolanda threw the deadbolt, then cracked the door just enough to greet the visitor. The voice in the hallway was too garbled to understand. She stepped back and swung the door wide open, permitting two people to enter the reception room. Neither of them was Tanzini.

They were detectives, easily enough to identify by the shields hanging from their necks. One was an African American woman, the other an Asian man who stood just behind her. She was almost as tall as me, with her hair in a short natural, dressed in a black pantsuit with cotton shirt and flat shoes. He was over six feet tall, with a trendy haircut, in jeans, a button-down shirt open at the collar, and a lightweight zipped jacket.

I rose from the table and walked out to greet them, intending to preempt their questions and wrap up their visit quickly. "Good morning, detectives. I'm Maureen Gould. This is my office. Is there something I can help you with?"

"Detective Dobson," the woman said. "And this is Detective Chong. We're here about Alfred Tanzini."

Cops showing up to a deposition is not a good sign. As far as they're concerned, the rest of the world can pause its business. If they wanted to talk to him, the deposition may never happen. It would take weeks to reschedule and could push the trial date off into the distant future. Meanwhile Esme wouldn't be able to earn money because of the injunction Tanzini had obtained forbidding her to work.

I knew from my years as an assistant DA, there was no saying "no" to the police. I hoped they'd only need a few minutes and then we could start the deposition late. "He should be here any minute, detectives, if you would care to wait." I gestured towards the couch.

A gasp came from the conference room. Dobson and Chong both glanced in that direction. Yolanda, who was standing behind the visitors, looked past me and subtly shook her head at whoever had made the sound.

Dobson zeroed in on me with a look she had clearly perfected for stopping people in their tracks. "I understand you represent Esmeralda Castillo."

"I do."

"Is she here?"

She was.

I turned to find Esme standing in the conference room doorway, one hand against the doorframe for support, the other covering her mouth. Her straight black eyebrows were gathered in worry. Her dark complexion had paled.

Normally, Esme was the kind of person people would describe as a "spitfire," small, slight, intense, perpetually in motion. The kind of woman who could work her way through culinary school as a janitor, then work fulltime in a restaurant kitchen, while baking cookies at night in her grandmother's kitchen, and then make early morning deliveries to coffee shops on her way into work. She was the kind of woman who could build a thriving business, Esme's Casa de Galletas.

The fragile, frightened woman I saw was not the Esme I knew.

Tanzini's attorney shouldered past Esme. As he stalked across the carpet, he reached inside his blazer. "Paul Lewis, attorney for Alfred Tanzini. What's this about?"

Dobson gave Lewis that drop-dead stare. He stopped short. I liked her.

"We'll need to speak with you shortly, Mr. Lewis," she said. "If you would make yourself comfortable, we'll be right with you." She nodded in the direction of the conference room.

Lewis glanced at his watch. "We're about to start a deposition. Can't it wait? You can call my office to make an appointment. Later in the week, maybe. Talk to my secretary." He extended his hand to her with his business card that he had slipped between his first two fingers.

The silent Detective Chong took the card, ran his thumb across the linen paper, eyebrows raised in an artificial show of admiration, barely concealing his disdain, then stashed the card in his pocket. I knew from my husband Jake, a former police officer now an assistant district attorney, that most cops disliked most lawyers. It isn't just an urban myth popularized in crime fiction. Lewis didn't pick up on the snub. He puffed up, apparently thinking the detective appreciated his good taste in stationery.

"You're all waiting for Alfred Tanzini, is that correct?" Detective Dobson asked.

"We are," I answered. "He should be here any minute."

Dobson shook her head. "I'm afraid Mr. Tanzini won't be coming. His body was found this morning."

Learn more: https://www.amazon.com/gp/product/B0D1HC1TDF